OUT OF MY LEAGUE

(THE UNDERDOG SERIES #1)

BREA BROWN

WAYZGOOSE PRESS

Edited by Maggie Sokolik

Cover design by Keri Knutson at alchemybookcovers.com

To my husband, who's taught me most of what I know about football, including the stuff I forget in the off-season. Thanks for being such a good sport and a patient teacher, not just in football, but in all aspects of our life together.

CONTENTS

AUTHOR'S NOTE

I love football (all forms), and this book is my love letter to the American version of the sport (played by the National Football League). As with most things I love, though, I don't fully understand it. So. Many. Rules! I don't go too far into the weeds on rules and regulations in this book (I realize not everyone loves the game as much as I do, and I didn't want to bore or alienate readers with extensive play-by-plays), but the game was a big part of the main characters' lives, so when I did mention it, I needed it to be authentic. I probably drove my husband crazy, asking him all these hypotheticals, not just about the rules of the game, but also about the regulations that guide players' behavior off the field. Something tells me he kind of liked being my main consultant, though.

I also did my own research, obviously, and read many interesting—and odd—articles about players' routines, health practices, and roles in the community. And yes, I had to brush up on terminology. I tried not to overdo it with the football-speak and worked hard to contextually define terms (I know you're a smart bunch and can figure this stuff out), but there were many places where it would have interrupted the flow of the story or seemed odd for characters so familiar with the game to explain things to each other. I'd like to refer you to the Wikipedia page for American football (http://en.wikipedia.org/wiki/American_football) as a quick, easy guide. That way, if you're inclined to know more than you already do, you can look it up. Otherwise, you can skim right over those terms (like I used to do while casually watching football each week), and nothing will be lost in the story. I promise. You don't have to be an NFL expert to understand what's happening in the following pages.

If you're a sports fan, I hope you find a lot to love about this book. If you're not a sports fan, I hope you can overlook the brief discussions of sport in this book and enjoy the overarching storyline, which is a fresh [I think] take on familiar themes: love and self-worth. If you hate sports and love, I weep for you, but to each his/her own. However, you may want to save yourself the six hours of boredom and/or frustration and put down this book now. Then again, these characters and their story may change your mind and be a surprising delight. You wouldn't want to risk missing out on that, would you?

So, happy reading! And if you feel moved to post a review on the site of your choice when you've finished reading, I'd greatly appreciate it. Thanks!

ONE

HOBNOBBIN'

If this were a movie, something big would be about to go down. Something bigger, that is, than that enormous linebacker doing the Running Man on the dance floor in front of me.

No, I'm talking something epic and life-changing. The ordinary woman invited to an exclusive NFL Christmas gala as the plus-one of her best friend, one of the Kansas City Chiefs' trainers, would look across the dance floor and meet the eyes of Keaton Busch (a.k.a., "Mr. Tight End," which describes both the position he plays and my sexist assessment of his fine figure). The rest would be filler until the happily ever after.

Or, if it were an action film, someone would come in here right now and shoot this mother up. Considering how the evening's gone so far, and the fact that Mr. Tight End is nowhere in sight, the latter seems much more likely.

Unfortunately, this isn't a movie. So nothing exciting is happening at this party.

I sit, abandoned, at a table for eight in one of Arrowhead

Stadium's premier event venues, watching huge dudes—most of whom I can't identify—gyrate to the pulsing music on the makeshift dance floor with their dates.

I don't recognize anyone. Well, I take that back. I knew Coach Dick Bauer when he got up and addressed the attendees, back at the beginning of the night, when it held so much promise. I also knew the Wise brothers, the team's owners. Everyone else here, they're a different story.

Despite being an avid fan of the team, I never realized how much I rely on the names and numbers on the backs of jerseys to help me identify the players. Here, in their formal wear, they look like clones at a giants' convention. I guess they're not quite identical; there's an impressive array of skin tones and hair styles (very multi-culti). But none of the guys are wearing under-eye black or sporting their helmets, and seeing them in real life is totally different than seeing them on camera, standing among other players, where they appear to be relatively normal-sized humans.

They're not. They're mahoossive. Even the kickers and punters, who usually seem so tiny on the field, are my height (5'11") or taller. In this setting, my friend, Rae, at 5'6", looks like an extra from *The Wizard of Oz* or *Charlie and the Chocolate Factory*. This is the only place in the world I can wear three-inch heels (which are killing me, by the dubs), and still feel tiny. So far tonight, I've seen a lot of nose hair. I defy the most dedicated fan to claim he or she can identify any of these guys based on that feature. I suspect second- and third-stringers and support staff comprise the majority of the attendees.

How disappointing! (Says the girl who's the least of the nobodies here.)

Obviously, not one of the players has given me a second glance. Part of that may be due to the fact that I'm attending the party with an openly gay woman. They all assume I'm Rae's date-date, not her straight friend who would love to dance with one or two ripped, rich guys. Since Rae doesn't seem eager to introduce me to any of these "sex-starved a-holes," and none of them will approach me to talk to me, there's no way to tactfully get that message across. A blinking "Straight" sign around my neck would come in handy right now, but it would ruin the lines of the red, beaded, one-shoul-dered number I'm wearing.

When Rae first texted me, asking if I'd be her "plus-one" to this shindig, I was thrilled. As a lifelong Chiefs fan, it was a dream come true for me.

It was too momentous an occasion to discuss via the text conversation she had initiated, so I called her to accept her invitation.

"Before you go all fangirl on me," she said, "this isn't just a social outing. These are my new co-workers. I need you to play it cool at this thing."

"I will be the epitome of cool."

Following the previous few months of lengthy silences and stilted conversations, usually in written electronic format, I was surprised she was asking me to go with her. The last thing I wanted was to add more strain to our friendship. So I resisted squealing in her ear when it became clear she wasn't playing an elaborate joke on me and was truly inviting me to something so amazing.

The squealing impulse remained close to the surface throughout that call, every time I thought of another player I'd have a chance to meet (Keaton Busch) or dance with (Keaton Busch!) or even drunkenly make out with but not go any further, because that's groupie behavior, and I'm so above that. (Keaton Busch!!) I knew any hint of a squeak or mention of the player she claims is a "doofus" and a "douche," and she'd rescind her invite, so I kept all noises in check.

Keeping silent wouldn't have been as big of a challenge if I'd known it was going to be like this.

My "date" disappeared a few minutes ago, following one of the players toward the locker room after he approached her to complain about his painfully pulled groin muscle. Ever the workaholic, Rae readily agreed to massage it for him. Anyone else, and I'd think they were speaking euphemistically, but the literalness of the situation is much more depressing.

I'm so over the entire night that when the air next to me moves as someone sits in Rae's abandoned chair, I refuse to look away from the sight of Giant Running Man. (The floor is shaking from the impact, and I don't want to miss when it finally gives way and swallows him.) That is, until I catch whiff of my visitor, like a rainy forest in the fall, and can't resist turning my head to see who belongs to that intoxicating smell. An equally mesmerizing smile is my reward for finding my manners. It's so pretty that I'm almost okay with it not residing on the face of Keaton Busch. (Dang it, where *is* that guy?)

"Hey, there," says someone who doesn't require a jersey for me to instantly recognize him.

Starting quarterback Jet Knox's face is plastered all over the city, most notably on the billboard I pass every day on my way to work. Plus I've seen him plenty of times with his helmet off. Somehow, his grin is more dazzling tonight than in any of the retouched photos of him I've seen in print. Sweaty post-game interviews don't do this guy justice. Close up, clean, and in person, he's a god.

My fluttery hands and twitchy mouth betray my nervousness at his proximity. He's no Mr. Tight End, but judging by my physical response right now, I'd probably faint if I came face-to-face with my biggest crush, so maybe it's a good thing he's MIA.

"Hey," I manage to squeak back softly enough to require the QB's ability to read lips in loud stadiums.

He leans closer to be heard over the thumping music. "You're Rae's friend, right?"

"Yep. Just friends!" I shout back. "Friend-friends!" Screw subtlety. It's too late in the evening and noisy in here for that.

He laughs loudly. "Okay, then. Thanks for clearing that up. But I already knew."

I manage to keep my vocal cords steady, hopefully sounding more flirtatious than desperate, when I say, "Oh, good. Word's getting around."

He either doesn't notice his effect on me or does a good job of pretending not to. In fact, he does his own share of squirming when he says, "I passed Rae and Joaquin in the hallway, and when I teased her for leaving her pretty date alone, she snapped my head off and said you weren't her date, and maybe I should come up here and keep you company."

I blush at several of the things he says, not least of which that he called me "pretty."

"You don't have to do what she says," I say, hating myself for not knowing how to graciously accept a compliment or muster a more characteristically sassy response. But... but it's Jet Knox! I'm officially star-struck. So much for playing it cool.

He smiles. "Yes, actually, I normally do. But it's our bye week, which is why we're having this party before Thanksgiving. And the only reason we have decent food and booze." Nodding toward the mountain of a man on the dance floor, he says, "Jackson wouldn't be allowed to attempt those dance moves. I'm pretty sure he's about to hurt himself. Or bring this whole place down."

I laugh, relaxing as Jet also seems to regain his social footing.

Looking relieved that I'm loosening up, he holds out his hand. "I'm Jet."

I allow my hand to be consumed by his and pretend it's not hilarious for him to be introducing himself to me, a nobody job counselor from Overland Park, Kansas. "I'm Maura."

"Nice to meet you, Maura." He plunks his massive mitt on the table and drums his surprisingly nimble fingers. "You don't look like you're having a good time. I feel bad about that."

Quickly, I reassure him, "Well, it's not anyone's fault. Especially not yours. But it's surreal—and intimidating—being here. Rae's busy, so she hasn't had a chance to introduce me to anyone, that's all."

He cocks an eyebrow at me. "Rae needs to get a life. No offense. I know she's your friend and all, but she's a little intense." At that, he chuckles nervously and scratches his eyebrow. "Don't tell her I said that, though."

I narrow my eyes. "She's one of the first ones on the field when you're hurt, right?" Grabbing the spot where his shoulder meets his neck, I imitate a trainer who's trying to diagnose a problem and pretend to squeeze maliciously. "Does this hurt?" I ask, wearing a serious expression and assuming a grave tone of voice.

He winces, sucking in a breath as if I'm causing him great discomfort, even though I probably couldn't hurt him if I tried. "Not until you did that. *Gaaaaah!*"

We chuckle at our dorky playacting, and I remove my hand

from his rock-hard muscle, suddenly hyper-aware I've touched someone I've only ever seen before on TV and in print.

I look down at my hands in my lap. "Anyway, I won't tell her what you said."

He stands, and I figure he's going to return to socializing with his teammates now that he's done his duty tour of the room, but his hand enters my field of vision, and he wiggles his fingers. "Come on. Let's dance."

Immediately, I stand and comply with his request, too grateful for the break in the monotony to play coy. Plus, I'd have to be in a coma to turn down an opportunity like this, if for no other reason than to brag about it to my brother.

After the song ends, the DJ plays an R&B request from one of the players to his "new, hot wife," so I step back from Jet. It occurs to me he probably has a bleached, buffed, waxed date wandering around here somewhere. A glance at my table tells me Rae's back from giving Joaquin his holiday rub-down. She's glaring at Jet and me.

"Forget her," my dance partner says, stepping forward and grasping me around my waist.

Instantly done.

Near my ear, his cheek pressed against mine, he says, "It's boring over at that table. There's no way I'm going to let you walk away from this party thinking we're boring. The NFL has a reputation to uphold, you know."

As he returns to his full height, his face glides across mine like satin against velvet. He pulls me closer so the beads on my dress catch on his silk tie. Someone capable of an emotion close to "worry" would step back to prevent snagging the accessory that probably cost half of my last paycheck. I'm too tingly, warm, and loose to fret, though.

Plus, he doesn't seem worried about his tie, so why should I be?

All I can possibly think about is those hands. And those eyes. And that chest. I'm vaguely aware of the song playing, but I won't remember it when it's over.

I smile dreamily. Wait until I tell my brother about this.

———

Too soon, I find myself sitting in Rae's SUV, looking out the passenger window while she grills me.

"What else did you guys talk about? What did he say about me? He always acts like he's forcing himself to be civil to me, like he hates my guts and rolls his eyes behind my back. Did he trash talk me?"

Since what Jet said about Rae was nothing close to what I'd call "trash talking," I'm not lying by keeping my promise to him. "No, not at all."

"Then what did you two talk about for so long out there?"

"Fade routes and slants. Oh, and the importance of a balanced running and passing game."

She scoffs. "Fine. Don't tell me. I already know, anyway."

Turning my head to look at her, I sigh. "I'm kidding. But really, we didn't talk about you at all. Except at first. He said you asked him to keep me company, when you passed him in the hallway on the way to the therapy room."

Wrinkling her nose and forehead, she says, "I didn't see him anywhere until he was out there on the dance floor with his grubby hands all over you. I definitely wouldn't have told him to talk to you. All those guys are major players."

"Yeah, darn good ones."

This gets her to laugh, in spite of her rotten mood. "You

know what I mean. Since that supposed conversation I had with him never happened, it appears Knox is also a liar. Shocking."

"Well, I'm hardly planning to get involved with him. We talked for a few minutes and danced to a couple of songs. Big deal."

Oh, and I gave him my phone number when he asked for it. But she doesn't need to know that right now. Or ever.

To prevent inciting more of my friend's wrath, I change the subject—somewhat. "So, other than throw ridiculously early Christmas parties, what else does the team do during its bye week?"

She frowns. "Most of the guys ignore their diets, stop working out, and open the door for injuries and illness, especially when the bye falls this late in the season. But supposedly, we maintain a training schedule and use the extra time to prepare for our next opponent. In this case, San Diego."

"San Diego. Nice," I say, as I stare at the naked trees lining the highway.

"I guess," she grouses.

I roll my eyes. "What is your deal tonight?"

She muffles, "It's nothin'," then removes her thumb from her mouth and glances over at me, but her eye contact is brief and returns immediately to the road in front of her. "Okay. Fine. Everyone thinks I'm a loser, like I'm a workaholic and a slave driver. I'm just the hag who wraps their sprained ankles and tapes their broken toes and nags them about their diets and workouts."

"So you thought cutting out of the party to *work* would prove you're not a workaholic?" I chuckle and push on her shoulder to soften my blunt assessment of her silly logic.

She grunts but smiles. "He needed help, but the other trainers—"

"Were busy having a good time with their guests and co-workers?"

"Yeah! Everyone knows they can rely on me to take care of things, even when it's not convenient."

I think about that for a second. "You know, your work ethic is admirable. But it's not winning you any popularity points, and that seems to be what you want the most right now."

"Maybe not the most, but equally as much."

I drum my fingers on the dashboard. "You can have both, you know."

"I don't know…"

"You can!" Warming to my topic, I swivel in my seat, pressing my back against my window so I can see her better. "This is your first season with the team. Maybe they just don't know you well enough to joke with you. How do you act when you're around them?" Carefully, I clarify, "Are you always so business-like?"

"I have to be professional. Do you know how hard it is for a woman to advance in this career? No matter how much people go on and on about equal opportunities and blah, blah, blah, *you* know what the reality is. I have goals." More quietly, she says, "I realize that's a foreign concept to some people."

Gritting my teeth, I let her comment slide and try to stay on topic. "You're not going to be passed up for promotion because you get along too *well* with the guys. If the guys like you, they'll request to work with you when they're hurt. Sounds like you need to make the first move. Maybe they're… intimidated by you."

Instead of contradicting me, she asks, "You think so?"

My heart breaks at her hopeful, approval-seeking expression. "Maybe."

"How do I break the ice? I feel like we have nothing in common."

"You like women, and so do most of them," I blurt, then laugh. "Sorry! It was the first thing that popped to mind. Probably not appropriate, though."

"Probably not," she says. "Seriously. What did you and Jet talk about? Maybe I can get a hint from that. A starting-off point."

My mind's a blank. I suddenly can't think of anything besides the one thing I can't tell her. My mouth works open and closed a few times before I finally admit on an uncharacteristic giggle, "I don't know! I remember him talking, but I was... gaga, I guess. I can't remember any of it. He smelled amazing, though," I mutter.

Since the majority of my statement is true (especially the last part), it passes muster with Rae, who laughs and says, "You're useless. Dangle a nice-smelling guy in front of you, and you turn to jelly. I guess I'll have to pay more attention to what the players say to each other on the sidelines."

"There you go!" I say, grateful to shift the focus of the conversation back to her. "When you're in the PT room or the locker room, or whatever, after the game or practice, and you're working on the guys, you can initiate some chit-chat. The weather's always safe. Hobbies? Significant others? Kids? Pets? After all, they're just guys."

How soon I'm able to spout that flippant advice after admitting how star-struck I was by Jet Knox. But that's different, because I like football. And hot guys. And sex with hot guys. Even if all I've done lately is *think* about sex with hot guys.

"Hello! Paging Maura Richards. We've reached your stop."

I shake my head and smile sheepishly at myself. "Sorry."

"Dreaming of Jet Knox's hard body?" she asks.

I reach for the door handle. "I'd be lying if I said I didn't wonder what he looked like in—or out of—a towel."

"I've seen nearly every one of those guys naked. Including Knox." Her tone is bored.

"And?" I barely catch the drool before it falls from my lower lip.

"Meh. He's cut—and hung. But it doesn't do anything for me, obviously."

"It could do something for me," I mumble, indulging in a mini-fantasy, then allowing myself to get a tiny bit excited at the thought of my number nestled in his cell phone. "All right. Well, thanks for taking me to the party. It turned out to be a decent time."

When I pop open the door, Rae grabs my left hand. "Hey."

I half-turn.

"Thanks for coming with me tonight. You made it more fun. Even though your taste in men is questionable and concerning."

Snatching my hand away from her, I playfully swat at her shoulder. "Shut it. Nothing's going to come from a couple of dances at a silly holiday party."

"Wanna bet?"

I'd say it's a pretty safe bet, but rather than argue, I merely shake my head at her and exit the vehicle, tossing a "Good night!" over my shoulder.

She waits for me to unlock and open the front door of my duplex, then give her the all-clear sign after I turn on the living room light. Sliding off the shoes that allowed me to at least reach the shoulders of most of the male partygoers, I return to my normal height and vantage point and marvel at how quickly I'm back to this bland life of mine. A thirty-minute drive. That's all it took.

"Nothing's changed at all," I say to the man who welcomes me home each night.

Matt Damon says nothing in reply, merely continues his focused study into the sight of his rifle in the second of three framed *Bourne* posters that fit in a perfect line in my entryway.

Despite how it may have felt for those few minutes in Jet Knox's arms, it was an illusion, a departure from the norm, like two people acting in a movie scene.

"That's a wrap," I say, shuffling down the hall to bed.

TWO

COLIN, THE EX-PAT

Vocations fall into the same category as soul mates, maternal instincts, and runners' highs: I'm sure they exist for some people, but not for me. There simply doesn't seem to be anything out there in the world I feel called to do. I spend forty hours of my life each week helping people find jobs, and yet, I have no idea what I want to be when I grow up.

I'm not alone there, though. Many of my clients are serial applicants. In some cases, they're not satisfied with their placements—ever. Sometimes, it's the other way around. You'd be surprised how many people truly are unemployable.

In the case of my favorite recurring client and friend, Colin Bennett, well... let's just say Colin has a short attention span.

"I'm quite keen to be in and out of whatever you've got by Christmas," the Brit ex-pat tells me now, leaning forward in his chair across the desk from me with his elbows on his knees.

I flip through the binder of temporary positions, tearing out the expired postings I come across. This is the fourth time I've seen Colin on the other side of my desk in as many months. Qualified—overly so, in most cases—he's not at all interested in a nine-to-five job that could lead to something permanent. I love the guy, but he's seriously fickle.

Colin hasn't always had issues with commitmentphobia, though. Just ever since I've known him. Which maybe means I'm spreading this disease to those around me, now that I think of it.

"It would be easier to be between jobs over the holidays, when I leave for my duty visit to Mum and Dad's, than to have to muck around with asking for time off."

"Oooh, that's right! You're off to the motherland soon, aren't you?"

"Indeed."

"How much are you dreading it?"

"Eh. It won't be too awful, I suppose. It's been a while since I've been back, and I have the air miles, so I couldn't say no, could I? Mum's been banging on about my coming home since Emily passed, and I've been putting her off, for one reason or another. I simply ran out of reasons after three years of stalling."

I look up and smile sympathetically.

He was newly bereaved when he first came to The Career Center to seek employment, so I never knew his wife. They met and fell in love online, when he was still living in London and serving on Her Majesty's police force. He chucked his pension and his entire life as he knew it to cross the Atlantic to be with his "one and only forever love." Even an unromantic person like me inwardly swoons at that notion.

Colin's experience in English law enforcement didn't translate over here, but that didn't matter. He took a job in the warehouse of the print shop where Emily was a graphic artist. Only one thing could separate them. And it did, after

Emily unsuccessfully battled a particularly vicious and efficient form of cancer. Colin couldn't stand to work at the shop anymore, so he came here to find another job.

"Any job. I don't care at this point," he'd said. "It doesn't cost much to merely exist."

Since then, I've found him countless temporary placements. I've also watched him heal and return to some semblance of the fun-loving and adventurous guy he must have been to leave everything and move to the States to marry Emily, but he's still not particularly interested in routines or permanence.

Now he rubs his face. "Mum has this picture of me as the grieving widower, you know? And I do miss Emily. Still. Every day. But Mum thinks I walk around with a hankie pressed to my eyes, and I know that worries her. The thing is, though, if I don't act that way around her, she'll harangue me about that, as well. There's no winning with her. It's going to be a miserable visit, but the first time 'home' has to happen at some point, and the sooner she sees I'm okay, the better. Until now, though, I haven't been able to show her I'm okay. Not convincingly." He stares down at his hand, fingering the wedding band he still wears. "Ah, blimey. I'm waffling. Sorry." He waves me back to my work, seemingly anxious for me to stop looking at him.

"It's okay," I'm quick to reassure him.

"Perhaps I should cut back on the coffee." The left side of his mouth lifts in a nervous grimace.

Suspecting he'd like a moment to try to recover his stiff upper lip, I return to the binder. "Jobs, right?"

His shoulders lower. "Yes. Perhaps something in retail? Surely places are hiring temporary seasonal help, now that it's December, and with Christmas coming up and all. I'd still prefer mornings and early afternoons. As much as I enjoyed sweating my balls off on that landscaping crew back in August, something a bit less physical may be in order." He shoots me an adorable smile as I flip faster.

"Let's see... Maybe something at the mall? Do you care what type of store you work in?" I check.

"Don't give a monkey's."

"Figured as much." I give up on updating the book as I make my way to the seasonal retail section of the folder.

He nods toward the docked laptop on my desk. "Any reason you're shunning technology today?"

"Network's down. I've been telling IT for months that the system is sluggish and seems like it's always on the verge of crashing, but do they listen to me? No."

Hmmm... Maybe I should go back to school to study computers. Nah. Too tedious. Although, the IT people make double what I do. Obviously, job performance isn't a factor in those earnings.

"Right. Well, whatcha got there?" Colin prods me after I've stared into space, fuming for a while.

"Oh! Uh, sorry." My eyes snap down to the page in front of me. "Do you have any engraving experience?"

He looks bemused. "You mean like etching inscriptions on lockets and pocket watches and things?"

I nod and tell him about a position for a clerk at a kiosk in the mall, where a computer does all the engraving, in fact. We both cringe at the minimum wage pay rate, but he likes the flexible hours.

After giving him a few seconds to mull it over, I take a deep breath and smile. "What do you think? You'll probably have to wear a Santa hat."

"Is that in the job description?" He sounds almost hopeful

as he half-stands and tries to read the paper from upside down.

I laugh. "No. But I recall seeing people wearing hats there when I was—" I remember at the last second that I was having a watch engraved for Jamie, my boyfriend at the time, nearly a year ago. "Anyway. I did some shopping there last year."

Time stands still when I'm with you.

Well, it did. Unfortunately. And that sucks, when you're biding your time, because you don't have the heart to dump someone during the dreaded Christmas/New Year's/Valentine's stretch. I wonder if he still has that watch. It was nice. I spent more than I wanted to spend, but that was the guilt talking.

Retaking his seat and shooting me a knowing look, Colin mercifully chooses not to comment on my sudden caginess but says about the possible holiday head-wear requirement at the kiosk, "I'm not bothered. It's no sillier than some of the other uniforms I've worn in the past." He taps his lips with his fingertips. Perhaps he's thinking about the hat he wore as a "copper," what probably seems like a lifetime ago. "I was hoping I could be one of those blokes who flies toy helicopters in people's faces. But this will do."

As I fill out the paperwork for him to take with him, he stands and wanders around my tiny, dingy office, then squints at the framed diploma on my wall.

He peers at the calligraphy, then looks at me. "Tell me again, Ms. Richards, what, exactly, does one study to get a film studies degree? What does one do with such a degree?"

In a snooty voice to match his, I reply, "One studies films, Mr. Bennett. Obviously, one subsequently becomes a job counselor."

Because watching hours and hours of Hitchcock, Scorsese,

and the Coen brothers and writing papers about point-of-view, the long shot versus the medium shot, and the significance of the well-placed jump cut don't have many practical applications around here. Heck, I'd have taken a projectionist job at one of the local movie theaters, if it had included benefits not in the form of free admission, popcorn, and candy.

Colin nods earnestly. "Ah, yes. It has served you well, then, that degree."

"I think so."

This conversation—or a version of it—is the longest-running joke of our friendship. It actually started it all, during an ordinary appointment. The first time he asked the question, I thought he was being what my dad would call a "wisenheimer." So my stiff reply wasn't said in jest, like today's.

He could tell right away he'd offended me and stuttered, "Right. Oh. Sorry. I-I didn't mean any offense. I was merely curious—"

Embarrassed I'd spoken to him so unprofessionally, I flushed. "No, I'm sorry. I-it's sort of a raw nerve for me."

At my college graduation party, the ink was barely dry on my highly impractical degree when my dad asked, "What's next, Mo?"

My older brother, Greg, jumped practically mid-sentence from another conversation to join Dad and me. "Yeah, Maura. I've been wondering the same thing. Are you going out to Hollyweird now?"

I couldn't bear to tell him, "No," flat-out, so I said, "Eventually. Probably. Maybe." At his disappointment with that noncommittal statement, I clarified, "I don't have a job yet, so it would be irresponsible to go out there without a plan."

Now, I was speaking his language. He nodded pensively.

"I still have my job at the Career Center, so I'll stay there for a while, save up some money, then relocate to L.A. or New York City."

When I stopped there, the two of them glanced at each other before Dad smiled and said, "Oh. That's nice, Sweetie. Good plan."

Greg was less diplomatic. "That's not really a plan, though. It's half a plan. What are you going to do when you get to New York or L.A.?"

I tried to lend a mysterious, carefree air to the half-shrug and eye roll that preceded my response, but I'm afraid the gesture betrayed my cluelessness more than anything. "Whatever. I'll apply for jobs in the industry."

"What industry?"

"Film-making," I answered, using the tone one would use with a child. "Or critique. Or teaching." By then, it was obvious I was reaching.

Greg lectured, "You don't want to wait too long, though. Nobody will hire you if you've been out of the business for any length of time. You'd be better off moving there right now, interning somewhere so you can get some experience, and taking any job you can find that pays the bills."

"But—"

"Really, Mo. You wait too long, and you'll lose your nerve."

Dad placed a gentle hand on Greg's arm. "Okay, okay. She gets it. Why don't you let the poor girl enjoy her party? She's only had her diploma for a day."

The two of them wandered away from me, but not before I heard Greg mutter, "I already had a job lined up before graduation," to which Dad laughed and replied, "Yeah, well, you're the go-getter."

Five years later, I'm still in Kansas City. I've become a seemingly permanent fixture in this temporary gig of mine, but I'm okay with my life. Job counseling isn't sexy, but it's a paycheck.

The first time Colin noticed my diploma on the wall, he said, "So, you display your degree, because...?"

Originally as a joke, I thought but didn't say. Instead, I said, "Most people don't read it, so it lends an air of authority. If nothing else, it proves I saw something through to the end, no matter how irrelevant it's turned out to be."

"Well, I think it's brilliant," he said, licking his lips and approaching my desk once more. "Truly. I'm a bit of a film buff, myself."

I was willing to leave it at that, but he winced. "Oh, blimey. That sounded quite patronizing, didn't it? You probably have more film knowledge in your little finger than I do in my entire— wherever that information is stored. Oh, bollocks. I'm making a real pig's ear of this. Never mind. I'll simply, er, take my referral and go now."

That's when, to my horror, I started laughing.

He nervously joined in.

Soon, we were both wheezing and wiping tears from our eyes and faces. When the hysterics subsided, I threw out, half-joking, "You should see my film collection sometime." As soon as the invitation was out, I regretted it. Blushing, I held out the referral card to him. "Never mind. Here. I'm sorry."

"No! I'd love to see it. Maybe with some other people around, though. For your safety, of course. Because—I say this as a former bobby—it's probably not wise to invite strange men to your house. I'm the strangest of strange men. My mum says so."

Relieved, I laughed. Three days later, he came over and, with Rae as a chaperon, stood in awe in the middle of my "movie room." He borrowed three films—and promptly returned them less than a week later. We've been friends ever since.

Today, nearly three years after that, I fill out the last two blanks on the referral card, attempting to make my horrible penmanship legible, and sign it with a flourish before sliding it across my desk.

He takes the two steps required to arrive in front of me and plucks the cardstock square from the surface.

"Right. Thanks."

I nod while clicking my pen. "No problem. If that doesn't work out for whatever reason, you know there's plenty where that came from. You could supplement those hours gift wrapping. There's a kiosk for that at the mall, too, and they're hiring."

He tucks the card into his back pocket. "There's a reason every gift I've ever given you was in a bag. The things I wrap look like they come from someone without opposable thumbs."

I laugh at his apt description but stop short when he suddenly slaps his forehead and says, "Oh, bloody hell. I've moaned on and on about my life and didn't leave time to ask you about that party you attended with Rae! I'm still a bit miffed she didn't ask me, since we're so close, and all."

Considering his barely civil relationship with Rae, the mental image of him at that particular event with her cracks me up. "Um, you dodged a dull evening. Other than dancing with the team's quarterback, Jet Knox, and giving him my phone number when he asked for it, it was a snooze-fest."

He snaps his fingers. "Pity. I was all set to hear some grand tales. But perhaps something will come of the exchange of digits?"

Scoffing, I reply, "Doubt it very seriously. It's been weeks, but I've heard nothing. There was no exchange. My phone number only, to be lost forever in a jumble of women's numbers in his phone, I'm sure."

"We need to work on your sense of romance."

"Romance only happens in the movies."

Conscious of the time and my next appointment waiting, I stand and circle my desk to give him one of the three hugs he claims he needs each day, "for emotional stability," and walk him out. "Let me know how it goes at the mall. I especially need an update on the Santa hat situation." Not wanting to give my waiting clients any ideas about hugs being part of the standard service, I let him go before I open my door. Ringing phones and outer-office chatter greet us.

"I will," he says. "Well, I'll try. That's a good enough promise, right?"

From him, yes, considering he has an aversion to texting I haven't been able to figure out.

He shakes my hand, mock formally.

Over his shoulder, I see my next client, another repeat customer. Frequently visiting my office is where Vanessa's resemblance to Colin ends, unfortunately.

I feel a headache coming on.

THREE

CHRISTMAS PLANS

Vanessa wasn't my last headache of the day, by far. The headaches didn't stop when I left work, either. The latest obstacle to my achieving a relaxing evening at home is a bumper-to-bumper standstill traffic jam on the interstate. And, to make this experience more delightful, my brother's ringtone, "Relax" by Frankie Goes to Hollywood, interrupts my fantasies of red wine and mindless television.

Since I may as well be sitting in a parking lot, it's perfectly safe to answer the call. I'm not happy about answering, but I know my brother well enough to know he'll keep calling until I do. Plus, I'm that bored.

"Gregory," I greet him drolly.

"Hey, Mo. Got a second?"

"From the looks of things, I have several. What's up?"

"I wanted to talk to you about Christmas."

Barely, I stifle a groan.

Mom and Dad are finally taking the cruise they threaten to take every year. While I'm happy for them, their plans leave me at the mercy of my older brother and his fiancée. Thanksgiving was nearly two weeks ago; I've been waiting and wondering when I'd be given the itinerary for "our" holiday plans.

When he doesn't continue right away, I prod, "Yes?"

He clears his throat. "Deirdre and I were thinking the three of us could get together on Christmas Eve. That way, she and I would be free to spend Christmas Day with her parents."

My gut reaction is to easily agree to this arrangement, but before I do, it hits me: that leaves me alone on Christmas.

My millisecond's hesitation makes him rush on, "I mean, if that's okay with you. You know what? Never mind. That's not going to work, is it? Well, is it?"

"Uh…" A picture of myself, sitting alone in my house, listening to carols on the radio station that plays them 24/7 from Halloween until the day after Christmas, drinking hot tea, and wrapped in one of the many hideous afghans our grandmother crocheted when she was still alive and had nothing better to do all day in the nursing home flashes through my head, and I barely choke out the "Okay" that was trying its damnedest to stick in my throat.

It's not okay. But neither is spending the day with Greg and Deirdre. So, he might as well make his fiancée and her family happy.

"Are you sure? I feel bad that you'll be alone on the actual day."

"Who says I will be?" I retort lightly. Before he can press me for details, though, I ask, "What time do you want to get together on Christmas Eve?"

"Seven. At my place. We'll have dinner, exchange gifts, and play a game."

This isn't a rough plan, either. He means those things *will* happen. In that order. I'll be out the door and on my way home by ten, my gifts in one hand and a wrapped plate of leftovers in the other. It'll be gloriously scripted and non-spontaneous. No surprises.

Greg and Deirdre are—How do I say this diplomatically? Ah, screw diplomatic—anal retentive. Both of them. Type-A bookends. God help their future children.

"Sounds... fun," I say weakly.

"We plan for it to be."

"Then it will be."

If he senses the snark in my tone, he doesn't call me on it.

"Hey, listen. The traffic's starting to move," I say, staring at the stationary license plate at eye level on the back of the enormous SUV in front of me. With that lie, I make plans to watch the Chiefs game at his house on Sunday, as usual, and hang up.

"Ho-ho-holy shit, this Christmas is going to blow," I declare to nobody.

———

I finally make it home after the snarl that turned my twenty-minute commute into a nearly hour-long nightmare. Dispensing with my shoes and my bra is Priority Number One. Then, with a contented sigh, I greet the man of the house.

"Howdy, Jason. Or are we Matt tonight? Either way, it's been a day. Where's my drink? How many times do I have to tell you to have that ready for me when I walk through the door? Honestly. You may be a crack spy, but you're a shit fake-husband-slash-sex-slave." Winking on my way past the last picture, I pat its wooden frame. "Only kidding. I love ya."

I don't talk to all of the framed movie posters on my walls. It just seems rude to ignore Matt, since he watches me take off my bra every day—with the exception of Bourne Number Three, who's a gentleman and keeps his back turned.

My poster collection is the only personal touch I've added to the living room's otherwise bland decor, with its stormy-gray walls and white molding. Light-blocking, white, wooden blinds cover the windows. Maroon embroidered sheers hang in front of them on pewter rods. The window dressing has one primary job: block out light during my weekend movie marathons. Privacy is a bonus. Not that I do anything in here that requires it.

I bought the matching microsuede couch and armless chair with ottoman in a slightly lighter gray than the walls but still dark enough to hide my clumsy food (okay, wine) spills. My dining area holds a lovely set that includes a table, chairs, and china hutch—empty of any fine china, mind you—but I prefer to eat in front of the television, unless I have company.

The place is generic, temporary, and noncommittal, like something from a box store circular. Or a timeshare condo that has to appeal to many different tastes. That's intentional. I didn't expect to be here long, so when making interior design decisions, I played it safe. I basically staged it, figuring it could be sale-ready in a matter of hours. All I have to do is take down my posters, and *voilà!*

That is, if I hadn't lost my nerve.

Over the years, the wall hangings have covered more and more of the gray. I've bought or salvaged them from stores and cinemas, and they're in every room, including the bathrooms.

"It's impossible to go with Patrick Swayze checking me out," Greg complained once after using the toilet.

I'd laughed. "Too bad. Johnny, Baby, and I have meaningful conversations during bubble baths."

Not really. But that tidbit served to annoy my brother and make him think I'm even flakier than I am, which was the goal. Actually, I don't normally keep the *Dirty Dancing* poster in the bathroom. When Greg's expected, I change out the *Crouching Tiger, Hidden Dragon* print that better fits with the cherry blossom shower curtain. Because I like to see my big brother squirm.

He deserves it—not just for abandoning me at Christmas.

At that mental reminder, I sigh again, this time not-so-contentedly, and plod down the hallway to my bedroom, where I peel off my work clothes, drop them in a pile next to the bed, stare at them for a second, then reconsider and hang up the stuff that's still technically clean but will become hopelessly wrinkled in that heap. My bra goes on top of my dresser (isn't that where they go?) to be worn tomorrow. And probably for several days after that, if I'm being honest. I pull on a large sleep shirt, turn off the bedroom light, and head straight for the kitchen.

After dispatching a frozen dinner into the microwave, I retreat to my movie room. My film collection fills up my spare bedroom, which I've turned into a miniature version of that endangered species, the video rental store. Above the door, I've even plastered the ubiquitous "Be Kind, Rewind" signage I purchased from a Blockbuster "Going-out-of-business-for-good-sayonara-thanks-for-nothing-Netflix-and-Redbox-and-the-rest-of-you-ungrateful-movie-loving-bastards" sale.

There are no posters in here, because built-in shelving covers every available inch of wall space. I'm also up to my second row of movies on each shelf. It's not an ideal system; it's cumbersome for cataloging and organizing when I add new films. I'm not sure what I'm going to do when I truly run out of space, which will be soon, at the rate I buy movies. I guess I'll—gulp—cull the collection. Or buy a bigger place. I'll worry about that when it happens, though.

Right now, my biggest concern is zeroing in on which film best suits my mood and will be keeping me company for the evening. Standing in the middle of the room, I close my eyes and tap my eyelids. It's likely I own any film that floats through my head, so I focus on my feelings.

After that depressing rush-hour conversation with Greg, *Home for the Holidays* with Holly Hunter is perfect. I walk straight to the section of shelving that houses the H's. Since the film is one of my favorites, I own it on both VHS (the original purchase) and in digital format, but I slide the newest version from its slot on the shelf and carry it with me to the living room.

The microwave dings as I press "play" on the remote, and that familiar Paramount summit appears on my screen, soon surrounded by the circle of stars that almost always gives me goose bumps. Because I'm about to have an experience. Good, bad, or indifferent. I'm going to meet some new friends or reunite with old ones. In this case, I know exactly what I'm about to get, and I'm going to love every minute of it.

It's going to be much more satisfying than that lonely meal for one that's bound to be volcanic on the edges and glacial in the center.

Before I can burn a single taste bud, however, my phone chimes next to me on the arm of the sofa. An incoming text from Rae reads:

Have you checked out KB's Twitter account lately?

The answer is, surprisingly, no. I still haven't forgiven Mr. Tight End for being a no-show to the Christmas party and dashing my fantasies. Allegedly, he was spending the bye week in his hometown of Cincinnati, to visit family and watch his brother, a Bengal, play the Thursday night game. I guess nobody told him his biggest fan would be at his team's Christmas party. That definitely would have changed everything.

With one hand, I text back, *No*, while taking my first bite of lukewarm lasagna.

I'll give you a minute

I navigate to Busch's Twitter page. All I see are the usual pre- and post-game pep- and smack-talk tweets.

I go back to my text conversation with Rae.

I don't see anything weird. What's up? Did he propose to me out there? I told him I didn't want all that publicity!

Ha. Ha.

Seriously. What?

He must have taken it down. Or was told to take it down. Some groupie asked him if he was single, and he replied, Send me your picture, and I'll let you know. Ugh!

I never said he was classy. Just that he fills out those pants mighty nicely, and I'd hit that

You'd be a match made in heaven

Make it happen, Lewisberg. KB, wrapped in a bow, delivered to my house, on Christmas morning. BAM.

NO. He makes Jet Knox look like a choir boy. And a Rhodes scholar

Knox will do, in a pinch

Have G set you up with someone from his work

I'd rather die

Nice, stable, normal human resources guru

You want me to date my brother?

One of his friends

He doesn't have friends

Colleagues?

Gross. Don't you have bags to pack for your trip tomorrow?

I'm all set. Ready to kick some Raider rumps!

That sounds like something stolen from KB's tweets

Eff you. I'm going to bed

Love you! G'night!

I want to tell her to say hi to Jet for me, but not only would that be pathetic, but it would break my perfect streak of not talking to her about him in any context other than football. It's getting easier. At first, I wanted to ask her all the time if he'd said anything about me to her, not caring if it made me sound like a teenager. But the more time passes, the more I realize nothing's going to happen there, and the chances of him remembering me are slim.

Not that I expected to get a call or text. After all, I'm me and he's Jet Knox. He's probably already deleted me from his contacts to make room for all of the other numbers he's collected in the past month. Which is just as well. As much as I like to joke about it and talk a big game, guys like Jet Knox and Keaton Busch are way out of my league.

Tuning back into my movie, I contemplate how Robert Downey, Jr. or Dylan McDermott are more my speed: cute, unattainable, and thousands of miles away.

FOUR

RAE & MAURA: A FRIENDSHIP

Rae and I have been best friends since she moved into the house next door the summer before we started sixth grade. She was a scrappy tomboy who reminded me of an older version of Scout in *To Kill a Mockingbird*. Freckled, wiry, and dirty, she introduced herself to me with a business-like hand-shake and a confident, "We're going to be best friends," when my mom dragged me over to the Lewisbergs' house to welcome them to the neighborhood.

I wasn't as positive. In fifth grade, I'd discovered boys. Which means by the time I met Rae, I was well indoctrinated in the cult of pre-teen girls, where image is everything, despite not having any idea at that age what image entails. I did know, however, that it involved regular bathing, cute hair, and trendy clothes, none of which seemed high on the new girl's list of priorities.

I couldn't resist an underdog, though. I'm a born-and-bred Chiefs and Royals fan, after all. When Rae declared us "best friends," I thought, *All right. I can work with this. She's a little rough around the edges, but what is life without a project?*

It didn't take long for me to figure out that Rae wasn't like other girls. Probably because she came right out and told me, the first time I tried to give her a makeover.

"I don't do girlie stuff."

"What do you mean, 'girlie stuff'? This isn't about being girlie. I like sports, too, and it's cool that you help your dad fix things, but if you let me do your hair and dress you in some of my new school clothes, I can show you how fun it is to—"

"That stuff's lame."

"No, it's not! All the girls at Kennedy are going to have these jeans this year." I held up my mom's latest purchase for me. "Aren't they cool?"

She wrinkled her nose. "They're pants. I have plenty of pairs."

"Not *these*, though. Yours are all... straight and stiff. Like something Greg would wear."

"As long as it's not a dress or a skirt, I'm okay with that." She slid down from my high canopy bed. "Let's go see what the guys are doing. Did I hear Greg say he got a new video game with his allowance money?"

"They're not going to let us play."

"So? Watching is fun, too."

I disagreed, but already at that young age, I hated conflict and avoided it at all costs, so I dropped my efforts to prissify my new friend. I revisited the topic several times over the next few years, as it became a bigger and more exhausting job to play protector and champion to Rae, the nonconformist.

Being different at that age isn't easy. It's not like I was the most popular girl at school, but I wasn't an outcast, either, so I took it upon myself to help Rae settle into life at Kennedy Middle School. I introduced her to my respectable-sized group of friends, who tolerated her until about halfway through high school, when I suddenly realized Rae and I were now a duo and were increasingly being left out of group activities.

It was about that time, during our sophomore year, that Rae disabused me of any lingering hopes of her assimilating.

Facing each other, we were sitting on the floor of my room one Friday night during a sleepover involving just the two of us, oohing and aahing over whichever baby-faced idiot teenaged celebrity we (supposedly) were into at the time, when she suddenly got quiet and closed the magazine between us.

"What's wrong?" I asked.

She shrugged. "Nothing. I don't feel like looking at that anymore, that's all."

"Oh. Whatever. Wanna go see what kind of chips my mom got?" I moved to stand, but she stopped me with a hand on my arm.

"Wait. I— I need to tell you something."

I could tell by the slightly sick look on her face that whatever it was would be juicy, so I settled in for some meaty gossip. "I knew it! You like Jeremy Ward, don't you? I've been telling Kimi for weeks that there's something going on there, but she keeps saying, 'No way! Jeremy's going out with Brandi,' as if that matters. I mean, if you like someone, you like someone. Danny Ashland's been going out with Heather-the-Feather Poole since eighth grade, but that hasn't stopped me from being, like, totally in love with him. So, when did you start to feel... you know... *wiggly* about Jeremy?"

She ducked her chin at me. "'Wiggly'? What the hell does that mean?"

Secretly, Rae's fascination with cussing made me uncomfortable, but I suspected that made me an unsophisticated goody-goody, so I tended to pretend I didn't hear the bad words. In this case, it was easy, because I was more intent on answering her question. "You know! Wiggly!" Sitting with my legs folded under me and my feet under my bottom, I squirmed and pretended to tickle my own stomach. "Like when you look at someone you like, and you feel all... fizzy."

For the first time in several minutes, Rae's face relaxed, and she laughed. "You're such a dork."

"But you know what I'm saying!"

She nodded. "Yeah. I do. Exactly."

"Then I'm not a dork. I'm good at describing things."

I was reveling in the satisfaction garnered by her conceding shrug when she dropped, "But Jeremy Ward doesn't make me feel like that."

"Whatever. Then why do you follow him and Brandi around all the time? I see you watching them when you think nobody's looking."

Her shoulders sagged, and she picked at the fringe on my area rug. I figured her big confession was about to happen— and I was confused as to why she was so hesitant to admit it— so it took me a while to comprehend what she meant when she said, "I'm not looking at him. I'm looking at"—she inhaled, reinflating her chest and sitting straighter once more —"Brandi."

Still so dumb (and young and Midwestern and wrapped up in my own narrow experience with life), I was on the verge of saying, "Why? Do you like Brandi's new haircut? It would look super-cute on you, too," when the penny finally dropped. I swallowed. Hard. "Brandi makes you feel all wiggly?"

Rae rolled her eyes. "Yes! Duh. I don't like boys."

She said it like someone would say, "I don't like onions," like it was no big deal. But to me, it was a big deal.

I also knew my next response was a bigger deal. In a

matter of seconds, I processed what she was telling me—what I already knew, if I were being completely honest with myself—and merely said, "Oh."

"Oh? That's it?" She scoffed, then muttered, "'Oh,' she says."

Recovering more fully, I laughed at myself, then said, "Well, I mean, girls don't do it for *me*, but hey! I guess we never have to worry about fighting over the same guy."

"Never." She shook her head and widened her eyes. "Danny Ashland? Barf."

I jumped to my feet and grabbed a pillow from my bed, swinging it at her head, "Hey! Danny is gorgeous!"

"And dumber than a box of rocks."

"He's not dumb, just quiet."

Struggling to stand while still under heavy attack, she crawled to my bed and pulled herself up by the eyelet comforter, almost laughing too hard for me to understand her when she retorted with her arms in front of her face, "Because he's too busy listening to the sound of his brains rattling around up there."

After the third swing and hit across her chest, she grabbed the pillow and wrenched it from my hands. Her short hair standing in a static-induced spike, she grinned at me. "Did you say your mom got chips?"

Not much later, Rae came out to everyone. Looking back, I'm honored I was the first person she told. At the time, though, as a stupid, selfish teenager, it was a burden I'd have rather not shouldered. Every time she told an adult or one of our distant acquaintances, they'd ask, "Did you know this? Why didn't you tell me/us?" How do you answer that? As a nearly thirty-year-old, with the benefit of hindsight, I can think of plenty of ways, some of them not polite. Back then, I was stumped and chose the non-answer, "I thought everyone already knew." It got me off the hook and shut people up, because nobody likes to admit they're clueless. It made me look like I *wasn't*.

Then, of course, came the ignorant questions from some (mostly male peers):

"Are *you* a lesbian too, now?"

Because it's contagious?

"Do you and Rae... you know?"

Because being gay means being attracted to and unable to resist everyone of the same sex, and the targets of their attraction are powerless to stop it, you know? They're trying to take over the world!

"Are you still going to be friends with her?"

Because she's no longer technically a human now, right? So you can cast her aside.

Of course, Rae's news wasn't news to most people close to us. I might have been the person she chose to formally come out to first, but I was far from the first person to know. Nobody in our group of friends was shocked. Suddenly, it made sense why she and I were being pushed out. Which pissed me off. But I wanted to hear it straight from them. I wanted them to admit that was the reason.

After months of mustering the nerve to ask, I approached one of them. Kimi confirmed my suspicions. "Rae's weird. She says things that make the rest of us uncomfortable, and she doesn't like boys, so she rolls her eyes when we talk about them."

I laughed. "Okay. But that's all about Rae. Why don't you guys invite *me* to hang out anymore?"

Kimi fidgeted when she answered, "You two are kind of a package deal now, right? You're *always* together. Like you're a couple, or something."

While that was factually inaccurate, I could tell by Kimi's wrinkled nose that if I were to deny her implication, it would somehow get back to Rae that I was disgusted by the prospect, and that would hurt her feelings. Not because she had romantic designs on me—she didn't and still doesn't and never will—but because she was constantly being rejected for who she was, by friends, family... everyone. I refused to let her think for a second she could add me to that list.

So I gracefully bowed out of the larger high school social scene (who wants to be friends with people like that?) and concentrated all of my friendship efforts on Rae. We went to UMKC together and were roomies for most of that time, after we had a choice.

After graduation, I bought my own place, deciding it was time to at least pretend to be a grownup and live on my own. Although I was the one who moved out, Rae's much more grown-up than I am, still. She has a *career*, after all, while I have a placeholder job that pays my bills and funds my silly movie hobby.

Living alone has meant that I've widened my friendship base to include people like Colin and... Okay, just Colin. Still, that's a one hundred percent increase in friends, which is pretty dramatic for me.

Dating has been easier, too. Not that I've done much of it or have been successful at it. But when I have dated, I've found that not having someone to answer to at home makes things less complicated. Rae never stood in my way of dating, obviously, nor vice versa, but when we lived together, it seemed like we felt the need to vet each other's potential partners, which could get dicey, considering she's *never* approved of the guys I've liked.

"Why do you always pick the dumb ones? I don't get it! Is

it so you feel smarter, by comparison? Because you're plenty smart, Mo. You could date a real brainiac and still be the smart one. Stop dumbing it down so much. What do you even talk about with these bozos? And don't say, 'movies.'"

But that's usually the answer. Because the dumbest person on the planet—and despite what Rae thinks, I've never come close to dating men of that description—can talk about films. They may not delve into the deeper meanings behind shot composition and selection, but they can at least pinpoint their favorite films and say why they like them. I've found that a good discussion about movies is a decent way to get a feel for someone's personality.

And while I'm not a cinematic snob, there are some red flag responses to, "What's your favorite movie?" It's not that I think I could never be with someone who replies, "The *Star Wars* prequels," but there's a good chance that's not going to be a lasting love. Depending on a few other factors, I might let him wave his light saber at me and call me Queen Amidala (in private) for a short time, though. Loneliness is a powerful motivator.

Right now, after a stint of dead-end relationships, with me being the dead end of the street,, I choose loneliness over the eligible guys my age who seem to be looking for uteri more than companionship. I've had a few first dates whose ticking biological clocks drowned out the paltry conversation to the point that all I could hear by the end of the night, no matter what the guy said, was, "Have my babies." Needless to say, there haven't been many second dates.

Rae's not experiencing that problem, because she's rarely dating at all these days. She doesn't have time for it, with her work and travel schedule. She doesn't have much time for me, either. Which is fine. She's not much fun to be around right now, anyway.

Prickly with everyone else in her life, she's tended to give me a pass—until recently. I've chalked up being at the receiving end of her more cutting barbs lately to the stress of her relatively new job. It was a highly contested position, so being chosen from the hundreds of applicants was a big deal. Plus, it's been her dream for as long as I've known her to work for the NFL, in general, not to mention our hometown team. Achieving and keeping a goal like that must come with plenty of pressure. Since I wouldn't know firsthand, I have to assume that's the case.

So, I get that she's on edge lately, even with me, the person who's been at her side through everything it took to get here. I also get that she needs to focus her attention on work and immerse herself in it. But the less time we spend together, the further apart we've grown. I guess it was an inevitability of growing up (which I'd like to go on record as saying pretty much sucks), and maybe there's nothing we can or should do about it, but that doesn't mean it's any less awkward while we're adjusting to our new dynamic.

Part of this new reality involves going to a party together, then not hearing each other's voices for more than a month and communicating exclusively via text message, if at all. Because that's happening. But you know what? That's life. She's living her dream, and I'm... living. Beats the alternative, right? Most days?

FIVE

BAH, HUMBUG!

"How are the potatoes? Do they seem bland to you? I think they're bland. Flat. There's nothing I hate more than flat potatoes."

"They're fine," I reassure my future sister-in-law. "And the duck is fabulous."

That's right. Duck. There will be no pedestrian turkey at this Christmas dinner. Or, heaven forbid, ham. Greg and Deirdre, the future Mr. and Dr. Snow-Richards/Richards-Snow (they're still debating the order of their hyphenated moniker), are duck people. We're eating by candlelight.

I've never felt more like a third wheel in my life. That always makes me belligerent.

When I'm finished eating, I set my silverware on my plate, lean back in my chair, pull out my huge pot-stirring ladle, and ask, "How are the wedding plans going?"

Deirdre answers, "Fine," then purses her lips so tightly they could be mistaken for her butthole.

Greg says, "Fine," then adds after a few seconds' pause, "if you ignore the fact that we still haven't been able to agree on the flowers. I want understated; she wants... gaudy."

She adjusts the position of her wine glass in relation to her plate. "The arrangements I like aren't gaudy! They're dramatic, which is going to be necessary, because the venue is so large. Your 'understated' bouquets will blend in with the woodwork."

"Why do you care about flowers, Greg?" I ask. "Seriously. That's so not the groom's territory."

"And that's a sexist statement."

"Answer the question."

"Sue me for not wanting the flowers to be towering over us in all the pictures, like something out of *Little Shop of Horrors*."

Deirdre looks at the dainty watch on her bony wrist. "Well, we're running out of time on that decision."

"Show me pictures of the two options, and I'll decide," I offer, straight-faced. "Break the tie."

The two of them laugh stiffly.

"Or you could postpone the wedding until you end your floral stalemate."

Deirdre's face goes from tight amusement to wide-eyed earnestness in 0.2 seconds flat. "The wedding is happening on the first Saturday in June, and that's not negotiable."

"Not at all," Greg concurs. "If we slide back the date of the wedding, that will affect all the other dates in our five-, ten-, and fifteen-year plans. Not an option."

I attempt—and fail—to stifle a snicker. If I didn't know them better, I'd think they were kidding about all of this. But they're dead serious. Scarily serious.

"Well, if the flowers are your biggest sticking point, then you've made progress since the last time we talked. You must have decided on your last name and which house you're going to live in, huh?"

Robotically, Deirdre starts stacking the china and gathering the silver. "Those decisions aren't as critical."

I continue to stir. "Oh, but with the housing market the way it is, you guys need to pick which house you're going to sell, right?"

"Hers is more marketable right now," Greg points out. "Fewer bedrooms, lower price point, easier to move. This place, on the other hand, is perfect for a growing family. It's hardly worth discussing."

Deirdre chuckles mirthlessly. "Oh, but it *is* worth discussing. This house is too big for us, but we could get more money out of it. Money that we could invest in our children's college funds."

"Where are these children of yours? Is there something the two of you haven't told me? What are their names? Bring them out to meet Aunt Maura."

Greg shoots me a look that probably was supposed to be withering but seems more indulgent when he can't catch his smile in time. "Maura."

"Oh! You've named one of them after me?" At Deirdre's panicked expression, I say, "Kidding, D! Gosh. I can't say it enough: you two need to chill. Take a deep breath."

"These are critical decisions, Maura, decisions that could affect the rest of our lives." Oh, Lord. She's using her Dr. Snow tone now. I can definitely hear her telling her heart patients about the importance of diet and exercise in this exact same voice.

Goaded by the condescension, I snipe, "Really, Deirdre? The wedding flowers could make or break your future happiness?"

"Someday you'll understand. When you're a bride, you'll want everything to be perfect. When you're ready to have children, you'll see how— how *loaded* every decision seems to be. Life is so easy when you have only yourself to answer to."

After she delivers what she believes to be the final word on that topic, she carries the dirty dishes into the kitchen, leaving me alone with Greg, who rolls his eyes at his future wife's back.

"Don't even," I warn him. "You're as bad as she is."

"There's nothing wrong with having goals and a plan. I can help you come up with one of your own, if you want."

It's a common misconception that I have no aspirations. I do. My main one simply happens to be for me not to be goal-oriented, and to keep my life as uncomplicated as possible.

Plus, Deirdre and my brother have enough goals and plans for all of us. It's important for society to be balanced. Those of us who are more, shall we say, "laid-back," keep the world from going haywire with all these driven freaks like Greg and Deirdre, the couple who manages to make the most intimate of Christmas Eve get-togethers tense.

I glower at him. "Plans aren't fun." Before he can contradict me, I rush forward with, "Oh, my gosh! Speaking of fun, I've been dying to tell you this for over a month, but with the holidays and work and... stuff— Plus, I didn't want to mention it in front of Mom and Dad at Thanksgiving, because they would have asked a bunch of uncomfortable questions, but—"

"You're moving to L.A.?"

My face falls. "No."

"New York?"

My jaw tightens. "Are you trying to get rid of me?" I say it lightly and with a slight smile, so I won't let on that he's ruining my moment. But he's totally ruining my moment.

"I'm trying to figure out what would be exciting in your world."

"Uh, gee. Thanks? How about you let me finish?"

He shrugs, then waits.

"You'll never guess who I hung out with at the Chiefs' Christmas party. Jet Knox!"

"The quarterback, Jet Knox?" he asks skeptically.

I tilt my head at him and make a face. "How many people on the team—on the planet—are named Jet Knox? Of course, the quarterback!"

"You're kidding, right?"

Offended he finds this so incredible, I pound the table. "I'm serious!"

"Wow. So, is he a cool guy? Man, I wish I'd known you were going to meet him; I'd have sent my Knox jersey with you for him to sign. Damn."

I don't tell him I probably wouldn't have agreed to do something that dorky. It's a moot point, anyway.

"Yeah. He was nice. Good sense of humor." *Smells great. Looks nice in a suit. Knows how to make a girl feel like the only woman in a room. Collects phone numbers he never plans to dial…*

"Who's this?" Deirdre asks as she returns to the table with pie and coffee.

Before I can open my mouth, Greg answers, "Mo danced with Jet Knox at the Chiefs' Christmas party! Can you believe it? How cool is that?"

I sip my coffee and roll my eyes, but I can't quite keep the delighted smirk from my face. It *was* cool, and he was hot. If this is going to be my one bite of the fame enchilada, I should probably get some chews from it. After all, something this insignificant has a pretty short shelf life. If I'm still talking about it more than a year from now, it's just embarrassing and pathetic. For now, it's fresh enough not to make people retch when they hear it.

For once, Deidre, the snow queen, looks impressed. She raises her eyebrows at me and says, "Hm. Any chemistry there? How fun would it be to date someone like him? Interesting, if nothing else..." I can see her wheels turning, and she says after swallowing a bite of pie, pointing to me with her fork and squinting her eyes, "Do you have any interest in journalism or PR? Because if so, he could probably help you get a foot in the door."

I sigh so enthusiastically that I almost shoot pie from my nose. She looks alarmed when I cough and sputter. After nearly a minute of this, her medical training is about to kick in when I hold up a hand and say, "I'm fine. But I don't have any ulterior motives with Jet Knox. I don't even know the guy. We talked at a party. That's it." Sip, sip, sip. Cough, cough.

"There's nothing wrong with networking," Deirdre says. "I was simply brainstorming."

Yes. Brainstorming. Toss ideas out there and hope one of them sticks or leads to a better one. Because, for some reason, she and Greg are obsessed with fixing me, figuring out the perfect formula that will turn me into a winner.

Dating Jet Knox would certainly do the trick. Then I'd never have to do anything else with my life.

Puh-lease.

———

So far this Christmas Day, I've listened to sixteen covers of "Last Christmas" and read two books. I've also consumed five cups of tea, but I've since moved on to spiked eggnog (I'm on my third cup). I've refused, however, to huddle under anything remotely resembling an afghan, to avoid doing exactly what I pictured myself doing in all of my lonely Christmas nightmares. Also, I'm not wearing fingerless gloves. (For some reason, I always imagined myself wearing fingerless gloves while sitting alone in my house on Christmas Day. Maybe it's because they add an air of utter despondence to the wearer. In any case, I'm not wearing them.)

For my viewing pleasure, I've watched the Christmas favorites, *Love Actually* and *The Holiday*, and I'm halfway through *Home Alone*. The rom-coms were obvious boneheaded choices to watch while alone and not just single, but hopelessly single. A part of me wanted to see if I was tough enough to handle them. I was. Barely. I turned on *Home Alone* to lift my spirits, since I always laughed so much at this movie when I was a kid. As an adult, though, it's a completely different story. It's downright depressing!

Think about it. The whole family hates this kid so much they don't realize they've left him behind until they're over the ocean on their way to a completely different continent! Meanwhile, he's all by himself in that big, empty house, fending for himself and defending the homestead against a couple of creepy burglars. The whole time, he's wondering if he'll be alone forever, because he took his family for granted and wished them away.

Poor Kevin!

Poor Maura!

I honk into my fourth tissue while stopping the DVD for good. I can't do it. I can't make it through the rest of this miserable movie. It's not at all funny to be home alone at Christmas. It's tragic!

Christmas is for being with people you love, your parents and siblings and grandparents (if they're still kickin') and—and significant other, someone who's glad to be with you and who put plenty of time and thought into your gifts, someone whose gifts required you to do the same, someone you can curl up with in front of a fireplace and laugh with while your family tells them funny—or delightfully cringe-worthy—stories about you and Christmases past.

It's hard to imagine Greg and Deirdre having a day like that at the Snows' house. From what Greg has said, D's apple didn't fall far from the proverbial tree. Not that he's ever complained. More like bragged about how sensible and staid and steady they are. In other words, boring!

Colin's holiday visit to England, on the other hand, seems to be exactly what Christmas should be. Based on the pictures he's emailed me, it's a Dickensian wonderland, with carolers, lights, garland, and stone churches. And snow! Some of the snapshots he sent also included people in them. There was one of him walking arm-in-arm with his mom (who looks lovely and happy to have her son with her, not fussy and haggard, like he always describes her), kicking through the powdered-sugar dusting on cobblestone streets. Another showed him wearing his goofy paper crown from his Christmas cracker and, still another, sitting by the fire in a bulky sweater, his hands wrapped around a mug of tea. It looks like he's having an amazing time.

I should have cashed in all of that vacation time I'll likely waste on Mondays I can't face and invited myself along. He probably would have welcomed the company, someone to share his parents' attention.

Unfortunately, I don't even have a passport. That's how lame I am.

Okay, this is ridiculous. I'm comfortable being alone with myself any other day. Why is this day different (other than the aforementioned reasons that I am now going to systematically disregard)? I don't depend on others for my happiness. I don't base my self-esteem on socioeconomic status or use career success as a yardstick of my worth as a member of the human race. One's importance has nothing to do with one's bank balance or letters after one's name or the number of friends one has or spends time with on evenings, weekends, and holidays. I'm a happy, carefree, modern *adult*. It's time to stop moping like an angsty teenager. It's time for...

I glance at my phone.

...Chiefs football!

When I turn off the DVD player, the sights and sounds of the pre-game show greet me. While it's not typical for there to be games on Christmas Day, the holiday falls on a Sunday this year. That sucks for the players, staff, and crew and their families, but it's good news for bored, lonely losers like me. I've been looking forward to this game all day.

We win the coin toss but opt for getting the ball first after halftime, rather than now. Usually, I agree with the decision to defer, but tonight, I'd rather not give Denver, one of our biggest rivals, the chance to strike first. Plus, watching an offensive drive is more exciting, and a successful drive ending in some points would go a long way to lifting my yuletide melancholia.

After allowing some quick gains, our defense finally seems to wake up, keeping the Broncos well on their half of the field, miles from the goal line (technically, eighty yards), with a long way to go if they want to keep the ball. A couple of bone-headed offensive penalties follow, pushing them back farther still.

"Ha ha! Losers!"

While I'm still gloating about that, one of our linebackers takes out Denver's quarterback, Pete Jay, before he can get rid of the ball.

"Sack!" I let loose in a delighted screech, followed by vigorous clapping.

That brings on the punting unit.

I sit on the edge of the couch and watch our punt returner signal for a fair catch before I rush into the kitchen to mix myself another glass of 'nog during the commercial break.

Returning to my perch, ready to root for my team, I say as the break ends, "All right, guys. Let's beat some Bronco butt! You can clinch the Division if you win this one." You know, in case they don't already know that. And can hear me.

After a long swallow, I watch over the rim of my cup while Jet trots onto the field. Now, *that's* what I'm talking about. Mr. Tight End, who? There's a new tight end in town, ladies. Licking my lips, I set my cup down on the coffee table without taking my eyes from the TV.

"I danced with him," I say out loud to the empty room. "Yep. A lot. He said some things to me. About… things. That I can't remember right now. But, oh! He called me 'pretty!' That's right. Jet Knox called *me* 'pretty.' And he smells good. Well, maybe not right at this second, but he smelled good when he called me 'pretty.' Yes, indeedy, he—"

I gasp when he drops back to throw, and the pocket of guys who are supposed to protect him from the other team disintegrates around him. "Oh, gosh! Watch out!" I bellow, putting my hands over my eyes and peeking through my fingers as a long-haired gorilla of a guy comes from Jet's blind side, swinging his arms in a determined effort to take off the QB's head.

On nimble feet, Jet scrambles out of reach and launches the ball down-field, where the original Mr. Tight End, Keaton Busch, has run a route and is wide open, waiting for the pass. Busch catches the ball, fakes out a defender in the open field, and runs for the end zone. He has one more man to beat, which he does, easily, when one of his teammates comes to his rescue and provides a phenomenal block. BOOM!

I jump from the couch and raise my hands above my head. "Aw, yeah! Touchdown, Kan...sas City!" I crow, swinging my hips and smacking myself on the butt. "Whoop-whoop! What's that, Broncos? Ride 'em? I think we just did!"

The camera cuts to a shot of Knox joining Busch in the end zone, where they bang their helmets together and hit each other so hard on their bottoms, I can feel the sting from eight hundred miles away. That's a whole lotta beautiful butt-slappin'.

"Yeah, baby!" I drain the last of my eggnog and point to the TV. "He called me 'pretty.'"

SIX

CATCHING UP WITH COLIN

Nearly two weeks later, all evidence of the holiday season seems to have magically disappeared. The city has removed the snowflake lights and holiday banners they hang from select street lights in early December. The New Year's confetti has been swept from the streets. All that remains is cold, gray winter, soon to be followed by short, wet spring, then hot, steamy summer, and...

I shudder at what awaits me in the fall, usually my favorite season but sure to be a different story this year, thanks to the news I received earlier today.

The buzzer on my desk startles me from my unfocused, despairing stare.

"Like, Colin Bennett is, like, here?" Becca, one of the many part-time receptionists, announces in typical questioning fashion.

I press the button on my phone and say, "Like, send him in?", standing and rounding my desk to greet him.

After he closes the door and faces me, he shakes his head and backs away from my impending hug. "Ah, you'd probably better not," he says in a thick voice. "I've caught a bug, so I'll have to forgo my three hugs today. I'd hate to get you sick."

I drop my arms and retreat behind my desk. "I hope you weren't sick while you were on vacation."

He shakes his head. "Picked it up on the return flight, most likely." After taking the seat across from my desk, he considerately scoots the chair back a foot or so. "Anything interesting out there?"

I riffle through the temporary postings I've already printed out for him to peruse, looking for the one I think he'll like the most. As I'm about to pass the stack across the desk, my cell phone rings, or—more accurately—moans, on my desk.

"Oh, crap," I mutter, fumbling for the device, trying to hit the button to reject the call and send it to voicemail. I eventually manage to silence it but not before Colin shows noticeable amusement at the noise and my response.

"What the bloody hell was that? A cat in heat?" His laughter brings on a coughing fit that lasts long enough for me to consider he might need a good whack on the back—for more than his health.

When he finishes spluttering, I slide a box of tissues toward him and say with as much dignity as I can muster, "That's one of my favorite actors, singing."

"'Singing'? Are you sure about that?" He hacks and honks into a tissue that he then tosses into the tiny trash can next to my desk. "It sounds like maybe one of his crazed fans got hold of him and is torturing him in their cellar. Or perhaps he has a severe case of food poisoning. I sounded a bit like that after you and I ate that egg salad that was off. You say that was an actor making that noise on your mobile?"

"Yes. He experiments with music in his spare time."

"That certainly sounded more like an experiment than a song."

"I put it on my phone as a joke, and I keep forgetting to change my generic ringtone back to something less… moany."

While we laugh at each other, I idly wonder who would possibly be calling me in the middle of the work day. All of my usual callers should be at work; plus, they have their own custom ringtones. I've written it off in my head as a wrong number when the phone, now in vibrate mode, buzzes in the middle of my desk to let me know I have voicemail. Both of us stare at the device for a second before I grab it and toss it into my deepest desk drawer.

Colin turns his head and looks at me from the corner of his eye. "What's going on?"

"Nothing," I answer honestly. "I'm trying not to be rude. You're here in a professional capacity—"

He snorts at the notion.

"—and I want to give you my full attention. And tell you about these jobs, so we have time to catch up before my next appointment."

Seeming unconvinced, he nevertheless humors me. "Hmm. Right."

"Anyway, I've found several things you might like—or at least be willing to do for the short amount of time they run."

His smile falters. "About that…" He averts his eyes. "I dunno. Maybe it's time I go for something longer-term."

"Really? Okay. Give me a second." I turn to my computer to navigate through the interface and widen the date parameters of my earlier search. While I wait for the sluggish results to populate, I say, "You never told me how the job at the mall worked out."

"You were right about the hat," he replies. "But I was told

I wore it well." After I laugh and chide him for not bothering to take a single selfie, he continues, "Also, I learnt that people have some odd sentiments engraved on mementos. And they engrave odd items, as well. For example..." He leans forward. "One bloke brought in a toaster. A toaster! And he had me etch"—he assumes a scarily good redneck accent—"'Luann, You melt my butter. Love always, Bubba.'"

"You're making that up."

He rests his hand against his chest. "I suppose you wouldn't believe me, since you don't believe in romance."

He may look completely guileless, but he's an amazing liar, especially in the interest of getting a laugh. He's fooled me countless times with funny stories that have wound up being utter fabrications, told merely for comedic effect. And that's fine. I don't mind being part of the punchline.

"It was a nice toaster," he adds seriously. "Four slots."

I whistle. "Bubba knows how to toast a girl's bread."

Colin stifles another cough brought on by laughter. "To answer your question seriously, though, about the job, it worked out well."

"Excellent. Now, about your new prospects..." Before printing anything this time, I describe some of the full-time jobs that meet his scheduling requirements and match his skills sets. He surprises me by going with appointment taker and greeter at a hair salon that caters to a slightly 'mature' clientele.

"It'll be nice to have Sundays and Mondays off. And free haircuts," he defends his choice.

I'm not here to judge, and he's more than qualified for the post, so I print and sign the referral, then hand it over to him. "There you go. Now, more important stuff. Your trip! How was it? The pictures you sent made me jealous."

He blows his nose. Smiling mildly, he answers, "Yeah. It was nice. Better than I expected."

"That wouldn't be too hard, considering."

His smile turns sheepish. "I suppose I presumed a bit much and expected the worst, but Mum and Dad were happy to see me, and when they saw for themselves, face-to-face, that I'm okay, they relaxed a bit."

"That's good. They can't help but worry about you, all the way over here, alone."

"I'm hardly alone." He crosses his arms over his chest and sits as far back in his chair as he can and keep all four legs on the floor. "Anyway, what's new in your world?" he asks, obviously finished with the basic recap of his overseas trip.

I flap my lips. "Absolutely nothing. The Chiefs made it to the playoffs; that's my major source of joy right now."

"That's American football right?" he feigns ignorance.

My rolling eyes give him his answer and seem to amuse him. He clicks his tongue. "Is it me, or are you uncharacteristically uptight today, Lady Maura? You were putting on a good show at first, but I can tell something's bothering you."

Checking the clock to make sure we're not keeping my next appointment waiting, I debate mentioning the problem that landed in my lap this morning. Saying it out loud may make it seem like less of a big deal, though, so I begin, "There *is* something bumming me out."

He leans forward. "Do tell!"

I nibble at the chapped skin on my bottom lip. "I've been put in charge of the fall job fair."

"Oh, I say!"

"It's not funny!" I snap, struggling not to smile at his smug amusement at my predicament.

He scratches his temple. "But it is, because a responsibility that large is a bloody nightmare for you."

"Still not seeing the 'funny' here."

"I can tell you're having kittens about it, but you know what? You can handle it. You'll be brilliant. Plus, that's ages from now. Late September?"

"Yes. It's going to be a cluster-bomb of the highest order. I have no idea where to begin," I moan, my stomach knotting more tightly.

"Give it a theme, to make it fun. Make a list of what you need to do. Take it one step at a time."

"Listen to you. Mr. Large and In-Charge."

"I'd be bricking myself if this was something *I* had to do," he admits with a laugh. "But since it's not my problem, I find it easy to detach and tell you what *you* need to do."

"Thanks. I really appreciate it."

"Any time. Who's organized these fairs in the past? Who's doing the spring one? I seem to remember you hold these to-dos more than once a year."

I squeeze the bridge of my nose. "Yeah. Arnold's doing the spring one, as usual. But he's retiring, the jerk. The powers that be decided I would be the perfect person to take up the baton."

"Have they only recently met you?"

"Hey! I'm a good employee. I guess I've been *too* good lately."

He hums something that could be taken as agreement or dissent, so I choose to interpret it positively.

"I'm shadowing Arnold this time around, for the spring fair, so he can show me what needs to be done, and when. Supposedly, I'll be good to go after that."

"Free food. That always brings them in droves," he suggests. "And perhaps a raffle."

"I don't want to think about it, much less talk about it."

"Then in the few precious minutes we have left together today, let's discuss something more promising, shall we?" His eyes sparkle. Or are they watering from his cold? "I seem to remember a certain footballer asked for your digits at that Christmas party. Whatever came of that?"

I struggle to maintain a passive expression when I say, "We don't call them 'footballers' here, and American 'footballers' apparently don't call everyone whose digits they procure."

Colin drops his chin in sympathetic indignation.

I wave him off. "Whatever. From what Rae says, he's another type of baller, and while I'm not interested in settling down, I'm also not interested in being a guy's regional booty call. I do insist on monogamy, serial or otherwise."

"Well, well, well. As you should. But if he were offering that?"

Considering that for a few seconds, I stare into the middle distance, then answer wistfully, "It would be nice to get laid again someday."

Oh gosh. No. I didn't just say that. To Mr. Widower T. Celibacy, of all people!

My back straightens, and I blink to attention, studying his face to gauge his reaction.

His eyes widen, and he rubs his forehead while suppressing a smirk.

"Not by you!"

Gaaaaaaaaaah! What?

He rests his chin on his knuckles, bites down on his pinkie, and winces, assuming a comically terrified expression.

"Not that I think it wouldn't be nice. Or that I think about it at all!"

Shut up, Maura! Shut the hell up now!

But I can't. I don't seem physically able, that is. My lips and tongue and vocal chords are operating independently of my brain. Obviously.

"I'm sorry. I'm freaked out right now and not thinking clearly and just saying whatever comes to mind. But having sex with you wasn't even on my mind, so I don't know where that came from."

He stands, taps his toe, and makes a big show of looking at a watch that doesn't exist on his wrist, while I snap, "You're the one who brought up Jet Knox! I was perfectly content to forget all about him. Keaton Busch would be a better time, anyway. He's such a funny guy with his touchdown dances and goofy selfies. What was your original question?"

When chuckling results in more coughing, he sobers, clears his throat, and replies, "I honestly don't remember. I was simply making small talk and indulging in a bit of a silly hypothetical. Then your filthy brain exploded on your desk, and—"

I plunk my forehead on top of where my filthy gray matter supposedly is and groan. The papers under my face move when I whimper, "I shouldn't have said any of that. I'm sorry." I lift my head. "It was rude. Now... it's like— Is it going to be awkward?"

He shakes his head and pulls a face. Folding his referral and jamming it into his shirt pocket, he says, "Not on my part." When I fail to look convinced, he scratches his ear. "Listen. It's probably crossed both of our minds, whether subconsciously or whatever, that we could toss some 'benefits' into our friendship and come to a decent arrangement, but eventually—for whatever reason—things would get messy, and neither one of us does well with 'messy,' so that's that." He looks down at his tie and flaps it.

When I say nothing to his speech, he stands with his referral and walks to the door.

"With that, m'dear, I believe I should take my leave." A loud sniff serves as the punctuation to that declaration. He opens the door. A rush of blessedly cooler air wafts in.

I take a deep breath and exhale loudly. "Okay, then. Good luck on your job interview."

Completely casually, as if we've been talking about job placement this whole time, he tosses over his shoulder, "And good luck on your... endeavors. Sorry I'm not the man for the job."

With a saucy wink, he tucks his hands into his pockets and exits the office without looking back.

————

If I were a different person, I'd be tempted to stress about my mortifying conversation with Colin. But he seemed cool. He's right that *nothing* is ever going to happen between us.

However, it *has* been a long time. If he had his heart set on adding some benefits to the mix, I'd consider it. I'm that horny.

Just kidding.

Not really.

A buzzing in my desk drawer distracts me from the buzzing in my underdrawers.

I retrieve my phone and see it's been busy in time-out this afternoon. Several missed calls and three voicemails.

I don't recognize the first number, but that doesn't mean

anything. If someone had a gun to my head and said I had to dial up any of my friends or family from memory or take a bullet, it'd be all over but the splatter.

The robotic voicemail lady announces, *"You have… three… unheard messages. First unheard message:"*

"Oh, hey. Maura. Jet here."

An immediate uptick of my heart rate suddenly makes it difficult to hear the recording. I bump up the volume with a shaky hand, nearly dropping my phone.

Jet Knox, Jet Knox, Jet Knox! If I had known, I probably would have answered the phone in the middle of Colin's appointment. I'm not proud of that, but I'm past the point of pretending I could ignore a call from Jet Freaking Knox. It doesn't escape me, though, that he sounds surprised to be calling me.

To his credit, he attempts to recover with, *"Uh, how's it going? It's been a while… Right? Thought I'd give you a call, since I'm back in town."*

Hmm. Well, at least he knows I'm a home-city girl. Of course, the area code on my phone number would tell him that.

"Maybe you'd like to—I don't know—go out, or something? I won't tell the coaches if you don't. It's supposed to be nose-to-the-grindstone now that we're prepping for the playoffs. But all work and no play kinda sucks. Give me a call back if you're up for it. Bye now."

Before the next message can play, I hang up and stare at the device in my hand, willing myself to stop panting and sweating like a walking hormone with a crush on a boy band member.

The fact remains that Jet Knox asked me—or someone he sort of remembers with my name—out on a date. Must not get too excited. Must not do anything uncool, like call someone to brag about this.

My fingers fly through the menus on my phone. When my brother answers, I say, without so much as a hello, "You're not going to believe this. Jet Knox called and asked me out."

"No way."

"Told you you wouldn't believe me."

"He has a playoff game on Sunday! He doesn't have time for dating."

"Even so, he called me at 1:30-ish and left a message on my voicemail. Maybe more than one. I didn't check the others."

"Where are you guys going, then?" He still sounds annoyingly skeptical.

"I haven't called him back yet."

"You're leaving Jet Knox hanging? For almost four hours? I'll bet you a hundred bucks that when you finally call him back, he's already made plans with someone else who was more convenient."

My stomach drops. "Oh. Shit. I didn't think of that."

"Do you honestly think you were the only chick he called when he had the urge to 'go out'?"

Well, when he puts it that way, I'd be an idiot to admit that, yes, I indeed thought that. "No! I mean, maybe. Why not? You're saying he went through the greater Kansas City area numbers in his phone until he got a 'yes'?"

"I guarantee it. I'm sure it didn't take long. He's probably already banging some girl in the hot tub on his bedroom balcony."

"You're sick."

"I'm realistic." After a few beats of silence, he says, "But you should still call him back, just in case."

"I don't know."

"I do! Trust me, you're not cool enough to snub Jet Knox. This could be the most awesome thing that's ever happened to you. And who knows? Maybe it'll lead to something. Like playoff tickets."

"I'm hanging up on you now."

His laughter flows from the phone's speaker as I stick out my tongue and press the red button to disconnect.

Bouncing my knee, I contemplate whether I have the guts to call the quarterback, only to have him screen my call or, worse, answer and tell me his offer has expired. A few extra minutes won't hurt, so I check my other voicemails, in case any of them are Jet, saying, "Never mind!" and will save me from further humiliation.

One of the messages is from Mom, announcing she and Dad are back from their latest round of globe-trotting and asking what happened to the plants I was supposed to be watering. (Oops. I guess they're dead, since I completely forgot about them.)

The other is from Rae.

"What're you doing tonight? I have a bona fide date, if you can believe it. Met her at the airport on our way to Denver, and we're meeting for drinks. Molly. She's a drug rep, or something. I guess I'll call you later and let you know how it goes. Bye!"

I take a deep breath and lean against my desk. The rest of the office is empty and dark. While I've been in here acting out my private drama, my co-workers have gone home to their lives. Boyfriends and girlfriends, husbands and wives, kids, pets, hot dinners, and favorite shows await them.

There's not so much as a frozen dinner waiting for me.

With a pang I realize I have nothing to lose by calling Jet. No pride left, for sure. And if he's already moved on from his earlier invitation, then I'll never see him again, and it won't matter.

Press it, Maura. That green square with the phone on it. Press it, select the number that belongs to one of the NFL's hottest players, and see what happens.

SEVEN

FIRST(ISH) IMPRESSIONS

After handing my eight-year-old Honda's keys to the valet, I stand under the trendy restaurant's awning, trying to be subtle about pulling my tiny panties from the crack of my butt, where they seem to want to hang out tonight, under my jeans.

Don't ask me why I wore the dumb things. It's not like I'm going to let anyone see them. I guess I thought wearing the sexy matching set would give me confidence. I underestimated the crack factor. There's no feeling confident or sexy or anything but uncomfortable when you're fighting a perpetual wedgie.

Underpants moderately in place, I tuck my clutch under my arm and clip-clop on my high-high heels past the doorman. Inside, I give the maître d' my name, as Jet instructed me on the phone.

"This way, Miss," I'm told right away, earning me some dirty looks from others who obviously have been waiting in line for a while.

For the first time in the past ninety minutes, I'm preoccupied with a thought other than, *This is crazy*. Part of me is still thinking that as I smile over my shoulder at them and say, "Sorry," although I'm not. I'm too amazed this is happening to me to be sorry about anything.

Well, maybe I'm somewhat sorry I didn't take Jet up on his offer to pick me up. But a rule's a rule. I never let a guy do that on a first date. Including—maybe especially—Jet Knox. Safety first. Don't want to chance getting stranded somewhere, at the mercy of a six-foot-four whack-job who outweighs me by nearly a hundred pounds. Still, it would have been gratifying to see the envy on people's faces if I'd arrived on the QB's arm.

Being swept to the front of the line and beyond, into the packed, buzzing bar and dining area, is satisfying enough. As it is, I keep thinking that any minute now, I'm going to wake up.

That wakeup call arrives at the same time I make it to Jet's table.

It's not until I'm standing directly in front of him that he clambers to his feet, realizing I'm his date. He hurries around the table and dismisses the maître d' so he can pull out my chair for me, hugging me lightly before I take my seat. Despite the dim room, I easily notice him size me up, looking relieved at what he sees after he returns to his seat.

Maybe I should be offended, but I can't fathom how many people he meets. It would be naïve to think he'd remembered *me*, some dullard he met at a Christmas party weeks ago.

He smiles across the table at me. "Drinking tonight?"

I glance at the huge glass of water in front of him. "Are you?"

He shakes his head ruefully. "Nah. I'm breaking enough rules just being here. But that shouldn't stop you. Please.

What would you like? He pushes the leather-bound drinks menu across the table toward me."

"Uh..." I rest my fingertips on the closed padded folder, then decide firmly, "No. That wouldn't be fair." Yeah, there's no use giving my hulking date any more advantages than he already has. "We'll both abstain, and still have a good time. I've been told it can be done."

He laughs loudly. "Okay, then. Let's test that theory."

"Let's."

After he orders less food than I expect, and I probably order more than most women he dates, he asks, "So, what have you been up to since the Christmas party?"

My rejoinder, "Oh, you remember that much now?" receives a guilty smile he tries to hide in his water glass.

"Of course. You're Rae's friend."

"You had no idea who to expect here tonight, did you?"

Instead of directly answering, he chuckles and chomps on a piece of ice. Still chewing, he opens his mouth to the side, just enough to ask, "Why are you bustin' my chops?"

"I want you to know I'm onto you, Number Fourteen."

Setting down his glass, he raises his eyebrows at me and swallows. "Oh?"

"Yeah. Oh." I sip my water and try not to laugh at the mock-indignant look on his face. Finally, I let him off the hook. "It's okay, though. I don't have any illusions. You're Jet Knox."

He pats his face as if trying to "see" himself with his fingers. "Thanks for clarifying that for me. What, exactly, does that mean to you?"

A warning gong sounds in my brain, but like most warnings in my life, I ignore it. "You meet lots of women, all eager to be with you. You're used to getting the star treatment from them."

The smile fading from his face, he leans back and tucks his hands into his underarms.

For the second time today, though, I can't seem to make myself shut up. "You can have any woman you want, and you know it."

"Wow. Your opinion of me isn't very flattering."

Trying to ignore the intimidating set to his jaw, I laugh off his statement while my heart thunders. I keep my hands folded in my lap, because if I lift them, their trembling will give away my trepidation. It's suddenly hit me who I'm talking to. This is not just any guy. I've been aware of that from the minute I accepted his invitation to dinner. But for the first time since agreeing to meet him here, I *know* it.

"I don't have any opinion of you," I breezily claim.

He tilts his head. "Could have fooled me. Sounds to me like you think I'm a tail-chaser who takes advantage of his money and influence and uses women like disposable razors."

"Huh-huh," I chuckle nervously, sipping more water. "Not exactly." *He probably has a few razors that have stuck around longer than some of his dates.*

"But pretty much, right?" He narrows his eyes and taps his fingers on the tabletop.

"Let's start over. What I meant was— Never mind. I shouldn't have teased you. But you may want to take a picture to go along with any future phone numbers you collect."

He relaxes and allows himself to look caught again. "Well, that." When I say nothing (I'm finally learning) and wait for him to explain, he continues, "I knew I associated the name 'Maura' with 'smart' and 'beautiful.' I figured, if you didn't call back, it was a sign I should stay home, like a good boy, and hang out with Quatorze."

"Quatorze?"

"My dog."

Normally, I'm not all that interested in guys' babe magnets, but having taken French in high school (because Spanish and Latin were too practical), I'm intrigued by this pooch's name. "What breed?"

He clears his throat and lifts his chin. "Bichon Frisé."

I stifle a giggle at the idea of this manly man owning and cuddling such a pampered breed, much less naming it the French equivalent of his jersey number.

"Go ahead and laugh. Everyone else does."

My sarcastic but good-natured "No!" cracks us up.

Eventually, he explains, "He was my girlfriend's. Well, fiancée's. Now ex. Obviously. He always liked me more than her, so she left both of us." His expression darkens.

Uhhhhh…

Looking down at the table, he clears his throat and composes himself, then attempts a lighter tone when he glances up at me once more. "Torz is small but mighty. One of the guys. He and I watch a lot of TV."

"What do you do with him while you're traveling?"

"I take him with me when I visit family. I have a dog sitter for the other times. Jacob lives in my guest house. He holds down the fort while I'm away. You know, since I'm hopelessly alone." His slight blush betrays the chagrin underlying his light tone.

Our food arrives before I can reply, and the waiter lingers, ensuring Jet approves of everything in front of us before he wanders off. After talking about the food for a while and trading amateur reviews, we eat in silence. Then, before he's finished eating, Jet props his knife and fork on the edge of his plate and leans forward onto his elbows. I pause mid-chew, waiting expectantly for him to say what's on his mind.

"Can I be honest with you without freaking you out?"

I swallow and croak, "Sure," hoping I won't regret it.

He sits back and rubs his chin. "This is my seventh year in the league. Don't get me wrong, it's awesome. I've been working toward this, especially now that we're heading into the postseason, since I started playing pee-wee football. Playing in the NFL is everything I've always wanted."

"But...?"

He shifts in his seat. "Man, this is going to sound so douchey, but I can't think of a way to say it that doesn't, so I'll just come out with it. The part I hate the most is... the groupies."

I'll bet, I think, unable to check the smile that spreads onto my face at his line.

"See? I told you it would sound like a douchey line, but I'm being real." He fingers his knife and stares down at it in an obvious attempt to avoid eye contact. "It's depressing as hell that someone who knows nothing about me would want to, you know, hook up with me. Or whatever. It's impossible to trust anyone. I hate being such a cynical jerk like that." He raises his sad eyes, and I regret doubting his sincerity.

Before I can say anything sympathetic, though, he says, almost defiantly, "I want to get married someday, you know? And have kids. But most of the women I meet are more focused on 'having fun.'" He says the last two words like they're the most despicable phrase in the world. "The ones who might be interested in something serious come off as gold-digging, desperate psychos. At the end of the day, I come home to an empty house—unless you count Torz. Trust me, Torzi and I aren't *that* close."

I beam across the table at him. "That's good to know."

"What, that I'm not a man-whore?"

"That, too. But, no, I was talking about your strictly platonic relationship with your dog."

He smiles briefly, then nods. "Really, though. I'm sorry for being so serious on a first date, but I don't want you thinking I call random numbers in my cell phone all the time. I don't have random numbers in my cell phone. I knew your number was important if it was in there."

His green eyes beseech me to believe him. I don't want to look away, but it's impossible not to blink at their intensity.

Trying to break the tension, I ignore everything else he's said. He's right; it *is* too serious for a first date. Instead, I focus on the last thing. "Fine, but you didn't know *why* my number was important."

Silverware in hand again, he points to his head with his knife and says with a half-smile, "Cut me some slack. I take a lot of hits out there. A helmet can only do so much."

Likely story.

"Realistically speaking, I probably don't have many more years in the NFL. I've always planned to retire before I'm too banged up. Of course, by then, I hope to be married, too."

Of course. Ha!

"And when my playing career is over, I'd like to start a family."

Well, duh. Double-ha!

"But not before then, I don't think. Because I'd hate to be on the road so much, away from my family."

What a swell guy.

"Then again, I'd love to get into broadcasting. I majored in broadcast journalism at USC. So, I'd still do a bunch of traveling with that, too, unless I got a studio gig, and those are hard to come by."

Please, tell me more. This is fascinating.

"But if I end my career on a high note, landing a studio job will be easier, so that's one more motivation for winning one of those rings."

Mon Dieu!

He has everything planned out. Everything.

I understand driven people know exactly where they're going and how they're going to get there, but whenever I encounter someone like that, I respond one of two ways: if I'm familiar with them, like Greg or Deirdre, I become antagonistic and sarcastic (see Christmas Eve dinner); if I don't know them well, I retreat into my shell.

Nodding and smiling is about all I can muster right now. At least I think I'm smiling. Probably more like grimacing.

Fortunately, before he can outline his life all the way through death (he probably thinks he has *that* all planned out, too), he ducks his head and says, "Oh, shit."

I half-expect Rae to be behind me when I turn to see what's interrupted his recitation.

"Don't look, don't look!" he implores, too late.

An average-looking blond guy in a black shirt, black pants, and skinny hot pink tie looks right at me and nods his head once. Then he makes a beeline for our table, shouting, "Yo! Knox!" When he arrives next to me, he peers straight down my top and says, "Hot date," like a statement, more than a question.

I'd be flattered, if he weren't an obvious creep and half the occupants of the restaurant weren't staring at us, thanks to him.

Jet smiles tightly. "Hey, Schoengert. How's it goin'?"

That's invitation enough, so our visitor pulls an empty chair from a neighboring table and plunks it next to me, sitting down. "Good, good. Just chattin' up the chicks, if you catch my drift. And who's this lovely lady?" he asks, somehow finding a way to lean closer to me.

"This is... my friend," Jet answers evasively. To me, he directs, "And this is Todd Schoengert, the team kicker."

But I've already recognized him. The guy's clutch. Hasn't missed a field goal all season. Shattered every record on the books. Unfortunately, I like the kicker much better on my television.

I slant away from him and cover my cleavage with my flattened hand. "Nice to mee—"

"Do you believe in love at first sight?" he interrupts me, intensely holding my eye contact.

"No!" I don't think I do, but I definitely don't in relation to anything having to do with this guy.

He waves his hand dismissively. "Me neither. It's a myth perpetuated by Hollywood to sell movie tickets, and it contributes to massive discontent in the ever-aging singles community."

"Well said," I say, trying to ignore the nerve his statement pings.

"Don't encourage him," Jet mumbles.

Todd turns his attention to his teammate. "Knox, you ever pee in the sink if you can't make it to the can?"

"Uh, no," my date replies, surprisingly unfazed by this seemingly random question and quick change of subject. "Can't say I ever have."

"What about the shower? You ever pee in the shower?"

"No, Schoengert. If you do"—he points to him—"I'm

gonna start keeping track of where you are after practices and games. I don't want to be stepping in your piss."

I study my fork and try not to laugh.

Then Jet says, "Well, it was nice of you to stop by and say hi, but…"

The kicker stands and pulls at his cuffs. "Yeah, I get it, man. We're a coupla rebels, out on the prowl when we should be restin' up, right? Like I told Busch, I won't tell anyone I saw you here if you don't tell 'em you saw me," he adds on a wink.

We give the guy a second to hear himself, during which time I try to be subtle about looking around the place for Mr. Tight End. Here? Seriously? I tuck my hair behind my ears.

"Aw, man!" Schoengert hisses. "I broke my promise to Busch."

Jet laughs. "Anyone who follows Keaton on Twitter knows he's not sitting at home tonight. See you tomorrow morning at the team meeting."

"Cool, man. Hey, nice to meet you, 'Jet's friend.'" Todd shoots double guns at me and winks before sauntering back to the bar area, where he sidles up to an olive-skinned beauty in a sleek halter dress. She turns away from him and escapes to the other end of the bar.

"Sorry about that," Jet says, wincing. "If I'd known half the team was going to be here, I'd have suggested somewhere else. And Schoengert…" He shakes his head and chuckles. "I hope you don't mind I didn't tell him your name. That's probably not information you want him to have. He's a blabbermouth."

"I noticed."

"And kind of a sleaze. But he's an awesome kicker."

"Right? He holds the current league record for successful

consecutive field goal attempts," I recite what I heard an announcer say last week during the Denver game.

Jet raises his eyebrows at me and grins. "Impressive, Richards!"

I pretend to inspect my nails. "I'm not one of those women who watches football to check out the players' cute butts." *Not exclusively, anyway.*

He laughs. "Anyway, you see why we all gladly put up with him and his annoying, random questions."

"You're only as good as your kicker, right?"

"Exactly! He's worth his weight in gold. I just wish he wasn't so socially backward."

"What're you talking about?" I dead-pan, swirling the ice in my glass of water. "You know, I'm beginning to think Rae's right."

"About what?"

"You're a liar."

He scrunches his eyebrows together and looks legitimately worried. And pale. "Excuse me?"

"C'mon, Knox. Everyone pees in the sink now and then."

His nervous, over-the-top laughter makes me wonder what he thought I was going to say.

EIGHT

INQUISITIONS

I'm not sure how to feel about that date. It was... nice. *Jet* is nice. Really nice. The nicest.

And that's such a bummer.

Because he's so *not* the man for me.

I was already feeling inferior in the presence of someone as well-known as he is. Add to that his brimming confidence, and I couldn't help but think, *Should I be more like that? What's wrong with me that I'm not? What's it like to be so certain of yourself, your likes, your dislikes, and your goals? How does it feel to get up every morning and be excited about what the day has in store, especially if part of the day includes work? What if work didn't feel like work, because it was something you loved doing?*

What disturbed me the most was that he sounded like someone at a job interview. But I'm not hiring a husband. Or a sperm donor for my unfertilized eggs.

Thinking about it as I lie in bed this morning quickens my heart and dampens my skin, partly because I'm beginning to doubt my sanity. What other straight woman would feel like this after a date with Jet Knox? The strongest positive feelings

I can muster about the situation are flattery and lust. I must not be right in the head.

That's why I can hardly argue when Rae calls me as I'm eating breakfast at my kitchen counter and says as an opening, "Are you crazy?"

"I might be. But maybe not for the same reason you're referencing." I push the sugary cinnamon squares around my cereal bowl, then drop my spoon when I realize how nonexistent my appetite is.

"What were you thinking, going on a date with Jet Knox, two days before his playoff game?"

Immediately as defensive as a linebacker, I reply, "Hm. Let's see. As I recall, I was thinking he called me and asked me out, and I didn't feel like sitting home alone on a Friday night, so I went."

"He's supposed to be resting, eating well, and getting as much exercise as possible, when he's not studying the playbook and watching video. He better not have had any refined sugar or alcohol on your cute little date."

"Of course not," I say without hesitation, immediately picturing the flourless chocolate cake we shared for dessert. She's the crazy one if she thinks I'm going to tattle on him.

Her exhale is so loud, it hurts my ear. "Whew. I hope even *he* isn't that dumb, to—"

"He's not dumb!"

Whoa! Where did that *come from?*

Fortunately, arguing Jet's IQ doesn't seem to be of any interest to my friend. "So, spill it. What did he eat?"

"Excuse me, but you're not my mother. Or his. Even if it was 'wrong' for *him* to be out, as you seem to think, *I* did nothing wrong. He's a grownup. I'm not about to ask a guy if he's making 'good choices' when he calls to ask me out. How do you know about this, anyway?" I already have a strong hunch where she got her intel, but I'd like confirmation, to ensure I kill the right person.

While I indulge in a fantasy that involves strangling Schoengert with his pink tie, she answers, "Did you really think you could go out with Jet Knox and not have someone—or several someones—take your picture with their phone?"

I mentally let go of the field goal kicker's tie.

"It's all over the Internet. Looks like you, Knox, Schoengert, and Busch had quite the night out together."

"We weren't together. It was a coincidence we were all at the same place. I didn't see so much as a glimpse of Mr. Tight End."

"Leave it to a bunch of meat heads to think they could go incognito at one of the most popular places in town."

"How was *your* date?" I ask before I lose my temper and say something I'll regret.

Unfortunately, she's not ready to let it go. "Do you understand the implications here? How are you going to feel if they lose tomorrow?"

I contemplate that for about a second before answering, "I'll be disappointed for the team—and the fans, including myself—but I won't feel responsible, if that's what you're suggesting. It was three hours. Jet's a grown man. A very well-grown man."

I don't get the laugh I was hoping for, but I achieve some semblance of victory when she takes a deep breath and says, "I'm sorry. You're right. You know how competitive I am."

I graciously accept her apology. "I don't think there'll be a second date, so stand down."

She sounds intrigued when she asks, "He didn't like you?"

"Why would you assume that?"

"Well, *he's* Jet Knox."

"Yeah, well, Jet Knox was freaking me out with his talk about domesticity and goals and the future."

This cracks her up. "Oh, geez. He didn't do his homework about his opponent before you guys met up, obviously."

I don't tell her that he wasn't clear who his opponent was going to be, period. I may have found it mildly amusing, but I'm not willing to admit to anyone else that it happened. I do have *some* pride.

"Right? Now, are you going to tell me about your date, or what?"

"It was fine," she says vaguely. "Short. Molly had to be up early this morning, so we had a couple of drinks and said we'd be in touch."

"And will you be?"

"Maybe after the postseason. I'm busy and could have a ton of traveling at the end of this month and beginning of February, if all goes well. I don't want to be tied down." The shrug in her voice tells me she's more apathetic about her love life than I am about mine, if that's possible.

"Well, aren't we the commitment-phobes?" I say wryly.

"Yeah, but what's the point in forcing something? You can't help it that you don't want the same things Jet wants, no matter how hot and rich he is or how much he seems to be into you—which is kind of creepy, if you ask me—and I can't help it that my career is keeping me too busy right now to invest a bunch of time in a new relationship. I would commit to the right person at the right time. Wouldn't you?"

"Uh, sure," I reply, feeling slightly guilty when Mr. Tight End's goofy grin flashes behind my eyes. Something tells me he doesn't think too far into the future—or think much at all, to be honest.

"Well, I would," she says. "And maybe you would, too, if you'd stop getting distracted by all the wrong people."

"Good grief. Who needs a mom with a friend like you?" I grumble.

She laughs. "Sorry. It's just— You know, some days I wish you'd pull it together."

"Get in line, sister."

————

I've set aside all serious thoughts about life and love and my future (or anyone else's) and spent this dreary Saturday afternoon using the gift cards I received for Christmas. After a productive afternoon on The Plaza, I stow my purchases in my trunk and head on foot to my favorite bookstore, where I've arranged to meet Colin.

When he texted his invitation to me this morning, I hesitated, but the outing at such a familiar venue for us seemed like his way of putting me at ease after what I said to him at the end of his appointment yesterday, so I accepted. Perusing shelves of books, people-watching, and discussing absolutely nothing of consequence sounds like the perfect way to move on.

Immediately upon entering the store, I head for the coffee counter to order my usual six-thousand-calorie, seven-dollar drink. While waiting for the barista to work her caffeine magic, I text Colin.

Are you here? I'm getting coffee.

It takes forever (but still not as long as it takes to get my drink) for him to respond.

Walking in now.

When he joins me at the counter, he asks, "Was your shopping successful? Don't keep a bloke in suspense. I want to know everything. Where'd you go? What'd you get?"

I laugh at his silly lisp. "I stayed close to here," I answer, referring to the swanky shopping district I can't afford any other time of the year but that he and I occasionally visit, since the people-watching can't be beat. "I had some gift cards, so I picked up a few of my favorite lotions that were on sale—"

"Take my breath away."

"—and I used the Victoria's Secret gift card from my brother—"

"What?" he wheezes. "Your brother thinks it's okay to give his sister a gift card to a lingerie shop?"

I laugh along with him. "I'm sure that was Deirdre's doing."

"Still. Inappropriate!"

"Ten bucks says it was a last-minute impulse buy after I told her about dancing with Jet Knox at that Christmas party. She's been obsessed. When she finds out I went out on date with him last night—" I cringe, then muse aloud, "Maybe I won't tell her and Greg. Ever."

Colin's eyebrows shoot up into his tousled bangs. "Hang on a mo. Lady Maura, you're holding out on me! You and I are going to have a chin wag." After I pay for my drink, he drags me with him to the end of the queue. "But first, I need one of those coffees."

While we wait in line—again—I try to tell him there's nothing to discuss regarding my Friday night, but every time I open my mouth to say something to that effect, he holds up a hand and says, "Wait! No. Don't."

As soon as we're seated at a table, I insist, "It was nothing."

"I don't believe that for a second. Did he wear his white trousers or his red ones?"

"He wasn't in uniform, you goosegog," I say with a laugh, using one of my favorite expressions of his. "He took me to a trendy place, not far from here. Well, we met there."

"Ah. Good girl. Safety first," says the former cop. "Although it would have been brilliant to ride in one of his flash cars. I'm already disappointed in this vicarious experience."

"I knew you would be! Would you like me to hook *you* up with him?"

"Hmm... I haven't had a good bromance in yonks." He stares into the distance, then snaps his focus back to my face. "But no. I couldn't possibly dream of stealing a man from you. Remember, you desperately need to get laid. Or has that already been taken care of?"

I roll my eyes at him.

"I'm asking, because I'm concerned about your sudden onset of sex-deprivation-induced Tourette 's syndrome." I kick him as he stretches his legs under the table and leans back with his hands behind his head, his elbows akimbo. "Ow. So, you met him at Chez Hookup, and then what?"

"Nothing. We talked. Well, *he* talked. A lot."

Colin sneers. "Oh, one of those? Enthralled with his favorite subject? Himself?"

"No, not like that. He seemed nervous, for one thing, which is *hilarious*."

"Why?"

"Because I'm me, and he's Jet Knox."

"He takes a bloody crap like you and me."

The corners of my mouth pull downward. "Ew. Speak for yourself, pal. You might want to get that checked out."

With a playful scowl, he clarifies, "He's a man, and you're an intelligent, vivacious woman. End of."

"Oooh! 'Vivacious'! Thanks! But he talked about hopes and dreams and aspirations. Lots of aspirations."

"Ahhh... That's a dirty word."

"I know! So you can imagine, I wasn't too engaged in the conversation."

"Blimey. Sounds like a miserable evening."

I think back on it and surprise myself by saying, "Actually..."

"No!" He sits forward and, resting his elbows on the table, taps his paper coffee cup with his fingertips. "How could that have been enjoyable, listening to an egomaniac drone on and on about his ambitions?"

"First off, he's not an egomaniac," I find myself defending Jet for the second time today.

He arches a skeptical eyebrow but doesn't say a word.

"And second, he wasn't droning. He's *passionate* about his future. At the time, I was on the verge of a panic attack, but looking back on it now, it was kind of... cute." My face warms.

Colin groans, but it morphs into a chuckle. With a twinkle in his eyes, he says, "Bloody hell. You're falling for this bloke."

Blush deepening, I say a tad too forcefully, "No, I'm not!" then tone it down. "But it wasn't the worst date I've ever been on, and he's not what you'd imagine a guy like him to be. He's driven in a way that, while sometimes scary, is also contagious. I could see how others might get caught up in his enthusiasm. He makes anything seem possible. Like he can make it happen by saying it. He's obviously a natural leader."

He points to my face. "And when you talk about him, your whole face lights up, and that little dimple in your left cheek pops."

"Shut up."

"I'm merely observing and stating my findings."

I follow the progress of a drop of coffee in the bottom of my cup as I tilt it back and forth. "Anyway, it's not going to lead to anything else, so…" I'm shocked when I realize I'm more disappointed than relieved by that statement, so I rush on. "Can we please talk about something else?"

His shoulders slump. "I suppose." After a brief pause, during which it seems he's giving me time to change my mind, he mentions, "My first day at the salon is Monday. I have to admit, I'm a bit nervous."

"Why? I'd figure by now you're an old pro at being the new guy."

One corner of his mouth rises as he says wryly, "True. But I worry I'll stick out rather a lot."

I hate to break it to him, but he sticks out anywhere in this town every time he opens his mouth. Instead of voicing this, though, I merely smile encouragingly. "They're going to love you. If it doesn't work out, you always know where to go to find another job. Right?" I look up and search his gray eyes.

"Right," he says. "Absolutely."

"And you seem like you're feeling better today than you did yesterday."

"I'm completely hopped up on over-the-counter remedies," he reveals, "but yes, fortunately, I sound a bit less like your mobile's ringtone and— Hang on. Was that *Jet Knox* calling you during my appointment yesterday?"

"Maybe," I answer coyly.

"Bloomin' 'ell... I was in the presence of greatness and had no idea."

"Please."

"And you tossed him in your desk drawer, like you couldn't care less."

"I didn't know it was him."

"If you had?"

"I may have answered the phone," I admit, quickly adding, "which is dumb. I'm glad I didn't know. Because I don't take personal calls during appointments with clients."

"I would have insisted. The better for me to listen in."

"Someone has a man-crush."

He looks down, then up at me through his lashes. "Who wouldn't? The way he grips that ball..."

Laughing, I shake my head at him. "You're hopeless."

He raises his head. "There's just so much material there."

Yeah, there is. For everyone.

What I don't tell him is that I immediately went online after I hung up with Rae and Googled the pictures of my date with Jet. Only a complete newb would care, right? But I wanted to see how I looked, and what people were saying.

Mistake.

Fortunately, nobody posting the pics has a clue who I am, so I was called "Knox's New Flame" (lame!) in most of the captions. The nicer ones, that is. The not-so-nice ones wondered if I was a distraction and went further to say I wasn't worth it. The meanest ones... Well, I refuse to repeat those. I'm trying not to think about them at all.

Now, suddenly feeling as if those labels are following me around, and any minute I'll be recognized as Jet's "Pre-Play-offs Poke" (yes, that was one of them!), I stand and dig my gloves and knit hat from my coat pocket. "I'm going to head home."

Colin blinks up at me. "What? But we haven't had a chance to see if there are any new *Murder, She Wrote* mystery novels with the exact same Angela Lansbury face Photoshopped on every cover."

I wince at skipping one of our favorite bookstore traditions. "Yeah, but I'm wiped out. By the time I fight the traffic and get home, I'll be ready to collapse."

"I didn't say anything to upset you?" He stands and hugs me, then pulls back and holds me at arms' length, searching my face. "I hope you know my teasing about Captain All-American is only in good fun."

Waving off his explanation, I say after a snort, "Does that sound like me? When I stop being able to laugh at myself, get the gun."

Still gripping my arms, he says, "In all seriousness, mate, he's a bloke like any other. I hope you don't think he's out of your league, excuse the pun. No, don't. It's brilliant. If you like him, you shouldn't be ashamed of that."

I shrug him off, but gently, so I don't let on how annoyed I am. "Colin. It's fine. I promise. Shopping wears me out, that's all."

"If you're certain..."

"I am." In an effort to convince him, I yank my hat onto my head and pull it over my ears, pulling a funny face. "*Au revoir, mon ami.*"

NINE

CHARMED

I may not be guilty of sitting around, stressing about the condition of my 401K or revising endless versions of my five-year plan (I've never had a first version of one), but that doesn't mean I never worry about *anything*. I do worry about stuff. Granted, it's usually more along the lines of whether the Chiefs are going to make wise picks in the Draft, but every once in a while, I stray into darker, more dangerous territory. Like, *Am I ever going to grow up?* or *Will I always be alone?* or *When was the last time I went to the grocery store?* Occasionally, I'll think about something truly scary, like, *Is it time to renew my car tags?*

This evening, after dumping my bags of purchases inside my bedroom door, taking a hot shower, and selecting the least romantic movie I can imagine (*The Hangover*), I struggle to ignore some of those deeper musings, and fail. Miserably.

I'm moderately more successful at ignoring the three voicemails from Jet on my phone (two of his calls I missed while shopping and talking to Colin, the other while I was in the shower), if you call not listening to them a victory. That doesn't mean I'm not thinking about them—or him—though.

I'm thinking about him plenty. Too much. Wondering what he thinks of this movie. Would he and I laugh at the same parts? Does he get the subtler jokes or only find amusement with the obvious, physical humor?

What about Bradley Cooper's other works? Has Jet seen *Silver Linings Playbook*? Did he find it as sweetly romantic as I did? Did it make him cry while trying to hide he was crying, because Rae was sitting next to him and would have made fun of him for being a sap? Probably not that last thing.

What *does* make Jet Knox cry? Anything? He seems like a pretty happy-go-lucky guy. But what about losing? If he lost, say, the Super Bowl, would he cry? Or just be mad? Or what if he *won* it? There's no shame in crying. I like people who feel deeply and don't mind showing it occasionally, around people they trust and care about. Did Jet cry when his fiancée left him to be a single dad to their dog?

Gaaaaaaaaaah! I shift on the couch under my fleece Chiefs throw blanket, blinking and trying to refocus on the movie. Tiger, missing tooth, Ken Jeong. Funny.

But before I can reorient myself to the plot, my cell phone moans. I stare at the device on the coffee table and implore my innards to settle the hell down at the sight of that name on the display.

Why can't the guy text or IM like a normal person our age? Then I could better react to what he says, and I wouldn't have to hear his voice, which is becoming my Kryptonite. No, that would be his eyes. But his voice makes me feel like a giddy moron. As does the way he smells. Thank goodness he's not into video calls, and there's no such thing as a smell-o-phone.

In a text message, I could also control the tone and pace of the conversation. I could pause between responses. Slow things down a bit. In a regular phone call, he's in control.

Which wouldn't be an issue for me, usually—control ain't my thang—but in this case, the person in control wants to go faster than I'm comfortable going.

The paradox, unfortunately, is that I can't get a handle on anything if I continue to avoid him, so before yet another call goes to voicemail, I tap the green button on my phone's screen, hoping my voice doesn't shake when I say, "Hi, Jet," and put him on speakerphone.

"Hey. Did you get my messages?"

"I did."

Please, don't ask if I listened to them.

"Oh. Are you busy?"

I pause the movie and consider my answer, finally going with a noncommittal, "A little."

Busy being terrified by my weird, obsessive thoughts.

"Well, I wanted to tell you I had an excellent time last night."

"Yeah. Me, too." *When I wasn't searching for a paper bag to breathe into.*

"Good! I'm glad. Mega-glad. I'd like to see you again, but…"

I hold my breath and close my eyes, praying for an insurmountable hurdle to our being together, other than his use of the term "mega-glad," which might be enough but would sound "mega-shallow" to cite out loud. An arranged marriage between him and the scantily clad woman who rides around the stadium on that white horse—Horse Lady, to me—would work. Or he's being traded to another team. In Europe. Anything like that. I don't want to hurt his feelings; I want him to feel like it was his idea to stop seeing me.

Unfortunately, he simply finishes his sentence with, "…it's going to have to wait until the off-season. Our date wound up on a couple of stupid gossip blogs. Can you believe that? Like there aren't important things happening in the world. Not that our date wasn't important to me, but... You know what I mean. Like, why do people care?"

I open my eyes, wondering if he's seen the awful things some of them have said about me. Or if I should admit I have. In the end, I pretend I don't care enough to mention it. "Right? Rae called me about it this morning and lectured me like a teenager who'd broken curfew."

"Aw, Maura. I'm sorry about that! It wasn't your fault. She shouldn't be mad at you!"

His genuine regret makes me smile. "I know! I totally blamed you."

He laughs. "Yeah, she was pissed when I saw her after the team meeting. If she wasn't so scary, it would be funny."

I smile at the image of her bearing down on him and can't resist teasing (okay, flirting), "Is Jet Knox afraid of a five-foot-six *girl*?"

"You better believe it. She has strong hands!"

For some reason, this strikes me as one of the funniest things I've ever heard from a guy.

He joins me in laughing at himself, then says, "You have a great laugh."

Nobody's ever mentioned it before, so his compliment surprises me. "Uh, thanks." I squirm, glad he can't see me.

"It always makes me smile. It makes me happy, I guess."

"Oh. Well. Okay." He doesn't seem embarrassed or self-conscious at all by this declaration, so it's up to me to be uncomfortable enough for both of us. "Anyway..."

Seamlessly, he picks up where he left off earlier. "I'd love to hear that laugh again in person. Soon. But— Well, I don't want to risk the team's chances of winning it all. Not that I'm thinking that far ahead. It's crazy to think past the next game, which is big enough. But the Super Bowl... That would be awesome, to say the least. It's wrong to get too far ahead of myself, though."

His stream-of-consciousness babble makes me shake my head. "Jet, I'm not Coach Bauer. Or one of your teammates. You don't have to temper your excitement with me. It would be weird if you didn't think about winning the Super Bowl."

Out of curiosity, would you cry if you won?

"I don't want to jinx it, that's all."

"You think I'm a jinx?"

"No!"

"Calm down. I was kidding."

"Oh. Right." He sighs. "I don't want to talk about going to the Super Bowl, because we still have some games to play before then." He pauses, but when I don't speak, he says, "I think you're awesome."

I soften. Marginally. He's such a sweet guy. And hot. (Don't forget hot.) Plus, despite his seemingly limited vocabulary, he's said two things to me in a matter of minutes that made me feel fantastic.

So fantastic that I blab without thinking about the consequences, "I like you, too, Jet. I'd like to see you again, when things settle down."

"Really?" He chuckles nervously. "Because I thought maybe you weren't that into me when you didn't return my calls."

Busted!

"Huh-huh. Well, like I said, I've been busy today."

"Yeah, I get it. I don't mean to sound creepy and clingy. That's not me." Again, the nervous chuckle.

"Okay."

"Seriously. I swear. I can tell you're not sure. But it's true. The pressure of the playoffs must be getting to me. I'm all, like, unsure and stuff."

"I believe you," I tell him, if for no other reason than to get him to stop trying to convince me.

"Good. Well, I'll let you get back to... whatever. Are you going to be watching the game tomorrow? Wait! Don't answer that. It'll make me more nervous, knowing you're watching."

"Oh my gosh!" I laugh. "You're a mess!"

Sheepishly, he says, "Sorry. It's probably a huge turn-off."

"Actually, I think it's cute."

I like it a whole lot more than the self-assured attitude he had at dinner last night.

"But it makes me feel like an idiot."

"I know you're not, though."

"No thanks to this phone call. I'm definitely going to hang up now, before I embarrass myself anymore."

I'm surprisingly disappointed, but I say, "Okay. I won't watch you tomorrow, if that'll help. But good luck."

"Thanks, Maura. Goodnight."

"'Night, Jet."

Oh, eff me.

TEN

MULTIPLE PENALTIES

Big, fat liar. That's what I am. Like everyone else in the city who isn't at Arrowhead, I'm glued to the TV the next day, of course. There's no way I'm missing this game, no matter what I told a certain someone on the phone. It's been too many years since my team has come close to the playoffs. But I'm not as certain about who I want to win as everyone else is.

On the one hand, I totally dig Playoffs Jet. He's nervous and self-deprecating and humble and cute. In that respect, I'd like to keep the playoffs streak alive. That means he has to win games, though. Each game he wins will give him more confidence and bring him closer to the Super Bowl. If he wins the Super Bowl, he'll be brimming with self-assurance and swagger. Plus, that will be one more thing he's checked off his life plan, meaning he'll be ready to move on to the next thing, perhaps something more personal, like—gulp—a committed relationship.

On the other hand, if the team loses today, he'll be free to see me again, as he claims to want to do. While I said I wanted to see him again, too, I said that mostly in response to his insecure ramblings. I *would* like to see *that* Jet, the one who sounded like a nervous wreck. If he goes back to being the suffocating man with the plan, though, I may have to give him his own ringtone ("Every Breath You Take" might fit well) and start screening his calls in earnest.

If I had three hands (which would be useful in so many aspects of life, by the dubs), I'd throw this into the mix: I'm a lifelong Chiefs fan. It was my team before Jet Knox ever entered the scene. Like I said, it's been a long time since we've been this far. It goes against everything in my nature to root against the team. The fan in me wants them to go all the way to the Super Bowl and win it, no matter what that means for my love life.

So here I am, breaking my promise to Jet, watching the game at Greg's. From September to February, football is a Sunday afternoon tradition for us. I hope that doesn't change after the wedding. I obviously don't care if Deirdre watches with us, but it would be just like her to make Greg spend Sundays working on the yard or the house. Or going antiquing. Or something equally horrid. It would be just like him to shove me aside and go along with it. Gross.

Today, the first thing he says next to me after kickoff is, "Are you nervous for your boyfriend?"

"He's not my boyfriend," I counter automatically, feeling like a teenager and hating how often I've felt that way lately.

Teasing me about guys has been one of Greg's greatest pastimes since high school. Especially because I used to have a bad habit of crushing on his friends. His Spanish tutor, Phillip, a shy, self-conscious, self-deprecating smart guy with a quick sense of humor and a quiet delivery. I contemplated learning Spanish so that he could tutor *me*. But I'd already learned every French curse word, and it was too much work to become trilingual in obscenities.

Greg persists now about Jet, "You went on a date with him, and he's called you since. That's a boyfriend."

Merde! Why do I tell him things? I must be a masochist.

"No, it's not. Of course, he's a 'boy' and he's a 'friend,' so maybe that qualifies."

He groans. "Not that old line. Jet Knox is a *man*, anyway. *The* man, if he leads the Chiefs to a Super Bowl win."

"Shh! Don't jinx it!" I admonish, smiling at how much I sound like Jet.

"You're right. One game at a time. It's gonna be hard enough to beat the Ravens."

I grab a handful of pretzels from the bowl on the coffee table in front of us and focus on the TV on the wall across the room.

The first series is a disappointing three-and-out, but Greg says, "Bah! The boys are just warming up. Your man looks tight out there, though. And not in the way you like."

Instead of protesting, I grit my teeth and hiss some insults under my breath. The more I resist, the more he'll tease.

Plus, he's right, unfortunately, about Jet looking tight. In more ways than one. I've always appreciated his striking figure in those little football pants, but now that I've had some one-on-one interaction with him, I'm looking at him differently. He's not just a professional athlete or celebrity or piece of meat. He's a person. I know things about him, like his hopes for the future, and his dog's name. And that my laugh makes him happy.

The Ravens fumble on their second down, and a Chiefs player falls on top of the coughed-up ball. When the pile clears, the ball is still in our hands, so the crowd goes crazy, as do Greg and I. And the players on the sidelines, including Jet. He looks like a jubilant kid as he slaps the butt of the guy who recovered the fumble. Then he quickly goes into attack mode, sliding on his helmet and fastening his chin strap. He has the same look in his eyes he had the other night at dinner, when he didn't appreciate the assumptions I was making about him: closed-off, cold, focused, and stony.

I still don't have a clue how I feel about him, as a person, but I suddenly don't have a single doubt about this game.

————

My instinct proves correct, but I'm hoarse from shouting all the way through the fourth quarter. After falling behind twenty-one points in the first half, the Ravens came back in the second half and tried to make it interesting. Jet was having none of that, though. Every time the opposition scored, he went out there and led the team on marathon drives that ate up clock and almost always resulted in more points on the board. He played out of his mind.

Before giving myself too much time to think about it at the end of the game, I pull out my phone and send him a text: *Great game! Yeah, I watched. Next stop: Beantown. No problem!*

Greg simpers after chugging the last of the beer from the bottle in his hand. "Texting the victor? You say he's not your boyfriend, and act like you don't want to be his girlfriend. You have a crush! What did you say to him? 'Watching you out there made me wet, Jet'?" he says in a high voice that sounds nothing like mine. "Hey, that rhymes!"

"No, you big, fat jerk. Grow up! I congratulated him on a great game and gave him some encouragement about the next one."

He rubs the side of his nose. "Oh, yeah. They're gonna get clobbered in New England."

"Who says?"

"Everyone!"

"Well, not me. I don't think it's an automatic win for those prima donna cheaters."

Now he laughs in earnest at me and tries to snatch my phone from my hand. "Oooh! Someone's super-defensive about her *boyfriend's* team. Maybe you should travel with them and be Jet's private cheering section. Or..." He gives up on his quest to grab my phone but puts his bare feet on me and nudges me with them, first on my legs, then edging up to my arms and, finally, my face. "...you could try out to be on the cheerleading squad next season so you and Jet could be together always." Fluttering his eyelashes at me, he makes kissy noises.

"Shut up. And get your nasty feet off me!" I swat at his hairy toes. "Gross!" I yell, jumping from the couch when his big toe almost goes in my mouth. "You are so disgusting!"

"My feet aren't gross. I got my first pedicure yesterday."

"You're so whipped."

"What? Who says it's against the law for a guy to have well-groomed feet?"

"You'd never get a pedicure if Deirdre didn't make you."

"She got me in the door," he admits, "but it was nice, once I stopped thinking about it too much."

"In case you're wondering, your spine is hanging up in Deirdre's coat closet in the house where you'll eventually be living, when she gets her way and makes you sell this place." I point smugly at him. "Mark my words."

With a stubborn shake of his head, he says, "Not if I have anything to say about it."

"But you don't; that's the point."

"No, seriously. We're going to put both houses on the market, and we'll let go of whichever one sells first. Hers will sell first. Guaranteed."

I blink rapidly at his overconfidence. "What have you done to this place?"

He smiles slyly. "None of your business. I don't trust you not to run to Deirdre and tell her."

That hurts, but I pretend it doesn't. "Idiot. You're both stubborn asses."

"I love this house! I've put a ton of sweat and money into it. C'mere." He leads me to the floor-to-ceiling windows overlooking the backyard and points. "Right there, I'll build the playset for the kids. I've already installed the privacy fence for the dog Deirdre and I are going to get after we've been married a few months. A Yorkie or a Chihuahua. We haven't settled on which one yet. Still need to do some more research. But I have it all planned out."

"Imagine that."

"Make fun all you want, but there's nothing wrong with knowing what you want and making it happen. That's what normal people do. They plan."

He plucks our beer bottles from the table and pads into the kitchen, where he rinses our empties before placing them carefully in their appropriate recycling container. Keeping his back to me, he says, "Adulthood isn't as scary as you think it is, you know. It's just *life*." Now he turns around and looks beseechingly at me. "It happens, whether you have a plan or not. But the plan makes it easier and gives it direction and purpose."

"My life has purpose, thank you very much!" I say hotly.

He tilts his head at me, and his eyes light up. "Great! Tell me all about it."

"Well... I— I— My job is important. I help people find work, which isn't an easy thing to do sometimes." I raise my chin, daring him to contradict me, since he and I both know the economy—especially the job market—isn't as bad as it was when I first graduated. When he says nothing, I continue more confidently, "Just because I'm not married with a bunch of kids and pets doesn't mean I'm not a valuable member of society. I contribute to the local economy. I pay taxes, damn it! I own a home, even if it's not an eff-off mansion like yours."

"You bought half of a duplex, and only because Mom and Dad gave you the down payment as a college graduation gift with the stipulation that you buy your own place rather than continue to throw money away on rent," he points out.

"So? I could have given them their money back and said, 'No thanks.'"

Which I was tempted to do. I didn't want to tie myself down to this area when I was sure I wouldn't be here long. Well, not sure. But hopeful. Then the more I thought about it, the more I realized I didn't know where I wanted to be or what I wanted to do, so I caved.

"That would have been stupid," he says. "At least you made the right decision there."

"Oh, yes. At least I made the right decision *there*, unlike every other decision in my life, right? Isn't that what you're implying?"

He puts his hands on his hips. "No. I'm not. Because you haven't made any other decisions. You're perpetually on pause."

"And you're perpetually a pompous prick. I can do tongue-twisters, too." My eyes sting, but I refuse to cry. No way. That would indicate I give a damn what he thinks.

"Now, don't get mad, Mo. What I'm trying to say is—"

"Screw you. Screw you and Deirdre and Mom and Dad. I bet you guys get together all the time to lament the hopelessness that is my life. Well, save your energy."

He points sternly at me. "Hey! Leave Mom and Dad out of this. They're always defending you. You'll be fifty, and they'll still be saying, 'Oh, leave her alone; she's young and trying to figure things out.' It's ridiculous. It's why you are the way you are."

"Which is…? Useless? Immature? Aimless?"

He merely shrugs, as if to say, *Take your pick*.

"You're a sanctimonious asshole," I spit, blinking away tears as I whirl away from him and head for the foyer, where my coat hangs neatly on a peg next to the front door.

"Mo! Come back. I'm sorry. I don't think you're useless. Under-utilized, maybe, but—"

I refuse to take the time to put on my coat, hat, and gloves, despite an awaiting outside temperature in the teens. "Forget it, Greg. It's good to know how you feel, finally. I've always suspected, but now I know exactly where I stand."

I grab the doorknob and twist fiercely. It comes off in my hand. After looking at it for a few seconds, I pitch it at him. The throw, a bullet, would probably make Jet proud. Greg catches it against his chest, then turns and follows my progress as I walk to the back door.

"A little obvious, don't you think?" I ask snidely about his childish sabotage. "But maybe Deirdre won't notice, since she's so preoccupied with adding pedicure clauses to your marriage contract. Effing nutjobs," I mutter on my way outside, slamming the door in my brother's face.

As I hike around the back and side of the house to get to the driveway, I struggle to keep the tears of rage and hurt in check. Unfortunately, "resolve" has never been my forte.

————

More than an hour later, when there's a knock at my door, and I open it to find a delivery person weighed down with what appears to be a hundred pink and white roses in a cut crystal vase, I snort and almost close the door in her face. But it's not her fault my brother's a jerk.

After I unburden her of her load and set the flowers aside on the tiny table in my entryway, she takes one look at my tear-puffy face and says as she thrusts a clipboard toward me with a delivery log to sign, "Oh. Now I understand."

I chuckle mirthlessly. "Yeah. But flowers aren't going to get him out of the doghouse."

Plus, since when does Greg send me flowers for anything? Or admit he was wrong, come to think of it? Never. And roses? He's so clueless. Maybe he *was* the one who got me that lingerie gift card.

I close the door on the courier and pluck the card from the mass of buds that are close to opening and becoming more beautiful than they already are.

This oughtta be good. He must feel awful to have plunked down the dough for these. The vase alone...

Maura,
That win was for you.
Yours,
J

ELEVEN

RELUCTANTLY WILLING

Two days later, I arrive at work with a whistle on my lips. I should be exhausted after my marathon phone conversation with Jet last night, but I'm buoyant. Bubbling. Beaming.

When I first received those flowers, my initial reaction was dismay. Because I'm weird. But then I realized if I'm going to worry about where all this is going with Jet, I'll have to do something to stop it, and that's too much work. So I'm going to go with it.

It's been the best decision I've ever not made. Decision-making is a major bummer and always stresses me out. It's so much better to simply do nothing and let someone else make all the moves. So far, I'm okay with all the moves Jet's making. He's sweet, funny, attentive, and thinks I'm "awesome." What's not to like about that?

Cassie (Carmen? Chastity? Oh, well, whatever her name is) hands my schedule to me and says, "Wow. Did you get your hair colored or something?"

I grab a strand from my shoulder and peer down at its

ends. "No." My voice distorts as I squash my chin to my chest to get a better view. "Does it look different?"

She shakes her head, befuddled. "Maybe. You look, like, lighter."

Continuing toward my door, I shrug. "Hm. Weird."

"Yeah. Anyway, your first appointment is here and waiting."

"I'll be right with them," I tell her, carrying my stuff into my office and settling in for the day.

My cell phone chimes as I hang my purse on the door hook. Unable to resist, I dig it out to read what I assume is going to be a text from Jet.

My stomach gurgles when I see, instead, *Roses? Someone's got it bad.*

Rae. Dagnabbit! How the heck does she know about that? There wasn't a whisper of it online. I know, because I signed up for a service that sends me alerts any time Jet's name is mentioned. (Who's the stalker now?) If he and I are going to be a thing, though, I don't want people knowing stuff about us that I don't even know, ya know? I want to stay ahead of the gossip. Maybe Jet told her? That poor, sweet, innocent man. He and I are going to have to have a talk. Rae is *not* his ally in this game. The sooner he realizes that, the better.

One of the best things about texts is that you can ignore a message and claim you didn't know it had arrived. In this case, I can only pretend so long, since Rae's all-too-aware of how regularly I check my phone. But I have a while before she becomes suspicious I'm avoiding her.

Not enough 5-hr energy n wrld 4 me 2 stay awake n this pats defense revu says the text from Jet that pops onto the screen before I can set down my phone on my desk.

The usual me would text back something flirty, but I need to get to work, so I don't have time to think about how it makes me feel that Jet Knox sends me illicit texts during playoff preps. My gut reaction is to discourage him. I don't want anyone to find out and treat me like a modern-day Yoko if the team loses Sunday. Silencing the device, I slide it underneath a pile of papers on the corner of my desk and concentrate on the stack of job descriptions already printed and ready for my first client. All thoughts of Rae and Jet will have to wait.

It isn't until after my first appointment ends that I have a chance to peruse the rest of my schedule. For the second time today, my stomach reacts unpleasantly. My entire afternoon is blocked out for a job fair planning meeting. It's for the spring fair, so I'm merely sitting in, observing Arnold. Still, it's an unwelcome reminder of the herculean responsibility I'm doing my damnedest to pretend doesn't exist.

The happiness I was feeling a few minutes ago dissipates like bubbles in a long, hot bath that's gone lukewarm.

———

When Carmen/Cassie/Chastity (I definitely need to figure out her name for real, no matter how temporary she'll be) buzzes me as I'm gathering my things to leave for the day and announces Colin's arrival, I experience a brief panicked moment. His new job only started yesterday! What could he possibly need so soon?

As soon as he opens my door, he says, "Sorry I'm so early. If you're not ready to go yet, I understand and don't mind waiting." At my blank stare, he prods, "Dinner? Oh, don't tell me, you've forgotten and made plans with Mr. KC?"

My shoulders relax. "Oh! No. I mean, yes. I mean..." In my angst and despair over the job fair planning meeting, I forgot about having dinner with Colin, my buddy, my pal.

Standing in front of my desk, he shifts his weight from one foot to the other, then slides his hands into the pockets of his fleece pullover before taking them out again.

After a deep, cleansing breath, I say, "I *did* forget, but I have no other plans. I'm just— I'm a little scattered right now. Let me get my things."

I pat the papers on my desk, trying to locate my still-buried phone, which has chirped and vibrated a few times throughout the day but has remained largely ignored, since I've been too busy to check it. Even now, it goes straight into my purse without a glance from me.

Smiling mildly, he says, "Excellent. Because I have some interesting stories to relay regarding the Blue Rinse Brigade."

I laugh at his colorful description of the clientele at his new place of employment. "I can't wait to hear all about it. Who's driving?" When he points to me, I dig my keys from my coat pocket and jingle them. "Let's go."

Once in the car, having determined our destination to be the "Irish" pub we often patronize relatively close to my office, he asks, "If you could try any job for a day, regardless of qualifications or location or pay or any of that, what would it be?"

"What?"

He repeats his question, then urges, "Come on. Anything. No limits."

I glance over at him and laugh at his eager expression. "I don't know!"

He lets that stand while I consider the question more seriously at a stoplight. Then it hits me.

"You've got something!" he says triumphantly. "I can tell. Come on, then. What is it?"

In spite of my best efforts not to, I blush and squirm.

He rubs his hands together. "Ooh, what is it? Pole dancer?"

"No!"

"Then come out with it already."

"Movie critic," I say, pressing on the gas when the light turns green. "With my own syndicated column. Or blog. Or whatever is the most modern thing with the biggest reach."

He hums approvingly.

"What about you?"

Seemingly surprised I've asked, he opens his mouth, then closes it.

"It's only fair that you play along, too."

"Promise not to laugh?"

Already cracking up, I say, "No way. This is *you* we're talking about. It's hilarious, whatever it is."

He rolls his eyes like a recalcitrant child. "Okay, fine. Taste-tester at the Boulevard Brewery."

I chuckle. "That *would* be a fantastic job!"

"I'd settle for tour guide, in a pinch, because you'd get to sample the finished product, I bet. If anything like that comes up at The Career Center, you must give me a ring."

"Will do."

"Promise?"

"Absolutely."

"Right, then. Well, thanks for indulging my little game."

"Was there a point to it?" Having arrived at the pub, I pull the car into an open spot and slide the shifter into "Park."

He shrugs while unbuckling his seatbelt and opening his door. "I simply wanted to see what you would pick if you weren't telling yourself you're not good enough." With that, he exits the vehicle and walks ahead of me to the pub's entrance, holding open the door for me.

Hurrying to catch up, I say on my way past him into the warm, dim bar, "Listen, Mr. Miyagi, I appreciate the sentiment, but I don't need a philosophical ego boost from you."

We're early enough that there's no wait for a booth, so after we've been seated and have ordered our first drinks, he picks up our conversation like there's been no interruption. "I'm not trying to inflate your ego. That suggests a certain level of insincerity. I'm simply trying to convince you to consider your worth. Or decide you're right where you're supposed to be."

Hoping to convey an air of boredom, I examine my ragged cuticles.

He takes that as a sign to continue. "Take Jet when he was… well, *a* Jet."

The concept of Colin knowing anything about American football, much less Jet's NFL résumé, piques my interest. "What do you know about that?"

Pointing to the ceiling, he answers, "Plenty, thanks to the almighty Internet. I know he was drafted by the New York Jets, and they made a huge deal about 'Jet the Jet' with billboards and promotions and gimmicks, but they were more in love with his name than the type of captain—"

"Quarterback."

"—he is, so he didn't fit their system. At all. He was doomed for failure the minute he stepped foot in the changing room—"

"Locker room."

"—his first season. But the fans were led to believe he would be the next Joe Namath, so they pinned all their World Cup—"

"Super Bowl."

"—hopes on him, and when he couldn't deliver, they very publicly demoted him after one-and-a-half seasons and promoted the backup capt— *quarterback* whose style better fit the team. Jet rode the bench as the Jets' backup for more than two years. At one point, when he was brought in to sub for the injured starter, and he threw an interception—which, after the fact, everyone said was his receiver's fault—he was benched again, in favor of the third-stringer."

He pauses to breathe, so I take the opportunity to ask, "Who are you, and what have you done with Colin?"

He laughs, banging his fist on the table. "I'm your friend! And after we talked at the bookshop Saturday, I decided a true mate would research someone his friend thought was so high above her."

"Well, Jet's not a loser, either, if that's what you're implying."

He wags his finger and pooches out his lower lip. "On the contrary. My point is, for the first five years of his professional career, Jet Knox was told over and over again that he was shite. But what was his response to that?"

I shake my head, not having a clue. I do remember the Chiefs got a great deal on him and that his first contract with the team was a measly one-year deal with all sorts of provisos and outs and an almost insulting salary, by today's standards, because he was so desperate to get out of New York. But having never followed the Jets, I'm unaware of anything more than what ESPN reported when he made the move.

Colin's all too pleased to educate me. "He was an absolute

star about the whole thing. He mentored his replacements; he kept morale up on the bench when games weren't going well; he never once said a bad thing about the Jets organization in the media; he didn't so much as pout on the sidelines. He took it like a hero and was a valuable member of the team, despite the fact that the team didn't want him anywhere near the pitch."

I'm too proud of my sort-of boyfriend to bother correcting my friend's terminology.

"That's pretty cool," I mumble.

"Very cool. This guy's credibility shot through the ceiling for me when I read that about him. He's classy, Maura. Classy."

"And this is supposed to make me feel *less* inferior around him?"

"It's supposed to inspire you!" He throws his arms wide, almost knocking our arriving beers from the precariously balanced tray in our server's hand. "Oops. Sorry, mate," he says, placing his hands in his lap. We order our usuals, and as soon as we're alone again, he continues, "It's supposed to prove that Jet hasn't always been the celebrated hero, but he didn't let anyone else's opinion of him affect how he felt about himself. He never stopped believing the possibilities."

From my purse, my phone chimes with an incoming text. Out of habit, I slide it from the bag and glance at the screen, noticing it's from Jet.

Colin stands. "Judging by that rosy glow on your face, that must be from the devil of which we speak." He grins. "Someone's ears must have been burning. I need to pop to the gents'."

I have the manners to wait until he's truly gone before reading the message.

Longest day ever. Have a minute to talk?

At dinner with Colin, I tap back. *Call you later?*

Gotta hit the sheets early tonight :(

8:00 too late?

Ha! No. Should I be worried about this Colin guy? ;)

The winky emoticon saves him. Because a whiff of jealousy from someone who's been on one date with me and that's Game Over. I've had my fill of possessive boyfriends; I promised myself I'd never go there again.

No QB controversy here

LOL. OK. Have a nice dinner. TTYL

Later

My phone is securely back in my purse, out of sight, by the time Colin returns. "All's well?" he checks.

"Very well. Jet wants to know if he should be worried about you."

He pretends to choke on his latest swallow of beer. "Me? Whatever for?"

I shrug. "Who knows? Men can be so weird."

Colin rests his hand, palm-up, on the table and wiggles his fingers. "Give me your mobile."

Wary, I balk. "Why?"

He tilts his head and shoots me a long-suffering look. "Are you saying you don't trust me?"

Since I do—mostly—I dig out my phone again and place it in his hand. He immediately snaps a silly selfie, complete with lolling tongue, then says aloud while he types painfully slowly, "This. Is. Colin. No. Worries." He taps "send" and returns the phone to the tabletop between us.

I'm still laughing when the phone lights up with an incoming message. Faster than I am, Colin snatches the device, but while cracking up at Jet's response, he holds it up so I can see.

I steady his hand and read:

Gay?

Before I can grab the phone back, Colin pulls it from my reach and swipes at his eyes. "No, no. That's perfect. We'll let that be the last word for a while. You can explain things more fully later." Nodding at something over my shoulder, he says, "Here comes our food. Let's eat and talk about my new job. The ladies are brilliant."

TWELVE

LOSING AND WINNING

When the Patriots do to the Chiefs what they've done to every other team this season, it's safe to say I'm the most disappointed fan in Kansas City. The ride is over, and it had only begun. Plus, now I'm going to have to figure out what to do with Jet. For real.

Or not. Doing nothing is working well so far. Why change my strategy, mid-game? Things will work themselves out. Surely, he'll tire of me before we get to the point that I have to do something drastic like step in and take control. Surely.

Rae asks me on the phone if I'm going to meet the fallen hero at the airport, but I laugh nervously and say, "Oh, I'll see him soon enough. When he's more rested."

It's only after I hear her relay this message to him that I realize he's standing right there with her.

He shouts in the background, "Come on, Maura! Let's get plastered in the airport bar. Like real losers."

"Mmmm." I pretend to consider. "Nah. Tell him I'll call him tomorrow. Or he can call me. Whichever. The office is closed for Dr. King Day."

"I'm not your messenger! You two need to work this out without me," she gripes before going ahead and telling him what I've said. I don't hear his reaction. After a pause, she says with a smile in her voice, "Uh-oh. He's pouting now."

"Is he still right there next to you?" I ask.

"No, he walked away. So I can't be the go-between for any more of your sweet nothings."

I change the subject. "Have you talked at all to Molly while you've been away?"

"Molly?" she asks blankly.

"KCI Molly," I remind her, laughing. "Gosh! How soon we forget. And you call Jet a player."

She chuckles. "Oops. Oh, yeah. That Molly. No, I told her not to expect me to be in touch until after our season is over. I knew it'd be crazy-busy on the road, and I didn't want her reading anything into my silence."

"Good move. But now the season *is* over. Are you going to call her when you get home?"

"What are you, my matchmaker? I don't know. Probably. I have a feeling Jet will be monopolizing my best friend's time, so I guess I'd better find someone to keep me company."

"Maybe we can go on a double date," I suggest flippantly.

As expected, she vetoes that. "It's one thing to hang out with Jet when we're on the road for work, but I don't want to socialize with him once we get back to town. He already knows way too much about me."

"Such as?"

"He could probably order for me at a restaurant."

I laugh. "You're almost as aloof as I am."

"Oh, I've told him he has a challenge ahead of him with you, and not to expect any help from me. No offense."

"I don't see how he could take offense to that," I say drily.

"But thanks for busting me out. I've been doing a good job of getting him to think he's making progress, and now you come in and with one statement let him know I'm only making all the right noises."

"He wants you to make all the right noises," she mutters. "Why would you want to lead him on? I don't understand you sometimes. Oh, shit. Here he comes again. I hope he doesn't sit next to me on the plane. Gotta go."

"Bye. Try to be nice."

"Take your own advice. He's not used to man-eaters like you."

After I hang up, I stare at my bedroom ceiling for a while, chewing my lips. Man-eater, my ass. To hear her tell it, I make a hobby out of using men for my pleasure, then kicking them to the curb. That's certainly not true. I rarely date at all, and not once since I chucked Jamie almost a year ago.

I haven't been ready.

It's not that I'm still hung up on *him*, but I'm definitely hung up on some of the things he said to me when I broke up with him. Before he stormed away from me at the park, where I gave him the bad news, he told me I was "emotionally stunted," and that I'd probably never be ready to "take things to the next level."

I hate that phrase. What does that mean? We were already sexually intimate. What other level is there? Rings on our fingers and a lifetime of boredom and resentment? Kids, pets, and a mortgage with both of our names on it? No thanks. Then it wouldn't have been fun anymore. It would have been work.

Why is everyone so determined to make more work for themselves? And why do I attract men who want all the things I don't? Where are all the commitment-averse guys that other

—some would say "normal"—women complain about? I'd take one in a heartbeat.

But that doesn't mean I'm heartless or that I'll never want to settle down. I'm simply not in a hurry to do so. I haven't found someone who seems worth the trouble. Until now.

Maybe.

Who knows?

It seems ridiculous to contemplate something long-term with Jet Knox. We've been on one date. We've never kissed. Not even a friendly peck "hello" or "goodbye" on the cheek. Other than that, we've talked on the phone a few times and have traded texts. Hardly hearing wedding bells.

But yeah, I'm a real man-eater.

Sometimes Rae's flair for the dramatic grates on my nerves.

———

"Tom McGown's not my boyfriend!" I proclaim, panicked, after sitting straight up in bed, where I fell asleep, fully clothed, on top of the covers. The lights blaze. My phone says it's a few minutes past three a.m. But something other than the strange dream about the former college football phenom (random!) startled me awake. What was it? A sound? A tapping?

There it is again!

Definitely tapping. More like knocking. Then the doorbell rings.

"Really?" I grouse, rubbing my face.

I live in a nice neighborhood, on a quiet cul-de-sac, but I still don't make it a habit to answer the door in the middle of the night. I'm so tired that I'm tempted to skip seeing who it is. They can call me or stop by tomorrow at a decent time.

But what if it's a cop, checking up on me after getting a call from a neighbor about someone snooping around? Or a firefighter, telling me the unit next door is on fire, and I need to evacuate? Or a neighbor, needing help with an emergency? Civic duty demands I at least look through the peephole to see who's there.

Growling, I swing my legs over the side of the bed and heave myself down the hall toward the front door. The knocking intensifies.

"Coming!" I bellow, glad the other half of the duplex is currently vacant. The person on my front stoop needs to cool it.

When I look through the peephole and see who it is, I almost turn around and go back to bed without another word. But I'm awake now, and I'll lie in bed feeling guilty—and other things—if I send him away.

The locks click under my fingers, and I swing the door open.

Jet's serious face relaxes into a disarming grin. "Maura! Oh, did I wake you up?"

"It's three in the morning. Yes."

"Your lights were on, so I thought you were awake," he says. "Or I never would have bothered you."

He keeps edging closer to me, so I step aside to let him in. "Did you just get back to town?" I ask as he crosses the threshold and looks around. I close the door and automatically redo the locks before realizing it looks like I'm locking him in and inviting him for a lengthy visit. Oh, well. He'll find out soon enough that's not the case.

"Yeah. I haven't been home yet."

"You should have gone home," I say bluntly, then back-track when I see the hurt in his eyes. "I mean, you didn't have to come see me right away."

"I wanted to," he says, as if I'm the one looking for reas-surance. "I've wanted to see you since the day after our first date. Now that I can, I couldn't wait. I was so relieved when I drove by and saw your lights on." He points to my *Bourne* posters. "Bad-ass." Advancing into the house, he whistles. "Whoa. This is..." He spins to face me again. "It's official. You're the coolest person I've ever met."

I'd have to be dead for that not to excite me. After all, he knows a butt-load of cool people. "I don't know about that..." I hem, standing directly in front of him, looking up into his twinkling eyes.

Gently, smiling affectionately, he reaches out and runs his finger along my face. "You have pillow creases on your cheek. You must have been out of it. In all your clothes."

I weaken a bit at his tender gesture. "Yeah. I guess I was." I lead him toward the kitchen, but he pauses several times along the way to look at posters, then stops at the locked, glass-fronted cabinet that straddles the threshold between my living room and dining room.

"What's in here?"

"My collection of official screenplays," I answer, trying to sound casual about my pride and joy, nearly one hundred leather-bound scripts in alphabetical order by title.

"No way. Like, the ones the actual actors used?"

"Or directors. In some cases. Supposedly."

"Are any of them signed?"

"A few."

"That's why you have them locked up, huh?" He drops to a crouch in front of the cabinet, balancing on his haunches.

"*Shakespeare in Love, Gladiator, All About Eve, Terms of Endearment*... Wait. These are Oscar winners!"

I kneel next to him, hanging onto the top of the cabinet for balance. "Yeah. I've concentrated my efforts—and funds—on purchasing the majority of the Best Picture winners. Of course, some of them are impossible to find or way out of my price range, but whatever."

"So cool. Ooh, *The Departed*. I loved that movie!" He straightens his legs and stands at his full height, then offers me a hand up. "Do you, like, wear gloves when you read them?"

Shaking my head, I laugh. "I don't touch them much after I put them in there."

"That's a seriously impressive collection."

"It's relatively puny by most standards. Now, my film library... That's another story."

He searches the living room, as if expecting to find it housed somewhere out here.

"Oh, no. It has its own room." Grabbing his hand, I drag him down the hallway and into the spare room.

When I flip on the light, his eyes bulge, and his jaw drops. "Holy crap."

"Yep."

"How do you— Oh, my gosh, there's more than one row on every shelf? There must be a million movies in here!" He walks to the nearest shelf and runs his fingers along the spines of the cases. "Dude! You have *Caddyshack* on VHS? That's old school."

"It's one of my favorites. I have a digital copy, too. But I got that tape when I was a teenager. Eventually, I'd like to replace all of my VHS copies with updated formats, but it's a slow process."

"Do you still have a working VCR?"

"Yeah, but it's about to die, and some of my tapes have been watched so many times, they've degraded."

"Bummer."

I shrug. "Most of my favorites have already been updated. I can't quite force myself to throw out the originals, though."

"Don't! Ever!" Still surveying the room, he says in almost an awed whisper, "This is one of the most amazing things I've ever seen in a normal person's house."

"Can you really say I'm 'normal' after seeing this?"

"You know what I mean. A lot of the guys on the team collect stuff—mostly sports memorabilia—but most of them have more money than they know what to do with. You…"

"Well, I haven't bought all of this. Some things were gifts. I scour garage sales and flea markets, bargain bins at stores…" I point to the "Be Kind, Rewind" sign above the door. "Going out of business sales." I stifle a yawn. "What else do I have to spend my money on?"

He follows me from the room and back down the hall to the living area. I continue into the kitchen, feeling like I should offer him something, although I'm not sure the usual hostess rules apply at this hour.

Without asking if he wants it, I grab a beer from the fridge and turn to give it to him. But he's right behind me.

"Hi," I say stupidly into his chest, offering him the bottle.

He takes it from me but sets it on the counter behind him without opening it.

I look up into his face and instantly regret it. I know that face. It's his heading-for-the-end-zone face. It makes me squirm.

"So, anyway… I'm sorry about the game," I say, cringing at my inability to scramble in the proverbial pocket.

"What game?"

I can tell by the set of his jaw that it's an effort not to think about it and worry it was a mistake to bring it up. However, I need to distract him from me. "You know what game. Less than twelve hours ago, you were on the football field, in all your gear, hoping to make it to the Conference Championship." I take a step back. He moves with me.

"There are more important things in life than football."

"Oh, you don't have to be brave for me." I chuckle nervously. "You didn't get where you are today by shrugging off losses. You're a competitor. You must be hurting."

"My shoulder's sore, but other than that…"

I cross to the other side of the galley kitchen. It places about two feet of space between us, but that's two feet more than before.

"Where are you going?" he asks, clearly amused.

"I feel like I'm about to be sacked."

He raises an eyebrow, his eyes sparkling. "For the first time today, I like the sound of that."

My guts jump pleasantly as my body betrays my brain. "I dunno. I'm tired," I supply lamely.

He sobers quickly. In one stride, he's directly in front of me again, his hands on my shoulders like a set of oversized pads. "I just want to kiss you, Maura. I've been thinking about it. A lot."

"Uh, okay," I murmur helplessly as he lowers his mouth to mine.

The kiss is soft but not at all hesitant. He knows exactly what he's doing. He's damn good at it. When it's obvious I'm not going to resist, he pulls me closer to him and presses his lips harder on mine. When my mouth drops open as I lose what little control I may have had over my muscles, he runs with the invitation.

My roaming hands on his chest, shoulders, and neck provide more encouragement. He transfers his hands to my butt and lifts me tighter against his body. Oh gosh. Only denim and a tiny scrap of cotton separate his fingers from the most intimate of my body parts. I hope he's not as aware of that as I am. I can't think of anything else.

Somehow, I manage to pull my lips away from his. He opens his heavy-lidded eyes and gazes into my face. A slow, lazy smile spreads across his glistening mouth. Without thinking, I rub my thumb across his bottom lip to blot away the moisture, but he grabs it lightly between his teeth and grins.

Letting go, he says, "That's definitely the best thing I've done all day."

Flattered, I nevertheless feel the need to check, "Better than that slant pass to Busch for a touchdown?"

"Keaton's never made me feel anything close to that."

I duck my head, wishing I could say the same. It suddenly seems super-awkward that I've fantasized about one of his co-workers.

Reluctantly, Jet steps away and runs his hand through his hair. "Well, I guess— I don't know. You probably want to get to bed for real, huh?"

If he's angling for a sleepover invitation, he's going to be disappointed. I try to let him down easy, though. "Yeah. But thanks for stopping by."

"Thanks for showing me your movie stuff. I'm sorry I woke you up." He smirks. "Actually, I'm glad I did. But it wasn't on purpose."

"It's fine."

More than fine. My body is screaming for more. That's why

he needs to leave right now. If he touches me again, I may explode.

Since his smirk is still firmly in place, I assume he knows it, too. He shows me mercy, though, and says, "I'll call you tomorrow. Maybe we can meet up and do something?"

I long to do something, but I try not to nod too eagerly while I walk him to the door.

As I'm showing him out, he turns in the open doorway. "I'll try to wait until late morning to call. But I can't make any promises."

Saucily, I bluff, "You can call whenever you want. I'm silencing my phone as soon as you leave."

"Don't keep me waiting too long," he requests sweetly, bending down to barely brush his lips against mine. "It's not nice to play hard-to-get."

Unfortunately, I'm not "playing" anything.

THIRTEEN

SWEET ENTICEMENTS

I manage to get a solid five hours of sleep before my doorbell rings again. I ignore it this time. It's a three-day weekend. I'm sleeping in. He's going to have to learn to call ahead. Standing on a cold front stoop after driving from wherever he lives to where I live is a good way to learn that lesson.

It was one thing last night, when I was fully clothed and half-asleep and thought he was a public servant or Good Samaritan alerting me to an emergency. But I'm not answering in my tank top and panties with bona fide bed head and morning breath. Uh-uh. For all he knows, I'm a sound sleeper and don't hear the doorbell that he rings four times.

In silent mode on my bedside table, my phone vibrates.

"Ratchin' fratchin' mother scratchin'," I grouch. However, all it takes is the memory of that kiss in the kitchen a few hours ago for me to weaken considerably and blindly answer the phone with a sultry, "Helloooo."

"Are you gonna let me in, or what?" Rae asks. "I brought you donuts. Thought you might want to dish about your early morning reunion with Knox."

Donuts? When my health-conscious friend offers such a nutritionally bankrupt breakfast, I don't pass it up, so I groan but say, "Use your key. I need to put on some clothes and brush my teeth."

"Whatever," she allows, and hangs up.

I toss the phone aside, then think better of it and slip it into my bathrobe pocket after I shrug it on.

By the time I run brushes over my teeth and through my hair, Rae's all set up in the kitchen, and a cup of coffee steams on the counter next to the brewer she got me for Christmas. Her own cup catches the thin, brown stream of liquid heaven currently trickling from the machine.

"Hasn't this thing revolutionized your life?" she asks, pointing to the space-aged coffeemaker.

"Absolutely. It's an awesome gadget."

"I wish I could take mine on the road with me."

I sip while perusing my choice of donuts. Oh, she went all out with this morning's selection, including those powdered sugar jelly-filled ones I love. She's sucking up, hard-core. But why?

She chooses a plain glazed pastry and dunks it in her freshly brewed cup of joe.

Silence rules as we savor our breakfasts, but after her last bite, she says, "So."

I dab powdered sugar from the corners of my mouth and repeat, "So."

"How'd you like Jet's middle-of-the-night visit?"

"How'd you know about that?" I ask what I've been wondering since she called me from my front door.

"He told me his plan on the bus back to the training complex."

"And how did he know where 'here' is?"

She rolls her eyes. "He's probably had your address programmed into his car's GPS since he sent you those over-the-top flowers."

"And he got my address for those... how?"

"You're listed."

"Under 'M. Richards.' Someone had to have helped him narrow it down."

Keeping her eyes steadily on mine, she says, "Okay, I did. So, sue me."

"And this morning, you didn't think it would be wiser to discourage him when he told you about his plan?"

She smirks into her coffee mug. "I figured it was his funeral if he came by here and woke you up at three a.m. Not my business."

"You suck," I say with a smile. "But the joke's on you, because it turned out to be a nice visit."

She raises her eyebrows and taps her blunt index fingernail against the ceramic mug handle. "Details."

"Well, not *that* nice, if that's what you're thinking. But he's a good kisser."

"Let me get this straight. He drops in on you at an ungodly hour without calling first, and you *reward* him? With a makeout session?"

Trying and failing to hide my amusement, I answer, "I showed him my movie collection first."

"Is that a euphemism?"

With a glare, I say, "He lost a big game yesterday, so I was nice. And there was no makeout session. We kissed. Right over there." I point to the place in the kitchen where it happened and have to concentrate not to get all swoony. "It was an intense kiss. But just a kiss. I felt sorry for him!"

"And after the consolation kiss? Nothing? He just went

home?" Suddenly pale, she grips the sides of the donut box, as if she's going to toss the whole thing in the trash, and whispers, "Oh, shit. Is he still here?"

"No! I told you, we only kissed. Anyway, is there an eighty-thousand-dollar car in my driveway? What's your problem?"

"He can't know about these donuts."

I roll my eyes. "Your secret is safe with me. He's turning out to be quite the gentleman, despite all the things you've tried to get me to believe about him."

"Apparently, he's digging this hard-to-get act you're putting on."

"It's not an act. I have no clue what I'm doing with him. He scares the crap out of me most of the time, because he's so intense. But he's also so effing hot!"

"Does he make you feel all wiggly?"

"Hell, yes! He's into *me*. That's flattering. I'd be an idiot not to enjoy the ride for a while, at least to say I did." Crude? Maybe. Honest? Yes.

She shakes her head. "He must enjoy the challenge. Lord knows he's not used to having to work for puss—"

"Hey, hey, hey!" I wag my finger at her. "I hate that word."

"That's why I use it."

A buzzing from my robe pocket gets both of our attentions.

"Speak of the angel," she cracks.

I pull out my phone and check the display before answering, "I'm already awake, if you can believe it."

His laugh makes me feel ridiculously fluttery. "Here you thought I'd be interrupting your beauty sleep."

"You have a habit of doing that."

"I'd hardly call one time a 'habit,' but if exaggerating is one of your faults, I'm glad to finally find one."

"Does that line actually work on anyone?"

"It's not a line. I'm serious."

"Then you'll be relieved to know I have plenty of faults."

Rae nods her silent agreement as she closes the lid on the donuts and puts her mug in the dishwasher.

I stick out my tongue behind her back. "Rae would be more than happy to tell you all about them."

"I'd rather discover them in person. Do you have any plans today?"

"No!" I quickly answer. "Not at all. Rae's here now, but she'll be leaving soon. She stopped by this morning to"—she makes a cutting motion across her neck and points to the donuts—"catch up," I finish lamely.

"I see." His smug tone indicates he knows we've been talking about him. "Well, if you're available later, I thought I might swing by to get you after the postmortem at the training complex."

"Where are we going?"

"Nowhere special. You showed me your place, so I thought I'd show you mine," he answers coolly. "And introduce you to Torz."

I mutter, "Gosh, that sounds serious," and he laughs in reply, but I'm not kidding. My heart palpitates. Maybe it's the coffee and sugar, though.

"What do you say?" he asks eagerly. "I'll come by at one-ish? The team meeting should be short. Nobody wants to talk about it, and it doesn't take too long to say, 'We'll get 'em next year, guys.'"

"Fine," I answer meekly. "Sounds... good."

"Great! I'll see you then, Maura."

"Yeah. See ya."

So, this is really happening.

———

This thing with Jet makes me feel like I have multiple person-alities. Or at least two. I'm afraid I'm sending him mixed signals. Since I'm sending mixed signals to myself, though, I'm powerless to transmit a more consistent message.

One of the Mauras can't get enough of the guy. He's funny and charming, he's a great kisser, he thinks I'm close to perfect, and—I'm just going to say it—he's rich and famous.

The other Maura is freaking out. He sends over-the-top flower arrangements, drops in unannounced and uninvited in the middle of the night, says suggestive things to me that could be interpreted as cheesy or sleazy, goes behind my back to get information about me, and is too damn sure of himself and everything he says and does.

As a result, I'll be creeped out one second and incredibly turned on the next. It's like he's holding a plastic grocery sack over my head, but I'm one of those weirdos who gets off on it.

Now, as I sit in the passenger seat of his sporty, low-slung car (Chiefs red, of course), I've finally figured out what the flashes of repulsion are about. I don't want to admit to myself that I could be falling for this guy, like Colin predicted. The last thing I ever want to be is predictable. Or impressionable enough for Jet's charms to work on me. I'm many things, but I'm not dumb. Only dumb women allow cheesy lines to charm them out of their panties.

That's where the me who's allergic to romance comes in. She shoves Horny Maura out of the way and cock blocks Mr. Knox. As she should. But I can't help wishing she'd go away. Maybe for an hour. Or one night.

She definitely needs to stop calling me a gold digger. Because I'm not one. There's nothing wrong with being attracted to a guy who happens to be wealthy. The two things aren't related in my brain at all. He'd be hot if he drove a cheap beater and lived in a one-room apartment. I genuinely like him as a person, despite wishing he'd slow down.

The state trooper we passed on the shoulder wishes the same thing.

Jet curses under his breath when the officer flashes his lights, and "bloop-bloops" his siren in greeting behind us. His face matching the paint job on his car, Jet looks over at me as he pulls onto the highway's shoulder and digs his wallet from his back pocket. "How embarrassing. You mind grabbing my paperwork from the glove box?"

I do as he asks and smile sympathetically as I hand it over. "There you go, Lead Foot."

He laughs. "Why didn't you say something?"

I shrug. "I'm not your mom."

Also, I thought he knew how fast he was going, given that handy gauge called a speedometer, *and* the fact that we were blowing past everyone else on the Kansas City freeway system like they were standing still. I figured, his ride, his rules, his speeding ticket. If he'd been driving recklessly, that would have been another story. But I never felt unsafe. In fact, I was enjoying the ride.

After he hands the officer his license, registration, and proof of insurance, he sits with his hands on the steering wheel, stares straight through the windshield, and waits for the cop's next instructions. I watch the trooper, who looks at the license, looks at Jet, and looks back at the license.

"Mr. Knox, do you know how fast you were going?" he asks as a matter of routine.

Jet gulps and grimaces. "Uh, no. Not really, sir."

This tightens the trooper's lips. "The posted speed limit through here is sixty. I clocked you going about ninety."

"That's fast," Jet says. "I'm so sorry. I wasn't trying to go that fast. This car… I wish there was an alarm or something on it that would grab my attention when I start to speed. I'm babbling. Sorry, Officer."

"Let me run all this, and I'll be right back," the patrolman says before walking away.

As soon as he's gone, Jet looks over at me and grimaces. "I'm so screwed."

I can't help but laugh at his worried expression. "Maybe you should be more aware of what you're doing when you're operating a deadly weapon."

He rubs his chin. "Wait until the front office hears about this."

"Ruh-roh. Is this a violation of some personal conduct policy?"

"Not technically. But I'm in for an uncomfortable lecture, at least."

"Way to go."

"Thanks." He reaches over and grabs my hand. "I guess I was distracted. And in a bigger hurry than I realized."

Before I reply or can do anything but stare at our joined hands while I marvel how a line like that could possibly do to my insides what that one is doing, the trooper returns, handing Jet's stuff to him through the window.

"Here you go, Knox. Just a warning today. But watch your speed, got it?"

"You bet! Totally!" Jet stumbles over himself in shock.

"Hey, tough loss yesterday, man. Damn Pats. If it's any consolation, they're probably gonna win the whole thing. Again."

Jet's hands freeze while sliding his license into his wallet, but otherwise he doesn't show he's surprised the officer is talking football. "I wish they hadn't made us look like such amateurs out there. We'll get 'em next year, though."

"'Atta boy. Well, you have a nice day." He nods at me. "Ma'am."

I wiggle my fingers at him.

As the trooper pulls around us and back onto the highway, he and Jet salute each other. Jet turns to me and grins. "That was a freakin' miracle. If anything, I thought he'd throw the book at me *because* of yesterday's game."

"No use kickin' a guy when he's down, I guess."

He restarts the car. "You have a point there. Yell at me if you notice I'm going too fast."

Hmm. I may have a few retroactive violations to address. But I merely smile and say, "Right-oh."

FOURTEEN

FORT KNOX

Between the gate at the entrance to the driveway, the gray stone, dark wood, and black ironwork, Jet's place looks moderately medieval. I almost ask him where the moat and drawbridge are, but I don't want to hurt his feelings, and it *is* an impressive place. Just not my style. At all. Not at all what I pictured for him, either.

Geographically, it's a five-minute drive (if that) from Arrowhead Stadium, so close it feels like we should be able to see it from the front porch, but his house is set so far back from the road and burrowed so deeply in mature woodlands that it's impossible to glimpse any other inhabitants from here, and vice versa. If not for the whooshing of traffic, the illusion of being hours from civilization would be complete.

Inside Fort Knox, he pockets his car keys and opens his arms wide. "Well, this is it. My home. About half the year."

"Wow. You're out of town that much?" I ask.

Before he can answer, tinkling tags and clicking claws announce the arrival of a white puff that runs to greet us. Well, not *us*. Jet. The dog I assume to be Quatorze pays absolutely zero attention to me. Not even a sniff of my shoes. Fine by me.

Jet lifts the oversized cotton ball and cradles it like a football, then cranes his neck to keep his face away from the dog's lapping tongue. "Yeah, when you add it all up and include time I spend out of town for other stuff during the off-season, that's about right." He laughs. "Torzi, cut it out!"

"That's a lot of time away from home." I nod at the fluffy pooch. "He must miss you."

Meanwhile, my hopes soar. I can handle a part-time boyfriend. *Yeesss. This could work.*

"He misses me when I'm gone for a couple of *hours*, as you can see. That's why I take him with me whenever I can. Don't let him fool you, though. When I'm not here, Jacob's his best bud. Right, Torzi? You know how to play people." He sets the dog on the floor and gestures toward the retreating animal. "See? He's done with me."

We head in the opposite direction, stepping down into a sunken living room. "I'll show you around," he offers.

I follow him through the living room, which features the biggest television I've ever seen in a residential dwelling, into a modern kitchen with carved dark wood cabinets, granite counters, and stainless steel appliances, and a dining room that could host a dinner party for the whole starting lineup, plus their dates. He shows me where I can find a bathroom— or three—if I should need them. Then he points into the backyard, where a hot tub and heated saltwater pool emit clouds of steam, a guest house beckons, and an outdoor kitchen hibernates, abandoned for the winter. Out-of-place in the perfectly manicured garden crouch two huge playsets, an alien spacecraft and a pirate ship.

"Holdovers from the previous owners?" I ask. "Or do you like to role play?"

"They're for my nieces and nephews, when they come to visit. Uncle Jet's house can't be boring, right?"

"No. That's not allowed." I'm suddenly dying to go out there and explore those things, though. Maybe later.

I'm also curious about his bedroom, but I'm relieved he doesn't take me upstairs for a tour of the second floor. That seems a tad personal for a first visit. (Apparently, I'm becoming a prude in my old age.)

Instead, he leads me back to the living room, where he sits on the couch and pats the cushion next to him. "I'm not gonna hurt you," he says lightly.

I wish I could promise the same thing.

Still, I sit and look around the room. "This place is…"

…*massive, like you.*

…*overwhelming, like you.*

"…incredible," I finally settle on, leaving off the *"like you"* that still fits. "I had no idea this was back here. And that you lived here."

"I'm not exactly listed." He grins. "But thanks. It's a place to sleep. And it's close to work. Plus, there's plenty of room for when my family comes to visit."

"You're originally from California, right? Are they still out there?"

"Some of them. Mom and Dad and my big sister and her family live there. One of my brothers lives in Minnesota; the other one lives in Texas. I have a younger sister who lives overseas. Her husband's in the Air Force. They're stationed in Germany."

"Whoa. Your family is huge."

He shrugs. "I guess. I never thought much about it." He grins. "It's tons of fun when they're all here."

"Does everyone get along?"

"Yeah! We didn't have a choice, growing up. Mom and Dad didn't tolerate fighting. Now, getting along is a habit, I guess. We give each other crap all the time, but that's all in good fun." He turns his head and squints. "Why are you looking at me like that?"

"Like what?"

"Like you're trying to figure out how fast you can get from this couch to the door."

I try to laugh off his too-accurate perception. "I'm not. But I had no idea you had such a big, close-knit family. I bet they're beyond proud of you."

"I suppose. As long as I'm not screwing up." He smiles wryly. "But yeah. 'Proud' is a good word for it. My mom can be overprotective, too. She worries."

"It must have been hard for her to see you go through such a tough time in New York."

"I wouldn't say New York was all *that* tough."

"The internet doesn't lie."

We laugh, then he says, "Hang on. Did you *Google* me?"

I blush but quickly remember it's not my embarrassment to own. "Uh, no. Colin did. I think he was looking for more material to tease me about you, but he wound up with a huge man-crush, instead. So the joke's on him."

Jet raises his eyebrows. "Seriously? That's hilarious! As far as I know, there's just a bunch of stuff out there about what a disappointment I was after the draft."

"He seemed more impressed by how you handled yourself through all of that." His response is a self-deprecating chuckle, so I say, "Nobody would have blamed you if you'd checked out."

"That's not who I was raised to be. New York hired me to do a job, and I couldn't get it done. If anything, I was trying to earn my keep, since they were paying me to sit on a bench."

"Well, you did it with more class and grace than most guys would have. I mean, good grief! Before you left New York, you wrote a letter to Jets fans, *thanking* them."

Okay, so maybe I did a *little* of my own research after talking to Colin. I have to admit, that little Limey got me curious about Jet the Jet.

"Yeah? So?"

"These are the same fans who cheered once when you were knocked unconscious at the end of a play!"

He laughs and scratches the side of his nose. "Well, I was out of it, so it didn't hurt my feelings."

"C'mon. Be serious."

"I am! When you're a quarterback, you're either the hero or the zero. Period. You're not a person to the fans; you're a— a tool, for lack of a better word. And if you work well and get the job done, they'll love you for it. If you screw up and make them look foolish to other fan bases, they'll cheer when you get your lights knocked out by one of the league's greatest pass rushers." He shifts his eyes toward his lap. "Or they'll—I don't know—fly a plane over the stadium with a banner behind it that says, 'Knox Sucks.' Because that happened, too. And I was awake for that one."

"That's horrible!"

He looks up and waves off my pity. "It's all part of it. And it's not like I was positive 24/7. I had some moments in private that weren't classy or pretty. Lost my fiancée at the time over it."

"Torzi's mom?" I ask, trying to keep it light.

He smiles sadly. "Ginny. Yeah. I'm afraid I was less-than-pleasant at home. Nothing major," he hastens to reassure me. "But moody. Quiet. Tired. I wanted to sleep all the time."

"Sounds like you were depressed."

"Not sure about that, but I had *lots* of free time to kill. I still had to know the playbook and stay in shape so I could be ready to go at a moment's notice, if need be. But I didn't have to do any of the public appearances I would have had to do as the Number One guy. So, when I wasn't working on the community service projects I'd already committed to, I didn't know what to do with myself."

"What type of volunteer work did you do?"

"Same stuff I do now. I'm a Big Brother, and I visit kids in the hospital." His face brightens. "It's one of the highlights of my week, especially in the off-season."

He's too good.

"You have that look again," he says.

I shake my head to clear it, then force a smile. "Sorry. Tell me something that proves you're not perfect. I can't handle perfection."

"I admitted I was such a dick to my girlfriend that she"—his jaw tightens, then he finally finishes—"left me. And our dog. That's hardly perfect."

"Okay, but all that other stuff…"

"Because I come from a big family and we get along, we're perfect?"

"And you volunteer with kids."

"Big whoop. I like kids."

"You're such a Boy Scout!"

"Nope. Never got into scouting."

"But you're *good*."

He lifts his shoulders toward his ears, then drops them again. "It's important to make the world a better place, however I can. Most of the time, that means entertaining football fans once a week. That's hardly world-changing. The least I can do is spend a couple of hours a week cheering up sick kids. Or helping someone with their homework. Or whatever else needs to be done."

"When I'm not at work, I watch movies. And eat ice cream."

He laughs. "Well, I'm not allowed to eat ice cream all that often. But I do a lot of hanging out, too. Watching TV. Swimming. Playing with Torz. After a while, I get bored. I guess it'd be different if I was hanging out with someone other than my dog. Hint, hint." He flutters his lashes at me but can't keep a straight face for long.

"You're a real charmer."

"I'm pathetic!"

"What are you saying, then? You hang out here, alone, all the time?"

He averts his eyes. "Um, pretty much."

"Interesting."

And hard to believe. This doesn't gel with any professional athlete stereotypes. Aren't they having orgies and wild parties all the time? Surrounded by stacks of money? I look around. Not a single bundle of Benjamins anywhere.

"I'm a normal guy," he insists. "Maybe *more* boring than most guys. Definitely not perfect."

Neither of us says anything for a while. Then he looks up at me, so serious, I suddenly do want to bolt for the door.

"Maura?"

"Jet?" I say in the same tone, but punctuated with a smile, trying to break the tension.

"What?" he asks. "You go first."

I laugh. "Nothing. Sorry." When he tilts his head, obviously confused, I blush. "You say my name a lot."

He studies my face. "I like saying it. It's pretty."

I duck my head. "Oh. Thanks."

"If it bothers you, I'll stop."

"No, it's fine." I mumble with a head shake, sorry I've made him self-conscious about it.

Fortunately, he doesn't belabor it. Unfortunately, his tone remains earnest when he continues, "I need to tell you something."

And things were going so well!

He picks at his jeans and turns toward me, digging his elbow into the back of the couch and resting his forehead in one hand. He rubs his hairline. His other hand grabs my right one, and he threads his fingers through mine. I stare at our woven digits while he focuses on my profile. His right knee brushes my thigh and makes me feel seriously—and dangerously—tingly in some private places.

"There's something I want to apologize for."

An apology doesn't fit into my idea of what I wish would happen next, but I stifle my sigh. "Go on."

"It's about something I said last night. This morning. Whenever."

"You definitely don't have to apologize for anything you said or did then."

"Maura. Really. Seriously."

My smart-ass grin fades as I meet those green eyes. I've seen that look many times on the sidelines when the team is down and facing their last drive of the game. "Fine. Go ahead. I guess."

"I'm sorry I said what I did about playing hard-to-get. I was kidding, but as soon as it was out, I realized it sounded like I was pressuring you or something. That's not it at all. It was rude, and sexist. I don't want you to feel like you can't say no." He lowers his chin, adding a meaningful look to those last two words.

Oh, I feel that way for many reasons, but not because I'm afraid he *won't* take no for an answer. Instead of trying to articulate that distinction, though, I keep it simple.

"I don't *want* to say no."

The left side of his mouth lifts in a sexy half-smile. "Well, that's different."

"Very."

My breath catches in my throat when his face comes closer, and I remember how he felt and tasted last night. I don't have to anticipate a replay for too long, as he brushes his lips against mine. My eyes flutter closed, and I become so relaxed, I worry I might melt off the couch. But he holds me in place, pulling me more tightly to his chest.

"Where are you going?" he asks quietly.

I open my eyes and say honestly, "Nowhere. I'm staying right here," before leaning into a deeper, much more intimate kiss.

His huge hands splay across my back, nearly spanning the entire width. In his arms, I'm tiny and delicate. It's an unfamiliar, yet amazing, feeling.

As his tongue probes my mouth, I release a moan on a tiny puff of air that makes him smile against my lips and would embarrass me if I weren't so turned on. His right hand slides upward to the back of my head and presses my face more firmly into his. I scoot so I'm practically in his lap, my hands roaming the wide expanse of his chest. When my palms graze his nipples through his long-sleeved t-shirt, he inhales sharply.

Separating from me for a second, he says on a breath, "Maura," before attacking my mouth once more. His hardness presses against my leg.

Soon, he transfers his attention from my lips to my throat. I wrap my arms around his neck and twist my fingers in his hair, shivering at his breath against the sensitive skin along my chin. My eyes roll backward in my head, which lolls heavily against his hand.

"Oh..." I breathe, letting him push me onto my back. He lifts my sweater, exposing my torso, which he covers with kisses that send tiny shocks southward.

When I'm thinking I couldn't stop him from doing anything, even if I wanted to (and I don't want to), a loud yap pierces our panting, and Jet exhales against my belly when a flying white furball lands between his shoulder blades.

He turns his head to the side and laughs. "Torz! Down boy."

The dog stubbornly disobeys his master and licks his upturned cheek.

Jet pushes himself upright, sending Torz skittering down his back, then scrambling across his legs. The dog plunks himself in his owner's lap, panting and grinning at me, as if to say, *Take that, 'ho.*

I squint at the pooch. *Why, you little cock-blocking son of a bitch...*

With a grunt, Jet stands, evicting our distraction, and hobbles to the back door, which he opens a Torz-width. "Out, cur. Go scratch on Jacob's door."

The compact canine complies, taking off like a shot across the patio and into the yard. Jet closes the door but watches his little buddy until he makes it to the guest house. I sit up in time to see a guy open the door to the cottage and wave toward us. Jet raises his hand in reply, then faces me.

"I'm sorry."

"Don't apologize! It's not your fault."

"He's used to having me all to himself."

"Lucky dog."

He narrows his eyes. "Hmm. Spoiled, definitely. But maybe Torzi knows best."

I smile bravely, but my libido sobs.

There, there.

I'm hoping Jet will return to the couch and kiss me again, but he looks around the room and says, "What do you want to do for the rest of the day? I'd say we could go out, but sometimes being out in public can get unpleasant after big losses."

I click my tongue. "People are such idiots."

"They're passionate about the game, that's for sure. Once—"

His ringing phone interrupts a story I'm sure would anger —but not surprise—me. He pulls the device from his pocket and grimaces at the name on the display.

"My mom," he says. "You don't mind, do you?"

"No. Take it. Please." I wave him away and move to stand, but he presses me in place with a warm hand on my leg as he lowers himself back down to the cushions.

"It'll be short. She's just checking in."

While he holds up his end of the usual parent-to-adult-kid chit-chat, I wander the room, peering at the framed photos on the fireplace mantle, recognizing him in a group picture of similar-looking people who must be his siblings and parents. As far as the guys in his family go, he's the smallest. "Yikes," I whisper. His older sister isn't exactly dainty, either. Judging by her size relative to Jet, she's at least as tall, if not taller, than I am. They make 'em big in the Knox family. Eek.

As I'm working my way through framed photos of kids I assume to be his nieces and nephews, including a few red-faced newborns, he says, "Listen, Mom, I gotta go.... Yes, I'm fine. Thanks for calling and checking up on me.... Ha! Well, I'm sorry—I guess?—that I sound happier than you expected me to sound. Look at the bright side: now I can go to the Pro Bowl and enjoy myself.... Yes, but I'll have to talk to you about it later, okay?... Okay. Love you, too. Bye."

Hanging up, he pokes his tongue from the corner of his mouth. "Sorry about that."

"I could have gone into a different room to give you some privacy."

"Nah. She wanted to baby me. And talk me down from the ledge. But you know what? I'm not on the ledge. We made it to the playoffs; that's further than I've ever been before. Next year, we'll get further. I hope. With hard work. But I'm tired from all the hard work of this season and don't want to think about that right now. I want to move on."

I retake my seat next to him. "You should have taken the time to tell her all that. I could have waited."

He shakes his head. "Probably should have let her call go to voicemail. Would have fit better with her idea of me sitting here in my underwear, pouting."

I get a vivid flash of what that would look like and have to stifle the fierce resultant tummy fizz. Fortunately, he seems clueless about his words' effect, and I nearly fall off the couch with his next seemingly out-of-the-blue question.

"Hey, how would you like to go to Hawaii?"

FIFTEEN

GETTING LEI'D

My initial reaction to his question, since we've been talking about how to spend the rest of the day, is, "Now?"

He laughs and shakes his head. "No. Sorry. That probably seemed so random. Do you want to go to the Pro Bowl with me? As my guest."

As if he's a doctor tapping a tiny rubber mallet against my knee, my reflexes kick in, and I turn him down, because it's a crazy suggestion. I still barely know him. I'm supposed to cash in half of my vacation time and jet to a romantic destination to have a once-in-a-lifetime sports experience that most fans would kill for?

Uh, yes. But no.

What if *he* ends up killing *me*? I'd be on one of those network TV news magazines, and they'd all shake their heads at the dumb Midwesterner who fell so fast and so hard for the pro football player's charms that she didn't see all the warning signs. I can hear that creepy guy on *Dateline* now: *"Maura Richards had no idea one of the only spontaneous decisions she'd ever made... would be her last."*

So I thank Jet for his amazing—and possibly deadly—offer but tell him I can't possibly accept. He seems to take it okay, even pokes fun of himself for asking, but for the rest of the day, he drops juicy teasers here and there about his upcoming trip. Or he tosses out something about the other players bringing their girlfriends or families. It isn't a hard sell—if he cajoled, wheedled, or whined, it would be easy to stand my ground—but it's enough to get me drooling at the prospect of going. Kansas City in the middle of winter isn't the worst place to be, but it's not Hawaii, either.

And by the end of the day (yes, it only takes a damn day. I'm weak!), I realize I'm only saying "no" because that's the less conventional answer to such an attractive proposition. Creepy *Dateline* Guy is on crack. Jet Knox isn't a killer. He mentors kids and has pictures of his nieces and nephews on his mantle. He loves his family and thinks a good time is hosting all of them at his house for a week. I probably have a better chance of being killed in his isolated house, alone with him, than I would in the middle of a hundred NFL players and their families at a Hawaiian resort.

So when he takes me home and kisses me goodbye inside my front door, I ask, "Is that trip to Hawaii still on the table?"

His face lights up like a handsome, well-chiseled jack-o-lantern. "You bet! Have you changed your mind?"

I nod. "Maybe. It sounds like fun."

"It is! It's also work for me, but not hard work. Fun work. It would be mega-cool if you were there with me. When you said no, I started stressing about who else I was going to ask. Picking one of my siblings doesn't seem fair, and I guess they could all go, but that gets distracting and hectic. Bringing my parents seems lame. Nice for them, but not very fun for me."

I place my finger against his lips. "Well, I guess now you

don't have to worry about making that decision. If you still want to take me."

His features relax, and his eyes zoom in on mine. What feels like a cocktail of soda and pop rocks bubbles in my belly. "Definitely," he answers. "More than anything."

"Then I guess I better buy a swimsuit."

"Or not. My suite has its own private infinity pool."

And with that teaser/promise/ultimate distraction begins the longest two-and-a-half weeks of my life. I want to go to Hawaii right now. Hop on a plane with no luggage, no stressing about what to bring and what I'll wear to the events when we get there. No endless phone calls from my brother, with his ridiculous requests for me to get this or that player's autograph or carry him around on my cell phone the whole time. No snide remarks from Rae about how I'm turning out to be much less of a challenge than Jet probably originally thought and wondering if that means he'll tire of me more quickly. No Creepy *Dateline* Guy talking to me every night before I drop off to sleep, reminding me that nobody believes they could be falling in love with a psychopath. *"Everyone thought Ted Bundy was a swell guy, too, you know."*

Oh, my gosh. Shut your hole, Creepy Dateline *Guy!*

We've finally made it, though. We're in sunny Hawaii. Getting lei'd on the tarmac after stepping off the Wise brothers' private jet. Checking into the hotel on the resort being taken over by some of the largest people in America. Staring at the bed in Jet's suite, wondering what will be happening here during the next few days. Escaping to the lanai to get some fresh air, under the guise of verifying that the private infinity pool is as amazing as promised. (It is.) Realizing that the dirty fantasies are as intense out here as they are in the bedroom. Returning to the room and trying to become as relaxed as Jet seems while he bounces on the end of the bed like a mattress tester.

"Seeing if it squeaks," he says with a cheeky wink. His face falls when I don't laugh, because I'm about to cry. "Hey, what's wrong?"

What *is* wrong with me? I shaved, I waxed, I buffed, I wrapped, I polished, I bleached. I did things to myself to prepare for this week that took a huge chunk out of my film fund and made me feel like a vain, shallow idiot. Now that the moment I've been dreaming about is here, I'm experiencing some major stage fright. Major. Like, the last thing I want to do is take off my clothes for this guy so he can compare me to every other naked woman he's ever seen.

What is that number, anyway? Probably huge. Probably mind-boggling. Probably stomach-turning.

If I let him add me to the tally, does that make me a glorified Pro Bowl escort? *"Take me to the Pro Bowl, and I'll have sex with you"*? It seems so— so... crass. And unfair. Because he and I have been on several dates now, and we've been to each other's houses, and if he was any other no-name guy, it wouldn't be a big deal. But he's not any other no-name guy. He's All-Pro quarterback Jet Knox. For the past couple of weeks, I've been able to somehow forget that. But now, surrounded by his contemporaries, all of whom are here in a professional capacity, no matter how fun it's billed to be, I can't ignore it.

He stands and approaches me like one would greet a skittish dog, minus the flat hand to the nose. Gently, he takes both of my hands in his and bends his knees to level his eyes with mine. "You okay? You look like you don't feel well. Maybe we should get something to eat. When my blood sugar—"

"I'm not hungry," I quickly say, averting my eyes, which land on the bed again, then dart to the tile floor.

"Then what's—"

I cross to the sofa and perch on the edge. He sits next to me, resting his hand on my back. "If you tell me what's wrong, I'll fix it. Is it the room? I'm not picky, but some people get bad vibes from a place."

I shake my head. "Not the room. Technically." His forehead wrinkles, signifying a mixture of confusion and concern, so it's the moment of truth—or concealment. I either need to tell him what's bothering me or downplay it and move on. It's not too late to take the blood sugar excuse and run with it.

But I can't. He deserves honesty, if nothing else, no matter how mortifying it is for me to say what I'm about to say.

"This place is amazing," I start. *Yes, yes. Always go with something positive first.*

"But?"

Oh. He knows this technique.

"But it's— Well, it's a little intense. Being here. With you."

He releases a breath I didn't realize he was holding. "Oh. Okay."

"I feel like there are expectations—I had them, too!—about this week, this room. Suddenly… It's a lot of pressure."

His response to that is to kick off his shoes, lean back on the couch, fold his arms behind his head, and stretch his legs in front of him. After he's been quiet for a while, I look over my shoulder at him, and I'm surprised to see him grinning at me.

"What? What's so funny?"

He lifts one of his shoulders but keeps smiling. "You are."

"I'm not trying to be funny. I'm trying not to freak out!"

But it's impossible to remain tense with him looking at me like that, posed like that, so I return his smile.

"You need this vacation more than I realized. It's a good thing I forced you to come along."

"You didn't force—"

"Exactly. So relax." He lowers his arms and pats his chest. "C'mere."

It's quickly becoming one of my favorite places, so I comply, resting my ear against his heart, which, I swear, has a resting rate of about thirty beats per minute. *Thud* (pause, pause, pause). *Thud* (pause, pause, pause). *Thud* (pause, pause, pause)…

"I want you to have a good time," he says, his voice rumbling under my head. "That's all. Whatever that means. No pressure whatsoever. If you're tense or worried or freaked out, that defeats the purpose of this trip."

I nod my understanding. "Okay. I'm sorry I'm being weird."

"Please. No apologies, no explanations, no worries." He cranes his neck to see my face, so I make it easier for him and look up. "You want a different room?"

"I told you, it's not the room."

"No, 'different,' as in, 'separate.' From mine."

"Oh." I consider it for a second, but that seems like such a pain, and likely impossible. This place is booked solid. This room is fabulous, now that I look around at more than just the bed.

I shake my head. "No. This is fine."

"I don't snore."

"I do."

He laughs. "Oh, great. Maybe *I* want a different room."

"I'm kidding."

"Me too. Relax."

I almost apologize again but worry it will make things worse. Instead, I say, "Thank you."

"For what? For being a decent human being?"

"You're more than that."

He shifts under me and sits up. "What I am is hungry. Let's order room service, then take a swim. Or go for a walk on the beach." He nods toward the sound of the waves we can hear and smell but can't see from where we're sitting.

"I like the sound of all of that."

"I'm all yours tonight. Tomorrow morning, the craziness starts, though."

"Then let's enjoy the calm before the crazy."

———

A couple of hours later, I emerge from the bathroom after changing into my pajamas and brushing my teeth to find Jet already in bed, propped against the headboard, reading *Sports Illustrated*. I pause, not because of his choice of reading material (it *is* somewhat remedial, but to each his own), but because he's on my side of the bed. Not that I'm going to make a big deal about it. I go around to the other side and get in, settling as quickly as possible, facing away from him, balancing on the mattress's edge.

This is bizarre. Stranger than I anticipated, somehow, and I figured it would be odd and awkward. I'm in bed with Jet Knox. I'm about to sleep with Jet Knox. Just sleep (I think). But still.

Behind me, I hear him close the magazine with a loud flutter and toss it with a slap onto the floor. With all of the noise, I look over my shoulder at him.

"You okay?"

His smile is uncertain. "Uh, yeah. You?"

"Fine."

"You know, I don't need all this space." He gestures to the expanse of mattress between us.

Arranging my hands under my cheek, I try to get comfortable again. "This is good." I close my eyes.

After a few more seconds, a shadow falls over me, and a weight settles against my shoulder. I open my eyes to see Jet looming.

"What are you doing?" I ask warily.

"Looking to see how you expect to stay balanced like that without falling out of bed in the middle of the night."

"I'm not going to fall."

"You're right." He hooks his arms over my side and pulls me toward the middle of the mattress.

"Hey!"

Satisfied, he turns off the light and slides farther under the covers on his back. "There. You're *not* going to fall."

"I was fine where I was."

"I would have worried about you all night. I would have been over here, waiting to hear the thump. The suspense was already killing me."

Laughing, I say, "If you wanted me to be closer to you, all you had to do was say it."

His laughter shakes the bed. "You got me."

"You're right, though; it's much more comfortable here." I wiggle my hips but immediately stop when my butt rubs against his leg. "Oops. Sorry."

"Are you kidding me? That was the highlight of my day."

"Good night, Jet."

"'Night, Maura."

As I'm dozing, he startles me awake by asking, "So, who are you more like, your mom or your dad?"

It takes a while for me to process his question, think about it, and formulate an answer, but he waits.

Finally, I answer, "Neither. Maybe I was hatched."

"So your parents are more like your brother than you?"

"I wouldn't say that. When they were younger, they were more like him, I guess. Which is why they can afford to travel all over the place now that they're retired. But the older they get, the more free-spirited they become."

"Like you."

I laugh at how he could come to that conclusion after all these weeks. "I'm hardly free-spirited. I'm just aimless, with my useless background education."

"Lots of people I went to school with got Film Studies degrees."

"Probably because it makes sense in California. In Kansas City, it's worthless."

"Can't be worthless or it wouldn't be offered. You didn't think it was worthless when you chose it. So, what changed?"

"Nothing. I knew perfectly well it was a frivolous field of study. But it was interesting and fun—and easy. I graduated with a 4.0."

"Well, I'm impressed."

"You shouldn't be. Anyway, that's a lie. I did get all A's in my major classes, but not so much in those general classes they force you to take. World history and applied math killed me. Don't ever ask me to balance a checkbook."

"I won't."

I adjust my head on the pillow, noticing it smells faintly like pineapples and Lysol. "I had every intention of making a career out of film critique. I envisioned myself writing movie reviews for *Entertainment Weekly* or whatever. But... I dunno."

I stop, then think, *What the hell?* It seems he's actually listening to me, not figuring out the whole time I'm talking what he's going to say next or what advice he's going to give me, so it's safe to tell him, "The longer I stayed in KC to save up money to move where that career is possible, the more it seemed like a crazy long shot, a silly kid's fantasy."

"Hm."

"Now, whatever 'skills' or training I once had are rusty, at best, or obsolete, at worst. I'm out of touch with the latest technology they use to make films; I have no clue how the entertainment industry works; I wouldn't even know where to begin to find a job doing what I went to school to learn. It's overwhelming and hopeless. So, I help people find jobs."

"Which is important."

"I guess."

"It is! It's hard for some people to find work. What you do is so much more important than what I do."

"Our respective salaries would suggest otherwise."

"Pay rates in this country don't make any sense, and you know it. You help people figure out what they want to do with their lives, support their families, and feel good about themselves. I toss a ball around a field once a week, sixteen—or so —weeks out of the year."

"Okay, but I could have done what I do without spending all that money going to school to get a degree."

"I'm not using my degree, either."

"But you probably will someday. You plan to."

"And hey," he says, ignoring my valid point, "you do use your degree. When we watch movies, you show me stuff all the time that I never would have noticed by myself."

"Rae hates that. She tells me to shut up."

"Well, I like it. I think it's cool."

"It's not making me any money."

"So? Does it make you happy?"

I consider it. "Yeah. It does."

"There you go, then. That's all that matters. Anything can make you money. Money is boring. Happiness rocks."

"Happiness *does* rock," I confirm with an audible smile.

His voice is sleepy when he adds, "You make me happy."

I blink into the darkness, realizing that's the nicest thing I can ever remember anyone saying to me. Before too much time passes and he thinks I don't appreciate the sentiment, I swallow the lump in my throat and reply, "You make me happy, too."

SIXTEEN

PLAYING HOSTS

I don't honor my brother's wishes to get an autograph from every single player. Nor do I carry him around on my cell phone so he can experience the Pro Bowl with me. I do, however, email him and Rae a report at some point every day, when I get a minute. Because putting it in writing is a decent way to convince myself it's happening. I want to brag a tiny bit. After all, I'm in Hawaii, surrounded by the likes of Michael Lewis and Pete Jay. Pete Jay! (Yes, his forehead is as stunning in person as it is on camera.)

The main objective of the trip, for me, is relaxation, but it's as much work as reward for Jet. Every day is tightly scheduled for him, and not surprisingly, he keeps apologizing about how hectic the itinerary is. There's absolutely nothing for him to apologize about, though, because I'm in heaven. It's eighty degrees in late January. This is a much better use of my vacation time than staying with my parents and Greg and Deirdre at Mom and Dad's timeshare in Florida for a week in the summer.

Watching Jet have such a great time with players who try

to take his head off during the regular season is its own special form of entertainment, too. Most of the guys, Jet included, are overgrown kids. Some of them take themselves too seriously, always wearing their sunglasses and headphones, followed by entourages, too cool to mingle with everyone at the social functions. But they're in the minority and are the butt of everyone else's jokes. Knowing many of the big names think those guys are ridiculous is a relief and has destroyed my assumptions of the men who have the most right to act like big shots. The majority of them are polite to a fault (three-time Super Bowl champion Pete Jay apologizes every time he slips and says a bad word), not to mention funny as hell.

It doesn't take long for Jet and me to fall into a comfortable routine, either. I'm never awake before him, but his gorgeous smile greets me every time my eyelids flutter open each day. Only the first morning was he still in bed, but he seemed embarrassed by that, so it hasn't happened again. Usually, he's wheeling in the breakfast cart, pausing at the foot of the bed and asking, "Here or by the pool? It's a beautiful day."

It feels weird to eat in bed when he's already fully dressed, so I meet him by the pool after using the bathroom, repairing the worst aspects of my early morning appearance, and changing into a swimsuit.

He squints into the sun, closes one eye, and beams up at me, his teeth gleaming in his unshaven face. "'Morning, Beautiful," he says while pushing a steaming cup of Kona blend coffee across the table toward me. Somehow (don't ask me how), some way, the endearment doesn't sound sleazy or objectifying, either. It's sweet and heartfelt. It feels… right.

After he leaves for his morning commitments, I head for

the beach. The resort has its own stretch of sand, of course, but guests with kids arrive around noon, so I savor the morning quiet with a book, then head back to the room when it starts to get crowded. It's not that I resent the noise—it's fun to watch the little ones dart in and out of the tide and pat the damp sand into "castles" and other sloppy shapes—but I worry I'm in the way. I don't fit in with the happy families, and it feels like I'm intruding on their private time together.

As one of the only ones not married (or legally connected through children) to the person who brought me, I often get the feeling the other women are sizing me up, trying to determine if I'm a temporary addition to the wives and girlfriends club or someone they'd better get used to seeing. Since I don't have a clue which one I am, either, it's hard to know how to act. Being too friendly seems presumptuous; being too stand-offish comes off as snobby. The last time I was part of a "girlie" group of friends, though, was high school. Look how that turned out. I'm sorely out of practice, and it shows here.

So I make polite conversation with the other WAGs at meals and group activities. Tomorrow, at the game, I'll be lumped together with the AFC West players' guests in a luxury suite, but I'm more comfortable around the players themselves, joking and talking about football like one of the guys. That probably doesn't do me any favors. Being here at all is sufficiently weird, though; I have to be myself, or it won't be fun.

It worries me enough to query Jet about it on our last moonlit walk. With our hands linked and swinging between us, like two carefree kids, I ask, "Am I being too... familiar with some of the guys?"

He laughs. "I don't know. Are you? Should I be keeping a closer eye on you?"

I nudge him. "Not like that. But am I coming off as a dorky fan trying too hard to fit in?"

"No! You're awesome. You're the best girlfriend here. Everyone loves you."

"I don't feel like the other women like me."

"I wouldn't know about that," he says quietly, kicking at the water.

"Maybe I shouldn't hang out with you and the guys later tonight."

"What?" He stops walking. "Aw, come on, Maura. Don't be like that."

"Like what? All I'm saying is, maybe I should give you guys some space and keep to the room. Watch a movie."

"It's our last night!"

"Yeah. That's my point."

"If I show up without you, they'll be disappointed."

"I doubt it."

"Keaton thinks you're hilarious."

Only a few weeks ago, that statement would have made it possible for me to die happy. But the more I get to know Keaton, the less I like him and the better Jet looks in comparison. (And yes, I compare them. It's only natural. Don't judge me.) So in this case, Mr. Tight End's approval doesn't outweigh the burden of so many others' possible disapproval.

"That's nice, but—"

"And if you stay in the room, people will think we had a fight, or something."

"So? Who cares?"

Instead of answering, he resumes walking and lets go of my hand. I keep stride with him. Finally, he says, "Whatever. Do what you want. But don't do it because some people are petty assholes."

"I don't want anybody thinking I'm flirting with their man. Or that I'm rejecting them in favor of hanging out with the famous people."

"You say who cares about what people will think about you not going out tonight, but you're willing to give up a good time because you *do* care what they think about other things. That makes no sense."

"I don't have to make sense."

"Whatever," he repeats.

"Jet, don't be mad at me."

"I'm not mad; I'm disappointed."

"Oh, geez. Anything but that," I say in mock horror, trying to bail us out of our first official argument.

"Then stop being dumb and worrying about what a couple of jealous mean girls might think about you."

I swallow loudly and halt in my tracks. The sand sucks at my feet, which sink as the tide laps around my ankles and zooms back toward the deeper water. It takes him a few steps to realize I'm no longer next to him, but when he does, he stops, too, and half-turns to look at me. "What's wrong now?"

"I'm not dumb."

He drops his head and jams his hands in his pockets. Walking back toward me, he says, "That's not what I meant."

"But that's what you said."

"I said you were *being* dumb."

"Same thing."

He lifts his head and shows me his profile as he stares at the black, glassy waves but chooses not to say anything else.

Pulling my feet from their quicksand anchors, I say, "I'm going to head back and call it a night. Big day tomorrow." I zip my hoodie further closed against the cool sea breeze and tuck my hands into the front pouch.

Jet grabs my elbow before I get too far.

"Maura, wait!"

"Let me go."

He does but keeps up with me. "I'm sorry."

"No apologies, remember?"

"But I owe you one."

"You don't owe me anything, Jet."

"Just don't be pissed, okay? I… I'll stay in the room with you tonight and watch a movie. You're right; tomorrow's a big day. I'll probably only feel like shit all day if I go out with the guys. Especially if you don't go with me. I want to spend time with *you*."

"You already told the guys you were in."

"So? I'll text Keaton and tell him we changed our minds. They'll understand. They'll think we're, *you know…*"

I can't help but laugh, so he relaxes but quickly adds, "Not that we have to. I'm just saying…"

Threading my arm through his, I rest my cheek against his triceps. "They're going to think whatever they want to think."

"Exactly. You were right before. Who cares?"

"I don't."

"Me neither. Now which movie are we going to watch? I've been dying to see that Jane Austen thing you mentioned on our first date."

"Beautiful liar."

He laughs and musses my hair as we stroll within view of the resort, then drops my arm and trots ahead. "Race ya."

———

Now that I'm back among average-sized people, I find myself starting every conversation looking over the other person's head. The first time I met Colin for lunch after returning from Hawaii, he kept looking over his shoulder and finally asked, "What's going on back there?" When I explained my new social affectation, he laughed. "Oh, great. As if I needed to feel shorter than I already am." He pointed to his face. "Eyes right here, Lady Maura."

That wasn't the only adjustment upon our return. Escaping the Kansas City winter was amazing; coming back to it sucked. Although we were gone less than a week, the frigid temps have been a major shock to the system since we stepped onto the tarmac at KCI. I thought I was being a wuss about it, but Jet squinted into the wind, hunched his shoulders, and said down at me, "This is the pits. Back to reality, I guess."

In more ways than one. It's unbelievable how quickly one becomes accustomed to luxury. I'm not only talking about beautiful hotel rooms and great service at nice restaurants. I'm talking about flying in a private jet. I'm talking about never having to ask twice—or sometimes at all—for anything. Having your every want and need anticipated is a heady experience. I understand better now how some of these guys become spoiled. It took me five short days to take it for granted. If that was my life all day, every day, it might be hard to stay grounded. It's given me a greater appreciation for Jet's down-to-earth demeanor.

But easily the worst part about being back is each morning.

Nobody wakes me up with breakfast and calls me "Beautiful" here at home. When I open my eyes after blindly swiping away the alarm on my phone, I see nothing. Nobody. It's awful.

I'd get a cat or dog if I thought I simply needed to see

another face in the morning. But not any face will do. I want to see Jet's.

Which is crazy. It's too soon, too fast, too... everything. Damn you, Hawaii!

Maybe he didn't turn out to be a psychopath, but he murdered your independent spirit in less than a week, Creepy *Dateline* Guy intoned that first lonely morning.

I hate that guy so much.

The more I get to know, Jet, though, the more I like him. That's not always a given with guys and me. He's finally coming down from the constant adrenaline high he must have been on going into the postseason, so he's less manic and more relaxed than he was when we first met. It's been a relief to get to know the real him. Sometimes I can forget he's, well, who he is. Sometimes.

As a matter of fact, without thinking the other day, I asked him what his plans were for my favorite day of the year, Super Bowl Sunday, and if he'd be rooting for the Cowboys or the Patriots.

When he answered, "I probably won't watch," it took a minute for me to figure out what he meant or how that could be an option.

Then I wanted to smack myself.

"Oh. Yeah. Sorry," I said. "But... you can't *not* watch it, right?"

He shrugged, flipping through the movie options on the TV in front of us.

I snuggled up to his arm. "Hey. You know what you should do?"

He looked down at me, his dull eyes brightening at my mischievous tone.

"You should host a Super Bowl party here. At your house."

Before he could shoot down the idea (I could tell it was coming, based on his dimming eyes and the set of his jaw), I said, "C'mon! You don't want people to think you're pouting, right?"

"I'm not. But it's short notice, don't you think?"

"It doesn't have to be a big deal."

"It would be the most depressing Super Bowl party, ever. Like, I'm downright cheerful about not making it past the playoffs, compared to some of the other guys. You saw it for yourself at the Pro Bowl. They're bummed."

"Don't invite those guys, then. You know who would *love* to come to your party and would get into the game and make it seem less sad? My brother. And Rae. And Colin. And, I guess, Deirdre," I tacked on.

He smiled. "You think they'd want to?"

"Uh, yeah! Greg's been dying to meet you, and you said yourself that you wanted to meet Colin. This would be the perfect opportunity. It'll be fun."

"What about Rae? I'm still not sure she likes me."

"She wonders the same about you. You guys need to get over that. It's exhausting."

He laughed at my bluntness.

"What do you say? I'll help you plan it, and everything."

Still looking skeptical, he nevertheless said, "All right. If that's what you want to do."

"Yes! You won't be sorry," I said with a quick, giddy peck to his lips.

Now, on the big night, I'm not as confident in my brilliant plan.

I have to admit, it feels weird to be hosting this party with Jet at his house. It's so *domestic*. But I'm trying to go with it. I'm definitely not dwelling on the fact that he's meeting my two best friends and half of my family in a few minutes. This is simply a fun get-together for one of the country's biggest sports nights. At the home of all-pro quarterback Jet Knox. My boyfriend.

Meep.

Oh, yeah, it's official. We have one of those ridiculous couple names. Jetaura has arrived.

Thanks to NFL guest lists, the media learned my real name at the Pro Bowl. When they determined I was a nobody (not a supermodel, actress, internationally renowned human rights lawyer, or reality TV star), they didn't have much use for the information. I wasn't worried, because by then, my parents knew I was dating Jet, and Jet's family knew about me, so it's not like ESPN would have been dropping a bombshell on any of our loved ones if it had been a slow news day, and the media decided to care who I was.

But Jet's already warned me that once the excitement dies down after the Super Bowl and before the Draft in May, football-related news is hard to come by, so NFL bloggers dig deeper and reach further for "stories," usually of a personal nature. Who's getting married, who's getting divorced, who's having babies (and with whom), who's letting their boredom get the best of them and running into legal problems—you know, the usual.

And now that they have a real name to go with my face, they might be more interested in my role in the dullest of soap operas, *The Off-Season*. By the time we got back from Hawaii, they already knew where I work, what I do, even where I live. It's all public record and not that big of a deal, considering they generally leave me alone as long as I'm not with Jet. When I am with him, I understand I'm fair game. It's part of the gig. I like the gig so far.

Jet's messing with the settings on his TV, scowling and complaining at the remote, when I bring the finger foods into the room, setting the veggie, meat, and seafood trays on the wet bar. As I'm shooing Torz away from the buffet, I hear Jet say through gritted teeth, "I *am* pushing the 'surround sound' button, damn it. Why isn't it working? Stupid piece of shit."

Keeping an eye on the dog, I sidle up to my co-host and ask, "You want me to try?"

He hands me the device. "I guess. Not sure what you're going to do different—"

I press the "reset" button, then "surround sound," and the icon pops up on the screen to let us know it worked, in case we couldn't suddenly hear the obnoxious pre-game show coming from the speakers installed strategically in all corners of the room.

"How'd you...?" Taking the remote back from me, he looks down at it.

"Happens with my TV all the time. You can't watch action films without surround sound."

He shoots me a shaky smile, then sets the remote on the end table next to his favorite oversized easy chair. "Well. Okay, then. Thanks."

"Are you okay? You seem tense."

Looking chagrined, he turns to face me. "Is it that obvious?"

"To me. What's wrong?"

Something over my shoulder catches his attention, and he quickly side-steps me. "Quatorze Knox! Get down from there!" he booms, rushing for the meat-and-cheese tray.

The dog hops down and skitters from the room, the tags on his collar jingling all the way up the stairs as he takes cover under one of the beds.

"Son of a bitch," Jet growls while surveying the damage.

I join him and remove the obviously licked food, then rearrange the untouched stuff. "It's okay. It's not like he sheds. A little dog slobber never hurt anyone. Especially if they don't know about it." *Ew. Not really, but whatever.* I smile gamely and continue removing another layer of meat, just in case.

"He's such an asshole sometimes."

Finished repairing the tray and disposing of the contaminated food, I grab Jet's hand. "Hey. Relax, all right? What are you so worried about?"

"What if your brother doesn't like me?"

I laugh.

"It's not funny. What if he doesn't?"

"He will. But even *if* he doesn't, there are a billion things he doesn't like about my life. Hasn't affected how I live up 'til now, so you wouldn't be any different."

"I couldn't come between family."

"Jet."

He looks pitifully down at me.

"Calm down. He's going to love you. They're all going to love you."

"I'm almost more nervous about meeting Colin, because you do care what *he* thinks."

"He already likes you, based on what he's read about you."

"By the way, am I supposed to know about that?"

"He doesn't care, as long as you think it's funny. Colin's one of the most honest, upfront guys in the world. Besides you."

He chuckles nervously. "It's just this place..." He motions to the room around us. "Sometimes it's embarrassing. With the guys from the team it's not, because all of their houses are like this. Well, worse, in most cases. But—"

"When the plebs come over to play, you feel self-conscious?"

"That's *not* what I'm saying!"

The horror on his face cracks me up. "Jet. Sweetie. Chill. I'm teasing you. I get it. There were times in Hawaii that the luxury felt perverse. Excessive."

"Exactly! That's what I'm saying. Like, what's the point of one guy having all *this*? I worry that's what people think. Like they judge me for having too much when so many people in the world don't have enough."

"Well, my brother's not going to think that. You're going to be his hero. He's all about capitalism."

He snorts.

"And you *earned* this. Plus, it suits a purpose for when your family comes to visit. You give back to the community and donate to charitable causes. And, you know what? You don't owe anyone any explanations!"

He smiles down at me as the doorbell rings. "You're amazing. Are you available for locker room pep talks?"

I tiptoe to kiss his cheek. "No. All those naked guys would make me giggly. Now, let's answer the door and get this party started."

SEVENTEEN

THE BIG SHOW

Punctual Greg and Deirdre are the first to arrive, of course, followed by Colin. Rae brings up the rear, arriving alone right before kickoff.

"Where's Molly?" I ask my friend during the first commercial break as we're cracking open our first beers in the kitchen.

Rae shrugs. "I didn't feel like bringing a date to this... whatever it is."

"It's a party."

She wrinkles her nose. "Um, let's run down the attendees here: a crumpet monkey who doesn't know anything about American football and keeps calling the field a 'pitch'; an ice queen who doesn't care about sports, period, and is only here to scope out Jet Knox's house—and possibly get some patient referrals from him; a guy who would willingly suck your boyfriend's dick for season tickets, or maybe just for the hell of it; and you, me, and one of my co-workers. Par-tay."

I clench my fists and my teeth, and then point out, "You didn't have to come. At least everyone else *wants* to be here."

"Oh, I wouldn't miss this for the world. This is going to be highly entertaining. But it was hardly a date night."

"If you must know, I suggested this so Jet wouldn't be watching the game alone, miserable."

Her expression slackens. "Well, that was sweet of you."

"Thank you."

"But he'd probably be better off alone."

"That's not true. Plus, this is a nice, casual, relaxed setting for Jet to meet my brother. Greg will be too into the game to interrogate us about stuff."

"I don't know why you're worried. Jet has all the answers Greg would love to hear. He has five-, ten-, and fifteen-year plans that make Greg's goal-setting look half-assed."

That's what I'm afraid of, I think but don't say. It's not that I'm afraid Jet will say something unsatisfactory to Greg; I don't want to hear the plans laid out yet again. I've done a great job of keeping Jet off that topic for nearly a month now, and that's a streak I want to keep alive.

We rejoin the group in time to watch the Patriots' first drive of the game. I perch on the arm of the sofa, next to Jet, and Rae retakes her seat in Jet's chair, which she claimed before he could (and he was too polite to ask her to vacate). It's just as well, since Greg would probably be heartbroken if he couldn't sit beside his host during the game.

"I hope they trip on their own shoelaces." Greg glances nervously at his couchmate before checking, "Right? I bet you can't *stand* these guys."

Jet laughs. "Well, I should probably root for my Conference. They're the best team, after all, the team that probably deserves to win."

"Yeah," I pipe up. "Plus, if you lose to the team that ends up winning the whole thing, it makes you feel like maybe there was nothing you could do about it. Like it was destiny."

Greg looks around Jet at me and tilts his head down. "That is one of the dumbest things I've ever heard. Do you think the Cowboys are going to feel that way if they lose today? 'Well, at least we lost to the predestined winner'? No way. Der."

Jet grabs my hand and smiles up at me. "I get exactly what you mean. And, I agree. I *would* feel better about our post-season loss if the Patriots won today."

Greg's mouth drops open, almost losing the cheese cube he's popped into it. After he recovers, he says, "I'm sorry, but I can't root for New England. They're dirty." He points to the TV and yells, "Chop block! Not called, of course. See? I rest my case!"

Smiling indulgently at my brother, Jet says, "Hey, man. I lived it. Trust me. But they're still the better team, and it's okay; we don't have to root for the same guys."

Behind Jet's head, I stick out my tongue at my brother and mouth, *"So there!"*

Greg simply laughs. "All right. Whatever. I guess that'll make it interesting."

Deirdre squints at the screen. "Are the Cowboys the ones in blue or the ones in white?"

"White!" we all yell.

Well, all of us except for Colin. He says, "Oh, I'm glad someone else asked. Now, why did that bloke get a yellow card a moment ago?"

"It's a flag, not a card," Greg says.

"Yes, but since you insist on calling football 'soccer,' I feel justified disregarding your sport's terminology."

"Real mature," Rae grumbles. "And he got a penalty for jumping offside."

"Oooh! Offside. I know what that means."

"It's not the same as in soccer," she tells him with a withering glare.

"I can still *infer* the meaning in this instance," he retorts. "I'm not *that* stupid."

After another short series that leads to a commercial break, Jet hops up. "Anyone need a drink? I'm heading that way. Colin? Maura told me you're a Newcastle man?"

Colin stands. "I'll go with you."

I'm dying to follow them, but I don't want to look clingy, so I continue to hold court in the living room, where I steal Jet's empty seat.

Greg says, "That's taken."

"Don't worry; you can still sit next to your new best friend."

He looks around the living room. "This place is awesome. Any chance of a full tour during halftime?"

"Put your eyeballs back in your head, you rube," Rae mutters.

"How much you think a place in this area goes for?" Without waiting for my answer, he shouts across the room to Deirdre, "Hey, hon. Maybe we should sell *both* of our houses and move to this neighborhood."

I slap his arm. "Shhhh! You're being tacky."

"Look who's Miss Cool now," Greg replies. "Someone goes to Hawaii for the Pro Bowl and hangs out with NFL stars for a while, and she's suddenly above it all?"

Deirdre laughs at his dig, which encourages him to add, "And you better never give me crap about my house again. *This* is an eff-off mansion."

I'm about to tell him to do just that when Jet and Colin

return. Clueless as to the topic of conversation while he was out of the room, Jet grins down at me after setting his beer on the coffee table. "Hey. Look what the football fairy brought me."

I flutter my lashes up at him.

"Tell her to move," Greg advises.

"Nah. There's plenty of room for all of us. Especially if…" He sits and pulls me into his lap, nuzzling my neck and tickling me.

"Gaah! Stop it!"

Rae half-turns and rolls her eyes at us. "You two mind over there? *Some* of us are trying to watch the game."

"Sorry, Rae!" Jet says, ceasing the tickle torture but keeping his arms wrapped around me. "Having fun yet?" he murmurs near my ear.

"Absolutely. Go Pats!"

He winces. "That's so wrong."

I laugh. "Hey, I'm standing by my 'losing-to-the-winners' philosophy."

"Go AFC!" he booms.

I cover my ear.

"There. That felt a *little* better."

Greg shakes his head at us. "You two are—"

"Brilliant," Colin supplies quickly, winking at me. "Now, someone explain to me what the bloody hell is going on in this match. I'm lost."

For the rest of the first half, Jet and Greg take turns explaining the basic rules, but after about the fifth *"Unless…"* from Jet, Colin throws up his hands and says, "It's hopeless. I'm too thick for this game. Too many rules!"

"Hey, if I can learn it and play it, nobody's too thick," Jet says with a wry smile as the two teams run into the locker room, and the stadium crew scrambles to set up for the half-time extravaganza.

"You're not stupid," Colin replies, "but you *may* be mad, going onto that pitch every week, with those blokes trying to flatten you."

"It's fun! And it's the only thing I know how to do. So, that's what I do. I've been doing it since I was five years old." He considers that for a second. "Well, I haven't been a quarterback all that time, but I've always played offense, so yeah. Defensive players have been trying to flatten me for almost twenty-five years."

Everyone laughs at that.

Greg leans over. "Hey, Jet. Would you mind showing Deirdre and me around the place? Both of our houses are currently on the market, so it'd be interesting to get a look, to see if we're priced competitively."

I nearly snort beer into my lap, but Jet keeps a straight face. "Yeah, Maura told me about that. Whichever house sells first is the one you're letting go of, right?"

Deirdre inspects her French manicure, but Greg replies, "Yep. That's the deal."

"I'd be glad to show you around. It's not anything special. Just big." He stands and leads the way from the living room. "It's nice for everyone to have their own rooms when my family comes to visit."

Greg, Deirdre, and Jet disappear, their voices fading up the stairs.

Rae heads toward the kitchen. "Your brother and his future bride are real pieces of work," she says.

"Right? For crying out loud, *I* haven't been upstairs yet in this place."

Rae freezes. She and Colin exchange a glance.

"What?" I ask.

"Nothing at all," Colin says firmly.

"Well…" Rae hedges. "Never mind. It's probably nothing."

I follow her into the kitchen with Colin on my heels. "No, there was a definite look exchanged between the two of you."

Assuming an innocent air, Rae roots in the fridge and comes out with another beer, which she pries open with the bottle opener on the counter. "I'm surprised, that's all, that you haven't seen… *everything*." She punctuates that with wiggling eyebrows, so there's no mistaking her meaning.

I peek at Colin and blush. He raises his hands in front of his chest. "Don't look at me. I don't find it odd at all."

"Good. Because it's not. We haven't known each other that long."

"You see or talk to each other every day. You've been to Hawaii together, where you shared a bed."

"But nothing happened." Although they both already know this personal detail, it's somehow awkward to remind them together, face-to-face. "So what's your point?"

"The guys I know and work with aren't *normally* this, um, conservative. Not when it comes to things of an intimate nature."

Colin flails his hands. "Blimey, say the word. *Sex!*" Then on a mutter, "And they say the English are repressed."

Rae lasers a deadly look toward him. "Fine. Players aren't slow to jump in the sack with people. Is that direct enough for ya, Princess Margaret?"

"Well, it's not only his decision, you know?" I counter.

"*You're* not usually this slow to jump in the sack with anyone either."

"I'm sorry that Jet and I are not behaving sufficiently sex-crazed for you. There doesn't seem to be any particular hurry, in this case. That's all," I say. "Not that it's any of your business."

Colin edges toward the doorway. "I may check out the half-time show after all. Maybe I've simply never given hip-hop a fair shake."

"Whatever." I wave him off. I'd prefer *not* to have this conversation in mixed company. I'd prefer not to have it at all, as a matter of fact.

As soon as Colin is gone, Rae asks, "Who usually stops things?"

"I don't know! One time the dog stopped us." She raises an eyebrow at that, but I shake my head to let her know it's not as exciting a story as it sounds.

"Hm." She swigs from her bottle but keeps her eyes on me.

"Stop looking at me like that."

Pulling her beer away from her mouth with a *thwunk*, she says, "Like what? Stop being so paranoid and weird. I'm just surprised, that's all. You're the one who brought up not seeing the guy's bedroom yet."

"And you turned it into a capital offense," Colin startles me by saying from the other side of the kitchen doorway, where he's obviously been listening the whole time.

I turn toward his voice. "If you're going to participate in this conversation, be a man about it and do it from the same room as the rest of us."

"I *am* a man; the lookout man. Carry on."

Rae defends herself, "I only mentioned it seemed out of character. For both of them."

Colin pokes his head around the door frame. "Maura's right. This is none of our business."

I bite the inside of my cheek but say, "Drop it, okay?

There's no story here. We're taking our time, letting things progress organically. If you want to know the truth—"

"No, we want you to keep lying to us about organic sex. Like we were born yesterday," Rae says.

"Why are you being so terrible about this?" Colin asks, returning more fully to the room. "That's not how friends act. You don't bully someone to confide in you, then interrupt them with sarcastic asides when they seem like they're about to open up."

She shoots him a middle finger. He responds with the two-fingered English equivalent.

"Enough!" I hiss at the bickering pair and glance nervously at the kitchen doorway I expect Jet, Deirdre, and Greg to walk through at any second. "The truth is, I'm scared. There. Are you happy?"

Rae scoffs. "Scared of what? It's not like it'll be your first time." She laughs but quickly sobers. "Oh, Lord. Did you tell Jet it would be your first time? He's stupid enough to believe that."

"He's not stupid. And no, I haven't lied to him. But the thing is, he's not just another piece of ass, all right?"

"Romantic," Rae grumbles under her breath, earning her another murderous look from Colin.

I ignore both of them and continue, suddenly needing to say it out loud, but needing to do it quickly, before I lose my nerve. "Every relationship I've ever had has fallen apart, and most of the time, I haven't cared, because I wasn't serious about those guys. But this time, I'm actually afraid of screwing it up. Like, lie-awake-in-the-middle-of-the-night scared. I care what happens next, despite being unsure what I *want* to happen next. So sue me if I'm delaying the inevitable for a while. I'm paralyzed, worried that whatever decision I make next will be the one that sends Jet running."

"Lady Maura, take my breath away! That's quite a statement."

"Well, it's true," I grouch at the floor. "And you know what? It sucks to feel this way. So if you don't mind, shut up about it."

Colin claps a hand on my shoulder. "You've got it. Not another mention of it. Didn't mean to upset you. Sorry, mate."

Eyes wide, Rae mutters, slightly less contrite, "Sorry. Geez."

Before I can accept either apology, the others arrive. Jet grins at Colin, Rae, and me. "Hey, guys! The second half has started. What's going on in here? Looks like a meeting of the minds."

We mumble separate things at our feet.

Greg saves us by saying, "That bed is incredible! I'm telling you, Deirdre and I are going to get one of those. It goes on for miles!"

Jet pulls beers from the fridge and passes them around. "Like I told Greg, I need a California King because I'm too tall for standard beds. But it's also come in handy for other things." He turns, closes the refrigerator, and wiggles his eyebrows at us. "Torzi's kind of a bed hog."

Everyone laughs but me.

———

The party's over, the leftovers are in the fridge, and the guests are gone. Jet and I lie on our backs on separate couches, recapping the game. Well, Jet recaps the game. He's still stunned—and not as disappointed as he thought he'd be—that the

Cowboys did what hardly any other team, including his, was able to do this season, and on the biggest stage possible: beat the Patriots. By a field goal. In overtime.

It was an epic match. But after halftime, I wasn't as interested as I normally would be. My kitchen conversation with Rae and Colin left me queasy, and the couple of beers I'd had until that point made me sleepy. For the rest of the game, I sat on the floor at Jet's feet, where I could doze, unnoticed, with my head against his legs. Occasionally, a roar from the others would rouse me, and I'd animate long enough to figure out what was happening, but for the most part, I didn't care.

And when I don't care about the Super Bowl, that's telling.

As the guests were leaving, Rae was too busy yammering at Jet about what a great game it turned out to be—"Much better than I anticipated, and—hey!—revenge for the injuries those a-holes gave us. How's that shoulder doing, by the way, Knox?"—to notice I barely said goodbye to her.

Greg and Deirdre were falling all over themselves to try to secure their next invite to Casa de Knox.

Colin, however, pulled me in for one of his three hugs of the day and said, "Tell him. You'll sleep better tonight for it."

I nodded my agreement, but I'm not sure I have it in me right now to have that conversation. Plus, Jet's in such a good mood. It would be a shame to ruin that with heavy talk about *feelings*.

More than anything, I'd like to go home and go to bed. But the thought of moving right now seems like an impossible task. Nodding and grunting at the right times during Jet's enthusiastic monologue is much more doable.

"And we've talked about it so many times, but the field goal kicker," he says from the other couch. "That's what it came down to tonight. Dallas's kicker was clutch; New

England's guy had a great night but missed that one in regulation that would have won the whole shebang for them. Bam. Most important guy on the team. *Not* the quarterback. The kicker."

"Uh-huh."

"Awesome. I still think New England was the better team —they lost a single game in the regular season. But Dallas showed up today, and that's all that matters."

"Yep."

"If I didn't know better, I'd say the Patriots underestimated their opponent."

"Totally."

"And when New England's coach substituted that Elvis impersonator in place of Hal Norton, that was cool, too."

"Right?"

"Maura."

I blink and turn my head to transfer my eyes from the ceiling to his face. "Huh?"

"You okay?"

"What? Oh. Yeah. Fine. Tired. Being around my brother is exhausting."

He sits up, swings his legs forward, and plants his feet on the floor. Resting his elbows on his knees, he asks, "Did he say something to upset you?"

"I'm not upset."

"You've been quiet since the beginning of the second half."

I resume my study of the wooden beams above us. "Beer makes me sleepy."

"Ah. Okay. Well, you're welcome to sleep here tonight."

"Thanks. That would be… nice."

He pops to his feet. "Let's go." Grabbing my hand on his way past me, he leads me to the stairs. "This way, ma'am."

When he shows me to one of several guest rooms, I don't question it. I'd assumed we'd sleep in the same bed, like we did in Hawaii. I'd wake up to the early morning smile I've missed so much since returning to real life. But I don't want to make a big deal about it.

He shows me the extra supplies in the en-suite bathroom like the businesslike proprietor of a boarding house, then steps back into the hallway after a platonic peck on my cheek.

With a bob of his head toward the door a few feet down the hall, he says, "I'm right next door, if you need anything. Sweet dreams."

Okay, then.

Alone, I strip until I'm wearing only my panties and the t-shirt that was under my Knox jersey, then brush my teeth and return to the bedroom, where I stare at the standard king-sized bed in the middle of the room. I can't help but wonder how it compares to the one in Jet's room that had my brother foaming at the mouth. Crossing the room and sliding under the covers, I moan at the sensation of the ten-thousand (give or take) thread count sheets against my bare legs. Oh, luxury, how I've missed you!

I miss my bedmate more, though. I turn my head and look at the empty pillow next to me. Without thinking about it, I've occupied the same side of the bed I slept in at the Pro Bowl, the opposite of where I sleep when I'm alone at home.

I sigh. *This sucks*.

EIGHTEEN

REALITY BECKONS

Before I can dwell too much on my disappointment, I hear hissing in the hallway. "Torz! Here, boy. C'mon, Torzi."

There's a scratch on my door.

"No! Torz! What the hell? Since when? C'mon. Here. Come."

Scratch, scratch. Whine, whine.

"Have you lost your mind? Get over here now."

Scratch, scratch, scratch, scratch, scratch.

I rise from the bed, cross the room, and flip on the lights. When I open the door, I come legs-to-face with Jet, who's bending over to pick up his stubborn dog and carry him to bed. For about the hundredth time, I consider what a lucky bastard that pampered pooch is.

Jet smiles sheepishly and stands at his full height. "Maura. Sorry. Torz is obsessed with this room tonight, for some reason."

I laugh. "If he wants to sleep in here, that's fine. I guess."

"Then who's going to sleep with me?" he quips, his ears reddening as soon as the words are out.

And there it is. The perfect opening. I grab it before I have a chance to let my fear dictate yet another decision. "I can."

Torz wiggles from Jet's grasp and shoots past me, flinging himself onto the bed and circling three times on the pillow I *was* using. Then he curls up for what looks like the duration.

We both watch him for a while before I turn back to Jet. "Well. I guess that's settled. I was lonely in there, anyway."

He studies my face, as if trying to interpret what I'm saying. I'm still on the fence about my meaning, so I keep it ambiguous, giving myself an escape route. "Do you want some company?"

With a stunned, "S-sure!" he leads me to the next door down the hall.

On the threshold to his room, I stop short. "Holy bed, Batman."

He laughs as he pulls back the covers to reveal layers of pillows. "Crazy, huh?"

I round the other side of the bed and look across the mattress at him. "You could fit a whole family in this thing."

"Funny you should say that. It comfortably fit five of my nieces and nephews for nap time once. Some of them are still pretty little, though."

"You got a picture of that, I hope."

"Definitely. Remind me to show it to you sometime. It's adorable."

We look awkwardly at each other across the expanse of sheets for a few seconds until I realize he's practicing a form of unchartered celibate sleepover manners and waiting for me, his guest, to get into bed first. If I tuck myself under the covers and stay on my side of the mattress, he'll lie there all night and not touch me, exactly like he did in Hawaii. But if I make the first move, he's all mine.

Suddenly, it's obvious he's just as afraid as I am; only he's afraid of rejection, not of making the wrong decision. Trusting him is one of the safest decisions I could ever make.

My heart races, but I climb onto the bed and walk across it on my knees. Instead of simply watching him watch me while I make what's sure to be a long, slow journey, I peel my shirt over my head. When I toss it aside, he takes that as his cue to scramble onto the bed and meet me halfway across the mattress, catching my face in his hands.

"Maura," he breathes into my mouth before devouring it.

I clutch the front of his t-shirt for balance while using my other hand to slide my panties to my knees. He pushes me back on the pillows and removes his clothes as if the play clock's about to run out. Frantically, feverishly, he yanks my underwear the rest of the way off and tosses them off the end of the bed.

Then everything slows. He stares into my eyes for what feels like forever, his hand trailing from my hip to my breast. I watch the pulse in his neck, much faster than usual, before moving my attention to his lips, his nose, and finally his eyes, still on mine.

"Maura?"

The thought of him stopping makes me want to cry.

"Yes," I whisper, then repeat louder, "Yes."

———

Several minutes (hours, days, weeks, lifetimes?) later, too spent to move anything else, I find the energy to purse my lips against his neck in a default kiss. Then, as more feeling returns to my limbs, I drag my arm up and cradle his head against it, raking my fingers through his hair. He shudders and shivers under me, where he ended up after much tumbling and rolling. Our heartbeats pulse where we're still joined.

He holds me firmly against him while he shifts to his side. Nestling my head under his chin, he runs his index finger up and down my spine. I fade and drift, my cheek against his rising and falling chest.

After a few minutes of silence, as I'm dozing from sheer exhaustion and deep satisfaction, he wakes me by softly saying, "Maura?"

Rendered speechless, I wait, but he doesn't say anything else. Figuring he's changed his mind about any pillow talk, I close my eyes and match my breathing to his, deciding I've never felt more wonderful in my entire life. It's not that my former boyfriends were slouches in the sack, but it was never like this with any of them our first time. It took several encounters—and a few miscues—for us to figure each other out. But this... This was inspired. The man is a sexual savant. And I wasn't too shabby, myself, if I do say so.

I'm far away, analyzing the phenomenon and chalking it up to amazing chemistry, athletic prowess (on his part), and extreme horniness, when Jet's breathing quickens slightly, and his heartbeat stutters against my ear. I open my eyes, prepared for him to shift position, ending our cozy cuddle session. But he squeezes me more tightly, kisses the top of my head, and says, "I love you," then tugs the covers over my shoulders.

My eyes wide, I stare at the crease where his arm meets his body until he loosens his grip on me by degrees as he falls asleep and I fall something else entirely.

———

It's still dark outside when Jet gently shakes me awake a few hours later. I open one eye but keep the other pinched tightly closed, hoping my face doesn't look as unattractive as it feels, mere inches from his.

"'Morning, Beautiful," he whispers, kissing my shoulder.

"What time is it?" I ask, trying as hard as possible not to open my mouth too much in the process.

"Five-thirty."

I roll onto my back and groan, closing my eyes against the day. "You've gotta be kidding me."

"You told me to wake you at five-thirty."

"I'm not mad at you; I'm mad at the morning."

He laughs. "The morning doesn't care. You want to sleep another half hour? I'll work out and take a shower, then get you up again." Rolling away from me, he moves to sit up, but I reach out and, making blind contact with his wrist, wrap my hand around it.

"No. Don't go."

"Okay." He settles against the pillows once more, on his side. His eyes leave tracers as they roam my profile. His foot runs up my leg, raising goose bumps.

I roll to face him and open my eyes.

His grin rewards my bravery. "There she is!"

"Hey. Good morning." I mirror his pose, propping my head in my hand, my elbow jammed into the pillows against the headboard. Torn between flattening my bedhead and pulling the sheet high enough to cover my not-so-pert bits, I wind up doing a half-assed job of both and probably look like I'm having a seizure.

He scoots closer to me, playfully tugging down on the sheet every time I nudge it up. I eventually give up and let him have his way, exposing my breasts to the chilly air in the room. My nipples tighten. He stares at them and says, "I should probably ask you how you slept, but I'm having a hard time caring."

"The key word being 'hard,' in this instance?" I tease, feeling more confident, suddenly. I inch closer and kiss his chin, but as I'm about to snake my hand under the covers, he pulls his head back, his eyes suddenly serious as they look into mine.

"Maura?"

Alarmed by the rapid change in his demeanor, I freeze. "What is it?"

Swallowing visibly and audibly, he says, "I have to tell you something."

Nothing good comes after that sentence. Ever.

Before I can panic that my worst fears are about to come true (or at the very least, he's going to tell me my breath stinks), he says, "Remember when I came over to your table at the Christmas party, and I said Rae had told me to keep you company while she was busy with Joaquin?"

The tightness in my chest loosens considerably, but not completely. "Of course I remember. I'm not the one who's taken too many hits to the head."

My joke fails to raise the tiniest lift of his lips. Instead, he balls his pillow under his head and shifts to get comfortable. "That never happened. Rae didn't tell me to do that."

I recall Rae claiming Jet was lying, and not caring then. I still don't. "So?"

"So... I lied. I feel awful about it."

"I don't care."

"I do. This is going to sound mega-creepy, but I saw you as soon as you got to the party. Then I realized you were Rae's date, and I was all, 'Dude...'" His jaw slackens, and he closes his eyes like someone who's received horrible news.

I laugh.

My reaction relaxes him, and he cracks a smile before continuing, "Then I overheard someone saying he'd embarrassed himself in front of you because he assumed you were Rae's girlfriend, but you were her friend. Her straight friend. So I was like, 'Cool,' but Rae kind of scares me, so I waited until she left you alone."

Tears leak from the corners of my eyes as I continue to shake with mirth. "You're killing me!" I rest my hand on his cheek.

He turns his head and kisses my fingers. "You're not mad?"

"No!"

"Oh. Good. Because I did what I did because I thought maybe you'd feel safer talking to me if you knew your friend had sent me. The crazy thing is that I lied about the whole thing so I wouldn't seem like as much of a weirdo, but that was worse than telling the truth."

"Yep."

He groans at himself.

"I have my own confession," I drop lightly, hoping I don't regret it.

"Well, well, well."

"I was still awake last night, when you said you loved me."

His smile fades, and he looks down at the mattress between us. "Oh. Well, that's okay. It's not a secret, or anything." He blushes, keeping his eyes down. "I just wasn't sure you were ready to hear it. But I had to say it. I felt like I was going to burst if I didn't. So I waited until you were asleep—or I thought you were."

When he lifts his eyes, he clears his throat and shoots me a wobbly smile. "I told you I was pathetic."

I trail my fingers down his cheek. "You're too good to be true."

He locks his gaze with mine. "I just love you, Maura. That's all."

When he makes slow, tender love to me, so different from our frantic first time, he reassures me that last night wasn't a one-time thing, that he doesn't use the "l"-word like a post-coital "thank you."

Afterward, as we lie side by side, I say lazily toward the sun-drenched ceiling, without moving, "Yep. I'm never getting to work on time."

He grabs my hand and kisses it. With his mouth against my knuckles, he says, "Don't go at all. Stay here."

I laugh. "No. I'm not playing hooky to have sex with you all day."

"You know you want to."

"Well, duh, but it's not any better than all the people who are going to call in sick due to their Super Bowl hangovers. I can't do it." With major effort and willpower, I swing my legs over the side of the bed.

Jet follows, scooting against my back and kissing my shoulder. "Quitter."

I laugh while idly wondering where the majority of my clothes are, before remembering I left them in the guest room bathroom.

"Is anyone going to see me walk half-naked from this room to the one next door?"

"The neighborhood already heard you," he teases.

"I still don't want Helen to see me," I say, referring to his housekeeper.

"She's not here yet. God, I'm already hard for you again."

"Jet!" I jump from the bed and retrieve my t-shirt and panties from the floor, putting them on in double-time.

He laughs at my prudish reaction, collapsing onto his back and wheezing at the rafters. The tented sheet proves he wasn't kidding and almost makes me reconsider my suddenly strict work ethic. Almost.

But I must be strong.

———

As much as I would have *loved* to stay in bed with Jet this morning, I couldn't. Arnold's been giving me more and more responsibility to prepare me for his departure in a few months. I thought the more I learned, the less freaked out I'd be about the fall fair, but the opposite has happened. The more I learn, the more I realize I still don't know, and the more I realize that as complicated as organizing and running these events is, the outcome is generally lackluster, and I don't want to be associated with something that lame when my time comes around. The system needs an overhaul, but I have no clue where to start. Therefore, I haven't.

After all, I have until September to organize and launch this stupid thing, and since it's only February, that means I have months to *not* think about it, according to my usual process. Whatever that is. But based on things said in the spring job fair planning meetings, this passing of the baton is a test of sorts. With Arnold leaving, I'll be one of the senior-most counselors (the turnover at this place is ridiculous, iron-ically enough), and the others already have their pet projects and responsibilities. It's time for me to step up and claim mine, if I want to keep my job.

And I guess I do want to keep it. Because I don't want to

leave and start over somewhere else. Plus, I do like helping people find employment. So if the status quo is no longer an option, I'd better get my act together.

I keep telling myself I'm too busy helping Arnold with the spring fair and learning what needs to be done to start planning my own event. That explanation isn't going to cut it with my boss for much longer, though. Cynthia's going to want to see some concrete plans.

As of this moment, I have zero.

As I'm about to leave for the night, eager to see Jet, Arnold corners me in my office and drones on and on about the pros and cons of having a full-service complimentary food cart at the job fair.

"I've had mixed results in the past," he says. "I guess I'll do it this time, and I'll send you a memo with the cost-to-benefits ratio, so you'll be able to make a more informed decision for the fall fair. By the way, how's that going?" He sits in the chair across from my desk, and I want to scream.

Instead, I stand and say, "Great. I have some, uh, ideas about, uh, things."

"What kind of things?"

"A theme, for one. Something to bring people in, drum up interest."

He chuckles. "That's hardly necessary. Paying jobs sell themselves."

"Yeah, but some of the jobs aren't all that attractive. A theme will drive people to the less popular booths. Maybe. I'm hoping."

"Sounds like a lot of trouble for nothing."

I walk around the side of my desk. "It'll be fun."

"What theme are you going for, then?" he asks, not moving from the chair.

"Uh," I take a stab at coyness when I say, "It's a surprise."

"A surprise theme?"

"No. I mean, I'm not ready to unveil it yet. I still have some details to work out."

Like all of them. This girl knows how to procrastinate.

"Remember, your budget's not that big," Arnold-the-killjoy points out.

"I'll skip the food cart and serve cookies and lemonade. Hey, Arnold. Uh, I have to go." I shift from foot to foot.

He rises slowly from the chair. "Sorry! Thought you'd be making up for coming in later than usual this morning."

I blush, remembering the reason for my tardiness. "Oh. That. Yes. I'll skip lunch tomorrow. But thanks for reminding me."

"Yeah, yeah," he grumbles on his way from my office.

I follow closely behind him as he crosses the threshold into the waiting area. Without warning, he turns to face me, so I freeze, to prevent running into his pot belly, and smile expectantly and politely.

He rubs his neck. "Out of curiosity, do you think your boyfriend might be interested in showing up at the spring fair to sign autographs? That would be something fun I could incorporate for free."

Buh-rother. My relationship with Jet has been a major distraction at the office. The part-time receptionists and job counselors, both male and female, hound me about him every chance they get.

"Is he ripped?"

"Is he, like, totally a perfect gentleman? Because he seems so nice at the press conferences, and one time, my baby cousin was in the hospital with dehydration from the flu, and he came up to the floor to visit the sick kids, and my aunt said he was, like, totally nice."

"What's his house like?"

"How many cars does he have?"

"Does he, like, hang out with all the other players, like, all the time?"

"Where does he take you on dates?"

And the football fans quiz me constantly about the Draft and the team's upcoming offensive and defensive strategies. Like Jet and I sit around and talk about that stuff. Okay, sometimes we do, but I'm hardly going to repeat it.

Now, to Arnold, I say, "I can ask. But off-season training will have started by then, so I can't make any promises."

"I appreciate your asking for me. Thanks."

I nod and smile. "Of course. Good night. See you tomorrow."

He leaves the building, raising his hand in a final (finally!) farewell without turning, which leaves one other counselor and me in the suite. Before she can engage me in the latest round of "What's it like to be Jet Knox's girlfriend?" I close my office door and jog for the exit.

NINETEEN

RECONNECTING WITH RAE

I've become one of those hideous people who neglects her friends when she's in a serious relationship with a guy. This is a first for me, since I've never been in a serious relationship with a guy, much less an all-consuming guy like Jet. I underestimated how much time we'd be spending together in the early off-season, when there's virtually nothing to keep him busy except staying in shape, doing his volunteer work, and occasionally spending a day or two fulfilling obligations with his endorsements. It leaves several unfilled hours in his week, hours he wants to fill with me, when I'm not at work.

For the past month, ever since the Super Bowl, Jet and I have enjoyed relative solitude, basking in each other's company in a cozy bubble where only the two of us exist—in our minds, anyway. It's not that we never socialize with anyone else, but the outings don't last long. Without realizing we're doing it, we tend to ignore everyone around us, until they give up and abandon us. Or vice versa. Not that anyone wants to be around us right now. We're admittedly toothache-inducing, with our snuggling, murmuring, and gazing, not to mention all our giggling at inside jokes.

It's been heady and fun, but I've started to feel guilty about my lack of input in my friendships with Rae and Colin.

Colin's easier to appease than Rae, of course. Once a week, I meet him for lunch. He regales me with stories about the Blue Rinse Brigade, and I tell him about the latest things going on in my life, and we're good. Rae needs more than that from me. I have to carve out *real* time with her, time that could be spent with Jet, or she doesn't feel I'm giving enough.

For the past several weeks, and the first time in my life, I've been asked by many different people to juggle many different things. Work stuff, friend stuff, Jet stuff, family stuff. I'm assuming it's something I'll eventually get used to and possibly master, with enough practice, but as of now, I suck at it. Hardcore.

Today, Rae emails me at work:

Do you remember what I look like? Because you're going all fuzzy in my head, that's how long it's been since we've hung out. Do you have plans tonight? Or any night in the next month? Year?

Able to hear her saying all of that in my head, I smile and type back:

I'm free as can be tonight. I'll call you.

It feels a bit cheap, because I won't be sacrificing Jet time to hang out with her (he's out of town, filming a razor commercial and making a quick stopover at his parents' for a couple days' visit), but it's better than nothing, right?

By the time Rae shows up at my house, I'm in one of Jet's

countless castoff Chiefs hoodies and a pair of yoga pants, my hair hanging in two braided pigtails against my shoulders. She takes one look at me and says, "You're wearing each other's clothes now?"

I roll my eyes at her. "He's not wearing anything of mine, obviously. But I like his stuff. It's comfy, and it smells good."

"And makes you look like a little girl in her daddy's clothes."

"Ew."

"Exactly. Where do you want this jug of wine?"

"In my belly," I answer, leading her to the kitchen.

"Your wish is my command." She plunks the wine on the counter and leans over to look at the casserole dish of enchiladas on top of the stove. "Those are vegetarian, right?"

"Of course. Quinoa."

She sniffs. "Yum." Turning to face me, her arms crossed over her chest, she says, "I think I've met someone... important."

"Molly?"

"Not Molly. Molly's so last month."

"For real?"

"Yes. It may shock you to hear this, but you're a tad wrapped up in yourself—and Jet Knox—right now and have fallen out of touch. With everything."

I release a self-deprecating chuckle. "Fair enough. Who's the new girl?"

"She's a *woman*, not a girl. She's one of the new trainers."

"Oooh! I like your strategy: get in good with the competition."

"She's not my competition."

"Because you're dating her?"

"No! Because it's not a competition. We're all there for the same purpose."

I cock my eyebrow at my friend. "Are you feeling feverish? Delirious?"

She glowers at me.

"I'm sorry, but you always speak about the other trainers like they're your rivals. Or you compare yourself to them. So don't shoot daggers at me. It's great if you've changed your mind and don't feel that way anymore." I grab plates from a cupboard. "What's this special person's name?"

"Are you going to be snide about it? Because, if that's the case, forget it."

I set our plates next to the stove and pull some wine glasses from the under-cabinet hanging rack. Placing the glasses next to the bottle of wine, I say, "I'll shut up now."

She tells me about Ana Paula, a trainer who was recently headhunted to KC from San Diego. I load a plate with two enchiladas and slide it down the counter toward Rae. She stops the dish before it collides with the bottle in front of her, then pours the wine. "She's from here, by way of Brazil, so she's glad to be back home."

"And you two have been out a few times, and things are going well?"

"Yep. We should all go out together sometime." Before I can tease her about her strict no-double-dates-with-Jet rule, she leads me into the dining area, where we pull out two of the four chairs at the round table I rarely use. Then she closes that subject so fast, I nearly get my nose slammed in it. "Now that that's out of the way, what's the latest with you and Super-Arm?"

I unfurl my napkin and place it in my lap. "Oh, so it's okay for *you* to be snide?" I cut my enchilada with the side of my fork and take a bite, realizing too late it's practically volcanic. Trying to cool the food while it's already in my mouth, I suck in some air and move the morsel from one cheek to the other, scorching my tongue in the process. Finally, I swallow the piece nearly whole.

"It's Jet Knox. You can't expect me to be serious about that guy. Ever. He's such a caricature."

Eyes watering, I take a drink of wine and say, "Hey, I love that caricature!"

"Eventually, you're going to figure out that he's not perfect. That's going to be a tough day for you. So, the golden boy's out in California, huh? Gonna visit the 'rents while he's there?"

I nod. "He's helping his mom and dad plan for the annual Knox family get-together in a few weeks." Cutting my next bite, I stare at it, steaming on the tines of my fork. "They all converge out there every April and have Pictionary tournaments and sing-alongs. Or something equally idyllic." After blowing on it a few times, I pop the cheesy bite in my mouth.

"Are you going?"

"Hell no. I'm planning to stay right here, in my own house, and sleep for two weeks. Well, when I'm not working."

She swirls her wine. "What are his parents like?"

"Never met 'em. I've only seen pictures."

"And? You've scoped out Jet's dad, right?"

"What? *Ew*. No!"

"You should. That's probably how Jet will end up looking when he's older."

I laugh and think of the pictures I've studied countless times on Jet's mantel. "He looks more like his mom than his dad."

Rae pulls back her head and wrinkles her nose. "I can't imagine a woman looking like him. Yikes."

"She's an attractive woman. Or probably was, when she was younger. She's a bit horsey now."

My friend slaps the table as she nearly chokes on her latest bite of food.

I point at her with my fork and try not to laugh. "Don't you dare repeat that. Ever."

"I won't."

"I'll deny it until my death, and you'll look like a liar, because Jet will believe me over you."

"I won't say anything! Geez! I'm insulted you'd think I would."

"You like nothing more than to get a laugh, especially at the expense of someone like Jet. A well-timed 'yo mama' joke in the training room would be just your style, and I don't want to be any part of that."

"Horsey," she says, still shaking her head and chuckling. "Man. You know, Jet has a bit of an equine look to him, now that you mention it."

"Only in one place that I can think of," I say to my plate with a smirk.

"There's no need to exaggerate. I've seen it, remember?"

"It was a joke. Sorry I brought it up."

"I bet you bring it up all the time." She wiggles her eyebrows across the table at me, then snort-laughs.

"I do, as a matter of fact. I'm excellent at it."

"Yeah, well, I'm glad you're finally getting it while you can, because once the season starts, that gravy train gonna run dry, girl."

My fork freezes midway to my mouth. "Huh?"

Eyes on her plate, she casually replies, "A lot of the guys don't have sex during the season."

"At all?"

"Rarely. They say it's a waste of testosterone. Which is dumb and not at all scientific. But whatever. There's no talking sense into some of these boneheads. They have so many ridiculous superstitions. You wouldn't believe it. Anyway, if nothing else, abstaining makes them crankier and meaner, so I guess it works in that regard, especially for the defensive players."

"What about stories of guys taking groupies up to their rooms during road trips?"

"Everyone falls off the wagon now and then. Not *everyone* subscribes to this practice. But a lot of guys do—the serious ones."

"Oh, man!" I groan, knowing nobody's more serious about the game than my boyfriend. There's still a tiny spark of hope in my horny heart, though. "Is this another stereotype you're attributing to Jet, or for real? Maybe he's not one of the abstainers."

She seems delighted to be able to reply, "He is, though. I've heard him talk to some of the married guys about it."

"So? Talking about it doesn't mean he participates."

"Commiserating," she clarifies. "Speaking from experience."

My optimism dissolves faster than soap on a rope. "Oh. Damn."

She grins, as if we're talking about something as harmless as giving up sugar for Lent.

I set down my fork and wipe my mouth. "This is no laughing matter, Rae."

That makes her laugh harder.

"I'm serious! I can't go"—I do the math in my head—"six months without sex."

"Four. I don't think any of the guys care during preseason. Chances of making it to the postseason are slim."

"Whatever! Four to five months!" I shudder at the horror.

"He's going to be gone a lot, anyway, so it's not like you'll have much opportunity." She smirks across the table at me. "A couple of months ago, you were all, 'Sex? Who needs it?' but now you're having panic attacks and preemptive withdrawals at the idea of going without it?" She shakes her head and clicks her tongue. "Addiction takes hold so quickly."

"It's not about getting off," I say. "It's about the connection, the affection, the… the intimacy."

"Bullshit. If that were the case, then cuddling would be enough. There's no stupid superstition against cuddling. Then again, guys generally don't cuddle unless there's something else in it for them or something's already happened. So, yeah. Dust off your king-sized vibrator and call it good."

"I don't have one of those!"

"Riiiight."

"And I'm not going to need one."

"You're going to tough it out, huh?"

"No! I'm going to convince Jet that abstaining is ludicrous."

"Peer pressure is not going to have any effect on *years* of practice. Honestly, I think the sex thing comes from high school coaches, who want their young charges to get enough sleep at night and focus on the game, not girls. Then it becomes ingrained in these guys. Especially a yes-man like Jet."

"He'll listen to me. He loves me."

Rae polishes off her last bite of enchilada, sighs contentedly, and replies, "More power to ya. Some of the 'health' myths these guys buy into are ridiculous. Jet's been receptive to my suggestions for changes to his diet. I don't think he cares what he eats, as long as he gets to eat. But some of his other wellness practices have been more difficult to break."

"Like?" This is the first I'm hearing of any weird rituals.

"Like, he and a bunch of the other guys still insist on puking before big games, and that pisses me off."

"What? That's disgusting."

"And horrible for them. If you can break him of that, I'd be ever so grateful."

"I'll try." I push my plate away. "He never told me about that."

"Well, it's not one of the things they brag about. Another guy, he eats seven 'lucky' Twinkies before every game. I guess he thinks diabetes is a sign of good luck."

I snicker. "Is he one of the pukers? Because I'd puke if I ate that many Twinkies."

"No. I wish. A ton of the guys are obsessed with candy, in general. Or those awful energy drinks that are basically battery acid disguised as soda. But Schoengert drinks the *nastiest* concoctions."

"Like what?"

"Like raw eggs with spinach, chocolate syrup, and hot sauce. That was his favorite last season. But he changes it up."

"Disgusting. What does that have to do with kicking?"

"Nothing! But he could get a kickin' case of salmonella. What do I know, though? I'm merely a health professional. I've stopped trying to educate them. They're all a bunch of nutjobs."

"Aw…" Hearing the ridiculous, albeit legal, lengths to which these guys go to give themselves an edge—including the lengths that could have a negative impact on *my* life—makes me realize how important winning is to them. It's not merely entertainment; it's their lives. "They want to feel like they have some control over the luck portion of the game."

Rae's not moved. "They're morons. You have no idea."

"Well, I love my moron. As long as he brushes his teeth after purging."

"How romantic." She wipes her mouth, then takes another drink of wine, finishing off the last of it. "I'd like to take this opportunity to say, once again, that guys are revolting, and I'm glad I've never allowed one to come in contact with my private parts."

"Yes, you're so much more evolved than those of us common hetero women."

"Damn straight. Actually, not."

TWENTY

INCOMPATIBLE LIVES

My social life has blown up. When we first met, Jet may have claimed to be a homebody, but his definition and mine are clearly different. When *I* said I was a homebody, I meant that I come *home* from work and park my *body* on the couch, where I stay until it's time to transfer that body to my bed. When Jet said it, I'm not sure what he meant. Maybe he thinks of this entire city as his "home." After all, he's treated like the lord of the manor everywhere we go. Or maybe he's more social now that he has someone to take out.

No matter the disconnect, there definitely is one. It's not that I don't like hanging out with his friends, but I miss whipping off my bra for Matt/Jason after work, changing into my fleece pajamas, and falling asleep on the couch to movies I've seen so many times, I could practically recite them *while* I sleep on the couch.

I've started to put my foot down about going out every weeknight, because the next day at work is miserable. I don't drink half the time—and never enough to get drunk and be hungover—but the amount of sleep I'm missing is enough to make functioning at my job a nightmare.

And I need to be at peak performance there. Yet another month has passed, and I'm still no closer to the epic idea I'll need to revolutionize our job fair system, in general, and kick ass with the fall event, specifically. Because somehow that's become the only acceptable outcome. I went from, "Nooooo! I don't want to do this at all!" to "This job fair will be talked about for years to come, or I will consider it a total failure."

Jet might be rubbing off on me—in more ways than one. It's like I'm starting to *care* about stuff.

I'm overwhelmed and exhausted and need at least one area of my personal life to quiet down so I can get a handle on what's going on in the professional sphere. If I can make it one more week... That's when Jet will be out in California for his yearly spring visit with his family. I'll have two weeks to focus more fully on everything else.

When I'm around him, it's hard to concentrate on anything but him—us—period. Normally, that's a good thing. A great thing. I love that when we're together, I don't think about anything stressful or draining. I just enjoy his company. It's wonderful. We take walks and swim. We talk about movies and football and try to one-up each other with cheesy jokes and riddles. He gets his from the kids at the hospital, and his little brother, Simon, at Big Brothers, Big Sisters. I have to resort to the Internet.

But all of that together time is making it a little too easy for me to continue to ignore the passing weeks and my lack of action on anything else in my life.

Of course, he has no idea he's enabling my procrastination. Because I haven't told him anything other than that I'm in charge of the fall fair. That was months ago. He probably thinks I have it all figured out by now. He would.

Today was another fine example of his unintentional, yet highly effective, distraction skills. On this fine spring day, our last Saturday together before he leaves for the west coast, he took me to my first Sporting KC match. I love the charged atmosphere at Chiefs games in Arrowhead, but those soccer fans were a whole other beast with their chants and songs and drum beats. The fresh air, sun, and electric crowd combined for a near-perfect afternoon.

I made him promise we'd take Colin next time. I doubt it's the same as it is among the English crowds, but I bet he'd still get a kick out of going. He'd be able to tell *me* what was happening. Jet only knew half the time. Not that it mattered. There was so much more to being there than watching the action on the pitch.

Now, back at his place for the evening, we've settled in to watch *Fight Club*. Well, sort of. It's sometimes hard to focus on the film with Jet lazily running his hand up and down my thigh like that while I sit sideways in his lap. But we've both seen the movie several times, so it's not like we have to catch every word.

At the iconic part where Brad Pitt explains to Edward Norton the now-famous Fight Club rules, Jet drops, "Oh, hey. I keep forgetting to tell you, I canceled my trip home."

When I'm incapable of replying to this bombshell, he grins, misinterpreting my speechlessness for delight.

And let me clarify: the slacker in me *is* delighted. *Oh, darn! I guess we won't have time to think about that awful job fair mess. But it's not our fault that Jet's so amazing and cute and funny and entertaining.*

Even the most delusional part of me, however, can't deny

I'm drowning. *Noooooooooo! Those two weeks were going to be the life preserver that allowed us to stop treading water and make some progress toward shore, or at least shallower waters where we can regain our footing.*

"But I thought—" I stop and take a deep, calming breath.

He tilts his head at me, like Torz does when we say one of his favorite words. Or when I mutter curse words at him.

I try again. "I thought you said you *always* go out there this time of year. Everyone *always* gathers at your parents' house. Because that's what you *always* do," I repeat, hoping I don't sound too panicked.

He picks up my hand, kisses my palm (which is suddenly clammy), and murmurs against it, "But you can't go with me."

"No, I can't."

"So I want to stay here. With you."

"Oh, that's not necessary. You should spend time with your family. You *need* that time."

"That's why they're all coming here for a late Spring Break, of sorts. This way, I won't have to schedule everything around preseason training, like I do when they visit in the summer." His eyes twinkle. "In fact, we're going to start a new tradition and do it like this every year. Kansas City is in the middle of the country, after all, and I have a bigger house. I don't know why we didn't think of it sooner."

I may pass out.

Still oblivious, he continues, *"Plus,* aren't your parents going to be back in town? We can get everyone together. It'll be so much fun."

Staring at his chin, I say carefully, "I think the first time I meet your parents should be a quieter thing. With the four of us. Don't you?" I brave a look into his confused eyes.

He pauses. "Does it matter?"

"Maybe." When he doesn't say anything to that, I edge farther onto the rickety bridge that is this conversation. "I'd prefer to meet them without an audience."

Or not at all. Ever. Would that be weird?

"Audience?" He laughs. "My brothers and sisters aren't an audience; they're family."

"Right. But they're still strangers to me."

"They're going to love you."

"You don't know that, and that's not the point!" I explode.

His eyes widen, and his head jerks backward at my outburst.

I rub my temples. "I'm so sorry."

His hand lands on my knee and squeezes. "Hey. What's wrong?"

"I'm— Nothing! I'm just really stressed right now."

"You are? Since when?"

"All the time," I say miserably, then backtrack when he seems more confused than ever. "Well, not when I'm with you. Which I guess is a lot of the time. But at work, I'm dying. Things are starting to pile up at home, too. With Greg and Deirdre's wedding happening in two months, that stuff is ratcheting up."

"How can I help?"

"You were supposed to help by going away for a couple of weeks."

As soon as the words are out, I regret them.

"I'm sorry," I quickly say again, placing a hand against the side of his face and kissing his lips. He could be a statue, except his eyes shoot to the side and down at the floor. Then his Adam's apple bobs.

"You can't do anything to help me, especially with the work stuff. I have to do it all by myself, like a big girl. But I've learned that event planning isn't my strength, and I still don't know what the hell I'm doing, so I'm paralyzed by my ineptitude, and I'm mostly doing *nothing* about it, rather than facing it."

I'm relieved my explanation seems to have gone a long way toward fixing my outburst, and he's willing to resume eye contact with me, but I add, "Really. I'm so sorry I said that about you going away."

"Well, you obviously feel that way, and if you do, I can go back to my original plans." He twists the drawstring of his hoodie around his fingers and frowns.

Oh, shit. Not the pout. It's the one thing Jet does that never fails to grate on my nerves. The puppy-dog eyes, the downturned mouth, the small voice. It makes me want to scream. Grown-ass adults don't pout. If he'd rail at me when he's hurt or mad or doesn't get his way, I could give it right back to him, but I have no recourse with the pout. If I give in to my irritation, I look and feel like a huge bitch. But it seriously pisses me off that the only acceptable reaction is a sympathetic one that encourages his childish behavior.

Today's no different, and I hasten to appease him. "No! No. I do want to meet your family. But I'm overwhelmed. By everything."

He smiles tenderly at me, and the pout is forgiven. I'd probably forgive him anything with him looking at me that way. "Aw, Maura. It's going to be okay. All of it. I promise."

For a second, I believe him. I press my forehead to his and nod. "Okay."

"I was mega-nervous about meeting your mom and dad, too, but it turned out fine."

And… we're back to freaking out.

"You're Jet Knox. They already knew you and loved you

before you ever sat at my mom's table and complimented her cooking and ate that huge slice of banana cake when you were so full, you wanted to puke."

"Well, when a woman's chanting your name and 'Eat! Eat! Eat!' it's hard to refuse."

I laugh and grimace. "Oh, my gosh."

"The Knox jerseys were a nice touch, too. I thought your mom was going to fall down when she struck that Heisman pose for me. I felt bad having to admit I never won one."

"And speaking of Heisman finalists, is my dad still harassing you about Michael Wilcox and the possibility of you guys drafting him?" I ask, referring to the University of Nebraska alum who's been slated as one of the incoming class of quarterbacks to watch.

Jet's sheepish smile is answer enough.

"That's it. You have to tell him to stop."

"It's not a big deal. He doesn't mean anything by it."

"He's so clueless! I wish he'd pick up on a social cue once in a while and not have to be told to cool it. I'll find a way to get him to stop bothering you about it."

"Be nice, though. I don't want him to think I was complaining about it. He's passionate about Chiefs football. I'm never going to complain about that." Jet tucks a piece of hair behind my ear. "I love Linda and Bruce. You're going to love my family, too. And they're going to love you. It'll be perfect."

"They'll be here next weekend? All of them?"

"Weekend after. Had to give everyone a chance to change their flights. They'll only be staying a week, instead of two."

Thank God for small miracles.

"Plus, Cyndi, Justin, and Mikey won't be able to join us

from Germany. But they weren't going to come out to California, either."

"Oh. So that makes"—I count the people in my head—"a total of fourteen guests?"

"Not guests. Family. You'll see. It's a blast."

In an effort to hide my concerns and end the conversation that's doing nothing to allay my fears, I turn back to the movie, where Edward Norton is getting his ass kicked. Something tells me I'm going to feel like that in a couple of weeks.

TWENTY-ONE

PROCRASTINATING PANIC

A week and a half later, nothing has changed. Except my anxiety level. Yeah, that's increased about five hundred percent. Because not only am I still grappling with issues at work—and now dealing with a boss who wants to see a plan (a real one) for the fall job fair before the end of next week—but I'm three days away from the Knox family invasion—and on my period.

In addition, today I received my invitations to Deirdre's bachelorette tea *and* bachelorette party, two events I have to somehow cram into my bursting May calendar. I've just hung up with Deirdre after RSVP'ing to both things.

The true purpose of my call was to get an explanation for this deviation from tradition, and to possibly get out of one of the events. It sounded hopeful, at first, when Deirdre said, "I wanted to do something to suit all personality types. Frankly, some of my friends aren't interested at this stage in their lives in going to a strip club, getting hammered, and sporting phallic novelty items. *I'm* not all that interested in it, to be honest, but my sister insists. It's her show, as the maid of honor. So we compromised and scheduled a tea for the more mature women who still want to show their support."

"So, I need to choose one?"

She laughed stiffly. "Oh, no. You're part of the bridal party, so you get to attend both, silly."

Silly, silly me.

Before anyone else can lay claim to another minute of my time, I change from my work clothes to my pajamas, grab a notebook and a pen, plus the movie, *Nine to Five,* for inspiration, and plop onto the couch. I'm not moving until I have a clear plan of action for the fall fair. Even if that means simply outlining the bare requirements, so I have something to show Cynthia next week at our meeting. That still won't be enough, but it will at least be *something* to prove I'm not completely blowing off this assignment.

Ignoring my buzzing phone on the coffee table, I start with a to-do list that includes contacting the usual employers about two weeks after the spring fair. We want to give them time to put the one fair behind them, but not enough time to forget how helpful it was (hopefully) and to secure their spots for the next one. I'll also need to make a decision on the food, but I put a question mark next to that, since it hinges on what else I do and how much budget I have left. The easier tasks include renting the huge tent that we set up in the office park's courtyard, arranging the catering (whatever it ends up being), and contacting the usual sources to place ads and other promotional materials, none of which I can create until I have a firmer plan.

Oh, gosh. List-makers are liars. This activity isn't making me feel better at all. It's merely highlighting how far behind I am! I toss the legal pad away from me, onto the floor. The pen soon follows, landing with a "thwack" on top of the skewed paper.

I cover my face with my hands, wishing I could have a good cry about everything. That's another thing that helps, according to normal people. But I don't cry about work. Work is something that facilitates life. It's a means to an end, not a source of angst. Or even joy. It just is.

And if my phone doesn't stop buzzing, I'm going to throw it through Jane Fonda's face on my TV.

Lowering my hands, I blink my burning eyeballs and frown at the insistent device. I know it's Jet, and I know if I don't answer his texts, he'll start calling, and he won't stop until I answer, because he'll worry I'm not answering. That could lead to a worse possibility: a visit. I can't temper my bitchiness with him face-to-face right now. The mere thought of how that will end (with more pouting) motivates me to pluck the cell from the table and tap, *Can't talk*, without reading through the messages he's been sending all evening.

A few seconds later, he replies:

You okay?

Just tired

I'll bring you dinner

That's okay. Not hungry

Too late

I'm staring at that message, wondering what the heck it

means, poised to reply with a string of question marks when I hear a car door slam, followed by my doorbell ringing.

Now I want to cry.

When I open the door, and he lifts in greeting a paper sack with the logo of one of my favorite sushi restaurants, my rumbling stomach outvotes my bad attitude, but I remain silent and passive while he unpacks the food on the coffee table.

Taking in the movie and the pen and pad on the floor, he asks, "Whatcha doin'?"

"*Trying* to work," I answer shortly.

"Fuel up, and you'll feel better."

Thanks, Coach! Ya think? Are you gonna slap my butt next?

Keeping my snarky comments to myself, I separate the disposable chopsticks Jet hands me and rub them together to smooth away the splinters, then examine my choices. All of my favorites, of course. And way more than I could ever eat.

Jet folds the bag and takes it into the kitchen. Returning with two beers, he sits next to me on the couch and, after setting my drink on the table and taking a few sips of his, says, "So. Rough day?"

I shrug, pluck a tempura-covered nugget from one of the trays in front of me, dip it in soy sauce, and, while I wait for it to stop dripping so I can transfer it to my mouth, reply, "They're all rough lately." I pop the roll into my mouth.

He watches me chew, then checks, "Good?"

Nodding, I finally locate my manners after swallowing and say, "Yeah. Thanks."

He nudges my shoulder with his. "Any time. Now about this job fair..."

I tense once more when he assumes his fix-it mode voice

but try not to show it as I select a cream cheese-, avocado-, and crab-filled piece.

"I could help you brainstorm ideas."

Oh, my favorite word. My brain has been a non-stop storm for weeks now. Surely, he knows that. Or maybe he doesn't. He's been busy getting ready for his family's visit, and I've tried to take advantage of that and leverage some space, so we haven't spent nearly as much time together lately. The time we have spent together, I've made a conscious effort to be present and positive—until now. I can't fake it anymore.

I wash down my food with three gulps of beer while I try to figure out how to kindly reject his offer. Finally, still stalling, I set down my bottle and ask, "You going to eat, or just watch me?"

He avoids my eyes as he picks up the next piece to feed to me. "This isn't for me. I ate before coming over." When I stare at him, ignoring the morsel he's offering, he clarifies, "Sushi's not my thing, remember?"

"Why didn't you get something both of us would like?"

He shrugs. "I was hungry after my afternoon workout, so I ate early. I wanted to treat you. I know you're having a rough time."

Ohhhhhhhhhhh. Right. I see now. Feed the menstruating bear, and you might stay off her shit list. If you're lucky and don't make any sudden moves.

His thoughtfulness should be endearing, but I'm too strung out to be coddled. It's suffocating.

When I say nothing to his veiled reference to my "rough time," he returns to the previous topic, one I'd hoped he'd forgotten. "I can ask some of the guys if they'd show up and sign autographs. We could probably swing it in the afternoon, after practice, since it'll be the middle of the week."

"You guys are already doing that for Arnold next month."

"So? We don't mind. It's fun."

"I want to do something different. It's a job fair, not a meet-n-greet."

"Sometimes you need to get people in the door. Everyone wants to meet NFL players."

No longer hungry, I toss my chopsticks in one of the half-empty trays and fall back into the couch cushions. "If everyone were as enthusiastic about getting jobs and working, think how great this country could be."

His jaw twitches. "It was just an idea. Shit."

"Well, I have my own ideas," I lie.

"Great!" He doesn't sound that happy about it, though. I'm glad he doesn't pick up that pad of paper and look at that lame list or ask me to share any of my nonexistent concepts.

"Don't pout, all right? I can't handle it right now."

"I'm not pouting!"

"You are. You do it so much, you don't even realize when you're doing it anymore."

He snorts. "Whatever."

While he most definitely pouts, I stare at the unwatched film playing in front of us. What would someone in a movie do right now? Rocky would jump some rope and run up and down some stairs. Jerry Maguire would hop on a plane to scout the next big thing in football. Dolly Parton would type a kick-ass memohhhhmygosh.

"Oh, that's it!"

"You know, I'm just trying to be sup—"

"Shhh! I'm being brilliant."

He bites the inside of his cheek. "Ewkay…"

Sitting forward, I place my hands on either side of my

head, as if to hold the ideas in place. "I know what the theme of the job fair is going to be."

"Theme? Like, 'getting jobs'?"

"No, something better." I drop my arms. "Colin suggested having a theme, and at the time, I thought, 'Whatever.' But all the job fairs we've hosted in the past—including the one I'm helping Arnold organize next month—have been so boring! And our answer to that is, 'Get some football players to sign autographs,' or 'Give away free food,' or 'Have a raffle for a stupid piece of shit nobody wants.'"

"I'm in," Jet quips.

"But that has nothing to do with getting a job. Or finding a career."

"Nope."

"So we have to make job hunting, itself, fun."

"Mmmm... Passin' out résumés and filling out applications. My favorite pastime."

I swat his shoulder.

"Ow!"

"Be quiet and listen."

"I'm listening!"

I jab a thumb at the TV screen. "What if, for each employer's booth, we have a picture—or several—of movie characters with the jobs that employer is offering?"

He closes one eye. "Um, give me an example."

"So, like, for the Highway Patrol, we'll have life-sized cardboard cutouts of famous cops and forensic scientists from movies."

"I can't think of any movie cops who aren't dirty," he says with a wince. "Or bumbling idiots. Like in the *Police Academy* movies. That's probably not what you had in mind."

I wave him off. "I don't need you to think of any for me; I

can think of a ton. And lawyers and doctors and teachers and—"

Jet nods at Dolly. "Secretaries?"

"Administrative assistants, yes! And chemists. Scientists. Politicians. Chefs. Writers. Lots of writers! Journalists."

"Sounds like you have a winner of any idea." He busies himself consolidating the half-eaten sushi rolls into fewer trays and stacking them for eventual transport to the refrigerator.

"I have to implement it, and it might be a huge pain in the ass, but I still have enough time. The marketing campaigns will practically write themselves."

"Great. See? You've got this."

Hit by yet another thought, I bolt to my feet and run around the front of the coffee table, between it and the TV, where I pace, kicking aside my discarded pen and paper. "And something else! Career planning is similar to film composition, you know?" Opening my arms to their full extension and stopping to face him, like a lecturing professor, I say, "The wide or establishing shot is your long-term plan, your five-, ten-, and twenty-year goals." I move my hands closer together. "The medium shot is what you're doing to get there: college, training, blah, blah, blah." I frame my face with my hands, Madonna-Vogue-style. "And the close-ups are of you, getting the jobs and advancing through your career with promotions, until you make it to the top!"

Jet watches me, pausing in his housekeeping. All traces of the pout are finally gone. "I like it. That's super-clever."

"I know! I mean, thanks. The theme's tag line..." I sweep my hand in front of me, plastering it on an invisible marquee. "'Be the Star of Your Life.' Yes! That's it. Nailed it!" I pump my arm twice close to my side.

"Hey, that's my touchdown move," Jet mock objects, laughing. He stands next to me.

High on inspiration, I throw myself at him. At the last second, he realizes what I'm doing and grabs me before I knock us both over.

"Oof! Whoa. Hey." He chuckles into my face and pushes a strand of my hair from my eyes. "We need to practice our end zone celebration. That was almost a disaster."

"Sorry about that." I gulp. "And I'm sorry about that other stuff, too. It was mean. You were only trying to help. I'm a real jerk when I'm stressed out. Good thing I don't care about too many things, huh?" I chuckle nervously while I wait for his reaction to my awkward apology.

He stares into my eyes. "Let's just forget it, okay? You figured it out, and now you can relax. I'm proud of you."

"I'm proud of me, too," I realize with no shortage of surprise.

He nudges his nose with mine. "I love you, and I can't wait to introduce you to everyone this weekend."

My euphoria fades, but I keep my smile plastered on my face and hope he doesn't see it deaden in my eyes. "That's right. Three more days." Blinking that dreadful thought away, I focus on his mouth, edging closer to mine. "I love you, too," I say, right before contact.

TWENTY-TWO

KNOX FAMILY INVASION

The Knox Family Circus arrives from the airport, kids and luggage and yelling parents tumbling from the two SUVs they've rented for the week. Through the bodies flowing into the entryway, Jet looks at me across the space and grins.

"Yep. This is about right," he says, wending his way to my side.

While his siblings wrangle their kids, we perform some distracted introductions, mostly shouting names and nodding over the din, followed by hugs for Jet as each person files past us. I take advantage of the chaos to observe and commit names to faces and personalities.

I already know from pictures that Keith and David are both easily four inches taller than Jet, but seeing it in person is a whole other story. They're not professional athletes so, therefore, they aren't as diligent about diet and exercise as their little (literally, in this case) brother. Keith, the older of the two, laughs and claps people on backs and lifts his siblings' kids, tickling them and making a big deal about how big they've grown. If I were a kid, I'd be terrified of that guy, but they seem to love him.

David watches on with a quiet smile, but Jet tells me he has a good sense of humor and comes out of his shell the more you get to know him. I look forward to seeing the similarities—and differences—between David, as the middle son, and his brothers.

As far as Jet's sisters-in-law go, once again, I'm enjoying the rare experience of feeling diminutive since they both measure in at more than six feet tall. Keith's wife, Lucy, rail thin and kitted out in designer *everything* from head-to-toe, gives her husband a run for his money on the Loudest Entrance Award as she herds her two kids with a hand on each of their heads toward the nearest bathroom, yelling about someone getting into the chocolate without permission.

Somewhat more sedate, David's wife, Tammy, holds a baby on her hip and periodically shushes her older child, a three-year-old boy whom she otherwise ignores while he repeatedly tries to climb her legs.

Jet's older sister, the tan, blonde, and buxom Bridget (nicknamed "Gidget"), walks through the door, takes one look at the confusion, and booms, "Everyone to their rooms! Meet in the living room in fifteen!"

The resultant silence is not only jarring, but it's eerie how everybody carries out her command, without question.

On her way past Jet and me, she mutters, "Someone's gotta take control here, or we'll never get anything accomplished this week." After hugging her little brother, she smiles at me. "Hey, there. I'd tell you not to be too afraid. But you probably should be."

Jet's parents, Gloria and Ned, stumble last through the door. The dutiful son grabs their suitcases and leans down for a kiss from his mom, who acts like it's been years, not mere weeks, since she's seen him.

"How's my baby boy?" she asks, wiping her lipstick from his cheek. "You're looking big and strong, as usual. Oh, I've missed you!" She pulls him in for a more intense hug, her eyes pinched closed with rapture. Still clinging to his shoulders, she opens her eyes to regard me, studying me like I'd imagine she'd admire a stylish fashion accessory worn by him. "Hello, Dear."

I manage to reply politely and eloquently. At least, I think I do; it's still difficult to hear myself over my ringing ears.

Jet quickly takes over, standing at his full height, introducing me more formally to his parents, and gushing about how excited he's been for this week.

"Well, I need to go lie down for about a day," Gloria quips. "Thank goodness we were on three separate planes. The drive from the airport was enough to kill me."

"What's the deal with the highway construction?" Ned gripes. "The detours were outrageous!"

Jet says something about winter pothole repair and promises to work out a better route back to KCI before their departure, then follows them with their bags up the stairs, tossing over the banister at me, "I'll be right back."

The rest of the day is a blur of simultaneous conversations and kids running in and out of the house. And laughter—lots of laughter. The Knoxes are happy people. Happy people who like to tease each other constantly, especially Jet and his brothers.

At the front door, as I'm leaving for the night, Jet brushes my bangs off my forehead and says down into my face, "Thanks for being such a good sport today."

"It was good to meet everyone and talk," I reply, resting

my arms on his shoulders and wrapping my hands around the back of his neck. "I have a feeling I'm going to hear a lot of great Jet stories in the next few days."

He groans. "I might have to lay down some bribes tonight to make sure that doesn't happen." He kisses me, then grabs my hand as I let go of him to open the front door. "Hey, I'll text you later and let you know the plan for tomorrow."

I nod, suddenly nervous about leaving. As soon as the door closes on me, the discussion will open *about* me. Not that I worry anyone will say anything negative to Jet—or that I've given them any reason to do so. It's just disconcerting to know I'll be a topic of discussion for part of the evening.

To avoid thinking about it, I go home and collapse into bed, and fall into a blissful, twelve-hour sleep.

———

The plan is for Jet and me to take the ladies and kids to Swope Park to explore the Nature Center and burn some energy outside during the late morning and early afternoon while his dad and brothers spend their kid-free time on the golf course.

After enjoying some alone time at my place when Jet picked me up earlier, I asked him why he wasn't golfing with the guys. He paid close attention to buttoning his shirt while sitting on the side of my bed, then answered, "I suck at golf."

I tugged on a pair of jeans and a V-neck t-shirt that didn't seem too wrinkled. "So? It probably makes them feel really good to be better than you at something."

"I don't like being a loser. Puts me in a bad mood. We'll catch up with them later, when the others go shopping. Unless you want to do that, too." He zipped his shorts and slid his feet into his suede shoes.

"No! I mean, no, that's okay." I was selfishly relieved when Jet chose not to join his dad and brothers on the links. Not only can I not play, but I suspect I wasn't even invited, to begin with. That would have put me in the awkward position of bowing out of the childcare duties, also not my forte, at the park, alone with his mom and sisters. But I would have. Because we're definitely not there yet. I'm not going anywhere with Jet's family without him.

We've been at his house for nearly an hour now, waiting for the moms and kids to be ready for departure. I try not to think too much about how he and I could have better utilized this time at my place. Rather, I stay out of the frantic fray, flipping through the latest issue of *ESPN The Magazine* from the coffee table.

Finally, Gidget, standing on the landing between the stairs to the second floor and the basement, shouts, "The train leaves in five minutes! If you're not in the car, you don't get to go to the park. Let's move!"

Children scurry from both directions, tripping over each other in their haste.

Gloria tuts. "Why do you insist on bellowing everything, Gidget?"

"It gets results, Ma," she replies, nodding to the line of kids at the front door and tossing a set of keys at Jet. "You're taking one group. I'll follow you."

He twirls the keys on his finger. "Who's riding with Maura and me in the cool kids' car?"

Five hands shoot into the air. The sixth one is quick to follow, as he blindly imitates his older brother and cousins. "Meeeeeeeeeeeeeeeeee!"

Gidget pulls her daughter's hand down. "You're coming with me, Miss Thing, after that stunt you pulled at breakfast."

Jet widens his eyes and winces. "Oops. Guess we missed something there. Okay. Maura and I have the other big kids, then."

"You're probably going to want another grownup in the back," Lucy suggests.

"Pshaw. We don't need no stinkin' grownups, do we kids?"

"Nooooooooooo!"

Gidget sniffs. "Jet's right; it's best that all the kids go with him. It's only fair. As a matter of fact," She pushes the breakfast troublemaker back in line. "I'll think of some other punishment for you. Go ahead with Jet and Maura."

Jet sticks out his tongue at Lucy. "It's unanimous. You have to go in the boring car. Better luck next time."

She rolls her eyes at him and smirks. "Don't say I didn't warn you."

Jet grabs my hand and pulls me through the crowd to the front door. "Okay, dudes and dudettes. Let's roll."

After the longest twelve minutes of my life, we pull into the parking lot of the Nature Center. Jet parks the SUV, pulls the keys from the ignition, and simply stares at me while the bedlam continues behind us. The look of utter betrayal on his face both breaks my heart and cracks me up. He soon follows my lead, but his laughter sounds more rueful.

Realizing the vehicle has stopped, the little monsters spring their seatbelts, hop down from their boosters, and start banging on the safety-locked doors and windows.

"Ow! Gage pulled my hair!"

"Patience stepped on me!"

"Milo's looking at me!"

"I'm hungry!"

"I hafta poop!"

"I want my mommy!"

"Sounds like the locker room back there," Jet says, making me laugh harder. Then he shouts over his shoulder, "Hey! What the heck? Everyone sit down and shut up."

"Ummm! Uncle Jet said 'shut up.'"

"That's a bad word!"

"You're mean!"

"You're not my friend!"

"Tell that weird girl to stop laughing at us!

"I hafta poop! Now!"

Jet runs his hand through his hair. "This is unbelievable. They all used to be so cute, and they loved me. What happened?"

"Oh, how quickly the tide of popular opinion turns," I half-joke.

Without warning, Jet whirls in his seat and startles the malcontents silent with a wide-eyed glare and flared nostrils. Outside the vehicle, the adult females peer through the windows.

"What's going on in there?" Gidget says through the glass next to Jet's shoulder.

He ignores her and continues to stare down the backseat contingent. Finally, after several seconds, he opens his mouth to make his proclamation, then closes it, sniffs, and says, "Aw, man! Did someone have an accident?"

A little voice replies, "I tole you I hadta poop!"

Jet and I spring from the vehicle like it's on fire and pull open the back doors, ushering out the kids.

With stiff arms, Jet hands the pooper to Tammy. "I hope you brought a change of clothes for this one."

Chagrined, she hands off her younger child to Gloria and frog-marches her oldest toward the Nature Center. Holding his hand against a disturbing bulge in the back of his pants,

Milo whines, "It was a accident! Uncle Jet wouldn't let us out of the car!"

Still reeling from the entire experience, I stand, shell-shocked next to the car. Gidget sidles up to me. "And that, ladies and gents, is the best form of birth control ever." With a nudge and a nod toward her little brother, she walks away.

On the other side of the vehicle, Jet fans the back door to air out the interior of the SUV.

Gidget turns and walks backward, winking and calling out, "You're welcome!"

We spend an hour in the echoey Nature Center, then head back outdoors for a picnic lunch and exercise on the playground until the golfers meet up with us for their turn with the kids. Going shopping with the women would mean a break from the loudest children I've ever encountered, much less had to spend any significant amount of time with, but the thought of traipsing along The Plaza after the past couple of hours nauseates me. I keep reminding myself that I get to go to work tomorrow. I've never looked so forward to a Monday in my life.

While Tammy, Gidget, and Lucy take the kids to the restrooms after lunch, Jet, Gloria, and I clean up our picnic trash and return the coolers to the SUV that we'll take back to Jet's. He sets up a chair for his mom, then sprawls on his back on the nearest blanket, feet flat on the ground, legs apart and bent at the knees. I sit next to him and lean back on my straight arms, tilting my head toward the warm sun and letting the breeze tease my ponytail.

"Mom, those kids are crazy," Jet says, arranging his hands behind his head.

Gloria clicks her tongue. "They're babies. That's how babies are, Jet."

"No. When they were babies, they were cute. Now they're beasts. Milo pooped his pants to spite me."

I snicker but stay out of it. Or try to. But Jet has other ideas.

"Ask Maura. It was terrible. They yelled at each other the entire way here. Sometimes they weren't even mad about anything. They were just... yelling. Like, they only have one volume."

Gloria arches an eyebrow at me. "Well? Was it as bad as he says?"

Aw, hell no. I'm not saying a damn word against this woman's grandchildren to her. Then again, I can't very well call Jet a liar. Because he's not. At all. As a matter of fact, he left out a few things. Before we made it to the main road, the girls insisted on singing along to the Disney soundtrack playing in the vehicle's CD player. At top, screechy volume. The boys covered their ears and demanded the girls stop. Then, when Jet turned off the music, the girls started to cry and scream at the boys.

Now he lifts his head from the blanket to see what's taking me so long to answer. Finally, I say, "I'm not around kids a lot, so I wouldn't know what's normal."

"This isn't normal," he says. "What's going on? Even Gidget's kids are nuts."

"They're on vacation," Gloria says. "That's what happens. Children need stability and routine. They're not as portable or adaptable as your little dog. They act out when they're out of their element, off their schedules. "

"Off their rockers, you mean."

"Give it a couple of days. They'll settle down. Now, shush. Your sisters are coming back. One day, when you two have kids of your own, you'll understand how difficult it is, and you won't want childless know-it-alls to judge you every time one of your little darlings acts out."

"I guess," he grumbles.

Wait, wait, wait a minute here! Did just she call me a "childless know-it-all"? And create a bunch of future mini-Jetauras? How did that happen? I didn't say a single judge-y thing! I was anti-judge.

Unjustly rebuked, I sit motionless with my hands in my lap while the other women return and shoo the independently ambulatory kids toward the playground. Tammy opens a bag chair, settles into it and unceremoniously whips out her boob to feed the baby.

The others talk about their upcoming shopping excursion (the first of many, I bet), but nobody consults me on anything, so I zone out and watch the kids climb, swing, and run, hoping all the activity wears them out.

After a few minutes, Jet's legs twitch and fall farther open, and when I glance down at him, I see he's fallen asleep. Lucky guy. He looks so peaceful and sweet. While I'm fantasizing about how amazing it would feel to snuggle up to him for a nap of my own, I hear my name.

My head snaps up.

Gidget chuckles. "Sorry. Didn't realize you were off in your own world. I was just saying, it feels like we already know you, because we read so much about you and Jet online."

I wince. "Oh. Yeah. I guess that's kind of weird, isn't it?"

"Not as weird for us as it probably is for you," Lucy replies. "I'd feel so paranoid about leaving the house looking anything less than flawless. Like, I really admire that you're out here in jeans and a t-shirt with no makeup and your hair in a ponytail. What if someone takes a picture of Jet, and you're in it?"

Reflexively, I reach up and touch my face. "I— I'm wearing *some* makeup."

"You are? You look so natural! And don't get me wrong; you're adorable. But I couldn't pull that off. Keith makes fun of me, because I won't so much as go to the mailbox without a full face on."

Before I can say anything else on the topic, something catches Lucy's eye over my shoulder, and she says, "Oh, no. The kids are fighting again. Lands, I'm gonna end up killing them by the time this vacation's over." She stands and stomps toward the playground yelling a string of first, middle, and last names to let them know she's coming and means business.

Tammy sets the now-sleeping baby in a patch of shade on the blanket next to me and cranes her neck to see into the distance. "Uh-oh. Milo's crying now. Keep an eye on Teddy, will you?"

Gidget watches the scene unfold for a few seconds, then heaves herself to her feet. "They're all in it now. Better go mediate."

Left alone with Gloria, essentially, since the other two humans with us are sleeping, I shrug. "Never a dull moment, huh?"

"Don't let Lucy bother you. She's from Texas."

I chuckle at that explanation, appreciating the support.

"You're exactly the type of woman Jet needs in his life. A stable, grounding force. Not some bimbo trollop who's going to cheat on him and leave him for someone else on the team."

Huh?

Oblivious to my befuddlement, she plows on, "And it's nice that you have your own career. It displays an important sense of self and independence. But it's good that you're not too committed to it, since you won't be able to keep it forever."

I gulp, hardly able to believe what I'm hearing. "Okay. Thanks. I mean…" I scratch my head near the base of my ponytail. "Hm."

"Being the CEO of a brand like Jet Knox is a full-time job."

Blinking, I replay that sentence in my head and verify that, yes, she called her son a "brand." And put me in charge of "it."

I nervously chuckle and trace my finger along the pinstripes in the picnic blanket. "Well, he has people for all of that."

"None of them will be more important than you. *You'll* be his main person."

Past the lump in my throat, I say, "Wow. So. You've thought a lot about this, I can tell."

She shrugs and says, while watching the tableau on the playground, "I've worked hard to get my son to this point. I can't have all my hard work undermined by someone who doesn't take his gift seriously enough. He's better off alone than with the wrong person." She smiles down at me. "But the good news is, you would be perfect. I've told Jet that."

"Oh. Uh, great. Thanks."

"You're welcome. My opinion is important to him, especially since I was right about *that* woman. But she had him fooled, and he loved her, so he had to learn the hard way. He won't make that mistake again."

Oh. My. Gosh.

The mama's boy rolls onto his belly and turns his head sideways on his arms, his eyes fluttering open, followed by a sheepish smile. "Oops. Was I snoring?"

I shake my head, wishing my nausea would abate. When it

doesn't, though, I scramble to my feet and mumble, "I have to use the bathroom. Be right back." Putting some distance between myself and that blanket helps somewhat, so by the time I get to the cement block public toilet house, I'm no longer in danger of puking or hyperventilating. I use the facilities, wash my hands, and splash water on my face.

As I'm patting my cheeks, blotting my forehead, and swiping the mascara from under my eyes, Gidget enters the building with her oldest, Brianna.

"Bladder the size of a pea," she explains, pushing her daughter toward an open stall, before looking more closely at me.

I smile shakily.

"Uh-oh. What did Ma say?"

Instinctively, I shake my head. "Nothing. No. It's not—"

She tilts her head in a mannerism so reminiscent of Jet it makes me want to cry. "You're freaking out."

"It's nothing. I must have gotten too much sun."

"No, you were fine before we all left you alone with her. We agreed ahead of time not to let that happen, and here we've failed on the second damn day. I'm so sorry."

Brianna emerges from the stall and tries to run out without washing her hands. Gidget stops her and oversees the scrubbing before giving her daughter permission to return to the playground without us, since the path between here and there is in full view of our party.

Then Gidget leans against the sink, crosses her arms over her chest, and demands, "Tell me."

"It's all a little intense, that's all." I toss my damp paper towel at the trash hole in the counter. "A few months ago, my life was ridiculously simple. That's how I liked it. Now, I'm half of 'Jetaura.' A name I hate, by the way."

"Isn't it the worst? I guess it's better than Met or Jaura. But I wish those couple names would die a swift death. When I saw yours and Jet's, I actually said, 'Ew!' out loud."

I laugh, relieved amusement is still a possibility and grateful to Gidget for reawakening it. Riding that gratitude, I say, "I love your brother."

"That much is obvious."

"What's not to love, right?"

She chuckles. "Well, he's stubborn, spoiled rotten, and has a horrible memory. Don't expect him to ever remember your anniversary. You know, if it ever comes to that," she adds quickly.

"Yeah," I say to my shoes.

Snapping her fingers, she says, "That's it, isn't it? Ma's already married you off to him?"

I nod.

"That's just her way. She's been trying to offload him since college. Don't let her—or anyone—rush you. Marriage is a big commitment. Marriage to someone like my brother comes with a whole set of issues the rest of us don't have to worry about. It takes a special person to handle that. Only you know if you're that person."

"That's just it; I *don't* know."

"You'll figure it out. But don't let anyone else's opinions influence your self-assessment. Not Ma's, not the public's, not even Jet's. *You* have to make the decision based on what you know of yourself and how you feel about Jet."

Suddenly I don't want to talk about it anymore, especially not with this person I barely know. The fact that she's his sister makes it even more inappropriate. Blushing, I jam my hands in my pockets. "Gosh. I'm so sorry. This is weird. You shouldn't have to talk about your family like this to me. You hardly know me."

"I like you, Maura. We all do, for what it's worth."

"Thanks."

"You make Jet happy. We love that big goober."

"I do, too."

"Maybe that's good enough."

When I snort and shoot her a skeptical look, she pats my arm. "It might really be that simple. Why overthink it?"

TWENTY-THREE

DRAFT DAY DOUBTS

That disturbing conversation with Jet's mom hasn't been forgotten, but it's faded to something less significant, an overbearing mother looking out for her youngest child's best interests. I took Gidget's pep talk to heart and returned to the group feeling less shaky. For the rest of the family's week-long visit, I stayed busy at my worthy-yet-not-too-critical job during the day, and Gidget guaranteed I was never alone with Gloria again.

Two weeks after the family's departure, too many other critical issues vie for my attention for me to dwell on Gloria's plans for my future.

Like Draft Day.

Both Jet and I are trying valiantly to pretend it's not happening. Driving here straight from work, I decided to take advantage of unseasonably warm early May temperatures to spend some rare alone time by the pool. I haven't talked to Jet yet; he was finishing his evening workout when I arrived. I saw him through the kitchen window a few minutes ago, so he's probably making himself a smoothie and on his way out to sit with me. In the meantime, I study Internet stories and images of him, gathering ammunition for the reassurances I'll no doubt have to regularly toss his way if the Chiefs draft Nebraska Heisman finalist, Michael Wilcox, as his backup.

Fortunately, I'm finding plenty of material. The love affair between Jet and the fans is stronger than ever. A winner on and off the field, he's given the entire city something to cheer about. He's the franchise quarterback we've been craving for a depressingly long time. Even the usually acerbic radio cynics can't find anything wrong with him. Most importantly, Coach Dick Bauer is his biggest fan.

I participate in these frequent Internet searches to keep my finger on the pulse of public opinion. Their opinions of both Jet *and* me. They love Jet. Me? Well, it's overrated to be beloved, right? And it's not that they hate me; they just don't know me.

Plus, the person who threatens to take an eligible bachelor or bachelorette off the market is always going to be the target of some mean-spiritedness. For the most part, I don't take it too seriously. I read the stories, because I want to make sure nothing serious *is* being said. As long as they're focusing on my ugly clothes and my average looks, we're good. The ones who speculate about wedding bells stress me out more, but since most of the speculation is wildly off-target, I brush that off, too.

The back door opens, so I quickly close the tablet and set it on the table next to me. Torzi, sleeping between my feet, raises his head for a second but returns it to his paws when he recognizes his master. Torzi and I have grown closer since the Knox family invasion. I rescued him from the kids more than once, when their version of playing didn't gel with the Bichon's more genteel idea of fun.

Striding across the patio, a plastic cup in each hand, Jet offers me the one from his right, and I sniff it, relieved when it smells like run-of-the-mill lemonade. Yesterday, he brought me one of his muscle recovery smoothies. I have no clue what my muscles were supposed to be recovering from (sitting at a desk all day? Driving in rush-hour traffic, perhaps?), but the smoothie was disgusting. I didn't ask what was in it, because I was afraid the ingredients list might intensify my urge to purge.

After a few sips of my tart beverage, I ask Jet, "Do I want to know what's in your cup?" when he sets it down in the shade of his chair and whips off his shirt.

"Strawberry, banana, and peanut butter," he answers, kicking off his sports slides. "Want a sip?"

"No, thanks."

He laughs. "Fine. They're not that bad, once you get used to them. You have to learn to block out the taste of the protein powder."

Before I can retort, he tosses his shirt on his chair and walks to the pool, where he dives in, surfacing a few seconds later past the halfway mark. He rolls onto his back and kicks water toward me, but the splash doesn't come close to leaving the pool, much less reaching me. He grins, anyway. "You comin' in, or what?"

"Nah."

"Suit yourself," he replies casually, flipping to his belly and transitioning to a lazy freestyle. I watch him for several laps but eventually close my eyes, because studying the muscles in his shoulders and back is working me up. After a few minutes, he climbs the steps to exit the pool, walks straight over to my chair and shakes water droplets over Torzi and me, like an overgrown dog.

Torzi immediately runs to the house. Jet calls after him, "Aw, c'mon! You're no fun! Man's best friend, my ass."

"You're obnoxious," I say affectionately.

Crossing to the weather-proof cabinet that holds the towels, he chooses a fluffy red one and pats himself until he's no longer dripping but still damp. He retakes his seat on his lounge, crosses his ankles, and tilts his head back, closing his eyes. "That felt good."

"Rough day at the office?" I ask, half-joking.

"My boss is a Dick," he says, eyes still closed, then smiles, lowers his chin, and looks over at me. "How about you?"

"Spent the day pricing print shops for my Hollywood cut-outs. May have to scale back my plans." He winces, but I reassure him (and myself) before he goes into fix-it mode, "It's okay." Swiftly changing the subject, I say, "What's the latest gossip? Any off-season shenanigans that haven't been sniffed out yet by the media?"

Jet thinks about it for a second, as if debating whether to tell me. He squints across the sparkling surface of the pool. "Pete Jay and his wife are getting a divorce."

"What? No way!"

"Way." He nods solemnly.

"That's awful." Monica wasn't one of the friendliest wives at the Pro Bowl, so I never got chummy with her, but this may be an explanation for her subdued demeanor. It wasn't that long ago. Maybe things were already ending between the two of them. "What happened?"

He shrugs and gulps another swallow of smoothie, then licks his lips. "Who knows? I'm not that close with the guy. I see him a couple of times a year, but we're usually trying to kick each other's asses in a game, not sitting around talking about our feelings, you know?"

I manage a good-natured laugh but defend my question. "I thought maybe you'd heard more details in the rumor mill."

"Nope. Probably the usual, though. You don't get to be where that guy is without making sacrifices in other areas. He's not just one of the best QBs around; he's busy with a ton of things off the field. Endorsements, business partnerships, hosting *Saturday Night Live*..."

"Is that what you want?"

"No!" He bends his knee and rubs at a spot that's been bothering him lately. Then he reaches across the space between our chairs and grabs my free hand. "No. I don't. That's too much. I'm perfectly happy doing my job on the field and doing my work in the community, then coming home. To you."

I smile at his sweetness, despite its technical inaccuracy. For one thing, he has endorsements, too. And more offers every day. For another, he doesn't "come home" to me every day. I still have my own place and spend as many evenings there as I do here. That's how I'd like things to stay for now.

Steering us away from that volatile topic, however, I say, "I'm glad they didn't have kids. Makes things easier, I guess."

After setting down his smoothie, he grins and drops to all fours on the patio between our chairs, then bites the swimsuit tie at my hip.

"Hey!" I set down my drink to avoid spilling it on us.

He kneels beside me, nibbling on my shoulder strap. "Divorce talk is depressing."

"But it happens. Often."

"Everywhere. To everyone. Not just football players."

"Yeah, but certain lifestyles make marriage more difficult. You can't deny that."

That brings to mind Ginny and the nugget Gloria dropped

about her cheating on Jet, something he seems determined to keep from me forever. I haven't had the guts to broach the subject, and today, with all of its other distractions, doesn't seem like the right time, either.

He sighs. "See, this is why I didn't want to tell you."

"I would have found out eventually, and I would have been annoyed that you didn't tell me," I say, returning my attention to the Jays' situation.

"Which is why I ultimately did tell you." He kisses my throat. "Mmm. You smell like coconut."

I laugh. "You're the master of distraction."

"It's what makes my fake hand-off one of the best in the league."

"Oh really, now?"

He abruptly stops smooching on me and sits on the side of my chair. "I better stop before I can't," he says, certain physical evidence reinforcing his claim.

"Why would you want to? Rae said your silly abstinence rule was only in effect during the season."

Looking over his shoulder, he regards me for a few seconds, then sniffs. "It's not silly. What would Rae know about it?"

"You may ignore the trainers, but they're still around when you guys talk about that stuff."

"And she ran right to you to report on it, huh?"

"No, it came up naturally in conversation. She wanted me to be prepared to make plenty of my own sacrifices come September."

"Great. I appreciate her help." He returns to his own chair and shrugs back into his t-shirt, droplets on his shoulders soaking through and freckling the dark gray material.

"Don't be mad at her for telling me the truth. If it were up to you, I'd still be clueless about it."

"Everyone knows it's a thing."

I tilt down my chin and look at him over the top of my sunglasses. "I thought it was a myth. Because it's ridiculous."

"It's not."

"I was assured it was a regular season *thing* only."

"It is. I'm just not in the mood, okay?"

"Some parts of you didn't get the memo."

He rubs the top of his wet hair. "Stuff on my mind, that's all."

"And you can't think and split my uprights at the same time?"

We both laugh at the crassness of that euphemism, but he sobers and says, "Probably not. I'm not a good multitasker."

After a few seconds of silence, I ask, "Are you really going to abstain all season long? Not that I'm worried about it."

Justifiably smug, he grins at me. "You're worried."

"Four months is a long time! I have needs."

Tossing his head back, he laughs, then turns his head to look at the pool again and avoid my eyes as he replies, "I do, too. Trust me. But my job has to take priority." He bravely looks me in the eye when he makes that risky statement.

That's it. Time to officially launch *Operation: Regular Season Satisfaction.* "You know, *National Geographic* did an article about this—"

"What?" He snaps his towel at me. "Get the heck out of here. You've been researching it?"

"Yes! This is important to me."

"Did they compare us to chimps?"

"No! It was a legitimate study about athletes and sex and

how it affects testosterone levels and—consequently—aggression in contact sports, like football."

"And? Don't keep me in suspense."

"Use it or lose it, apparently. Sex *raises* testosterone levels. Like energy produces energy."

"Come off it."

I grab the tablet from the table. "I'm not making this up!" In a matter of seconds, I've navigated to the article. I hand the device to him.

"You have it bookmarked? Holy shit." He looks down at the screen and skims the story. "Ha! They say there wasn't anything conclusive about *psychological* effects in the study."

"So?"

"It's a mental game almost as much as a physical one."

"But if the physical part isn't harmed by sex, and the rest is all up here"—I tap my head—"then it's a matter of changing the way you think. We can work on that."

"It's not worth it." When all I do is glare at him hard enough to singe every hair from his body, he qualifies, "Whoa, that came out wrong. What I'm trying to say is that I'm not going to be able to change fifteen years of thinking based on one article."

"Oh, I have plenty more where that came from. Maybe Pete and Monica needed to have more sex."

He hands the tablet back to me. "Pete Jay's sex life is none of my business. But I've developed a system for *me*. It works. And if something ain't broke, you don't fix it."

"Is making yourself puke before games part of your awesome, unbroken system?"

"Damn it, Rae," he curses under his breath.

Before his annoyance turns into a full-blown pout, I journey from my chair to his. Stretching myself between him and the arm of his lounger, I kiss his chin. "I told Rae I still love you, in spite of your gross pre-game habit. Don't be mad."

"I'm not."

I poke at his mouth with my index finger. "Your lips are all white and pinchy, like they get when you have to throw the ball away on third down."

"I'm about to tickle you."

"Oh, now. Don't waste your testosterone on such silliness."

He wedges himself sideways to get a better angle at my midriff, but his action throws off the weight balance of the chair, which tips us onto the stamped concrete patio, me on top of him, the chair on top of both of us.

We're both laughing too hard to say anything (or get up) right away, but I recover first and say, "Oh, crap. Are you okay?"

He smiles into my face. "Yes. Are you?"

Before I can answer, his phone rings on the table above us. A few seconds later, mine competes for attention. Soon, a new, more insistent chime sounds from Jet's cell. It's a noise I've never heard before, but his slackened face tells me he knows exactly what it means, and it ain't good.

"What the hell is that?"

Gently, he pushes the lounger away from us and slides out from under me. After offering me a hand up, he rights the chair and looms over his phone, staring at it for a few seconds before prodding it with his pointer finger, as if it's a small, dead animal that may be diseased.

My phone rings again, but I barely glance at the lit-up screen long enough to see it's my dad. I figure I can call him back.

Jet cranes his neck to read the latest notification to come through. "Well, I have a new backup."

My phone continues its frenetic activity, this time with an incoming call from Rae. I blindly reach over, reject the call, and push away the device. "Big whoop. These people act like nobody's ever drafted a quarterback before. You're not worried, are you?"

"Nah. I'm in good shape; I know the playbook inside and out; Coach loves me; and the guys respect me as a leader. There's no controversy here. People just like drama." But the confidence in his voice isn't mirrored in his eyes.

Damn it. I wish I'd thought to turn off our phones earlier.

He scrolls through the first of many comment threads about the breaking news. Resigned, I slide on my shorts, gather the rest of my things, and head for the house.

"Hey, where you going?" he calls after me without looking up.

"Inside," I toss over my shoulder. "There's some leftover chocolate cake calling my name."

————

By the time Jet follows me into the house, his phone is nestled in his t-shirt pocket, and I'm sitting on the kitchen counter, next to the sink, licking cake and frosting from a fork. I load up the next bite and offer it to him.

"No thanks. I have to be a good boy."

"Overrated," I muffle around a mouthful of chocolate.

"You're a bad influence," he says, scooting up to me and settling between my knees. He kisses my mouth and dips his tongue in.

After I pull away, laughing, I say, "You're still technically consuming the cake, even if I've chewed it first."

"Nope. There are no calories in food from someone else's mouth. It's science."

"It's disgusting."

"No, delicious." He runs his tongue along his teeth.

I swallow. "I'm sorry about the Draft pick."

With a mighty, cocoa-scented exhale, he says, "Not you, too."

"I'm not looking for drama where there is none. If I thought you didn't care, I'd leave it be." I set aside the rest of the cake and tuck my hands in my armpits while I wait for him to reply.

Instead of doing so right away, he picks up the dessert, steps back from me, and shovels cake into his mouth.

Oh, crap. It's worse than I thought.

After several bites, he stops and tosses the now-empty container and fork into the sink, as if appalled at himself. He wipes his mouth with the back of his hand, jams his fists onto his hips and says at the floor, "Fuck. I— Why do they need that guy, huh?"

"They don't."

"But they obviously think they do. Or why draft him?"

"Insurance."

He looks up. "I hate that I'm threatened by that. When am I going to stop feeling like I'm everyone's second choice, like I'm a placeholder for when someone better comes along?"

Gripping the edge of the counter, I look down at my knees.

"Maybe I wasn't upset enough when we lost that playoff game," he speculates. "But I *was* upset. I just didn't think it served anything to mope about it. And I had you. And I-I was too happy and hopeful to be sad or mad about it. I thought it made more sense to move on and look ahead to next season. But maybe I moved on too soon. Maybe the coaches and the front office and the guys, maybe they think I don't want it enough, that I'm satisfied with making it to the playoffs and getting our asses handed to us. But I'm not."

"Nobody thinks you are."

He shakes his head and looks down at his feet.

"C'mere," I implore him. When he shuffles back in front of me, I put one hand on each shoulder and squeeze, locking his eyes with mine. "You're amazing. You *are* the franchise's quarterback. This kid is exactly that: a kid. They're going to be counting on you to show him what you know so that one day, when *you're* no longer interested in the job, they have someone to take over seamlessly, someone who learned from one of the best at the peak of his career."

He ducks his head.

I run my fingers through his hair. "And you're not *my* second choice. I'm not waiting for anyone better to come along."

His chin lifts.

Suddenly terrified, I bob my head once to underscore what I've said.

His eyes soften. "Aw, Maura." He parts my lips with his.

"Now, *you* taste like chocolate," I say after a few languid seconds.

He lifts me from the counter and carries me from the kitchen. "You taste like heaven."

TWENTY-FOUR

CHIEF AND CHEF

Three weeks later, Jet invites me over for dinner. Because of his training schedule, we haven't seen each other for days, which is just as well, because one of those days coincided with Arnold's spring job fair, and I was busy with setup, execution, and tear-down. We've both had exhausting weeks, so I'm surprised when I arrive to find Jet in the kitchen, cooking.

"Where's Beau?" I ask him after a lazy hello kiss.

"Not here," he answers with a wink. "Why? Do you need to talk to him about something? Exchange recipes? Ask him his opinion on gluten?"

"No, I—" Torzi trots into the room and stretches himself to his full length along my leg, nudging at my knee with his cold nose. I scratch absently at his furry mop of a head. "I didn't know you could cook."

Jet grins. "I can't."

"Oh."

"Don't look so scared. My mom walked me through it. She promised I couldn't screw it up."

He dumps the boiling pasta into a colander in the sink,

then gives the strainer a firm shake. I admire the muscles in his forearms, sticking out from the rolled-up sleeves of his light purple dress shirt. Based on the shirt and his dark dress pants, belt, and shoes, he hasn't been home for long, although I don't remember him mentioning any meetings after practice, especially none that required dressing up.

"You look nice," I say, fishing for information.

"Thanks," After dumping the drained pasta back in the pot, he blots sweat from his forehead with the towel draped over his shoulder.

Okay, then. Must not be that exciting.

"So, what is this foolproof dish you've prepared so lovingly for me?"

"Spaghetti and meatballs."

I suck my upper lip into my mouth and bite down on it.

He laughs. "Okay, it's something a third-grader can probably make, but I never learned to cook. Never had to. I made the meatballs from scratch, using Mom's recipe, so it's not like I tossed a jar of store-bought sauce in a pan and called it good."

Putting up my hands in a soothing gesture, I say, "I'm not judging." I glance into the dining room and emit a low whistle at the sight of the crystal, silver, and china sparkling in the candlelight. "You went all out in there!"

His ears redden. "I thought you deserved a little extra effort tonight. I haven't been very attentive lately."

"I've been too busy—and tired—to care."

"That doesn't make it okay." He removes the large pot of bubbling red sauce from the gas range and sets it on a hot pad on the counter. "Why don't you take off your shoes and relax at the table while I fix our plates in here? The wine's already been poured."

"If you're sure you don't need help…"

"Nah. I've got it. I think. Probably. I'll be less nervous if you're not watching me."

I laugh at his self-consciousness, the likes of which I haven't seen since those heady days after our first date. "Okay. Call me if you need me."

With Torzi on my heels, I walk into the dining room and take the seat obviously intended for me, with the long-stem red rose strategically straddling the pewter charger. "Ooh, là là." Torzi jumps onto the chair next to me and sits primly as if awaiting his own service. I kick off my shoes under the table and hold the flower to my nose.

Hm. Smells like a rose.

I twitch my schnoz, then offer the bloom to the dog for his own inspection. He sniffs and sneezes.

"Pretty much," I say, setting the flower on the table, out of the way. "It's the romantic thought that counts, though, right?"

"Are you guys talking about me in there?" Jet calls from the kitchen.

"Nope. Just taking time to smell the rose."

He enters the room with plates lined on his arms, like a seasoned waiter. I hop up to help him set everything on the table.

"Wow. That's a ton of food."

"You don't have to eat it all. I think my mom's recipe feeds twenty."

Or his two brothers.

I filter at the last second and retake my seat, inhaling the fragrant steam coming from the pile of pasta, sauce, and meat in my shallow bowl. Jet places a small plate of salad next to each of our bowls and a basket of Italian bread chunks in the middle of the table, next to the butter dish, then stands back.

"I think that's it," he says but remains standing next to the chair at the head of the table, catty-corner from mine.

I wait while he shifts from foot-to-foot. He leans over and spins the bread basket a quarter turn.

Keeping my eyes on him while unfurling my napkin in my lap, I ask, "Are you okay?"

"Yeah," he answers distractedly, still focused on the bread. "I want it to be perfect, that's all."

"Well, I'm starving and tired, so it doesn't need to be perfect."

He finally lowers himself into his chair, but he steeples his hands over his bowl and stares at me.

"Umm," I say. "Am I supposed to say something?"

He nods at my food. "Take a bite and tell me what you think."

I'm afraid; very afraid. It smells good enough, but what if it's awful? What if it's the worst thing I've ever tasted? I stare down the giant meatball in the center of my mountain of spaghetti noodles and swallow tightly. "Uh, okay. Let me cut into this gigantic ball o' meat."

"Yeah, sorry about that. I guess I didn't take into account that my 'handful' would be a lot bigger than my mom's."

I'm relieved when I cut the meatball and it not only falls away tenderly, but the meat inside is cooked through. "Okay. Here goes," I say, pretending my trepidation is fake. I dip the beef chunk in some sauce and deliver it to my mouth, expecting the worst. My shoulders relax when I'm able to shoot him a sincere smile and say after swallowing, "Excellent."

"Yeah?" He lifts his own fork, finally brave enough to see for himself.

Torzi whines next to me.

I send him a sympathetic glance. "Sorry, bud. I don't think so."

Jet swallows his first bite, then points his fork at the dog. "Go," he commands.

After a protesting growl-grunt, the dog does as he's told, prancing off in a huff.

"He wasn't hurting anything," I say, taking a sip of wine.

He rolls his shoulders, as if trying to loosen up. "I'd prefer to be alone with you, without him making his wise-ass comments over there."

I laugh and reach for the piece of bread balanced on top of the other slices in the basket. Jet freezes, mid-chew, and watches my hand. I snatch the slice and playfully clutch it to my chest. "What? Did you want this piece?"

He smiles sickly. "No."

Wondering what his problem is, I say coyly, "Because it's mine. If you want it, you'll have to come over here and get it from me."

His eyes flicker back to the table. I follow his nervous glance. That's when I see the corner of the baby blue cube peeking from the center of the basket.

The piece of bread in my hands tumbles into my lap and bounces onto the floor. Torzi swoops in, snatches the dropped food, and sprints away with his scavenged goods.

Neither Jet nor I take our eyes off the bread basket.

"What's—" I finally manage, pointing at the blue box. "Is that— Wh… what is that?"

His hand shakes when he reaches to lift the basket from the table and holds it in front of me. When I make no move to pluck the Tiffany ring box from its yeasty nest, he does it himself. Dropping to his knee next to my chair, he pries the squeaky lid open, revealing a huge diamond-and-platinum engagement ring.

"Maura, I love you. I had a whole speech planned out to say when I gave you this, but now I can't remember any of it. I do remember I'm supposed to ask you one question, though: will you marry me?"

If I keep staring at that giant rock, I won't have to look at his face. Or into his eyes. So, I keep staring at the ring.

Finally, when I can't possibly get away with staying silent, I breathe out and say sadly, "Oh, Jet."

He shifts on his knee, which pops. "That's not exactly the tone I was hoping you'd use when you saw this." He runs his tongue along his teeth. "In fact, that sounds—"

I look away, at the wooden floor next to his knee. He bends farther, trying to make eye contact, but he'd have to lie down to achieve it.

I mumble, "Not yet. Not now."

Closing the box with a snap, he pockets it and returns to his chair, his hands on either side of his plate, which he seems to be studying, as if a decent explanation is in the noodles. "Not yet," he repeats.

I cover one of his hands with mine, but he yanks it away.

"Not never, either," I say. "Just—"

"When?"

My mind races. "Well, I don't know. But we've only been together for four months!"

"Closer to five. Our first date was at the beginning of January. It's almost June."

"Okay, whatever."

"Not 'whatever,' Maura." He finally looks up at me, but I

wish he'd look back down. I wish I could look away. "I love you, and you say you love me—"

"I do! It's not like I've been lying about it. I do love you."

"Then I don't understand. Who cares how many months we've been together? I already know I want to spend the rest of my life with you." He pinches at his eyes. "Aw, damn. That was part of what I was supposed to say when I opened the ring box."

"And that's lovely, but I'm not as sure about 'forever' as you are. I'm not as sure about *anything* as you are."

He drops his hand, revealing reddened eyes. "I've been waiting. I've been patient. I've been trying not to shout proposals at you for months. But lately, you've said some things that made me think you were ready. Still, I waited some more, to be safe. But you're still telling me no?"

"No! Not 'no.'"

"But not 'yes.'"

"Not *yet*." I gesture toward his bulging pocket. "That ring... It's a perfect example of what makes me unsure about all of this."

He digs it from his pants and opens the box, looking down at the glimmering jewel. "What's wrong with it?"

"Probably nothing. Technically. But it's ginormous!"

"So? I spent one month's salary, like they say."

That one bite of meatball is about to stage a comeback for the ages. "No, you didn't. Tell me you didn't."

"Yes, I did! Because you're worth that and so much more."

I cross to the windows and pull the curtains closed, despite the fact that Jet has no nearby neighbors, and his house isn't visible from the road. "Put it away."

"What's your deal?" He sets the open box on the table between us.

I jab a finger at it. "You think I'm going to wear a ring that costs the equivalent of one month of *your* salary?"

"I was hoping, but obviously that's not happening."

"When that stupid marketing campaign came out about spending a month's salary on forever, or whatever the hell they said, they were speaking to guys who make 50K a year, not twelve mil."

"See? Everyone knows my personal business. You spouted off that figure like it's your social security number."

"It was in the papers constantly after your last contract negotiation."

"Well, I have no idea how much *you* make."

"Forty-five thousand and change. Before taxes."

"Am I supposed to feel bad about that?"

"No! But you need to understand the huge difference between your reality and mine."

Resting one hand on the side of his face, he plunks his elbow in his other hand and rubs his ring finger against his lower lip. "I hate talking about money; it makes me uncomfortable. Money has nothing to do with my wanting to marry you."

"Well, it has a fair bit to do with why I'm not ready to marry *you*."

He drops his hands to his sides and thrusts his upper body forward. "Because I'm too rich? That's idiotic."

"Thanks."

"You already called *me* stupid for spending so much on your ring."

"That's not my ring. Which is what I've been trying to explain, if you'll let me."

With a quick poke of his finger, he closes the Tiffany box with a thwack, nudging it away from us, toward the other side of the table. Then he crosses his arms over his chest. "I'm waiting. Again. As usual."

With extreme effort, I ignore that dig and go back to my original point. "You think you know me, but that ring proves you don't. I could *never* wear that ring."

"Fine! I'll get you a different ring. I'll get you a glass piece of shit from a gumball machine, if that will make you happy. What do you want from me, Maura? Because all *I* want is to make you happy."

I fish my shoes out from under the table and slip my feet into them. Standing, I say, "You're hurt and upset, and I'm not going to be able to get you to understand where I'm coming from tonight."

"I *do* understand, more than you do," he says hotly, standing too. "You're rejecting me out of habit. You can't control how you feel about me, and since it scares you, you run away any time there's talk of making us permanent."

"You're wrong."

"No, I'm not."

"Yes, you are! I don't think it's *possible* to make us permanent. That's what scares me, okay? This... this *relationship* is unsustainable in so many ways, most of all because you don't see that."

He blinks, opens and closes his mouth a couple of times, and finally says in a near-whisper, "I don't know what you're talking about."

I droop. "That's part of what I love so much about you. You think anything is possible. That's amazing. But it's also incredibly frustrating. And intimidating."

"So I can't win."

Exasperated, I drop my chin to my chest and shake my head. "It's not about winning."

"And you're also not saying 'not yet.' You're really saying, 'never.' You just don't have the guts to say it to me right now."

As my blood pressure rises, so does my chin. "Don't have the guts, huh?"

"No." He jabs his fists against his hips, his elbows sticking out from his sides. "I don't think you do."

I chuckle mirthlessly. "Hm. Let's see if I can find the guts to tell you how I'm really feeling, then."

He smacks himself on the chest. "Lay it on me, babe. I'm a big boy. I can take it."

I roll my eyes. "Okay, for a start, maybe I don't want to be married to someone who's gone all the time. Maybe I don't want to live here at Fort Knox, rattling around the empty rooms. Maybe I don't want to be the CEO of the Jet Knox 'brand.' Maybe I don't want my appearance to be criticized every time I leave my house. Maybe I don't want to be married to a titty baby who pouts every time he doesn't get his way. Maybe I don't want to go without sex for four months straight because my husband thinks it's bad juju to ejaculate during the football season!"

My heart pounds while I wait for him to react, but he simply gapes, nostrils flared. Finally, he blinks rapidly, but he still says nothing.

Already regretting ninety percent of what I've said, I rub my temples. "Jet. I'm sorr—"

"Whatever." He turns away from me and starts clearing our congealing plates from the table.

"No, I—"

"You should go home. I want to be alone."

"But—"

"Just leave, Maura!"

Even though I was ready to go voluntarily a few minutes

ago, it hurts to be kicked out. Tears stinging my nose, throat, and eyes, I say, "Okay, but I'm sorr—"

"No." He closes his eyes. "Don't. I don't want to hear any apologies or see your pity."

With that, he exits the room and begins loudly and not-so-gently "doing" the dishes.

I let myself out.

TWENTY-FIVE

BRIDESMAID BLUES

I've been dreading this day since Greg and Deirdre announced their engagement two years ago and asked me to be one of Deirdre's bridesmaids. Their wedding has been every bit as tedious as I feared. The only person having a worse day than I am is Deirdre's sister, the matron of honor, who has to wait on the demanding bride, God help her.

Detachment is what I need, but that tends to make me stare off into space and incur the Wrath of D, so I've tried to strike a balance between awareness and indifference. I'm living for the moment when the happy couple drives to the airport to catch the plane to their honeymoon, and I'm free to go home, soak in the tub, and take all of these pins out of my hair, releasing the elaborate updo that's been giving me a headache all day.

Just a few more hours.

Jet informed me via text the day after I rejected his proposal that he suddenly had a scheduling conflict with today's ceremony. In the week since then, there's been absolutely no contact from him. I've been afraid to initiate communication, because what if I call him or text him, and that opens the door for him to officially break up with me? Not knowing for sure what's going on has been horrible; knowing for sure —if he's decided I'm a waste of his time—would be worse.

So I've tried to pretend like everything's normal. Only it's been far from it. It's not normal for my phone to sit mostly silent throughout the day or for me to jump and run to it every time it makes the slightest noise, only to be disappointed when it's a just a text from Rae or Colin or my parents or the most demanding bride and groom in the universe. It's not normal to get notifications about Jet's movements that make no mention of me. Or worse, stories that mention my sudden absence and gleefully speculate about the demise of our relationship. It's not normal for me to sleepwalk through my work day, wishing everyone would just leave me alone. It's not normal for me to lie awake at night, crying until my eyes swell shut, my snot production kicks into overdrive, my throat aches, and my head pounds.

It's not normal for me to care this much.

Being so self-absorbed on Greg and Deirdre's special day sucks, too, but Greg's less-than-sympathetic reaction last night to the news that Jet wouldn't be here today makes me feel justified in my selfishness. As if I'm not dealing with enough, he chewed me out at the rehearsal dinner, going on and on about "Deirdre's numbers" and the stress of both of their houses selling at once (serves him right!) and having to move as soon as they get back from their honeymoon. Since I can't do anything about most of his beefs, I focused on what I could control and reassured him the seating chart would be fine, because Colin agreed to step in as my date, in Jet's stead.

Nobody could take Jet's place, though. (Duh. As if I didn't already know that.) Away from the other attendees, Greg hissed, "The city's most eligible bachelor asks you to marry him, and you turn him down? What the hell is wrong with you?"

It's a valid question. I've had a lot of time to contemplate it—or any number of closely related queries. I think I've figured it out, too, and it has very little to do with a million-dollar ring that needs its own bodyguard or any of that other stuff I spewed at Jet when he shoved that thing under my nose. Sure, those things matter and contribute to a larger whole, but they're also surface. After a week of tearful soul-searching, I have a much better handle on the deeper problem. Problems.

Now, I need to work up the nerve to call him and explain.

The blaring organ startles me from my deep introspection. I've missed The Kiss (I'm okay with that), and it's time to reverse process and take our places in the receiving line. Joy. I make a private bet with myself that I'll hear no fewer than a dozen instances of, "Your turn next!" from well-meaning relatives who have no idea what else to say to me.

As I turn to inch my way toward the center aisle, where I'll have to take the sweaty arm of Deirdre's nerdy cousin, Kevin, I catch sight of Colin, who gives me a campy wink and thumbs-up from his seat in the same row as my parents. I smile at his encouragement.

I'm still smiling, in spite of the sweaty arm under my hand, when, making my way toward the back of the church with Sweat Hog, I see him. Standing in the third-to-last row, on the aisle. In his big-and-tall suit and the green tie that matches his eyes so perfectly. With his carefully combed hair and his clean-shaven face. Wearing a sheepish smile. Mouthing, *"Love you."*

I drop Kevin's arm like I've been caught cheating. He

glances over at me and utters something I can't hear, but I wave him on without me and stop at Jet's row.

"You came," I blurt, standing in front of him like a simpleton.

He laughs, then glances toward the rest of the wedding party. "Yeah. Uh, you better get in line there, Richards, before Coach D notices you're out of formation."

"But you showed up." I fling my arms around his neck and hug him, then quickly let go. "Don't go anywhere!" I point at him with my fussy bouquet as I short-step away in my tight dress, toward the receiving line. "I'll be right back."

"Right back" turns out to be nearly thirty minutes later, by the time every wedding guest has gone through the line and I've told my family I'll catch up to them at the hotel that's hosting the reception.

Exactly where I left him, as commanded, Jet slides down the now-empty pew to make room for me and my swooshing taffeta.

"Hey there, Beautiful," he greets me. "You look amazing."

"Thanks. I'm miserable. But better now that I've seen you. Were you here the whole time?"

"Yep. Saw you walk down the aisle and everything."

I press my hand to my forehead. "I've been so out of it. I can't believe I didn't see you!"

He pulls my hand to his lips. "Maura, I'm sorry," he says against my knuckles. Lowering our hands to his lap, he continues, "About everything. About yelling at you; about pressuring you; about pouting when you didn't say 'yes'; about giving you the silent treatment all week. About that ridiculous ring. What was I thinking?"

I chuckle through my sniffles.

He looks up at me. "Aw, man. Don't cry. I… I let my disappointment and hurt pride get the better of me, and I completely ignored the fact that you were hurt, too, and I was being a selfish jerk."

"I'm okay."

"And I'm so sorry my reaction to what you told me was to break commitments—and dishes."

I wipe under my eyes before my makeup slides down my face. "Yeah. I may have heard that last thing."

He winces. "It was mega-childish. And messy."

"I'm sorry, too. Some of the things I said were horrible."

"I was baiting you. You didn't tell me anything I didn't already know."

"The way I said it was inexcusable, though."

"I forgive you. Do you forgive me?"

Nodding, I rasp, "Of course. I'm sorry I'm not ready."

"You can't help that." He traces his finger along a seam in my dress.

After a bracing breath, I say, "You know, you were partly right about one thing." I thread my fingers through his and look down at our joined hands. "I do run away from commitment and responsibility out of habit. While there are some practical things you and I will need to discuss before we ever stand in a church like this one and say vows before God and everyone, the biggest thing holding me back is plain old fear."

"There's nothing to be afraid of, Maura. I'll never hurt you. You'll never regret—"

I look up and place my finger against his lips. "Shh. Listen to me for a second. I'm not afraid of any of that." Gulping spasmodically, I suddenly worry I can't say it without breaking down. But I have to say it, no matter what.

"I already feel like less than a whole person," I say, my chin wrinkling and the corners of my mouth tugging downward. "I always have, like I'm not justifying my existence on this planet. I'm just taking up space."

I pause to clear my throat, trying to loosen the tightness threatening to choke me. "It terrifies me to think I could become your wife and spend my days being an even bigger waste. Like, at least now, I'm a contributing member of society. I have a job, where I help people, and I pay taxes. You know?" My eyes fill and overflow. I look down at my lap.

He cups his huge hand on the back of my neck.

"What will be my purpose?" I wail nearly incoherently what I've been thinking so often all week. "What will be the point of me? To be on some stupid NFL Hottest Wives and Girlfriends List?" I stop short when it hits me I wouldn't even qualify, considering my competition.

"Those lists are bullshit." He cringes at himself and says toward the cross at the front of the sanctuary, "Oops. Sorry, Jesus." Returning his attention to me, he moves his hand from my neck to my upper arm and pulls me tighter to his side. "I see us doing all kinds of great things together.

I twist at the waist and look fully into his eyes. "I don't, though. And that scares me. I see you traveling all the time and me sitting in an empty house, watching movies. Or next to the pool with Torzi, reading stupid celebrity gossip magazines."

"Torzi can't read. And what about your job? You'll still have that to keep you plenty busy."

Gloria's face flashes through my mind, but I shake her away in time to hear the following nugget fall from Jet's mouth: "Then you'll be the mother of our children, which will definitely be a full-time job."

I choke-hiccup on a sob and break down again, covering my face.

"Oh, no. What's the matter?" He wraps me in a full-on hug, crushing my arms between us.

I push away so I can look at him. This difficult revelation requires eye contact. "Jet, I... I'm not sure I want kids."

His swallow is both visible and audible. "None? Ever?"

Shaking my head, I answer, "No." Then louder, "I don't know. Maybe not. The responsibility freaks me out."

"It should. Most people take it too lightly."

"It's more than that, though. I get panicky thinking about it. The whole thing. Pregnancy, childbirth, parenting. Alone." My breathing speeds up in direct proportion with my racing thoughts and tumbling words.

He hugs me again. "Hey. *Shhh.* We don't have to talk about any of that right now."

"It's important to you, though. You love kids and want your own someday. You made that clear on our first date. So it's only fair that I'm upfront with you about this, because"—I choke but manage—"I know it's a deal-breaker if I *don't* want them."

His hands encircle my upper arms. Gently, he pushes me away and searches my face. "Deal-breakers are for first dates and casual acquaintances. I'm so past the point of deal-breakers with you, it's not even funny."

"You are?"

He nods and half-smiles. "Oh, yeah. You'd have to tell me you've decided to become a Raiders fan. Still probably not a deal-breaker."

"Gosh. Well. You never have to worry about *that.*"

"See? You're stuck with me." He swipes a straggling tear from my face with the back of his hand. "They're going to wonder what I did to you when we show up at that reception."

I straighten and gasp. "Oh, crap! The reception!" Standing, I pull on his hand. "We have to go. Poor Colin. I've abandoned him. But I couldn't find him after he went through the receiving line."

"He told me he was going home," Jet tells me, standing and stretching. "Said he enjoyed the 'good weep' he got from the ceremony, but mentioned something about his 'pipe and slippers.' Does that mean anything to you?"

I crack up. "Yes. That's his way of saying he's spending the night in."

He offers me his crooked elbow in the middle of the aisle. "Then shall we?"

Threading my arm through his, I say, "Yeah," but I hold him in place when he tries to walk toward the sanctuary's exit.

Bemusement brightening his eyes, he backtracks and asks, "What are you doing?" Bending at the knees to bring his eyes level with mine, he swipes his thumbs along my lower lids, then rubs the mascara residue with the sides of his index fingers. "There. All better."

Rising on my tiptoes, I brush my lips against his. "I'd love to marry you someday. I think."

"I'm here when you're ready. You're worth waiting for." He wraps his arms around my back and gathers me against him, lifting me off the ground as he lowers his mouth onto mine.

TWENTY-SIX

SCANDAL

Early September isn't technically autumn and doesn't even feel like it here in Kansas City, but we trick ourselves into believing the mornings are cooler, the sun is a bit mellower, and the days are slightly shorter, all hallmarks of the best time of year. Because football is on its way.

The city buzzes. The fountains flow red. The Chiefs flags fly. Tailgaters dust off their hibachis, shake out their banners, freshen up their skin paints, stock up on booze, and practice their trash-talk. Stats and projections zip over Internet, TV, and radio lines. Hopes run high.

"This is the year," fans declare without a hint of doubt. "Knox and Busch are the best duo in the league. The running game is strong, making us unpredictable. Our offensive line has never looked better, thanks to free agency and Draft pick-ups. Our defense is stout. Our kicker is the clutchest of clutch. This is it! See you at the Super Bowl, suckers!"

We've already primed ourselves for action with four preseason games, mostly serving as a final try-out for second-stringers and practice team hopefuls. But now we're ready for the real deal.

It was an amazing summer, and I'm sad to see it go. Between training camps, fall job fair preps, and a mini-vacation to the Gulf Coast for a long weekend, it was busy but happy. And over in a flash.

Now, we're on the brink of another NFL season. Surviving those sixteen weeks (seventeen, including the bye), plus possible postseason play in January and early February, will be the ultimate test of my relationship with Jet, to date, and a rehearsal for the rest of our lives.

When I think of it that way, it's a bit daunting. But that's what this season is. And I'm not going to lie. I'm worried.

I roll over and bury my face in Jet's pillow, inhale his scent, and moan. He left for the training facility for his first day of regular season practice a while ago. I need to get up and get ready for work, since I have a long commute this morning. Thanks to our final off-season sleepover, though, my limbs don't seem to want to work in concert. They don't want to give up this feeling. The moment I move, the sex drought official begins.

Of course, that's the least of my worries. I'm focusing on that like a horny teenager because it's easier to make sex the scapegoat for everything than deal with the real challenges, which are plentiful. There are so many other what ifs, enough that without the "love" factor, I would have bolted a long time ago. Too many variables exist that could lead to failure. We all know I'd rather not try at all than try and not succeed. It's what's kept me in this town and has served as the theme for my entire adult life.

What Jet and I have is too important to play it safe, though. Walking away will require outright defeat. Because the horror of living without him outweighs my usual crippling fear of failure. That's scary enough in itself. I've never cared about another person (not related to me) that much. Especially not a man.

If this doesn't work out, I'm finished with romantic entanglements. I'm going to take a page from Colin's playbook and fondly remember my one true love but never go there again.

In the meantime, while I'm still in the game, it's important to stay focused on the important things. Scratching my various carnal itches isn't one of those important things. Not really, in the grand scheme of things.

What *is* important, at least in Jet's world, is that the first match of the regular season is a less than a week away. It's an away game in Miami, but that doesn't dampen our spirit; it simply heightens the anticipation for the Week Two home opener, a prestigious Monday night rematch against the Patriots.

GO CHIEFS!

At that rousing thought, I drag myself from the warm, tousled sheets and stagger to the shower on weak legs. I may not be in the strategy meetings or out on the practice field or treating injuries, but I'm still a member of the team. An important member. I'll be providing emotional support, in both victory and defeat.

My spine straightens, and my chest inflates. Under the hot stream, I strengthen physically and mentally. I can do this. I can *be* this.

I'm also about to be seriously late for work.

Dressing in the clothes I brought with me last night, I grab my purse and rush downstairs to the kitchen, where I pour coffee into a giant stainless steel travel mug and snatch a scone from the kitchen. With a quiet "See ya" to Beau—it's still awkward to encounter "staff members" first thing in the morning, especially when so freshly sated—I run to my car to drive back to reality.

———

About halfway through my second appointment of the day, my purse starts making noise on its door hook.

My client half-turns to see where the dings and beeps originate, so I blush and say, "So sorry. I forgot to silence my phone this morning. As I was saying about these prospects…"

But Rae's tinny ringtone blares next. Then Jet's.

Mortified—and somewhat worried—I jump from my chair, round my desk, and cross to the door, where I reach into my handbag and blindly silence the device, breathlessly apologizing once more to my clearly put-out guest, a first-timer who has no idea how unusual this is. *Way to make a great first impression, Maura.*

Returning to my desk, I waste no more time on excuses or apologies but get back to business. I devote my full attention to the woman looking for a paralegal position for her first job after five years out of the workforce as a stay-at-home mom for her son, now a kindergartner.

After sending her on her way with three referrals to large law firms, I greet my next client. My phone beckons me from my purse, but I can't satisfy my curiosity right now. I have a jam-packed schedule until lunch. Whatever Jet and Rae want will have to wait. Knowing them, they're bickering about something and trying to drag me into the middle of it. I can't justify neglecting my clients to indulge their childishness.

Finally, lunchtime arrives. I close my office door and retrieve my phone from my purse. While crunching on carrots and apple slices (recent online speculation about my "baby bump" has spurned a healthy eating phase that might last the week, if I'm particularly disciplined), I view my mile-long notifications list with wide eyes. I skip the stuff from the feeds and go straight to my waiting text messages. But all of them, from both Rae and Jet, are terse variations of, *Call me when you get this,* so I dial into my voicemail, holding the phone slightly away from my ear, as if afraid of what's going to come out.

The first recorded message is from Rae, whispering, *"Uh, shit's happening. Have you heard anything from Jet? Call me."*

Jet's next. *"Hey, it's me. You've probably already heard the news, but I'll call you again when I get a chance. They're bringing us together for another meeting before the press conference, so I have to turn off my phone. But I'll try to call after that. If I'm allowed. Whatever. Love you."*

What. The. Hell?

Rae: *"Okay, so is this effed up, or what? I can't talk specifics, but we just had a meeting with* everyone, *and it's not good. I could probably get fired for calling you, but what the heck was that guy thinking? Idiot! I've never liked him, but everyone puts up with his bullshit, because he wins games. Jet's face was scary during the meeting. We're not allowed to talk about it here, though. Are you under a gag order, too? Call me, text me,* something."

Jet: *"They're sending us home early, since we can't get anything done here with the media crawling all over the place. I'm worried you haven't gotten in touch, but maybe you're busy? Coach's press conference is next. Then we have one more debriefing so they can tell us— again—not to talk to anyone. What a mess. See you later?"*

For the first time ever, I wish I had a TV in my office. A quick scroll through the feed notifications on my phone tells me Keaton Busch is the "idiot" at the center of whatever this is, but I'd have to click on the link to get the full story, and

I'm somewhat afraid of what I'll find when I do that. Obviously, I'm about to be disappointed, but not surprised, by yet another of my favorite players. Something tells me I'd be better off to wait for Jet to get home and tell me the unfiltered version.

Before I can receive any more cryptic texts, I shoot a message of my own to both Jet and Rae.

> *I've been slammed here at work, so I have no idea what's going on. Gonna try to keep it that way. Is anyone dead?*

A few minutes later, Rae texts back: *Busch probably wishes he was*

Jet: *We shouldn't text about this.*

I'm willing to leave it at that for now. *OK*

Rae: *Whatever. Cat's out of the bag. Keeping mum shows support for that moron*

Jet: *I'll tell you about it later, Maura*

Jet replies with as much finality as you can put into a text bubble on a phone screen.

Rae: *Talk over dinner? At Jet's? What's on Beau's menu tonight, Knox?*

Me: *Don't know. I eat whatever he puts in front of me*

Rae: *Any chance he can toss me a salad?*

My heart drops. I love my friend, but the idea of listening to her sarcastic asides while Jet gets me up to speed tires me. On the other hand, there's no way to tactfully tell her I'd rather be alone with Jet tonight, and he's too nice (and afraid of her) to dare reject her self-invite.

Sure enough, after a slight pause, Jet replies: *OK*

Rae: *See you later, then. 6:00?*

We all agree to that time, and I exit from the text interface.

For several seconds afterward, I stare at the Internet icon on my phone's screen, but I resist tapping it. I'd rather hear the news, whatever it is, from friends.

Chastity buzzes me to announce my next appointment, saving me from any further temptation.

Of course, there's no way for me to avoid the news for the rest of the day. It's the talk of the office. My co-workers are obsessed. Being who I am and whom I'm dating, they assume I have the inside scoop and won't stop trying to tease details from me, no matter how many times I tell them I don't have any more information than they do. Probably less, since I'm getting the details in drips and drabs. My brother won't stop sending me news story links I don't have the time or inclination to read. Every person who walks through my door and sits across the desk from me spends the first five minutes of their appointment discussing it. It's a titillating topic, a scandal that has even stronger legs than the guy at the center of it all.

Mr. Tight End stands accused of running a sex-for-money game involving groupies and other NFL players all over the league and has been suspended without pay pending further investigation. The charges are simple; implications are anything but.

This is beyond disheartening, even considering my admiration for Mr. Tight End as a person waned long ago. Coach Bauer encourages all the guys to have fun and show their personalities, but Keaton takes it to a whole new level with his inappropriate social media posts throughout the week and lewd gestures on the field, many of which have earned him hefty fines. His touchdown dances are fan favorites, and I used to love them, too, but now I recognize them as another piece of his somewhat obnoxious "Look at Me!" persona, something that shouldn't have a place in a game about teamwork and collaboration.

The veteran players, including Jet, chalk it up to the guy being relatively young and trying to make a name for himself. Last season was only his fourth; he spent his rookie season sidelined by injury. For the most part, his teammates have encouraged what they deem his "youthful enthusiasm" and have let Keaton be Keaton.

I bet they're not as amused by their resident goofball now.

TWENTY-SEVEN

CONFLICTING TAKES

My stomach lurches when I drive past Arrowhead Stadium on my way to Jet's and see the media encampment sprawled out in the vast parking areas usually filled with happy tailgaters.

Oh, Keaton. You dumb, beautiful, sleazy assclown. What have you done?

Despite thinking they'd be leaving the training complex early, Jet and Rae have put in a full day, and then some, so I'm the first one to arrive at Castle Knox. After taking it upon myself to send Helen and Beau home, I kill some time setting the table.

When Jet arrives, he walks past me, through the living room, sniffing the air on his way to the kitchen. "Smells great," he says shortly, as if I'm in any way responsible for the beef stir fry waiting for us.

Rae, closely behind him, points to his back and mouths *"Hangry"* with a roll of her eyes as we follow him.

I slow and hover on the threshold while he lifts the lid from the wok.

"Is this ready?" he asks, stirring, then scooping an enormous portion into a shallow bowl without waiting for my answer.

"I see today's events aren't killing your appetite," I say, trying to lighten the mood without downplaying the seriousness of the situation.

"This is the first real food I've seen since breakfast, thanks to all the B.S. going on." He moves down the counter to the heaping bowl of rice and makes a major dent in it, piling it on top of his beef and vegetables, like snow on a mountain peak.

Rae snags the wooden bowl of salad meant for her and nods her head toward the dining room on her way past me. "Come on. I'll tell you the latest."

She looks all too eager to fill me in. I remain in the kitchen with Jet, sidling up to him and pressing my nose against his upper arm. "Why does she look so smug?"

He shrugs. "Proves her point that all men are scumbags?" he hypothesizes, placing a kiss on my forehead. "I'll eat, and she can report."

I follow him into the dining room and sit to his right, facing Rae across the table from us.

"You're not going to eat?" she asks, around a mouthful of lettuce and sprouts.

I shake my head. "Maybe in a minute. I have a feeling I might not want to have anything on my stomach while we talk about this."

"Good point," she allows. "Jet and I have been listening to the details over and over all day. We're desensitized."

"Speak for yourself," he mutters into his bowl. "What's happening is sickening. But my body needs to eat."

She waves her fork dismissively at him. "Whatever."

Before she can rehash what I already know, I tell them the few details I've gleaned throughout the day, then admit, "I'm still not clear about how it all worked, though—how extensive it is or who was involved."

I glance at Jet, who wrinkles his nose and says with a full mouth, "Not me!"

I can't help but laugh at his interpretation of my look. "I'm not accusing you! I'm— Wow. Uh..." I shake my head and tease, "That was a quick denial, though."

He finishes chewing, swallows, and grumbles, "Just sayin'."

Rae clears her throat, happy to provide the gritty facts. "The participants pay into the game at the beginning of the season—this would have been the third year, apparently—and score points by having sex with people in the cities they visit for games. The person with the most 'scores,' at the end of the season takes home the pot of money."

She stops, but I blink, my mouth gaping. Again, I peek at Jet, who continues shoveling rice into his face like he's in an eating contest. He doesn't take his eyes from his bowl, so I return my attention to a gloating Rae, who smirks at my speechlessness.

"Yeah. That's how we all looked for about the first half of the day, when the news broke."

"Where's Keaton during all this?"

"Oh, he's been called to the Commissioner's office to answer for his crimes. We're just now getting wind of it, because the person who blew the whistle on him also sent her story to the media so there'd be no chance of the league sweeping it under the rug." She taps her temple with the handle of her fork. "Smart chick."

"One of the, uh, 'scores' blew the whistle?"

Rae nods. "A woman in Dallas. She had no idea what she

was a part of when she went back to Busch's room. I guess she figured she was simply hooking up with an NFL player."

"Groupies," Jet hisses behind his napkin while mopping his mouth.

Rae either doesn't hear him or ignores him. "Turns out, part of the 'game' is providing proof of your score, and when Busch, who was drunk, according to this woman, tried to take her picture, she objected, so he explained to her why he needed it. He told her the whole thing, then logged into the spreadsheet where he kept track of the points system and had all the players listed by their *real names*. What a dumbass!"

"Well, jocks aren't known for their intelligence." At Jet's warning glower, I clarify, "Lots of blows to the head, right?"

He growls something unintelligible, to which Rae replies, "Oh, don't get all man-hurt, Knox. You have to admit, the guy's a bonehead. He was so drunk and proud of his stupid scheme, he repeated the whole spiel for her when she pretended not to understand. She recorded it on her phone. Gosh, I'd give an ovary to see that video."

"Not a huge sacrifice for you," I point out.

She shrugs. "Well, it's not worth an important body part. But I'd be willing to give up *something*." Having told the story, she returns her attention to her salad.

But I still have questions. Lots of questions. Like... "What's going to happen to Keaton? Is he going to be released from the team?"

I'm looking at Jet, but when he doesn't answer right away, Rae snorts. "Probably not."

Finally, Jet sets down his fork and speaks. "The investigation is still pending."

"Seems pretty clear to me," Rae says. "If the woman was able to give everyone access to a video of him talking all about it, *and* a spreadsheet with names and other details, what more is there to investigate?"

"I dunno. I'm not a lawyer. But I don't think the team can release him from his contract—"

"Yes, they can!" Rae practically shouts. "Due to other recent indiscretions by similar jerks, the league purposely left the updated personal conduct policy vague to cover all manner of sins, including stuff like this, that they surely couldn't have predicted. Because this is stupidity on a grand scale."

Jet's lips tighten to a whiteness that almost matches his teeth, but he angles himself more toward me and addresses me directly. "I don't know the details of Keaton's contract. But I have a feeling we're about to see some second-stringers all across the league getting their big breaks."

"How many guys were involved?"

"Too many. A couple dozen." He rattles off some of the bigger names listed in the preliminary report.

"Wow."

"Yeah. I can't believe it," he says. "What the hell were they thinking?"

"Uh…" Rae raises her hand, like a student with the answer. "The correct question is, 'What were they thinking *with*?'"

Again, he ignores her. "And Keaton! I knew he was a man-whore, but this? Why would he feel the need to do something so, so…" He collapses against the back of his chair. "I'm too mad to think of the right words. We're less than a week away from our first game of the season. We don't need this distraction."

Rae sneers across the table. "What's wrong, Knox? Misogyny's okay in the off-season, but when it starts to affect your win-loss record, you have a problem with it?"

His face reddens. "What? No! That's not—"

"You watch." She stabs her forefinger into the table. "We'll find out this has been going on a lot longer than three years, that he took over organizing it from someone else. He's not nearly smart enough to come up with the concept himself. I bet this is pervasive and has been widely known about and kept hush-hush."

Jet slaps his hand on the table. "By who? I know you're not saying what I think you're saying."

"Maybe *you* didn't know, but I guarantee a bunch of people did. People high up, even. They turned a blind eye to it, because 'boys will be boys.'"

"That's bullshit."

"Is it? We all knew he was trouble. We all knew he was drilling every willing vagina he encountered, and nobody said anything."

"That was his business."

"Why? Because he still showed up every Sunday and caught your passes?"

"Because being promiscuous isn't against the law." Jet plunks his elbows on the table and, resting his head in his hands, massages his scalp.

Rae scoffs. "In other words, because he brought shame to the team and the league, *that's* what makes him a bigger creep than you already thought he was? If he'd had a kid with a different woman in every city, like so many guys do, it would have been business as usual?"

Jet drops his hands and looks incredulously at her. "What do you want from me, Rae? Step off my balls a little, huh?"

I raise my voice to drown out the beginning of my friend's heated response. "Guys! We've witnessed a billion of these scandals."

"Exactly," Rae points out. "Stupidity is an epidemic with these pro athletes."

"But it's not the responsibility of the entire team to defend or support the person at the center of the scandal," I remind her. "The team has to keep doing what they're paid to do: win games."

"Thank you," Jet directs at me. "This is already a big enough headache and distraction; if we all chime in with our personal beliefs about what's going on, not only will there be a ton of conflict in the locker room between teammates who don't agree with each other, but nobody will be focused on winning."

"There are more important things than winning games," Rae says.

"You think I don't get that? They don't pay me to preach, though. Let's not forget, all of these acts were consensual."

Eyes locked on his, she replies, "That we know of. I bet there'll be more than one person who steps forward and says some over-sexed asshole forced himself on her in a desperate attempt to get his weekly points."

"And if that's the case, I hope they throw the book at that guy. And Keaton. But I'll have to keep that to myself, won't I?"

"Why? You guys better not close ranks and refuse to say anything against these animals."

Seeing Jet's fists clench and unclench, I laugh nervously. "You two! Stop it. We're all on the same side here, okay?" I toss a warning look at Rae. "Chill out."

Jet breaks the face-off by taking his empty bowl into the kitchen. A few seconds later, he returns to the doorway, his expression stormy. "I've had a long day, and I'm tired. I don't feel like defending myself in my own damn house to some feminazi who wants to paint everyone with a dick with the same nasty paint brush. Screw that. I'm going downstairs to work out, since I sat on my ass all day in meetings and debriefings."

After he leaves, I say, "Thanks a lot," to Rae, who looks anything but contrite.

"Are you kidding me? He's being an asshole. He's laying the groundwork for every time he says 'No comment' or 'Keaton Busch is a good friend of mine and a great teammate.'"

I sigh at her deep-voiced imitation. "He's in a ridiculously difficult spot, though. Surely, you see that. The people who pay him tell him what he can and can't say."

"The same people tell me what to do, too."

"But you're never going to be tested. Because nobody gives a crap what your opinion of the situation is. No offense."

She scoffs. "No offense."

"*I* care," I quickly amend. "But you and I are in agreement that this is symptomatic of a much bigger problem in our society. Guess what? Jet feels that way, too."

"Does he? Or is he upset that his colleagues were stupid enough to get caught, and this is a major distraction from Game One in Miami?"

"You probably need to stop talking now. You're mad because he lost his temper and said some heated things, but—"

"This is so typical." She stands and glares down at me. "You're going to take his side and be all 'stand by your man' with your twenty karat vacuous smile?"

I rise, too. "I'm not smiling."

"You will be soon enough, standing in the background, lookin' so proud, like all you ever wanted out of life was to shop and have babies. Unbelievable."

I clamp my lips together and stare at her, then ask quietly, "Is that how you see me?"

Arms crossed over her chest, she answers, "I had hoped it wouldn't come to that, but I'm beginning to think it has." She gestures to the house around us. "You like all this. You like coming home to a fully cooked meal in a spotless mansion, swimming year-round in the heated pool, and screwing your boyfriend in a different room every night of the week, if you want. You love rubbing elbows with celebrities and not only knowing all the gossip but being the subject of it. '*Wedding Bells for Jetaura?*'" she asks, assuming an entertainment reporter's perky tone.

Before I can deny that ridiculous claim, she rushes on, "And you know what? If that's what makes you happy, go for it. It would be nice, though, if you'd admit it and stop acting like you're above it, like you're still the same old Maura you used to be. Because you're not. Not even close."

She steps through the archway that leads to the front of the house. "Thanks for dinner and such scintillating conversation. It's been enlightening."

TWENTY-EIGHT

GAME DAY JITTERS

I thought it would be better to watch the first game of the season with other people, so I've stuck to my usual routine of hanging out with Greg at the new Richards-Snow residence (which is very nice, but nowhere near Jet's house, geographically or otherwise). I invited Colin along for extra support. But now that we're all here, and the game is well underway, I'm not so sure. I'm probably not much fun to be around.

"THROW IT ALREADY, JET! SONOFABITCH! GET OPEN, NEW GUY, YOU DUMB ROOKIE AMATEUR!"

A Cheez Doodle sailing from the direction of the other couch, where my brother is sprawled, hits me in the face. Without diverting any of my attention from the TV, I return fire a piece of caramel corn.

"Would you two please stop throwing your food at each other like animals?" Deirdre snaps, picking up the snacks from the floor before one of us can stomp it into the rug. "Or is it a crime for our new house to stay nice for a while?"

"Yeah, Greg," I say, smiling against my beer bottle. "You're such a pig. Is it too much to ask the offensive line to do their damn jobs and protect my boyfriend?" I'm normally a big fan of the passing game, but I've definitely developed a greater appreciation for the run game. I'd prefer Jet hand the ball off to someone else who can get clobbered by a burly defenseman.

Around a belch, Greg says, "Jet's hanging on to the ball too long. It's like the clock in his head is running in slow motion."

"Everyone seems kind of out-of-sync out there," I grudgingly admit.

Colin pats my knee. "It's first-game jitters. They'll settle."

The huddle breaks, and Jet waves his arms at his guys to remind some of them where they need to be. The game clock ticks down to zero, and a flag comes out for a delay of game. I press my hand to my forehead. "What the hell is their problem? It's like nobody knows what they're supposed to be doing!"

"Including Jet," Greg mutters, shielding his face from the flying popcorn that never comes.

I'm too worried to lob any more snacks. Plus, I wish I could protest and give examples to the contrary, but he's right. Number Fourteen isn't looking sharp.

I refuse to analyze the reasons for that as one of the linesmen flinches before the next snap, and Jet stoically walks backward another five yards with his team.

"It looks bloody hot there," Colin offers as an excuse. "It's not even the end of the first period—"

"Quarter!" Greg and I automatically correct.

"—but look at them! They're all listless and dripping." Colin wrinkles his nose disdainfully.

"That's Miami for you," I say.

He waves his hand in front of his face. "That changing room is going to smell ghastly at halftime."

"Don't think about it."

"Maybe they got food poisoning at the hotel during second breakfast," Greg supposes.

The speculation is doing nothing to sooth my nerves. "The game's just started. Shut up. Everyone's getting into a rhythm. At least the pocket is holding up better now."

"If Jet can't get a pass off, it doesn't matter if he has all the protection in the world."

"It's not his fault! Nobody's getting open!"

To prove my point, Jet's next pass sails inches from his tripping intended receiver's fingertips. Fortunately, there weren't any defenders farther down the field, waiting to intercept. Unfortunately, that was third down, and we're backed way up, so we have to punt it away.

"He's throwing it too hard," Greg says. "The ball's like a bullet."

"Which one is it?" I snap. "Is he not throwing it, or is he throwing it too hard?"

"Both."

The camera follows Jet as he rips off his helmet and sets it on a drying post behind the bench. He slides on a sun visor and immediately grabs one of the sideline tablets to study the pictures from the last series. The quarterback coach sidles up to him, but when they start discussing things, the camera switches to a shot of the punter kicking a boomer down the field.

"Hey, at least *that* guy showed up today," Greg says. "Good thing, too, since I think he's going to see plenty of action."

I stand and head toward the kitchen for another beer, but reply, "You know, if you're going to be a dick, I'm going to go home and watch this alone."

"I'm not being a dick! I'm stating the facts," he shouts after me.

To be fair, I'm likely a bit testier than I would be if this was the opening game of the season that everyone was expecting two weeks ago. I guess we'll never know, though. I'm nervous about Jet, but the past week with the Keaton Busch scandal (dubbed "The Bedroom Bowl" and all sorts of other crude plays on words with the tight end's last name) has fried the nerves of everyone connected to the team. For the guys on the field today, it's a major direct factor, considering the front office made Busch inactive (you should have seen and heard all the jokes about *that* this week) until an official decision is handed down by the league. The reporters want to keep the story alive, but they're hitting brick walls with players, coaches, and owners, so they're seeking out peripheral people like me, hoping one of us will slip up and give our opinions about the offenders' behavior, since we're not technically under the NFL gag order. I did blindly sign a confidentiality agreement over the summer, though, so I'm not saying a word.

Unfortunately, the media's not giving up. It's easy for them to gain access to me. They call me at work, wait for me at my car in the parking lot, and park in the cul-de-sac in view of my house, waiting for me to emerge for the mail or come home at night. I've stayed at my parents' house twice this week. I'd stay at Jet's, but I'd have to sleep in one of his guest rooms, and that's too depressing for words.

Not helping matters is my continuing standoff with Rae. We might as well be under a gag order with each other. I've heard nothing from her since she stormed from Jet's house Monday night, and I'm sure as hell not going to be the one to reach out, after what she said to me. It probably says something not-so-flattering about me that I've tolerated her utter disregard for other people's feelings all these years, but reached my limit as soon as she aimed her vitriol at me.

I'm more upset, however, with the way she talked to and treated Jet that night at dinner. It wasn't fair he had to bear the brunt of her ire for something he didn't do and would never condone. Her disrespect was unacceptable.

Now Deirdre follows me into the kitchen. "I don't know how you do it," she says, nudging her head toward the living room. "I couldn't watch at all."

"It's not that bad," I lie, because I don't feel like going into it with her. It's disturbing how much I suddenly sympathize with Gloria.

One night during Jet's family's visit, after dinner, we were sitting around and laughing about yet another one of Jet's false memories regarding Knox family history. Stretching from the top of the arch leading into the living room, he blamed it on too many concussions.

"Don't kid about that!" Gloria scolded. "Every time you fall and your head hits the turf, I want to cry."

David snorted. "Why do you still watch, Mom?"

She pressed her hand to her chest. "He's my baby, and I'm proud of him!"

Keith and David made good-natured gagging noises, while the ladies mock-scolded them.

"Aw, Mom!" Jet drawled, abandoning his stretches and bending down to give her shoulders a squeeze. "You worry too much!"

Jet's physical safety isn't *my* only concern. I also feel obligated to defend everything he does—or doesn't do. I'm worried about what he's thinking and feeling. And already anticipating what I should say, if anything, if they lose this game.

This caring shit is for the birds.

Anyway, there's still plenty of game to play. Unfortunately.

Suddenly, from the other room, Greg bellows, "FUMBLE! GET IT, FAT BOY! RUN! RUN! RUN!"

I make it to a spot where I can see the TV in time to watch Demarcus Jackson, one of the biggest defensive guys on the team, cross into the end zone and collapse on his back, huffing and puffing while clutching the ball to his chest.

"YES!" I yell, hopping and sloshing beer on my Knox jersey.

From his standing position next to the couch, Greg performs his ridiculous touchdown dance, writhing like a chubby, balding belly dancer, kicking his feet like a drunk, uncoordinated Cossack, then performing the Tomahawk Chop (so many cultures offended) before jerking his pelvis back and forth. "Touchdown! Kansas! City! Who needs offense? We'll let the defense do all the work today."

"Hey!" I protest for the sake of propriety. Really, though, I'd be okay with that.

The camera follows Jackson to the sideline, where the first hug he receives is from his quarterback, who grins and slaps his teammate on the butt.

"Aww! Look how much they love each other!" I say, giddiness and relief closing my throat.

Colin giggles. "'Kiss me, you beast!'" he says, providing a silly dialogue for the exchange between the teammates. "Oh, my! He did nearly kiss that bloke on the cheek. Jealous, Lady Maura?"

"Nope. They're buddies. They get emotional out there." I retake my seat. "I'm so glad we have points on the board now. Much less pressure."

"Jet still needs to step it up. That score's not gonna hold

forever. The defense can only do so much." Greg says, resuming his spread-out lounging position and digging his hand back into his bowl of Cheez Doodles on the floor next to the couch.

"Yeah, but special teams can get in on the fun, too. It doesn't all have to be on Jet's shoulders."

"That's why he gets paid the big bucks, Mo."

We're still arguing the meaning of "team sports" several minutes later, after a quick three-and-out from Miami and a commercial break, when the Chiefs' offense takes the field again.

"Oh, man. Your boy looks determined now, doesn't he?" Greg catcalls.

Yes, he does. He's definitely wearing the face that says he's ready to increase his team's lead. Or he's constipated. Or he's listening intently to the speaker in his helmet. Or all three. That face means business. I love that face.

Satisfied with the play call, he takes his position behind the center for what appears to be a run play, so my shoulders relax further. But after taking the short snap, he fakes a hand-off to the running back, obscures the other team's view of the ball with a sweet spin move, then when all attention is focused on the "runner," turns back around to scout his options down-field.

Except one of the defensive linemen wasn't fooled. He got past his man and is barreling toward Jet.

"Eeeeeeeeeeeeeeek!" I squeal, covering my eyes.

Colin grips my forearm, his fingers digging into the skin near my wrist. "Oh, blimey!"

"Knox gets it off just in time to Tiffenauer before getting a faceful of Javier Wahl. Oh, my! Tiffenauer is still on his feet at the twenty… the

ten... finally brought down at the seven yard line. It's Chiefs first and goal. But Knox is slow to get up."

Greg thumps his chest. "Thatta boy, scab! First down!"

"Uh-oh." Colin intones.

"What happened?" I ask, turning my head to look at my friend while resolutely refusing to peek at the television.

He winces, sucking air through his teeth. "They're showing the replay now, but it appears before he was knocked down, Jet hit his hand on that scary bloke's helmet."

Unable to resist looking for another second, I lower my hands and watch the scene unfold. Jet's up, and he's in the huddle, but he shakes his throwing hand intermittently, then grabs it with his other hand and presses it against his thigh.

"Rub some dirt on it, tough guy!" Greg yells.

"Shut up, Greg!"

He looks sharply over at me. "What?"

"If he's shaking his hand and holding it, it hurts. He's not a wuss."

"Okay! Fine. Shit. Are you going to be like this all season? You're no fun anymore."

I shush him and focus on the screen. After a couple more failed attempts at the end zone with run plays, the kicking team comes out, and Schoengert knocks in the chip shot for three points. One camera sticks on Jet, creeping as close as it's allowed to get and zooming in for a shot of Rae palpating the heel of Jet's hand and instructing him to wiggle his thumb.

"Rae!" Colin shouts, then mutters, "Sorry," in my concerned direction.

I nibble my thumbnail while watching Jet follow Rae's directions with gritted teeth and a bounce of his knee. "Oh, gosh. It's his thumb," I say with a groan.

"Not good," Greg concurs.

"What's that mean?" Colin asks. "They'll ice it, right? Wrap it, maybe? Inject it with something? But he'll still be able to play, surely."

I collapse against the sofa cushions behind me. "If he can't grip the ball, he can't play."

Greg tosses the official NFL football he always keeps close during games (don't ask) across the room to Colin. "Try holding it like they do without using your thumb."

Colin complies and immediately sees the problem. "Bloody hell. That's not on."

I stare at the ceiling as the game goes to commercial. "This is bad."

"I've seen guys miss a game and come back okay," Greg tries to reassure me.

"And I've watched as much football as you have. It's not always that simple."

"There's no need to get hysterical," Deirdre pipes up, "until you know for certain what you're dealing with. Even then, panicking is hardly going to help things."

"The doctor has spoken," Greg intones. "Nothing to worry about."

"She's a cardiologist, not a— a hand doctor," I petulantly point out.

Meanwhile, the game returns, the announcers speaking in excited tones as they discuss Michael Wilcox warming up on the sidelines. They cut away to video of Jet walking toward the locker room during the break, his helmet dangling from his left hand, his right hand cradled protectively against his body, his head hanging.

"So, Knox is getting checked out in the locker room, and Michael Wilcox, the rookie backup, is warming up. What do you think about Dick Bauer's decision to go with the rookie, Charlie?"

"*I think it's surprising, Dan. We've all been given the impression that veteran QB Rick Hess was the official second-stringer, and Wilcox was still learning the system, but apparently Coach Bauer thinks the young Heisman finalist deserves a chance.*"

"*I'm not sure I agree with this decision. Maybe if the score was more lopsided and it was later in the game, but there's still a lot of game left, and the score's close.*"

"*Well, I suppose Bauer could be bringing him in for a series or two to see how he handles the situation.*"

"*Still risky. Especially considering Tiffenauer's subbing for Keaton Busch on short notice, which come to think of it, may have been a contributing factor in Knox's injury. It looked like Tiffenauer wasn't where Knox expected him to be.*"

"*You have a good point there. And speaking of Jet Knox, we'll check in with Jessica on the sideline in a minute, as soon as she has word on his condition.*"

The attention returns to the action on the field, but I don't hear or see anything for the next several minutes. All I can do is worry, helpless, not knowing any more than what everyone else does. Obviously, it could be worse. In no situation is this hand injury life-threatening. But depending on the severity, it could be season-threatening. At the very least, it's a nightmare. As is waiting for an injury update on someone you care about.

Several plays go by. Then, during a time-out, the guys in the booth pitch it to an inordinately perky sideline reporter.

"*Charlie and Dan, there's not much coming from the Chiefs' locker room right now, but they did confirm that Knox has an injury to his throwing hand and is undergoing X-rays. His return in this game is listed as doubtful. That much they're sure about! Back to you guys!*"

Colin snorts. "He's doubtful; that much they're sure about? Where do they find these people?"

Dan and Charlie drone about X-rays and hand injuries like they're automatic career-enders and it was nice knowing Jet, but where's the new guy? It takes them a shockingly short period of time to start spewing Wilcox's college stats and reversing their earlier concerns about putting the greenhorn into the game. To hear them now, it's a wonder Wilcox wasn't given the starting job a long time ago.

The offensive play calling, however, remains conservative to the point of coma-inducing, so the rookie doesn't have a chance to do anything noteworthy for the rest of the half.

The announcers are underwhelmed. *"Despite Wilcox's relative success in preseason play, it appears Dick Bauer's not going to try anything cute here with his rookie backup and is burning time off the clock to get us to halftime."*

As soon as the clock hits zero in the half, I bolt from the couch.

"Where are you going?" Greg asks. "There's still half a game to go!"

"I don't care. I'm going to Jet's house."

"Why? What's the point in that?"

"I can't watch this game anymore, and I'm not going to make you guys turn it off."

"Good luck with that, anyway," Deirdre says under her breath.

"Exactly. So, I'm going to go to Jet's and wait for someone to get in touch with me."

"They can get in touch with you here," Greg says. "On your cell. We have the technology. Do you really want to be alone right now?"

"Yes! Stop asking me stupid questions."

Colin rises. "Are you positive you're okay? I can drive you, or...?"

I take a deep breath and smile bravely. "No! Of course, I'm fine. But I want to be alone when he calls."

Greg waves his hands at me. "You're weird. Give us the scoop when you know anything, so we can sell it to the *Star*."

It takes every bit of willpower I have not to run to my car. When I get in, it takes still more control not to dial Jet's cell phone. I'll only be forced to leave a frantic message, and that's the last thing he needs to hear when he's able to check his messages later. I do send one text through my tears, though:

I'll kiss it better when you get home.

TWENTY-NINE

INSULT AND INJURY

"Look, Rae's here!" Jet says after kissing me hello.

"I see that," I reply coldly, wishing they'd sent a different trainer with him.

"I told her I could drive myself home, but she wouldn't let me. It's only a thumb!" He waves his bandaged hand in the air.

Rae rolls her eyes and nudges Jet's dropped duffel bag out of the way with her legs. "He's high. Valium and Vicodin. Don't let him operate machinery. Or go to the bathroom alone."

He thrusts his wrapped hand under my nose. "I have a boo-boo. Did you see the game?"

"Uh, yes. Didn't you get my text?"

"Huh?" He pats his pockets. "Oh, no! My phone! Where'd it go?"

"Never mind," Rae says. "You don't need it right now. Let's get you settled."

Leading them into the living room, I ask, "What's the damage?"

Rae waits until we're all seated and Jet's greeted Torzi, who's been keeping me company for the past several hours, before she answers, "Don't know yet. X-rays were negative, so we know it's not broken, but they'll need to do an MRI tomorrow to get a better idea of ligament damage. The key is to keep it immobilized and the swelling down until then. It's not the worst hand injury I've ever seen," she finally finishes. "Probably a bad sprain."

I sigh at her less-than-precise diagnosis and prognosis.

"I can't make any guarantees or predictions. You're going to have to wait and see what the specialists say. And maybe, eventually, a surgeon."

"Surgeon? You think he needs surgery?"

Jet edges closer to me on the couch and pets my hair with his healthy hand. "Babe. Babe. Babe."

I turn my attention to him, so he'll stop calling me that.

"Babe. It's gonna be okay," he slurs with a dopey grin. "It doesn't hurt at all. It'll be fine in a day or two."

"Jet, honey, you're stoned," I coo. "That's why it doesn't hurt."

"For realsies?" He whirls and looks at Rae. "Am I gonna get in trouble for this? I'm not allowed to do drugs, Rae."

"These are legal drugs, dumbass. Keep that hand still!"

"Is it in there? I need that hand to throw footballs." He doesn't seem all that concerned, though, which I chalk up to the Valium doing its job. Instead, he switches back to petting me. "You're soft, like Torzi."

Rae stands. "This should be a fun night for you."

"You're leaving?" I don't want her here, but I also don't want to be alone with the patient. "I have no idea what to do with him!"

"Put him to bed. It's better if he sleeps, because then he won't move his hand. He needs the sleep."

"I could sleep," he says agreeably, standing.

"What do I do if it starts to hurt again?" I ask Rae.

"His 'scripts are in his bag. The instructions are on them. He re-dosed his pain meds on the plane. Around six-thirty, I think."

"You think? I probably need to know exactly."

"I wrote it down. Duh. It's all with the pills. He doesn't necessarily need to keep up with the Valium dosage. We needed him to be relaxed for the trip home." She turns toward the door. "You'll be fine. This will be great training for your future. Football players get hurt. When he's finished killing himself on the field, you'll have little diapered Jet Juniors to nurse through illness and injury."

My temper spikes, but I have more important problems than her snide predictions into my future. After a three-count, I ask, "What about this diagnostic appointment tomorrow? What time is that?"

"Have him ready early. They'll send a car."

"What about *his* car?"

She whirls on me on the top step leading from the living room to the foyer. "For fuck's sake, Maura! You're going to have to put on your big girl panties and figure this shit out for yourself. This is the life you've chosen. I was just the lucky person who was chosen to babysit one of the team's biggest *ass*ets and deliver him safely home."

I lift my chin. "I wish they'd sent someone else, someone willing to give me some advice, instead of letting her personal feelings get in the way of her job."

"It's not my job to hold your hand." She nods behind me at Jet, who's lying on his back on the couch, laughing while he lets Torzi lick the inside of his mouth. "As soon as Brain Trust is lucid, he'll be more of a help. He knows the drill." Reaching into her jacket pocket, she pulls out Jet's phone. "Oh, and here. I didn't want him texting his dong to random people or something else equally scandalous while drugged." Before I can thank her (however grudgingly) for covering that detail, she says, "Sweet message, by the way."

"Hey! That was private!"

"Whatever. There are several from his mom on there, too. If I were you, I'd respond as him and tell her 'you're' fine; otherwise, you're about to have Gloria on your doorstep, on top of everything else. But whatever. Your call."

"My mom's name is Gloria!" Jet says around Torzi's tongue, then pushes the dog away and sits up. "What are the chances?"

When I turn to shoot him a long-suffering look, he waves coyly, fluttering his eyelashes at me. "Hey, baby. You know how horny it makes me when you wear my jersey. Why don't you come down here and let me prove it?"

Rae pulls open the front door. "And that's definitely my cue to go." She shows me her back and says as she steps onto the porch, "Get him to bed ASAP. That'll make your job a whole lot easier."

I want to punch her in the back of the head, but instead, I simply reply, "Thanks for bringing him home."

She says nothing to that, merely retreats down the landscaped, lighted path to her car and quickly circles it to get to the driver's side.

Seething, I stare after her taillights for a few seconds, then, eyes closed and arms wrapped around myself, strategize my next steps. I'll keep an eye on Jet's phone for updates about those tests in the morning, and afterward, we'll have the hired car take us by the training facility to get his car.

I open my eyes. Under the porch light, I give myself a silent pep talk.

You've got this, Richards. He's a grown man, after all. Get him upstairs and in bed. How hard can it be?

A crash from inside the house behind me has me spinning and running faster than an All-Pro punt returner. It'll be a miracle if both of us survive the night.

————

We do survive the night. And the next morning, and the whole next day, most of which we spend at the hospital. It doesn't take long for doctors to confirm Rae's suspicions that Jet sustained a deep sprain to the ligament connecting his thumb to the rest of his hand, but after his diagnosis, the celebrity patient doesn't seem in a hurry to leave the hospital.

When he first suggests we stop by the pediatric ward, I'm not particularly thrilled. After a long, restless night, part of which I spent helping two-hundred pounds of dead weight get to the bathroom when his meds upset his stomach, I want to get him home and take a nap. But I don't object to visiting the kids, because it seems important to him, and I figure if it takes his mind off things for a while, then it's worth it.

As soon as the elevator doors open on that pediatric floor, he's a different person than he's been all morning. The patients think it's cool that Jet Knox has a boo-boo, too. He explains to them what the doctors have told him about his hand and how it means *he* can't play like he wants to, either, for a while.

Then he spends one-on-one time with each child. In most

cases, he makes the kids laugh by cutting loose and acting silly. Other times, for the less outgoing patients, he tones it down, talking quietly and gently next to their beds, or listening intently to what they have to say. In one instance, he holds a ten-year-old girl's hand while she cries. At another bed, he reads a story to a boy too young and too sick to know or care who Jet Knox is.

We spend hours on that floor. Jet the hospital visitor is amazing.

Jet the patient is a pain in the ass.

I know, that's a horrible thing to say. He's hurt; he's worried about his throwing hand and his job; he's dealing with a lot. I should be more understanding. But I thought he'd be a better trouper than he's been. I figured he'd be his usual go-getter self, the guy who doesn't take "no" for an answer, the guy who's all about solutions. It's not that I thought he'd be like he was when he first came home, high and manic and silly, but I didn't think he'd be so down and short-tempered, either.

The doctors say if he follows their recovery instructions and does the exercises they've prescribed, he could be back in the game in as little as three weeks, missing only two games, thanks to the team's early bye this year. But one of the games he'll miss is that Monday night home rematch against the Patriots he's been looking forward to since losing to them in the playoffs. I can only imagine how disappointed he is.

Since he's not talking to me, I've had to resort to just that, my imagination.

Maybe he's simply tired and hungover from the drugs. Maybe the pain is getting to him more than he wants to let on.

Or maybe, like so many people online, he thinks this is my fault.

Anyone else notice that Knox sucks now that he has a girlfriend?

Someone doesn't have his head in the game.

It's like Tomossi and Samantha Wallace all over again. Remember that mess?

Less time with the chick and more time with the playbook and on the practice field, please.

If Jet's demeanor is any indication, he *does* agree with them. He hardly talks to me at all. He says "Please" and "Thanks" when I help him with things that require two hands with opposable, working thumbs, but the monosyllables are killing me. I might as well be one of his handlers, an employee, someone he barely knows, paid to get him from place to place and make sure he's comfortable.

Going back to work has been somewhat of a relief. I took Monday off, but you can only call in so many times because your boyfriend sprained his thumb, even if he is the beloved Jet Knox.

Fortunately, he's back to a semi-normal schedule, too, despite not participating in full workouts or practices. Mentoring Michael Wilcox, his temporary replacement, is his main job duty now. I bet he's thrilled about that.

Again, I wouldn't know. That information is apparently classified, and I'm not one of the people on a need-to-know.

————

My idea of a perfect Friday night at the end of such a crap-tastic week includes pizza, a good movie from my collection, and my solitary, sweats-clad ass on my couch. Unfortunately,

Jet and I are expected to attend tonight's Red Friday, the team's official pep rally for the home opener.

That means I make myself presentable to play Happy Couple around thousands of strangers, many of whom hate me right now and blame me for their hero's fall, which they're treating like the end of the world, rather than the temporary setback it is.

At the rally, Jet turns on the charm for his teammates and the fans, signing autographs (unrecognizable, considering he can't hold a football, much less grip a pen), while I'm expected to socialize with the other wives and girlfriends, or WAGs. And the cheerleaders.

One such conversationalist is Dixie, the Southern-accented woman who rides the white horse, Warpaint, at home games. I have to listen to Horse Lady gush about her myriad "blassin's," which include dressing up in a crop top and chaps to bounce around in front of drunk spectators. Nursing my red plastic cup of hard cider, I play my own private drinking game, taking a gulp every time she utters any variation of, "Ah'm so blassed!" In order to prevent being completely blasted by the end of the evening, I take small sips, so I'm only moderately tipsy by the time we leave.

Fortunately, the players aren't expected to stay late, so Jet and I are home by nine. Well, at Jet's home. He seemed to be driving home on auto-pilot, and in my pique, I didn't realize it until we were almost here. Instead of asking him to take me home, I figure I'll sleep in a guest room and borrow one of his cars in the morning. No need for discussion, since that's, apparently, something we no longer do.

When we enter the house, and I walk straight to the stairs with a listless, "Good night," he says, "Hey," drawing me up short.

I pause halfway up the flight, looking down on him while Torzi catches up to me.

"You're going to bed already?"

"Yeah."

"Oh. Okay. I have to do my physical therapy real quick."

"No rush," I reassure him, clomping the rest of the way to the second floor.

My sole requirement is a bed, so I choose the first room at the top of the stairs. There, I listlessly kick off my cute new cowboy boots and shed the casual red dress I bought weeks ago in such joyful anticipation of this night. The balled-up dress gets tossed in the general direction of the wing-backed chair in the corner. My denim jacket stays on the floor where I dropped it.

Stripped down to my underwear, I find a new toothbrush in the bathroom and unwrap it. While brushing my teeth, I study myself in the mirror over the sink. I look miserable. Which makes sense. Because that's exactly how I feel.

Maybe this is my reality check. Maybe I'm not cut out for this life, being another actor in a show that runs four months —sometimes longer, if the players are lucky—then spending the rest of the year preparing for the show's next run, all the while ignoring the audience's heckles and making sure they never glimpse what's going on backstage.

When I return to the bedroom, Torzi is patiently waiting for me at the foot of the bed. As soon as I slide under the covers and settle on my side with my back facing the closed door, he burrows beneath the sheet and curls up in the space between my legs and torso.

I absently stroke his head. "You keepin' me company tonight, Bud? Maybe you have some tips. You've been keeping the home fires bright and warm for a while now. Is this how it always is?"

He licks my hand, so I move it to discourage the behavior that always grosses me out, but I continue talking, because, no matter how ridiculous I feel talking to a dog, it still feels better than holding it all inside for another minute.

"You might not have realized this about me yet, Torzi, but I'm not a big fan of responsibility. This NFL support person gig is a big responsibility, you know? It's hard to keep everything in perspective. But that's our job. To make sure Jet's not letting everything that goes along with this life mess with his head. Right? But how do you keep it from messing with *your* head?"

After a few more attempts at licking and my consistent rebuffs, the dog gives up with a resigned exhale. Surprisingly quickly, I doze, then fall deeply asleep.

I wake up slowly when something damp presses against my neck.

I swat at it. "Torzi, no. Cut it out." But instead of my hand making contact with the springy fuzz I'm expecting, it meets skin, and eyelashes.

"Ow. Hey, it's me."

My eyes fly open, but I remain motionless on my side.

Above and behind me, Jet asks with a smile in his voice, "What have you and Torzi been doing in here?"

"Sleeping," I grunt, pulling the covers further over my bare shoulder.

He slips into the bed and cozies up to my back, placing a peck between my shoulder blades. "I've been looking all over for you. Why are you in here?"

"I'm tired and want to sleep."

"There's a bed in my room for that, too."

"I know."

"You're not going to be bothering me." Goosebumps pop on my skin as he kisses a line down my spine.

I hadn't considered I might be disturbing *him*. Instead of admitting it, I say softly, "This week has been so horrible."

"Yeah. Being on the DL sucks."

"Well, being the girlfriend of someone on the DL sucks about fifty times harder. You haven't talked to me all week."

He thinks about it for a while, then says, "Well, you've been doing your thing, and I've been trying to do my thing, which isn't my thing at all. So that's all."

"You think it's my fault you got hurt."

"What?" He pulls on my shoulder with his wrapped hand, urging me onto my back. His nest disturbed, Torzi jumps down from the bed and shimmies through the cracked-open door into the hallway.

"What the hell are you talking about?" Jet asks.

Now that I've said it, it's even more horrible. My stomach clenches. My eyes fill. My ears ring. I hope he doesn't expect me to say it again, because I can't talk at all, much less repeat the awful sentence that's been pinging around my brain for days. Fortunately, he moves on without forcing me to reiterate my suspicion.

"Who told you that? No, let me guess. This has 'Rae' written all over it."

I shake my head. Rae has said less to me than he has since she brought him home last Sunday. "Nobody has to tell me anything. It's obvious. When you're forced to talk to me, it's more like grunting."

"I'm talking to you right now."

"You're *arguing* with me right now. It's the longest conversation we've had since you told me your pain pills constipate you. What's worse is that you act fine around other people. Tonight, at the rally, you were that happy-go-lucky guy I fell in love with. Around me, you're practically silent."

He sighs. "People will jump all over it if I show that I'm worried or stressed out. But here at home, I don't have to pretend. I've been so glad this week that you haven't asked me a million times how I'm feeling or what I'm thinking about. Because I'm feeling like shit. I'm thinking this is New York all over again. Sidelined for something stupid, then it turns into a permanent thing."

"That's not going to happen this time."

"Maybe not, but you never know. You can't take it for granted. So, that's what I've been thinking about. It doesn't make me very chatty."

I sniffle, contemplating whether I buy his explanation.

"What's this about me blaming you? I was the one who didn't see that guy coming until the last second. I'm the one who forced the pass, even though I knew I didn't have enough clearance for my follow-through. I'm the one who decided to do anything not to take that sack. My hand came down on his helmet. How is that your fault?"

I swallow painfully. "That's what everyone's saying."

"Who's 'everyone'?"

"Just… people. Fans. They think I'm a distraction, that I'm bad luck."

His voice steely, he says, "There's a reason I don't read or listen to any of that crap. It's toxic. I don't want to hear it secondhand from you, either. They're all a bunch of idiots."

"Those idiots love you, though. They think you're great. I'm the one they hate."

"Nobody hates you."

"Yes, they do. They think I'm ruining the team's chances at another postseason run."

"If anyone's done that, it was that bastard, Busch. People are nuts, talking about the postseason. We've played one game so far! Which we happened to win. So why is everyone pressing the panic button?"

"We lost you, in the process."

He pulls back the covers and sits on the side of the mattress, pointing his back to me. "You tell me this won't be like New York, but in the next breath, you try to take credit for ruining my career. Which one is it, Maura?"

Openly sobbing and clutching the covers on either side of me, I moan, "I don't know! I'm sad and confused and so alone. I don't know what to think or feel. You're so c-cold, and so m-mean, mad at me because I happen to see and hear the horrible things people are saying about me."

"You seek it out! You have alerts on your phone to tell you when anyone's talking about us. You're torturing yourself with this shit. Who cares what they say?"

"I care, all right? I can't be a curse for an entire city."

"You're not. I'm doing everything exactly the way I always have. But accidents happen. Injuries happen. And the one that happened to me last week had nothing to do with you."

"But people's perceptions—"

"Screw their perceptions! The people who matter know the truth. At least, I thought they did. But I guess you'd rather believe a bunch of asswipes who have nothing better to do than trash-talk and read into things that aren't there." Rising from the bed, he stomps to the door, yanks it open, and walks through it, slamming it behind himself.

THIRTY

REASSURANCES AND UPHEAVAL

It doesn't feel like I sleep at all, so I'm surprised when a soft knock on the bedroom door wakes me the next morning. The person on the other side doesn't wait for me to answer; rather, he walks right in, bearing a huge tray with one of those silver domes, like you see in the movies.

While Jet sets the tray on the unoccupied side of the mattress, I sit up and rub furiously at the mascara-coated, puffy bags under my eyes. He comes around to my side of the bed and squats next to me.

"'Morning, Beautiful," he murmurs with a sad smile that threatens to undo me all over again.

At my shaky chin and welling eyes, he tilts his head and sighs, then motions for me to sit on the side of the bed, facing him while he remains perched at my level. When I do, he grabs my right hand in his left and rubs his thumb against my knuckles. "Oh, Maura."

I sniff the tears away and look at my knees. "I'm okay. I didn't sleep much."

"Me neither." With his bandaged hand under my chin, he

lifts my face to look at him. His stubbled cheeks are pale, which highlights the dark circles under his eyes. "Hey. We're in this together, right? You still want that? Because I do."

All I can do is nod.

Smiling, he says, "Good. That's what I should have said last night. I shouldn't have yelled at you. I shouldn't have stormed out of here like a—"

"It's okay." I cradle his face in both of my hands. "I let my imagination run wild, instead of talking to you. I overreacted."

He shifts from his feet to his knees, brackets my hips with his arms, and rests his head on my lap. "I was afraid when I opened that door this morning, you'd be gone. I thought I blew it. Again."

His rare allusion to Ginny isn't lost on me, but I don't want to talk about her. I feather his hair. "I wouldn't do that." Then, to lighten what's becoming an impossibly heavy vibe, I point out, "I don't have a car here."

He laughs and looks up at me. "You're right. I guess I accidentally kidnapped you last night."

I press my thumbs to the rings under his eyes. "I love you."

"I love you too. Please be here when I get home later."

I nod my compliance. "Still don't have a car."

"You know where all the keys are. Use whichever one you want, if you need to do stuff or go anywhere. But I want to come home to you tonight."

"I'll be here." It'll be one of the only times this season we get to spend a Saturday night together, thanks to the home opener being a Monday night game.

I lean down, and he reaches up, our lips meeting nearly exactly in the middle of the space between our faces. It's a short kiss, but it's probably packed with more meaning than nearly any other we've shared.

When it's over, Jet rises to his feet and clears his throat.

"Well. Enjoy your breakfast."

"Wait!" I swivel at the waist and raise the dome on the tray to see that, sure enough, there's only one plate of eggs Benedict, bacon, and toast under there. "You're not going to eat with me?" I glance at the sun streaming through the balcony doors. "It's such a beautiful morning. We could eat outside."

He shakes his head regretfully. "I have to get to the training complex." His smile is rueful when he explains, "You know, so I can watch everyone else work out." He winks.

I chuckle. "Oh. Right."

As if on cue, my phone lights up and vibrates on the bedside table, signifying an incoming notification. We both look at the device like it's a bomb about to explode. His face darkens.

Before he can say anything, I promise, "I won't read it. I won't read anything. As a matter of fact, I'll delete those alert settings altogether."

"I just want you to be happy, Maura."

"You make me happy."

"If anything important and *real* comes up that you need to know and we need to handle, I'll tell you. Right away."

"I trust you."

He rewards me with a lopsided smile and a longer goodbye kiss, then walks to the door. As soon as he opens it to leave, Torzi bounds in, leaping onto the bed. I pull him away from my food and into my lap, then lift his paw in a wave to Jet, who laughs at us and says, "You two stay out of trouble."

"You do the same."

Like I ever need to worry about that.

———

On a typical Saturday during the season, like last week, I don't see Jet at all. He goes to practice early, and if the team is playing an away game, they fly to their destination city to get settled at their hotel, where they attend more pre-game meetings and hit the sheets early (alone, presumably). For home games, the routine is the same, minus the flying. The players even stay in a hotel, like they would in another city. It's all part of the mental aspect of game prep, designed to lessen the impact of away games on the psyche.

When I originally looked at the schedule, back when being Jet's girlfriend was new and somewhat stifling, I counted the Monday and Thursday night games, as well as the bye week, and committed the dates of their associated Saturdays to memory. Not because I was looking forward to them, but because I wanted to prepare myself for those extra days of girlfriend obligation. To think, the old Maura dreaded those anomalies in the schedule, worried about sacrificing precious alone-time. The old Maura was a clueless moron.

The new me recognizes these rare Saturdays as gems to be cherished, gifts to be highly anticipated. This first one isn't turning out quite the way I'd planned, but it's not too late to turn it around. My original plan for this first Saturday together is back on track after a temporary derailment.

This early in September, it's still pretty warm out, but I'm eager for fall. Thanks to the stress of the job fair and the prospect of the love affair of my life shattering under the pressure created by the world in which it exists (drama much?), I've forgotten how much I love this time of year.

Today, I reclaim my favorite season. I'm making this year's first pot of chili, one of the few dishes I do well. I've recently returned from an afternoon with Colin and Torzi at the farmer's market, where I picked up fresh ingredients. I'm excited to cook, then spend the rest of the night relaxing with Jet.

"This is the life, Torzi," I say down at my supervisor as he waits adorably and patiently for me to drop something delectable. He licks the air, and I add, "When I don't think too much about it, that is. Let's face it; not thinking about things is my specialty. So, maybe this will work, after all."

He lies on the wood floor and rests his chin on his paws.

"You're right; I need to relax, and talk to Jet more often when things upset me, right? Because if I'd told him what I was worried about, right away, I could have avoided a miserable week. He's a simple guy. But complicated at the same time. I've never been with anyone like that. It's confusing sometimes."

I glance over at the dog and see he's asleep. Or pretending to be.

"Oh. Sorry. Excuse me. Didn't mean to bore you," I grumble with a chuckle. "If I'm not feeding you, you're not interested, huh? I get it. And here I thought we were connecting."

He dozes through my fake rant.

I finish browning the beef and drain the fat, then dump it and the rest of the ingredients—tomatoes, garlic, onions, jalapeños, beans, tomato sauce, chili powder—into a huge pot on the stove. After stirring everything together, I place the lid on the pot, then turn the burner below it to "low" for a long simmer.

Only after I've cleaned up my prep mess do I wander into the living room, where I lounge on the couch and pull my phone from my pocket. True to my word, I deleted the notification settings, but that doesn't mean I can't go straight to the usual sites and browse the message boards and comment threads, if I truly wanted (or needed) to seek out the information. Like any addiction, the temptation has lessened the longer I've remained strong and kept my mind on other things. I'm not missing out on anything but heartache by staying away from those sadistic sites.

Now I check to see if I've missed any calls or texts while I've been diligently ignoring the device. When I see that both Rae and Jet have tried to get in touch with me, my smile fades, my mouth dries, and my stomach shrivels. An overwhelming sense of déjà vu grips me. A few weeks ago, before the Bedroom Bowl debacle, having Rae and Jet both text me during the day wouldn't have been out of the ordinary at all. But this is the first communication I've received from Rae since Jet's injury.

It could be a coincidence that she picked today to reach out to me, and her call came in at roughly the same time as Jet's, if the communication had occurred around lunchtime. But the time stamp on the calls, while similar, is from not that long ago, which was much later than when everyone would normally stop for a break.

And as I take a closer look at the phone, I notice it's bursting with missed calls, voicemails and texts, the latest of which, from Jet, simply states an address and a hastily typed:

Meet me here. Bring Torzi

Scrolling through the rest of the texts from earlier doesn't clarify anything. It's all a bunch of *Wow!*s and *Are you okay?*s and *Call me*s from Greg, Colin, and my parents.

Hoping the voicemails will explain more and save me from

having to resort to Internet sources, I dial into my mailbox, which tells me the first one came through at about three o'clock.

"I take back everything bad I ever said about Jet," Rae gushes. *"Wow. Good luck with the media, though. And heads up, not everyone is as thrilled about what he said as I am. But hot damn! If I wasn't me, I'd kiss that boy on the mouth. Or maybe not, since I know what he does before games. You should definitely do it for me, though. For women everywhere."*

She pauses.

"And uh, I guess this is sort of an apology. No, a real apology. I'm sorry about what I said to you—and Jet—when the Busch story broke. I wanted to apologize when I brought Jet home after the Miami game. I actually volunteered to take him home for that very reason. But you were so mad at me, and I was tired, and it all went to shit before I knew what was happening. Anyway. You probably hate me, and I get it. But I'm still sorry. Okay, enough of the mushy stuff. I'm making myself want to barf, and your voicemail's probably about to cut me off. When you see Jet, though, tell him he's absolutely my favorite man right now. Bye."

So, Jet did something to make Rae happy. This could be bad. Very, very bad. It's one of the signs of the Apocalypse.

I suddenly need to pee. And puke.

What I need most, though, is to hear Jet's voice, and I need him to tell me he didn't do something stupid. My prayer is finally answered after several inquiring messages from various family members, both mine and his.

His strained voice follows the robot lady's intro.

"Hey. This is me, having to deliver on my promise already, unfortunately, to give you a heads up when something important happens. I screwed up hardcore."

Nonononono. That's the opposite of what I wanted to hear!

"Please don't be mad at me. I can explain. Maybe. No, I really can't, but I'm going to have to in about ten minutes. I'm on my way to this place called The Ranch, near the airport, where they send players after we've been naughty." He laughs nervously. *"I'll text you the address. Can you meet me there? They're going to want you to lay low, too. If the media can't find me, they'll go after whoever they can to get a quote. I'm so sorry. I hope you get this before anyone approaches you. You don't have to talk to them. As a matter of fact, don't. It'll only make things worse, probably. Listen, I gotta focus and follow my GPS. I've never been here before. Call me if you need help finding it. I love you."*

I hang up in the middle Gloria's next voicemail, which is the last one. After a deep breath, I send a mass text to Colin, Rae, and both of our families that says, *We'll call you later, as soon as we can.* Then I turn off the stove and launch into action.

THIRTY-ONE

SAFEHOUSE

Jet's waiting for me on the front porch of the log cabin nestled in the woods on Gray Lake. The Hummer's GPS brought me straight here, no problems. After parking the behemoth, I'm prepared to jump from the embarrassing vehicle, but Jet meets me in the gravel driveway and wraps me in a hug that keeps my feet several inches off the ground.

"Brought the tank in case you needed to run over reporters?" he asks with a surprising grin.

Holding tightly, I say with my chin on his shoulder, "Yes, actually. Finally, this ridiculous thing comes in handy."

Jet's been driving the Audi, which I normally use when borrowing one of his cars. The more intimidating midnight blue Mercedes is my second choice, but when I parked it in the garage after returning from the farmer's market, the gas light came on. At the time, it was no biggie—I figured I could refill it tomorrow. Then all hell broke loose. I didn't have enough gas to get to The Ranch, and I didn't want to chance being spotted while gassing up. I can't drive a stick, so the

Corvette was out. That left the obscene H2 as my only option. Although I hate the SUV, its invincibility, full gas tank, and built-in GPS seemed to suit my purposes best tonight.

A plane coming in for a landing at KCI less than two miles north of us would render my explanation inaudible, anyway, so I let it go and merely enjoy the hug Jet seems reluctant to end.

Finally, as the noisy plane exits the airspace above us, he sets me on my feet and smiles shakily down at me, then accepts my help unloading Torzi's supplies. I hand him the duffel bag he asked me in a later text to bring to him. Looping the bag's strap over his shoulder, he greets the dog, who's too chicken to attempt the leap from the car to the ground.

Jet plunks his buddy from the leather front seat. "Hey, Torzi. Thanks for agreeing to come out here and keep me company." He wraps his free arm around my shoulders, rests his wrapped hand against my upper arm, and leads me to the porch steps. "You, too."

On our way up the steps, I ask, "What the heck *is* this place, anyway?"

"A safe house, of sorts. It was mentioned in the confidentiality agreement you signed last summer."

Hmmm. Maybe I should have actually read that thing.

"Not sure how it got its name," Jet continues, "since there aren't any livestock or horses here, but it's where the front office sends you when they need to isolate you, usually because you're in trouble. The media and general public don't know it exists, so it's a nice, private place to meet with players and chew them out. Basically." He nods at the sky. "Plus, it's close to the airport, if they need to get someone out of here in a hurry."

I gulp and glance behind us at the other cars parked in

front of the house. Three luxury imports, all black, flank Jet's familiar silver Audi, like they're blocking him in and preventing his escape.

"So, it's a luxury principal's office?"

How heartily he laughs at my feeble joke indicates things may not be as serious as I thought. I still don't know anything, since I kept the radio off and my phone mostly out of sight after sending my text reassurance to everyone. I also had no desire to turn on the TV and get up to speed before I left Jet's.

I did take the time to put the chili in the fridge, but I didn't eat any of it first. I can't imagine being hungry for a while.

Inside the house, I expect to come face to face with "the others," probably a bunch of suits, maybe a Wise brother or two, and possibly Coach Bauer, whom I've met on a couple of occasions, all more pleasant than I anticipate this one to be. But the place is silent.

"They're all in the conference room, discussing my fate," Jet explains. He sets Torzi on the floor, bounds up the stairs, and returns a few seconds later without his duffel bag, his steps light.

"You don't seem worried or upset," I say, letting him take my jacket and hang it on a rack near the front door.

He shrugs. "Well, the worst is over, I guess. I've already been told how idiotic I've been and that they expected more from me and how I'm supposed to be the team's leader. They've threatened to strip the captain's 'C' from my jersey, but since I didn't do anything illegal or that shameful, I doubt they'll do that."

"What *did* you do?" I ask, unable to stand not knowing another second.

He tilts his head and drops his jaw. "Are you serious? You still don't know?"

"I promised you I'd get my news from you. I avoided all forms of media on my way here." I squint my eyes. "Don't abuse your power."

He laughs and leads me to a door under the stairs, which opens into a small library with a desk, a sofa, and some bookshelves. The southwestern and Native American decor in this room screams 1995.

We sit on the throw-covered leather couch, each of us sideways, facing each other. Torzi hops up between us, then settles in my lap.

"Honestly," I say, scratching the dog's head, "I was afraid of what I'd hear. I wanted to hear it from you first. I can get caught up on ESPN later, to fact-check you." I'd smile to let him know I'm teasing, but I'm still too worried to manage it.

Suddenly serious, he rakes his good hand through his hair. "I— I said something I shouldn't have said. It wasn't a wrong thing to say, but *I* shouldn't have said it. Especially to a reporter."

When all I do is wait for him to spit it out, he inhales a huge breath, then spouts on the exhale, "She put in an interview request, saying she wanted to talk to me about my injury and get an update on my prognosis—schedule, and all that. In the locker room, after practice, she *did* ask about that stuff. Then she started to bait me about Busch. You know, did I partially blame him for my injury, since his absence may have made me feel off my game and may have led me to force plays? Was I aware of what was going on with him and other players around the league, while it was happening? Was I ever approached to participate in—or *did* I participate in—the Bedroom Bowl? As if! Did I think the punishments handed down so far were too harsh? Was the NFL making examples of these guys because of past scandals related to women? She was relentless! And so, finally, I— I snapped."

When he pauses to catch his breath, I pull my mouth sideways. "Ruh-roh." I grab his left hand and squeeze it.

He audibly swallows. "I went on a full-blown rant about overpaid assholes who break the law and act like animals, and how the world has made them feel like they're above it all, just because they can throw or catch a ball or run fast. They're going to have to bleep out a few things."

"Is that all you said?"

He pooches his lips and scrunches his nose. "Oh, hell no. I was just getting started. I said a bunch of stuff about human rights and feminism, and then I said how sick I was of the decent guys being left to answer the 'bullshit questions' that should be directed at the dirtbags who can't keep it together. I addressed the groupies in the audience, too."

"Oh, dear."

"Yep. I was like, 'Do yourselves a favor: stay away from these guys. Have a little self-respect. You're worth more than that.' Oh, and I ripped pro athletes a new one, too. I said, 'And guys…? Grow up. Show some self-control. Real men don't act like horny animals.'"

I snort. "That explains why Rae wanted me to do this…" I lean forward and kiss him, intending for it to be a peck, simply to lighten the mood, but he pulls me against him, sending Torzi running away from us with a disgruntled yip.

I wrap my arms around him and kiss him harder, my eyes rolling back in my head as he flicks his tongue into my mouth. When we separate, I laugh nervously. "I had no idea you wanted to kiss Rae like that."

He scratches his forehead and chuckles, but his smile

quickly fades as he returns to his side of the couch. "And then... Then I said the thing that might get me in major trouble with the league."

"Oh, gosh. There's more?"

"Yeppers. I said we obviously have a problem in professional sports, because crap like this keeps happening. Or something like that. I'm not sure. After a while, it was all a blur. I... I... I couldn't stop talking. It's like everything I've thought since all this started had to come out. This reporter activated the launch sequence."

I can't help but laugh through my nausea. "Well, it's not the end of the world, right?"

He looks balefully at me. "Might be the end of mine."

"I doubt that. For what it's worth, I'm proud of you. I still love you. Maybe I love you more. If that's possible."

He half-smiles. "That's actually worth a lot."

"Okay, good. What are you most worried about, then?"

"That everyone else will hate me. Not just for opening my big mouth and adding to this stupid mess but for *how* I said it."

"And if that ends up being the case, then what?"

He shrugs. "I dunno."

"Are they going to cut you from the team?"

"Nah. Nothing like that."

"Then it's basically about what people are going to think about you? That's your biggest worry?"

Picking at his bandage, he smiles sheepishly. "I know what you're getting at. But it's not the same. The fans don't have to like *you*. They have to like *me* to go out there week after week and cheer and support, in good times and bad."

"Take a deep breath for me."

He does.

After a few seconds, I prod quietly, "Next worry?"

"That after my hand is better, they'll still keep me on the bench."

"Coach Bauer's not going to punish the whole team and make things worse by doing that."

"If Wilcox lights it up while I'm gone—"

"Your expected return game is against a division rival. They're not going to leave something that important to a rookie *and* a substitute tight end. No way. Keep going."

Eyes still downcast, he says, "I'll probably be fined by the league. But I don't care much about that."

I ruffle his hair. "Cheer up. It feels bad right now, because it just happened, but this will blow over. It'll blow over faster if you keep your focus and do what the big wigs tell you to do."

He lifts his eyes to mine. "I don't want to lose my 'C' because I screwed up and lost my temper. But I probably deserve to lose it. I wasn't much of a leader today."

"I guess I should reserve judgment until I see this epic rant of yours for myself, but based on what you've said, you showed great leadership by speaking out."

He shakes his head, which he lowers again. "No, Maura. I didn't. The instructions were to say, 'No comment,' every time we were asked about Busch. I blew it. You'll see. I'm such an idiot."

"Hey!" I scoot closer to him, nearly in his lap, and poke him in the chest. "You're not an idiot. No matter what you said or how you said it or who's pissed off about it or what it means for your job or your wallet. You're a guy who's been pushed to his limit, and you cracked a little. That doesn't make you stupid; it makes you human."

He shrugs, obviously still not convinced.

"And anyone who says you're stupid has to answer to me. I'll pull a Stacy Henderson and call into a radio show and rip everyone a new one," I say, referencing the frequent PR nightmare that is the wife of the Eagles' embattled QB.

The horrified look on his face when his head snaps up makes me laugh. "You wouldn't, would you?"

I roll my eyes. "No. But I don't want you saying or even thinking that about yourself. You're funny and kind and sensitive and smart in ways that mean more to the people who love you than anything you could gain from a book or lose after a few too many knocks to the head. You have heart."

He jabs his thumb and forefinger into his eyes while his head bobs up and down. "Thanks. I— I really needed to hear that."

I pull him to me and rub his back while he rests his forehead against my shoulder and sucks in a shuddering breath. "I mean it. Now, do I need to go into the conference room and repeat it for those goons?"

Releasing a shaky laugh that indicates he's uncertain about my seriousness, he says, "No. That's okay. How *they* feel about me isn't as important."

I kiss his ear, then whisper into it, "That's more like it." When he shivers and straightens, I say, "Now go call your family and tell them everything's going to be fine. Because it is. They need to hear that from you. They're worried about you."

———

Before we can make any phone calls, however, a union rep, the team's general manager, Jet's agent, and Coach Bauer call Jet into the conference room to speak to him privately about the decisions they've made. They aren't in there long before everyone reemerges, smiling and clapping Jet on the back like they're all best buddies and saying their goodbyes.

As soon as we're alone again, I ask, "What happened?"

"Slap on the wrist from the team. The league will be in touch to discuss fines for speaking publicly after being ordered not to, and also for some of the choice words I used."

"Are they still planning for the San Diego game to be your first one back?" I hold my breath.

He nods and raises his right hand. "Yep. Health permitting."

Whew! That's the away game I've chosen to attend this season. The plans have been set since the summer. San Diego in September the weekend after the job fair that's kept me up nights all year? It was a no-brainer. I need that weekend.

Rather than make this all about me, though, I return to the issues at hand. "And you have to stay here until…?"

"Just tonight. But when I go to work in the morning, I can't say *anything* to any members of the media. Not so much as a 'good morning.'"

"That's going to be hard for you."

"Well, it's rude!" he says with a wink. "But I'll have to chance being seen as a jerk."

"Let's find something to eat. I'm starving," I reply, hoping to distract him with food.

But we make the horrifying discovery that there's nothing to eat in this place except dry cereal. Apparently Keaton, the house's most recent "guest," likes Lucky Charms. A lot. He also overestimated the length of his stay, because he left behind several boxes, all opened, but not much else.

Before the big-wigs left, they reminded us about the confidentiality agreement that prohibits us from telling anyone where we are. One of the Wises, himself, said if we needed anything to text him, and he'd have his assistant bring it to us. It's late, though, and neither Jet nor I are the type of people to rouse someone from their home this late to cater to our whims. I'm kicking myself for not bringing the chili with me.

Trying to make the best of it, we take our two boxes of stale cereal upstairs to the bedroom to watch the ten o'clock news so I can see for myself how bad Jet's slip-up was.

The first time through, Jet cringes at the sight of himself, his hair still wet from the shower, his shirt not quite buttoned all the way. I think it's hot, but I'm too nervous about what's still to come to make any crude comments.

He places his hand on his cheek, and throughout the viewing, his fingers creep closer to his eyes, but he never covers them completely.

And you know, what he said was... heated. But either this particular channel did a ton of editing (possible, since they played some video over his sound bite), or he filtered himself better than he thought. I've heard one *bleep*, and it was for a relatively minor curse word, not any of the "biggies."

Next, they cut to their unsuccessful attempts to elicit reactions from teammates, but the most any of the players said was, "I'm trying to stay out of it and keep focused on Monday's game." The one variation on that theme was Jackson, who spouted the scripted line, but before they turned the camera away from him, shot it a double thumbs-up and winked.

Finally, they show some man-on-the-street interviews to

measure public opinion. With the exception of a few gruff manly-men saying things like, "He should worry more about his pass percentage and how he's gonna avoid the Chargers' blitz," people seem overwhelmingly positive and supportive, especially the females. Not a solitary one of the interviewees had a bad thing to say about him. As a matter of fact, they bandied around words and phrases like, "hero" and "real man" and said, "It's about time one of these guys finally had the guts to say something."

When it's over, I pause the program, fully intending to rewind and re-watch the segment, and turn to him. Popping a crunchy marshmallow into my mouth, I say, "See? Not so bad."

"I can't believe nobody said I was a stupid ass-face."

I laugh. "Not yet. The ladies love you."

He blushes. "What does that have to do with anything?"

"Everything. Women rule the world. You should know that by now."

We watch it four more times, until we both nearly have it memorized, inserting phrases like, "That's what she said," and analyzing what's going on in the background (including a towel-clad Schoengert we didn't see the first few times).

"Wait, wait, wait," I say. "Rewind it. I want to see that part where you bob your head like a self-righteous diva. It's priceless."

Reclined against the pillows, right arm behind his head, he extends his left arm to hold the remote out of my reach. "No. I can't handle seeing it anymore."

"Then close your eyes and cover your ears." I strain and snatch the remote from his hand, eliciting a sickening crunch from the box of cereal in his lap.

He groans but keeps his eyes and ears open.

"See? Right... there!"

I slow it down when his head moves subtly back and forth, then hit play so I can hear him say it in real time:

"This is a human rights issue, not just a women's rights issue. When you have no respect for people, you treat them like dirt. And maybe that results in a sex-for-money game or maybe it makes you think it's okay to beat someone up. Or rape them. Or kill them. It's all connected."

"Amen, bruh-thuh!" I say with his touchdown fist pump.

He snorts. "I was super into it, at that point. I guess."

I hit "stop" for the last time and turn off the TV, tossing the remote away from me on the bed. Setting our cereal boxes on the floor, I cuddle up to his chest. "I think it's adorable. You're adorable."

He rubs my back. "Team leadership doesn't think so."

"They'll get over it. Especially after you kick some Chargers butt in a couple of weeks. All this will be forgotten."

I push against him to sit up and stretch. He tugs me back toward him. I laugh. "I have to get going. It's a forty-minute drive to my house from here."

"What? You're not staying here tonight?"

I yawn. "I hadn't planned on it."

"Aw, c'mon! What about the big, bad reporters?"

"They've already forgotten about me. They don't care that I think you're the sexiest feminist to ever walk the planet."

He pulls me closer and slides his good hand up my shirt.

"You don't have work tomorrow."

"No, but—"

"I was counting on you to take Torzi back to the house in the morning."

"Am I on your payroll now?"

He nuzzles my neck. "No. Let's not get that rumor started. But..." He stops his advances, and I struggle to focus on his face. "I thought when you agreed to come out here, you were planning to stay all night, to keep me company."

"Umm..." I consider adding sexual frustration to my exhaustion and balance it with my desire to stay right here with him, after such a long day.

"You don't want to drive all that way tonight," he continues his persuasion. "Plus, the Hummer doesn't fit in your garage."

"You're reaching now."

"Please, Maura?"

Gaaaaaah! Those damn eyes. That mouth. And that hand. And...

"I don't want to go."

"Then don't!"

"But I don't think I can stay, either." This time, more resolutely, I pull away from him, going so far as to stand, and remind him, "Tomorrow's going to be another long day. You need to get some rest."

He ignores that argument. "What I need right now, more than anything, is for you to stay here with me. Tonight. All night. Please. I don't like to be demanding, but I need you."

I groan. "You're killing me, man."

Leaving the bed, he stands in front of me. Keeping his eyes on mine, he reaches down for the hem of my shirt and pulls it over my head. Automatically, I raise my arms so the garment sloughs off, and he tosses it aside, but I ask, "What are you doing?"

He answers me with a well-placed and well-timed, deep

kiss, during which he shows off how much he can still do, one-handed, by unhooking my bra.

I break my lips from his with a wet, sucking sound. "Jet. What about...?"

He grins down into my face, breathing heavily. "Being on the DL comes with *some* advantages."

THIRTY-TWO

DISAPPOINTMENT

We're both up well before the sun the next morning, setting out on the drive to Jet's to give us plenty of time to eat breakfast together, preferably something other than Lucky Charms. Beau has already been alerted via text message that we're on the way and hungry. My mouth is watering for the Greek omelet he promised me.

Our mini motorcade makes the trip in record time thanks to the early hour. Neither of us talks until we're several bites into our meals.

Finally, around a swallow of coffee, I say, "Oh, thank God. I feel human again. I was weak."

Jet winks at me across the table. "Stale cereal wasn't very good fuel for last night."

"Yeah, you better eat up, big boy. You have a rabid media contingent to face today. In a couple of weeks, I can't wait for you to show everyone your stuff. In sunny San Diego." I close my eyes and inhale the steam rising from my cup. "It's going to be amazing."

He neither confirms nor denies my prediction, so I open

my eyes, expecting to see him too busy eating to talk. But he wipes his mouth on his napkin, places it next to his plate, and says, "About San Diego…"

Pushing down my sudden nervousness, I say, "I've never been to California before, so that'll be fun. And Greg, Greg is out of his mind with—"

"Listen. The front office asked me to ask you not to attend the San Diego game."

I set down my cup with a clang. "Wh… what? I mean, why?"

He frowns and slumps, picking at his napkin and avoiding eye contact with me. "They feel like it's not a good time."

"Because I'm a curse, right? A jinx." As the blood drains from my face, the tears flood my sinuses.

His head snaps up. "No! No!" He hops from his chair and kneels next to mine, like he did three months ago. Only this time, he's not holding a ring. He grips both of my hands in his good one.

"It's not about that at all, Maura. I swear."

I close my eyes, willing myself not to cry. I've cried more in the past six months than I have my entire adult life, and I'm sick of it. My emotions have emotions, and they're all crowded close to the surface 24/7, ready to overflow.

Part of it is plain old exhaustion. I get that. But that's why this news about San Diego is that much more crushing. My face numbs at the idea of abandoning the weekend I've been anticipating for months.

"Then why?"

"They didn't give me a reason, and with everything that's happened, I didn't feel like I had any room to argue." He presses his finger under my chin, so I lift my head and open my eyes. He looks as miserable as I feel, but that only makes it all seem more hopeless.

"To be honest," he continues, scratching the side of his nose, "it might be for the best. I'll probably be nervous about my hand, no matter what. What if I screw up again? What if I can't grip the ball? What if I have a horrible game? I don't want you there, seeing that, being embarrassed by me."

"Never. Never, ever, ever embarrassed by you. I'll be watching, no matter what. I'd rather be *there* than at Greg's. Or, more likely, alone, since Greg will never speak to me again after I tell him we're not going."

"Oh, come on. If he blames anyone for this, it'll be me."

"I already have the plane tickets! And the hotel reservations. And the rental car reservation. And my vacation time. Everything."

"There's still time for you to cancel—reschedule—everything. Pick any other away game, and I'll—"

"I want *this* away game, your comeback game, in your home state. I want to wear my Number Fourteen jersey and sit in that luxury box and cheer you on, for everyone to see."

Looking down, he tells a spot on the floor next to his knee, "I want that, too. I do. But this comes from above. I'm sorry. I hate it. It makes me sick to disappoint you like this. I've been dreading it since they asked me to tell you."

"You've been keeping it from me since last night? Since before we...?" I'm too mortified to say the words out loud.

He nods and swallows. "Yes. I'm sorry. Every time I tried to tell you, you'd say something that would remind me how heartbroken you'd be, and I couldn't make myself say it. It had been such a long, weird, awful day, and neither of us slept worth a damn the night before. I thought it was better to tell you when we were both better rested."

"Was last night my consolation prize, then? I can't go to San Diego, but you broke your rule for me instead, thinking a great screw from you would make it all okay?"

He bites the insides of his cheeks and looks toward the ceiling.

I bury my face in my hands. "Oh, shit. I'm sorry. That... That was a horrible thing to say."

"It's okay."

"No, it's not." I transfer my hands to either side of his face. "I know you're just as disappointed as I am. But damn it!" A sob hitches in my chest.

"Aw, Maura!"

"It was my birthday present to Greg. For once, I was able to give him something he really wanted. And—"

"Shhh." He pulls me to him again and rubs my back. After a few minutes, when I've calmed a bit, he lets go of me, soaks up my tears with the back of his beige bandage, and says, "Hey. What if Greg can still go? What if we transfer your ticket to your dad? It sucks for you to miss out, but it's better than a total loss, right?"

I sniffle. "Can we? That sounds like a big, complicated mess."

"I'll take care of everything, if that's what you want to do."

"And you won't be distracted or nervous if my brother and dad are there?"

He laughs. "No. I probably won't think about them at all. No offense."

"None taken."

"So?"

I close my eyes and suck in as much air as I can, hoping the oxygen will extinguish, rather than feed, my bitterness.

I'm not the only one not getting my way here. Jet would

rather his injury never happened. He'd rather Keaton had never orchestrated the scheme that's caused such a distraction and led to his own heated comments. But wishing all of that away won't make it disappear.

We might like to downplay this life and say, "It's only a game," but the amount of money at stake every week is eye-watering. It's easy to become blasé about that and say, "It's only money," but it's an industry like any other, and if Jet doesn't want to sacrifice those aspects of his life necessary to participate, there are others out there, like Michael Wilcox, waiting for their chances.

That doesn't make it any easier, however, for me to give my blessing for someone else to have my glorious weekend. Nevertheless, I finally nod and say, "Do what you need to do so Greg can still have his birthday present. I'll be okay."

I'm jerked forward in my chair as Jet pulls me into a huge hug I'm not expecting. More for balance than anything, I return his embrace, wrapping my arms around his shoulders and burying my nose in his neck. He still smells like the air outside The Ranch, dewy and woodsy and cool, with a hint of leaf smoke.

His hand on the back of my head, he murmurs, "You're amazing. I'll make it up to you, I promise."

I pull my head back slightly, so I can say, "There will be plenty of other games."

He pauses, then reminds me, "This is the only time we're going to San Diego this season, though."

Pushing myself back but still perched on the edge of my chair, leaning on him for support, I search his eyes and say, not so confidently, "But we'll have lots of other seasons, right?"

His face relaxes into a wide grin, his eyes sparkling. Barely above a whisper, he confirms, "Yes. Absolutely."

———

After Jet leaves, I spend the morning catching up on some sleep and updating my parents on the latest. A conversation with Colin will have to wait until later. And Rae, to whom I'm still *technically* not talking, despite her rushed apology and one-eighty on her opinion of Jet, will find out everything at work today. That leaves a potentially painful pow-wow with my brother.

I wait until right before noon, to limit the length of the conversation. The Sunday games are about to start, and he'll want to get off the phone to monitor his fantasy players.

As soon as he verifies my boyfriend still has a job and still expects his comeback game to be against the Chargers, he asks, "So in San Diego, do I wear a Chiefs jersey, or is that too obnoxious?"

"Since when have you ever worried about being 'too obnoxious?'" I say, sitting sideways in Jet's favorite chair, wearing Jet's favorite jersey, and gently kicking my white knee-sock-clad feet. "Plus, we both know you're already packed, so why are you acting like you're still undecided?"

"I just want to have a plan."

"Of course, you do."

"You have no idea how much I need that weekend." He lowers his voice. "It's the only thing keeping me going."

My throat throbs with the realization that, only a few hours ago, I felt the exact same way.

Fortunately, he doesn't wait for me to respond but continues, "Hey, don't say anything to Mom and Dad, and don't you dare tell Deirdre I told you, because she's not ready to tell anyone, but... we're pregnant."

The phone slips from my hand and clatters to the floor in front of the fireplace. "Shit!" I try to reach it without leaving the comfort of the chair, but it's too far away, so I slither to the ground and snatch it, rolling to all fours and slapping the device to my ear in time to hear Greg say, "Hello? Are you there?"

I try to sound completely chill when I answer, "Wow. That's great! Wow. I already said that. But I thought—"

"Yeah, it's sooner than we planned, but I guess on the honeymoon, with the change in routine and everything, Deirdre's birth control got slightly off-schedule, and—"

"Um, I don't need to know all the details. Congratulations, though."

I can practically see his hangdog expression when he says, "Thanks. But it's already intense. I wasn't expecting her to be so uptight."

"This is Deirdre we're talking about. Isn't 'Uptight' one of her three middle names?"

He chuckles. "Okay, I'll give you that, but not usually about medical stuff. She's clinical, you know?"

"Yes. I do."

"I thought she'd take pregnancy in stride, too. But that hasn't been the case."

"Ah. Well, I hear the first time is hard. So, I guess this trip comes at a good time."

"The best."

I do the math in my head and say while wiggling back into my butt indentation in the chair, "She's almost out of the first trimester now, right? Maybe it'll get better soon."

He doesn't sound convinced when he says, "I guess. We're

going to tell everyone after you and I get back from California, so it's not like you have to keep it a secret for long."

"My lips are sealed." *This is it. Time to make the new plans official. Let's go, Richards. Say it. Out loud.* "Say... So. About that weekend in San Diego..."

He snorts. "I knew it."

"What?"

"You're totally going to ditch me, aren't you?"

"Ditch you? How did you—"

"I knew you and Jet would somehow find a way to get around all those rules and tight schedules to spend time together."

"Oh. No, that's not—"

"It's okay. I get it. You guys are in luuuuurve. Whatever."

"Greg, it's not like—"

"So how'd you swing it? And does this mean I need to get a different room? Because I'm *not* okay with you two going at it in the queen bed right next to me. That's nast—"

"I'm not going!" I blurt, the statement feeling every bit as awful as I thought it would.

"Wait. What?"

"I'm not going to California with you. Jet's having everything of mine transferred over to Dad's name. My plane and game tickets, our hotel reservation, your VIP passes at the stadium. All of it." For once my brother is speechless, so I explain without prompting, "With everything that's happened, the front office thinks I'll be too much of a distraction."

Because, let's face it: whether or not they said it outright to Jet, that's the reason. There's no other explanation. He pretty much confirmed it would be the case when he said he was worried about choking with me in the stands.

"That's bullshit!"

"Well…"

"I guess Jet's in no position right now, either, to argue with them, huh?"

"He sort of agrees with them."

"Are you kidding me?"

"It's okay," I lie, hoping if I say it enough times it'll be true, and I won't feel my throat closing up with tears every time I even think about it. "A lot of thought has gone into the decision, which is complicated, and I understand where they're coming from."

"But this is your dream weekend."

"Nah. It's your birthday present."

"Well, it sucks now. Going with Dad? I love the guy, but he doesn't know any of our inside jokes, and he doesn't dance with me after touchdowns."

"I don't, either."

"But you want to. I can tell. Dad's all about spouting stats and discussing the business side of football. That's boring!"

"Greg, this is the way it has to be, okay? I need Jet to have a good game and come home in one piece more than I need to be there."

"Are you going to watch at all?"

"I… I'm not sure," I reluctantly admit what I've been debating all morning and probably won't decide until this isn't as raw.

He scoffs. "This is effed up. You haven't missed a game since… since I don't know when. Never, maybe. Not since adulthood, anyway."

I don't need him to point this out to me, but it under-scores the depressing nature of the situation. "It's not that I don't want to see what I'll be missing; it's also going to be torture to wonder during every offensive play if Jet's going to survive it."

"He's ruined football for you. He's ruined my weekend, my birthday present."

If he didn't sound so childish, I'd cry.

But I relish the opportunity to turn the tables on him and say to him, for once, "Oh, Greg, grow the hell up."

It's the best I've felt all day.

THIRTY-THREE

DARK CLOUDS

Now that my vacation plans have been eighty-sixed, my main motivation for getting through the past couple of weeks has been non-existent. I've walked through life on auto-pilot, robotically finishing the last-minute details for the fall job fair. Which is today.

And I wish I could say it's going to be the *tour de force* I imagined, but "Be the Star of Your Life" is about to fall spectacularly to Earth, leaving a huge crater where my so-called career used to be.

I've been keeping an eye on the weather forecast for a week, watching the green blob on the radar creep closer and closer to the KC metro area. When I tried to lobby for an indoor event, Cynthia, not often interested in pulling rank, wouldn't budge on her long-standing policy of holding all job fairs in the office park's courtyard.

"We have to take advantage of the beautiful setting and the visibility from passersby," the director said dismissively, not looking away from her computer monitor to address me.

"That's why we go to the trouble to set up that huge tent. If it rains, it's not a big deal."

While the tent will keep fair participants perfectly dry, the humidity is going to kill the cardboard standees I made, some with my own money when I ran out of official job fair budget. I tried to explain my setup would be more sensitive to weather conditions than anything Arnold's ever done, but Cynthia waved me off. "I suggest you do something lower maintenance then, Maura."

Um, too late!

And now it's like someone took over my body (and head) and suddenly gave a shit. What has it gotten me? This morning, a puffy face.

As usual, Jet calls me at 6:30, as he's heading to the training complex. His call typically serves as a delightful wake-up, the next best thing to opening my eyes to his smile. This morning, however, I've been awake for a while. Awake and panicking.

"'Morning, Beautiful."

"Have you seen the weather?"

"Uh, yeah. Hard to miss it. It's a monsoon out here."

I whimper into the phone at how cheerfully he says that, like it's the most delightful development.

"What? Oh, yeah. Shit. Your job fair's today."

"Yes," is all I can manage.

"I didn't forget. I'm just— With everything going on the past couple of weeks, and being cleared to play this weekend..." He clears his throat.

Thanks to Jet's diligence with his physical therapy and the team's early bye week, he's completed his recovery right on schedule, and ready to start this Sunday.

And none too soon. As much as I've reassured him over

and over (and over and over) again about the security of his starting status, I have to admit Wilcox did a phenomenal job while Jet was on the bench.

After a shaky start during the Monday night home opener against the Patriots, where the rookie displayed some under-standable nerves during the first two series, he settled down, in large part due to Jet's calming influence on the sideline and in the helmet speaker. Wilcox led the team to an eked-out win that came down to a missed field goal by the Patriots at the end of regulation. The Chiefs' win the following week at home against San Francisco was much more authoritative, however, and I could tell Wilcox was getting mighty comfortable out there as Mr. Starting QB.

We can't have that.

The backup's growing confidence hasn't been lost on Jet, either. The long stretches of silence have returned, but this time, I'm not taking it as personally. It's still unnerving, but I realize he has a lot going on, most of it between his ears.

Now, for the first time in weeks, he's the cheerful one. "Aw, it'll be okay. It's coming straight down, so it'll be fine under the big top."

"The booths will be fine. The people will be fine. My standies aren't going to hold up."

"Oh. That sucks."

"To put it lightly." I release a shaky breath. "All that work. All that—" I almost say "money," but I don't dare go there with him, so I bite it back and amend, "All those ideas! And I'm only serving cookies and lemonade, because I was counting on the theme to bring people in, not the promise of free food. When I pictured the day, it was sunny, and the tent was crowded, and everyone was impressed with my life-sized cut-outs."

"I'm so sorry. This is a major bummer. I wish I could help."

Running my hand through my bed-head hair, I say miserably, "Unless you can make it stop raining."

"Nope."

"Then I'm screwed."

"Well, what's your backup plan?"

"I don't have one. This is it. It works one way." I sit up in bed and punch my mattress. "Why? Why, why, why is this happening? I never plan *anything*. This is why. Because planning is a ton of work for nothing."

"I don't know what else to say. People will still get the information they need to get jobs, right? That's the most important thing."

"I guess."

"And you're still hotter than Arnold."

"Jet, that's not helping, all right?"

He chuckles. "Sorry. I thought it would make you laugh."

"Today is supposed to be about my brains, my creativity, my... my brilliance. Not what a great piece of ass I am."

"Sheesh. Okay. I didn't realize you cared *that* much. You've hardly talked about it."

I bite back the retort that I'd be hard-pressed to get a word in edgewise about my life lately, since everything going on in his world right now has taken center stage.

It's not technically true, anyway; he's right that I don't talk about my work. I haven't wanted to let on how much I care, how hard I've tried, or how important the success of this day has become to me.

"Well, I do care, okay? I care about something, and I tried hard to succeed. Never again! Because it's a huge pain, and when it ends in disaster and heartbreak, not only have I wasted all that time and effort, but I look like an idiot, because I've failed."

"Hey, as long as you're keeping it in perspective."

"This is important!"

"I'm not saying it's not. But it's kind of a first-world problem, you know?"

"Says the guy who plays a game for a living."

"Touché," he concedes on a chuckle.

For some reason, his willingness to laugh at my insult infuriates me further. "You know, it may seem like being your girlfriend is my biggest priority and the greatest accomplishment of my life, but—"

"Nobody thinks that."

"Everyone thinks that. 'Oh, good. Maura's finally got her shit together and snagged a top-notch boyfriend. We were so worried she'd never do anything with her life. Now we can be proud of her.'"

"You need to calm down and hit the shower. When you get to work, none of this will seem so bad, and you'll figure it out."

"Don't tell me what I need to do, okay? I don't need your stupid game plan."

"Well, on that note, I need to get to my first meeting."

"I have to go, too. The sooner this day starts, the sooner it's over."

"I'm sure it'll be fine. I can't wait to hear all about it later, okay? You'll be great."

His patronizing tone only serves to make me more petulant. "Doubt it." I mumble, picking at my bedspread.

His initial response is silence, followed by a snort. "Whatever, Maura. You'd rather be miserable, then go for it. Goodbye."

I toss my phone into the pile of covers next to me and flip it the bird.

———

On my way to work, I experience a brainstorm. A big brainstorm. One to rival the thunder and lightning all around me as I run from my car to the office. As soon as I hit the door, I toss my company credit card at the first part-timer I see and send her to the nearest office supplies store with a list of everything I'll need to save the day.

I have two hours to follow through on my improvisation, so while I wait for her to return, I remove the already-soggy floor stands from my cutouts. When Chastity returns with the pins and adhesives, I assign four or five booths to each of the part-timers dedicated to helping me today, and I take the rest. In double-time, we pin, tape, tack, and Velcro the life-sized cardboard figures to the black curtain backgrounds of each employer's booth.

And although we're now officially open but still not finished with every booth, it's no biggie. "Keep working; we're almost done," I tell Becca and Rory, tossing Mrs. Doubtfire and Doc Hollywood at them. "They're labeled on the back with the booth numbers where they belong." Thank goodness I was at least *that* organized.

Leaving it in their capable hands, I turn my attention to the employers, checking they have everything they need, and the arriving applicants. As people enter the tent, I approach the ones who look lost or hesitant, say hello, and introduce myself, then ask if they're interested in a specific field or simply browsing. Based on their replies, I funnel them toward the most appropriate booth or booths and move on to the next clueless attendee.

After a couple of hours, I'm parched and tired, and my feet are absolutely killing me, but I'm also stunned at how many people are here. Generally, the spring fair brings out more folks than this one. The weather's better, for one thing. For another, more people are walking around with freshly inked high school and college diplomas, ready to start their careers and make some money. But today I've seen easily double the people Arnold had at his fair in May. *Without* any pro football players here signing autographs.

I smile smugly to myself and wink at Matthew McConaughey. He'd tell me I'm doing "all right, all right, all right!"

"I say. Did you wink at that handsome cardboard barrister over there?" comes a familiar voice from my left.

I whirl on one of my new tall heels.

"What are *you* doing here?" I ask, despite being glad to see Colin's friendly face.

He sips from a straw in a fast food cup. "I thought I'd pop round on my lunch break to see how you're getting on."

"Great, after a rough start."

"The rain literally put a damper on things?"

"Uh, yeah. But it wasn't as big of a disaster as I thought it was going to be."

"Things rarely are," he says sagely.

I roll my eyes. "Yeah. Trust me. I'm going to get a huge helping of 'I told you so' from Jet later, too."

"Did he dare try to calm you when you were in a high dudgeon?"

Pushing on his shoulder, I give him his answer in a dodging, "Shut up."

"That'll be a jolly good talk between the two of you later. Can you conference me in?"

"No."

"Bugger."

I shoot him a sideways scowl, then momentarily excuse myself to step away to help a newcomer.

When I return to him, he says, "I watched an entire American football game last Sunday by myself, but it's not the same without your expertise. Since you're going to be in town, after all, is there any chance you'd like some company watching Sunday's match?"

My face falls. "Oh. Um... Well, I might not watch."

"That's not on. You have to watch."

"I don't *have* to. It's too hard."

"Jet's counting on your support."

"He doesn't have to know. I'll catch the highlights later." I rock on my burning toes. "You know, I'm trying to be a good sport about the whole thing, but watching is something I'm not sure I can stand."

"Because you get jealous of those large, sweaty men jumping on top of your boyfriend?"

In spite of my sadness, I laugh. "Yes. That's it, exactly."

"He's a strapping lad. He'll be fine." He wraps his arm around my shoulders and pulls me to him in a side hug. "Come on, be a sport. If nothing else, it'll be a chance for the two of us to catch up. We haven't talked in an age."

I sigh at the highly effective guilt trip. "Fine. It's the late game, since it's on the west coast. Three o'clock kick-off."

"At Jet's house? With my favorite imported ales?"

I push him away from me but laugh. "Okay."

"Excellent. I'll see you then. I'd better be heading back to the exciting world of hair art, for now."

"Thanks for stopping by. Grab a cookie on your way out."

"Biscuits?" He cranes his neck to see across the tent, toward the small refreshments table, where Catherine Zeta-Jones beckons in her double-breasted chef's jacket. "Ooh, matron. Well, I say."

He slinks off in the direction of the food, and I step up to the latest potential job seeker who looks overwhelmed.

———

I'm high. High on something I've so rarely experienced in my life that I don't recognize it at first: success. I understand how *some* people might become addicted to this and want to keep doing things to experience it over and over again. They might even choose professions in which striving for victory is a regular—even weekly—occurrence.

After Becca, Rory, and I finish cleaning up everything but the giant tent that will be dismantled and carried off by the rental company tomorrow, the sun peeks out, just in time to set. I shake a good-natured fist in its sinking direction as I toss the last of the bedraggled standies (see ya, Erin Brock-ovich and firefighter Joaquin Phoenix) into the cardboard recycling dumpster behind the office. Then, whistling, I turn toward the parking lot, vaguely aware of but not caring about the blisters on my feet. Soon, I'll be home, and I can soak in a hot bath.

After I call Jet to apologize for being so terrible to him this morning.

The poor guy was trying to make me feel better, and I bit his head off. How did I like it the couple of times he did that to me while he was recovering from his hand injury? Not at all. But I gave it right back to him today without considering that. I didn't have physical pain to blame for my irascibility. I can't claim I was worried about my job, either, like he's been.

Today's elaborate plan went above and beyond what it would have taken to secure my position at The Career Center. I pushed the limits to show off, and once I committed to the plan, I was willing to do anything to avoid defeat and save face. Like forcing a pass to escape a sack on a trick play gone bad. But the only thing risking injury was my pride. Thanks to some quick scrambling, I avoided that. Now it's time to admit my part in the busted play, apologize to my teammate, and learn from the experience.

I'm rehearsing in my head what I'm going to say to Jet when I call him, as I round the corner of the building, expecting my car to be the only one left in the lot. But it has company, in the form of a much prettier friend who makes her look dirty, rundown, and old. Leaning against the red Corvette, holding a massive bouquet of gerbera daisies, is exactly the man I want to see.

We break into grins at the same time. I'd run to him if I could do it without limping and whimpering. Instead, I settle for the slower walk that hides my pain. It looks cooler, anyway.

The setting sun glints off the windshields of the cars and the cellophane around the flowers. I blink at the brilliance that eventually disappears as I draw nearer to the objects.

"Hey, Beautiful," Jet says, then flinches and corrects, "I mean, Smart Girl."

I laugh and deliver a peck to his smooth cheek while receiving the flowers. "Nice save. But I like your traditional greeting."

"You didn't this morning."

"I didn't like anything this morning. This morning sucked.

I sucked." Looking down at the brilliant reds, yellows, and oranges in the blooms in my arms, I say, "Thanks for these. They're gorgeous and just my style." I set them on the hood of my car so I can hug him without anything crackling or smooshing between us.

He wraps his arms around me and squeezes so tightly, I worry I might pass out. After a few seconds, his grip loosens enough that I can breathe again, but he doesn't let me go. Near my ear, he says quietly, "I do love you for your mind, too, you know."

My index finger swirls in the back of his hair. "Okay."

He pulls his head back slightly to look down into my face. "I do. This morning, you made me feel like a real jerk. Like, guys aren't allowed to tell the women they love they're hot or sexy or any of that anymore, because that means we don't value you as people. But if we never told you how beautiful we think you are, that wouldn't be right, either."

"I normally like it. But this morning wasn't the right time. I was freaking out."

"Yeah, well I was, too, after I hung up with you. I couldn't concentrate on what the coaches were saying. I stared out the window at the rain, worried about you, and wished I could be here to help you."

Feeling bad for him now, I calmly, gently say, "Why don't you accept that you're not going to be able to fix everything all the time? That would be a good start."

He exhales loudly and lets me go altogether. After a pause, he replies, "Okay. So, how did it go?"

"It went fine." My smile returns when I amend, "Better than fine. Cynthia was impressed. Which means I probably have this responsibility for the rest of my life." My eyes land on his broad chest. I stare at it while I follow my logic, and my euphoria fades a bit. "I'll have to keep topping myself, and that's stressful, but I'm not going to think about that right now."

I blink and return my attention to his face. The gleam in his eye and knowing smile spread a warmth through my chest that the damp, chilly evening can't touch. "Enjoy feeling good for a few minutes. You deserve it."

"I will. I'm just relieved it's over and that my vacation starts"—I tap the imaginary watch on my wrist—"now."

When my San Diego plans were nixed, I debated canceling my vacation days altogether and saving them for when Jet *will* be making this up to me. On a beach. In the middle of winter. That will have to wait until after the season, though, and my vacation days will have reset by then. I'm also so burned out that I need this time off, even if I sit in my house the whole time, sleeping and watching movies.

Actually, that sounds pretty awesome right now. Maybe not as good as kicking off the week in California, at a professional football game, but dwelling on that impossibility has brought me nothing but misery the past couple of weeks.

Jet rubs my shoulders. "You deserve it, too. And your cardboard friends? How'd they hold up?"

"With tape and Velcro and pins. On the booth backdrops."

"Great idea!"

I tap my temple. "Thought of it on my way to work."

"You're so smart."

"Yeah, I know." We laugh at my affected smugness.

"Can I take the most amazing job counselor to dinner?"

My stomach growls before I can give him a verbal answer, but when I picture what dinner out would probably look like tonight, four days before his comeback game, I wince and reply, "Now that the adrenaline's wearing off, I don't know if I can sit upright for much longer, much less smile through seven hundred interruptions while we try to eat."

He tucks my hair behind my ear. "There goes that exaggeration again. We'd probably only be bothered about a hundred times." Leaning down, he bumps lips with me. "Then how about we go back to my place? Beau made something for me for dinner before I impulsively came out here to meet the victor. Chicken-broccoli-rice something-or-other. It's not gourmet, but it'll taste good, and the only one who will interrupt us at home is white and furry and can be locked in a different room until we finish eating."

"Sounds amazing. I need to get my weight off my feet before they—"

Without warning, he lifts me from the ground, presses his mouth to mine, and silences me with one of the most eyeball-spinning, head-lolling, panties-dampening kisses I've ever experienced. Despite its intensity, though, it's short, and I groan with frustration when he withdraws.

He waits for me to open my eyes. Then, with a half-smile, he asks, "How's that?"

"Good start," I approve as he sets me down. Too bad that's as far as it's going to go. Instead of whining about it, though, I simply smile bravely at him, turn to retrieve my flowers, and say, "See you there."

THIRTY-FOUR

SAN DIEGO SURPRISE

"And that's the game, folks," I say with gleeful authority, standing to collect our empty beer bottles.

Colin lurches to his feet. "Wait!"

I freeze in my stretch, my arms suspended over my head, my back arched.

"Don't you want to watch to the end?"

Relaxing my posture, I yawn. "This *is* the end. That's called 'the victory formation,' and watch..." We both keep our eyes on the television as Jet cozies up to the center, receives the snap, and immediately kneels on the turf.

"Why's he doing that?" Colin asks.

"To run out the clock without the chance of turning over the ball." I point to the screen with the beer bottle in my left hand. Jet stands with his teammates in a loose huddle, watching the play clock tick down to ten. Then they line up in the same configuration, wait until the clock hits "one," and snap the ball again. Once more, Jet rests on one knee. "See? Every time they do that, it kills forty seconds from the clock. So you can eat up as much as two minutes of play time with three downs and not risk a turnover."

"Ah!" He grins. "Clever. Now that you mention it, I've seen teams do that before halftime, too."

"Same thing, only that's generally called 'taking a knee,' since it's not about winning at that point; it's mostly about getting to halftime more quickly. Sometimes losing teams do it to end their first half misery."

"So it's a throwaway play. That looks incredibly frustrating for the losing team."

"It is," I reply with a smirk. "I *hate* when our defense has to sit back and watch it happen. But I love watching Jet do it."

Colin clears his throat. "You like to watch him kneel?"

I laugh. "I didn't mean it like that, but"—I think more about it—"yes."

When I move to leave the room again, he quickly and loudly asks, "But wait, wait, wait! How does that differ from spiking the ball?"

I stop again and face him. "Spiking the ball is also a throwaway play, but it counts as an incomplete pass and stops the clock, which you definitely don't want to do, in this instance."

"Makes sense."

He fidgets and glances from me to the television as Jet takes the final knee, underhand tosses the ball to the ref, and jogs off the field, toward the bench.

"Game over," I announce, turning once more toward the kitchen.

"Maura!" Colin rushes over and removes the bottles from my hands.

I'm so taken aback by his odd behavior, I don't resist, but I do ask, "What the heck are you doing?"

"Let me worry about clearing up." However, he sets the

collection of glass containers on the nearest surface and leads me by the arm back to the couch.

"What? No! You're a guest."

"We're both guests, technically. In effect."

"Uh, I guess. But I invited you here."

"I invited myself. Which was terribly rude, come to think of it. So the least I can do is clear up. You simply have a seat and relax." He pushes me down onto the sofa. "You must be knackered after watching that game."

Sitting on the edge of the cushion while he plumps a pillow behind me, I eye my strange little friend and say, "It wasn't as bad as I thought."

Sure, it was hard at first to see what a gorgeous fall day they're having out there in San Diego, especially considering we're experiencing yet another soggy Sunday here in Kansas City, but I can't begrudge them the nice weather. For the most part, I'm glad Mother Nature has conspired to provide my brother and dad a picture perfect day.

Life is good. It's trite, and it's a cliché, but it fits. Life is amazing. I'm in love and loved back in equal—if not greater—measure. I'm young and healthy and gainfully employed at a job I don't hate and sometimes even enjoy, on the best of days. It's petty and ungrateful to sulk because one weekend of my life didn't go as originally planned.

Now that I've had a few days away from work, I don't feel so run down. With the job fair behind me, I'm lighter, in general. I did it. I'll do it again, only next time with less angst, because I'll know I can.

As for this game, I did approach it with some trepidation. I probably assigned more significance to the win than was necessary, division rival or not. While I eventually did decide I'd watch it, no matter what, I wasn't keen on having to regulate my behavior or my responses to the unfolding action due to the presence of someone else.

But it hit me the third time I tried to back out of hosting Colin, and he wouldn't hear of it, that his insistence at coming here today was about more than a game he may or may not be all that interested in watching. He wanted to be here to support me, his friend. Sometimes being a good friend—or sibling or child or lover or person—is not only about giving; it's also about accepting the care of the people who love you. For whatever reason, Colin needed to nurture me today. The least I could do was let him.

His behavior throughout the afternoon has only confirmed that suspicion. He's watched me more than the television. So I've made it a point to show him I'm fine.

He kept me preoccupied at the beginning of the game, as we got settled in with our drinks and snacks and caught up on life. The Blue Rinse Brigade is as colorful as ever, and his storytelling skills only make them more hilarious. He seemed relieved that I took such delight in his stories and was in good spirits.

The odd thing is, though, as the afternoon turned to evening, and I became more and more relaxed, with the help of a couple of beers and a game in which the Chiefs didn't trail for a single minute, Colin became more, not less, fidgety. At one point, when I was dozing before halftime, as I have a habit of doing, he clapped his hands and whistled to wake me. Not only did that bring Torzi running, but it scared the crap out of me. When I insisted I needed to rest my eyes while the commentators droned on about Jet's comeback and the other games happening around the league, Colin was equally dogged about keeping me awake, plying me with sugary snacks and demanding I show him how to make coffee with the fancy machine in Jet's kitchen, then nearly forcing me to drink the strong brew.

"You have to stay awake to explain things to me."

So I did. But while I allowed him to coddle me throughout the game, this latest behavior is too weird to let slide.

"What is your deal today?" I finally ask.

"My deal?" he repeats guilelessly, blinking, then rapidly and repeatedly shifting his attention from the TV to my face.

I glance at the screen, but the coverage is lingering on a wide shot of the field, the helmetless players from both teams mingling and greeting each other, saying, "Good game," and "Hey, how's it going?" The usual. I don't see Jet, but it's a shot taken from so far away, on one of those cable cams, that I don't expect to be able to see him. Plus, the sideline reporter has probably pulled him away for a post-game interview.

Returning my focus to Colin's face, I ask, "What's going on? You've been shifty all day."

He widens his eyes and puffs out his cheeks, but before he can issue a denial, it dawns on me. "Wait a second. Did Jet put you up to this?"

He pales. "Jet? No. What makes you— That is, why on earth would you think— Er, put me up to what?" Again, his eyes flick to the television.

I follow his attention, and just as I'm about to persist with my line of questioning, accusing him and my boyfriend of having me on mope prevention watch, the shot changes to a view of the visitors' bench, where Jet and Rae are sitting, with seven guys from the team standing behind them.

"What the fuh…?"

"Oh, *this* is interesting," Colin remarks innocently, grabbing the remote and cranking up the volume. "Is that Rae with Jet? How odd! I wonder what's happening."

I shoot him a dirty look from the corner of my eye but keep my attention glued to the action, as the booth announcers pitch it to the sideline reporter, whom we only hear, not see.

"Thanks, Dan and Charlie. We'll have some post-game remarks from Chiefs quarterback Jet Knox in a moment, but first he's asked us to help him relay a special message, so… here we go."

"What the fuh…?" I repeat, only at a higher, Torzi-deafening range as my heart threatens to turn inside out on itself.

Jet flips up a piece of poster board from his lap that says in bold, Chiefs-red letters, *Maura, will you marry me?*

My hands fly up to cover my nose and mouth.

Rae turns up the white sign in her lap, which reads, *Say yes! You know you want to!*

I laugh into my hands and muffle, "Oh, my gosh! I'm going to kill all of you."

Colin wraps his arm around my shoulders as the players in the line behind the bench raise posters that each contain a letter and the punctuation of the question, *PLEASE?*

Dropping my hands, I nod like an idiot, then mouth into the room, "Yes!", not clear how the heck this is working or how Jet will get my answer. If there's a camera in here, I'll puke. What else has the TV crew seen and heard today from this room?

Before I can panic too much, though, Rae holds up her phone for Jet to see the screen.

"She said yes!" He springs from the bench and pumps his fist next to his body in his touchdown celebration move, which is the signal for the guys behind him to go crazy, rubbing his head, slapping his back and butt, and shouting, "Congrats, man!"

It all took less than fifteen seconds, probably, but it feels like the world is moving in slow motion. I turn to Colin, who holds up his phone, the word *Yes* in a text bubble on the screen. At the top of the screen is Rae's name and number.

He hugs me while I wipe my eyes and sniffle. "You guys!" I screech over his shoulder, smacking him, hard, on the back.

He laughs and admits, "I've had that typed into my phone all day. I didn't trust myself to be able to enter it fast enough with shaking fingers." Holding up his hands, he confirms they're still trembling. "I didn't want to be the weak link in the plan."

Jet's voice rings out in the room, thanking the sideline reporter for her help, so I turn toward the television again, still squeegeeing tears from my face. He stands in the typical post-game interview stance, bent down slightly to hear the questions and speak into the microphone of the much shorter reporter.

"*Jet Knox, that was the gutsiest play call of the day. What was going through your mind when you held up that sign?*"

He laughs. "*Uh, actually, I was thinking, 'She's going to kill me.' But it was too late to back out, and I love her and really wanted to ask the question, and if she said no, I'd just keep finding other ways to ask.*" He flashes his mega-watt grin at the camera. "*I'm glad it worked out, though.*"

"*This was a big game, in general, for you, with your return to the field after your injury in Game One. Were you worried about your post-game plan being a distraction from what you wanted to do here today, get a win against your division foe, the Chargers?*"

His hand on his hip, he smiles down at the reporter and shakes his head. "*Not at all, Gina. Maura's not a distraction; she's an inspiration. I go out there and play my heart out every game, because that's what I love to do. Nobody loves this team more than she does. Her support only makes me better.*" He kisses his fingers and holds them up to the camera.

Gina chuckles. *"Well, this is like something out of a movie, something she'll remember forever. Thanks for talking to us. Congrats on the win… and the engagement."*

"Thanks, Gina." To the camera, he says, *"Love you, Beautiful. GO CHIEFS!"* and then jogs out of frame. The shot follows him as he hugs Rae, who's waiting for him, and disappears with her into the tunnel that leads to the locker room.

Stunned, I stare at the screen for several more minutes, through more sideline interviews and the pitch back to the desk in the studio, where the guys there marvel that "Jet Knox has some serious courage" and say they'd never have the guts to try that. I remain catatonic through most of the following commercial break.

Finally, after giving me my moment to recover, Colin pats my knee and says quietly, "And you said romance only happens in movies."

THIRTY-FIVE

"SO BLASSED!"

I still haven't recovered by the time Jet returns home, slinging his overnight bag onto the entryway floor with a thump and a rustle of nylon against tile.

"Maura? You still here?" he calls, striding into the living room, where I'm sitting in virtually the same spot Colin left me, staring vacantly at the wrap-up analysis after the night game.

Not sure what to do with myself, I rise to my feet and wipe my damp palms on my yoga pants, suddenly wishing I'd thought to change into something nicer than yoga pants and this football jersey. Especially when I see Jet's still wearing his post-game press conference dress shirt and trousers. Feeling inexplicably shy, I train my eyes on his huge, shiny shoes.

"Hey," I say, but it comes out in a choked whisper, my voice rusty from disuse.

"Hey, Beautiful." His strides shorten, and he pulls up, approaching me more slowly, cautiously, like he's waiting for my permission to proceed.

I clear my throat and attempt a smile, but to my horror,

the dam breaks on all of the emotions—both good and bad—that have been plaguing me for the past month. Heck, probably the past *nine* months.

No longer hesitant, he steps up to me and pulls my face to his chest. "Hey, hey. What's the matter?"

"Nothing!" I say, not certain if that's the truth, since I'm not sure why I'm crying, to begin with. I just know it feels good. And humiliating. I wish I'd been able to get this out of my system before he got home. But I was still in such shock. It took seeing him, his smile, his unsure eyes... Those effing eyes! How am I going to manage a lifetime with this guy and those eyes?

Weaving his fingers through the back of my hair, he gently massages my neck at the base of my skull. "Oh, man. Your answer's no, isn't it?"

"No!" I try to pull my head up to look him in the face, but he's stronger than I am, stronger than he must realize.

"Okay, but it's not 'yes,' right? It's still 'not yet.' But Colin didn't want me to look like an idiot on national television, so he texted 'yes.'"

"Jet, no. That's not—"

"Gosh. What a nice guy."

Finally, I manage to use my entire body to push away from my fiancé and say, "My answer is really yes."

The color I didn't realize had left his cheeks returns, and he exhales so hard I worry about his lungs. "Oh, whew! When you started crying, I thought you didn't—"

I swipe at my tears. "I don't know why I started crying. I mean, I did when it all first happened, but since then, I've been numb."

"Numb? That's not good."

"I guess I still can't believe you did that. And that Rae and

Colin and all those guys were in on it with you. And that not a single one of you realized what a horrible idea that was." I laugh, so he does, too, looking relieved.

Pulling me against him once more, his hands against my lower back, he asks down at me, "Are you mad at me?"

"No."

"Not even a little bit?"

I shake my head.

"Okay. Then it was my idea."

"And if I had hated it?"

"Then it was Rae's idea."

I brush a lock of hair from his forehead. "What am I going to do with you?"

"Marry me?"

"After that."

"Live happily ever after with me?"

I close one eye and look toward my forehead. "Before that."

He cups my butt in his hands and bends at the knees. "I have a few ideas," he murmurs, his breath feathering against my lips.

I laugh. "Yeah. Well, you'll get back to me on that in about three months, right?"

"How about three minutes?"

"Don't tease me, Number Fourteen."

"Does it feel like I'm joking?"

No, it does not. Not at all. That's a serious appendage.

Still, I check. "So, like that, the rule you follow so religiously—unless you're on the DL—is a thing of the past? Or is this a one-time-only reprieve? Because I don't want your pity or your charity. If you're tough enough to go without, I am, too. I'd prefer not to fall off the wagon and have to start all over again."

His head drops back, and he laughs at the ceiling. When he lowers his eyes to mine again, they're dancing. "Wow. This is quite the one-eighty *you've* made on this rule. I figured you had a bet running with Rae about how soon I'd crack."

"I know you better than that. You're stubborn, like... like a horse!"

"A horse, huh? Like Warpaint?"

Assuming a strong Southern accent, I answer, "Why, yes, as a matter of fact, you big stud."

He nuzzles my neck. "Mmmm. Someone mega-smart once showed me the results of a study that said my rule might be complete and utter horse hockey."

"Well, I declare! And what did you make of that?"

"I think we need to do our own study and test that hypothesis. Extensively."

"My stars! It gives me the vapors when you talk scientific."

He snorts against my neck but catches himself before losing a grip on his amusement. When he lifts his head, and I flutter my eyelashes at him, he almost cracks up again.

I'm right there with him, not sure how much longer I can keep this up, but I manage to choke out, "I'm still waitin' on an answer, Professor Hoss."

We both collapse into giggles at that improvised detail. Breathless, he grips my forearms and bends at the waist, laughing at his shoes. "Oh, damn. I was okay until 'Professor Hoss.'"

I recover more quickly and, dabbing at my eyes, resume character. "Now, Professor, we ain't got no time for silliness. This is serious work. For science."

He stands at his full height and transfers his hands from

my arms to my face. The smile still plays on his lips, but his eyes are earnest as they roam my features, and he says, "I love you, Maura Richards, and I can't wait to be your husband, to come home to you after every win, after every loss, after each grueling practice or press conference or public appearance."

"Aww. Bless your heart!"

"I meant what I said to that reporter. You inspire me to be better, to work harder, to play smarter. You're the first person who's ever made me feel like I'm more than just an arm. Out at The Ranch, when you said I had heart…" The corners of his mouth turn down, and he blinks rapidly. "I've been waiting my whole life for someone to see that."

I stand on my tiptoes and kiss his chin but keep the Horse Lady accent to prevent any more crying. "I saw it right away, the minute you sat down next to the saddest, most pathetic, loneliest party guest and tried to cheer her right up."

"My heart may not have been the only thing at play there."

Smacking his chest, I say in my normal voice, "Big talker."

"And when you called me out on our first date for not quite being able to place your name with your face, I thought, this woman is going to change my life. And you have."

Now he takes a knee and pulls a familiar baby blue ring box from his pocket. "So, I know I already asked you in front of a million people, but I want to ask you again, with just the two of us. I want to look you in the eyes when I say it. Maura, will you marry me?" He opens the box with a squeak of its hinges and reveals an enormous glass cocktail ring crammed between the two pillows that make up the bottom of the box.

I roll my eyes and mutter, "Oh, my gosh," on a giggle.

He looks down at the ring, then back up at me. "There wasn't a chance in hell I was going to risk screwing that up again. You'll be picking out your own ring."

I pluck the costume jewelry from its nest and slide it onto my finger, then hold out my hand, turning it side to side to inspect it. "I think this one is perfect."

"So, is that a yes?"

"Absolutely."

He rises to his feet and embraces me. After a deep kiss, he startles me by sweeping me off my feet and carrying me toward the stairs. As we ascend, I throw back my head and drawl, my voice echoing in the high-ceilinged area, "Ah'm so blassed!"

ACKNOWLEDGMENTS

Huge thanks go out to the usual suspects, including friends, family, people I haven't seen in a long time who still keep up with my writing (thanks to the magic of technology), members of social media groups, and readers who follow me on Facebook and Twitter. Your encouragement has been the difference between publishing and quitting some days, so thank you!

Specifically, I'd like to thank Laura Chapman, fellow author and football lover. She and I may root for different NFL teams (Packers for her and Chiefs for me, just FYI), but that only made our conversations about the game more interesting. She also hosted me on an incredible weekend in her delightful hometown of Lincoln, Nebraska, where I was an honorary Huskers fan for a day. She introduced me to her cats and some of her friends and family, red beer, and Runza sandwiches (if you've never had one, they're uh-may-zing). The Chapman clan made me feel very much at home, which was heart-warming and something I'll never forget. (Thanks, Bruce, Linda, and Sarah!)

Most importantly to this project, however, Laura encouraged me to dust off and revamp an old, dismissed manuscript that was previously destined for the hard drive graveyard. She spent a lot of time reading rough, rough, rough drafts of most of this book, hot off the brain, then more time reading a more polished version. Thanks for being a rock, L.C.!

Other beta readers (you know, those brave souls who read a fully written manuscript and tell the author exactly how they feel about it?) for this book were Erin Baker, Jami Deise, Bethany Dodson, Nicole Ford, Kylie Frankel, Mary Macklin, Kaley Stewart, and Natasha Walsh. Each reader provided a special perspective, and as usual, their responses made this book better than it was when I sent it to them. As a matter of fact, it's almost an entirely different book altogether. Thanks, ladies!

I dedicated this book to my husband, but I feel like a more thorough thank you is in order. The man not only helped me come up with *The Underdog Series* title (and its funny runner-up, *The Pigskin Passion Series*), but he answered some random questions at some ungodly hours of the day without batting an eyelash. He also didn't roll his eyes once (that I saw, anyway) when I compared Jet Knox's quarterback stats—completely made-up, remember—to the *real* football players we watched on Sundays, Mondays, and Thursdays. He even acted like he cared when I lamented having to change my fictional NFL scandal to something less similar to real-life goings on, even though it didn't affect his life at all, and he probably could have done without that half-hour angsty conversation when he was trying to eat dinner after a long day at work. We've been on the same "team" for a long time, and it works because he accepts my kookiness, and I appreciate his level-headedness. I love you, Clint, which is why I had the Cowboys win the Super Bowl in this book. You're welcome!

Finally, I'm going to offer a preemptive shout-out of gratitude to reviewers, and not just the ones I hope will chime in after reading this book, but every person who's written a review for any of my works. Whether you're an individual who just likes to share your thoughts about the books you've read or someone who has a more structured platform, like a blog, your words matter. You influence readers' choices about how they spend their free time and which characters they spend that time with. When you're recommending my books to others, I appreciate it. And when you're conveying your disappointment with one of my works or with a certain aspect of a story or character, you're helping me consider ways in which to grow and be better, both as a writer and a person. (Or you're ruining my day. But don't worry so much about that, as long as you don't make it personal.) So don't assume your opinion is worthless. If you enjoy telling other people about the stories you've read, do it! Voracious readers love recommendations from other reading enthusiasts.

Thanks for reading!

ALSO BY BREA BROWN

The *Secret Keeper* series:

- *The Secret Keeper* (Book 1)
- *The Secret Keeper Confined* (Book 2)
- *The Secret Keeper Up All Night* (Book 3)
- *The Secret Keeper Holds On* (Book 4)
- *The Secret Keeper Lets Go* (Book 5)
- *The Secret Keeper Fulfilled* (Book 6)

The *Underdog* series:

- *Out of My League* (Book 1)
- *Rookie of the Year* (Book 2)
- *Opportunity Knox* (Book 3)

The *Nurse Nate* series:

- *Let's Be Frank* (Book 1)
- *Let's Be Real* (Book 2)
- *Let's Be Friends* (Book 3)

Stand-alone novels:

- *Daydreamer*
- *The Family Plot*
- *Plain Jayne*
- *Quiet, Please!*